CENTRAL LIBRARY

Inverclyde Libraries

34106   002670730

THE PULL OF THE MOON

THE
PULL OF THE
MOON

Diane Janes

SOHO
CONSTABLE

Constable · London

Constable & Robinson Ltd
3 The Lanchesters
162 Fulham Palace Road
London W6 9ER
www.constablerobinson.com

First published in the UK by Constable,
an imprint of Constable & Robinson, 2010

First US edition published by SohoConstable,
an imprint of Soho Press, 2010

Soho Press, Inc.
853 Broadway
New York, NY 10003
www.sohopress.com

Copyright © Diane Janes, 2010

The right of Diane Janes to be identified as the
author of this work has been asserted by her in accordance
with the Copyright, Designs & Patents Act 1988.

All rights reserved. This book is sold subject to the condition that it shall not,
by way of trade or otherwise, be lent, re-sold, hired out or otherwise circulated
in any form of binding or cover other than that in which it is published and
without a similar condition including this condition being imposed on the
subsequent purchaser.

A copy of the British Library Cataloguing in Publication Data is available
from the British Library

UK ISBN: 978-1-84901-272-0

US ISBN: 978-1-56947-639-0
US Library of Congress number: 2009043666

Typeset by TW Typesetting, Plymouth, Devon
Printed and bound in the EU

1 3 5 7 9 10 8 6 4 2

Mixed Sources
Product group from well-managed
forests and other controlled sources
www.fsc.org Cert no. SA-COC-1565
© 1996 Forest Stewardship Council

For Bill

Gravity is the attraction of one body to another . . .

. . . As the moon orbits the earth it moves not only
the oceans but the ground beneath our feet . . .

ONE

Marjorie swims at the leisure pool every morning – a steady breast stroke which keeps her face clear of the water and her hair dry. We've both been going there for quite some time, so Marjorie assumes we know all about each other. We chat, you see, while we get changed or pause for a breather between lengths: for I too have become the sort of woman who swims without getting her hair wet.

Marjorie is a widow, who passes her non-WI evenings in front of a television set. She asks me if I've seen programmes, then discourses on them irrespective of my reply.

'It was very ingenious,' she says, 'the way they hid the body inside the snowman. A very ingenious murder.' She pauses for my reply.

There's a lot of things I could say. Like murder isn't ingenious. It's sandpaper in the mouth – an ice cube down your spine. It's fear you can taste and feel. Thunder flashes going off in your head.

I don't say any of this. Instead I say: 'I never watch murder mysteries.'

Marjorie gives me a knowing smile. A series of wavelets plinks against us, the aftermath of a fellow swimmer's tumble turn. Marjorie raises her eyes heavenward. What's the hurry? her expression asks. I wonder if Marjorie has ever splashed or raced, or skinny-dipped.

'Sometimes I have to turn them off,' she says. 'It's no use watching something, then lying awake half the night, hearing every little noise.'

I realize she is still talking about television programmes. She thinks I'm too windy to watch alone at night. I let her think it.

'Another couple of lengths,' I say. 'Then I'm getting out.'

We set off together, but I soon outpace her, even doing the stately breast stroke which never threatens to engulf my coloured hair in chlorinated water. My hairdresser has warned me about this. Chlorine strips out what he calls my 'semi-permanent', thus exposing the grey faster. Thirty-five years ago I never thought to be careful of my semi-permanent. Didn't have to watch my weight, or consider hiding my creased neck under a scarf. Everything changes.

Just as the size of my waist has expanded, so the gaps between the thunder flashes have lengthened. Their velocity has decreased, their deadly brightness grown dim. I thought the Cat Stevens lyric would be prophetic – *Wherever I am, I'm always walking with you* . . . It is no longer so. Every day turned into every other day, every other day into occasionally. Occasionally doesn't come around so often any more.

I drove past the house a couple of years ago and it looked quite different. New windows, fancy wrought-iron gates; it had even sprouted a conservatory on one side. The wood at Bettis has become a nature trail. It has a car park with picnic tables. How we would have scorned that. I didn't stop, but I could imagine it. Waymarked walks and community arts projects. Little notices forbidding the leaving of litter, ghost hunting, or fornication on the forest floor. Well, okay, I made that last bit up.

The house where Danny lived has gone completely.

There's a neat quartet of semis there now. Semi-detached and entirely permanent. Everything changes. Even Cat Stevens isn't Cat Stevens any more.

Marjorie catches up with me in the changing room. We keep our eyes discreetly focused away from one another, our shared taste in Marks & Spencer's knickers not remarked upon. Instead Marjorie discourses about her youngest's husband. He has just paid for a new car *and* a fitted kitchen. 'He would do anything for our Lyn,' she says.

Anything for love. That's what the song lyrics tell us. Everyone from Meatloaf to Lionel Bart's Oliver professing their intention to do anything – anything at all – for the object of their affections. 'Would you risk the drop?' asks Nancy. 'Anything,' coos the besotted young orphan. Not the drop of course. Not quite that. They'd stopped hanging people by 1972.

I half listen to Marjorie's eulogizing with appropriate nods and smiles. Marjorie accepts this as a kind of victory. I have no children, so I cannot compete. She turns away to fold her towel. She is fully dressed now: tartan slacks and a pastel polo shirt, courtesy of the Edinburgh Woollen Mill. The fact that I already choose the same underwear as this woman may be a frightening portent of things to come. I'm already doing the sensible shoes. My God, I'll be morphing into pleats and a shortie mac before I know it.

I am glad to escape from Marjorie. Normally she is at worst no more than mildly irritating, but today she has trampled into dangerous new territory, prising open the door on to an 'occasionally' – one of those increasingly rare moments of stark reality, which can be provoked by any unexpected reminder – some innocent unconnected prompt – a phrase from a song, a headline in the paper. A few weeks ago it happened in a busy street. I saw a tall young man walking ahead

3

of me, with wavy dark hair and a leather jacket which was well worn and creased at the elbows. I opened my mouth to call out. Closed it again. Danny would not be a young man now. *I look but you're not there . . .*

The walk from the leisure centre to my flat takes twelve and a half minutes. I find that the postman has already deposited his daily handful of litter through my door. The top item is a gaudy flyer for a furniture store – the sort of thing you come across dropped on the pavement. This morning I have won a guaranteed cash prize, been selected to attend a special holiday promotion and deemed worthy to apply for both a credit card *and* a loan. Machine Mart and the Hawkshead Clothing Company have both favoured me with their latest catalogue, while a charity I have never heard of solicits my support via a depressing picture of underfed Africans.

At the very bottom of the pile is a plain white envelope, addressed by hand. When picking up everything else, I somehow leave this envelope lying on the hall carpet where it sits reproachfully, for all the world as if I've neglected it on purpose. I have to bend specially to pick it up, transferring the other mail into the hand holding my swimming bag, so that this letter is carried into the kitchen separately from the rest, already acquiring a status my other post does not possess.

Propped unopened against the silent radio it tries to catch my eye, this letter, with its second-class stamp and smudged postmark. The writing is old-fashioned, with elongated loops on the y and f of Mayfield. All the letters slant to the right, uniform as sequence dancers, but there is an unsteadiness about them, as if some have spent too long in the bar.

Reluctant to concede to the self-important air this missive has assumed, I pour my juice, sort and discard

4

my other post, put bread into the toaster, reach down the jam.

I know the writing. Recognized it immediately. We still exchange Christmas cards every year. A weird ritual – and my own fault it has continued. I could have stopped it years ago – inadvertently failed to supply a new address. Why didn't I? Guilt? Fear? The ultimate gesture toward non-existent normality? For several years now, I have written her card wondering whether I will get one in return. She must be well over eighty. One year soon there will be no card. Then I can stop sending.

In my head Cat Stevens sings some more: *I'm always thinking of you, always thinking of you . . .*

Every year I expect the cards to cease, but they keep on coming. Season's Greetings. Christmas Wishes. Every December. Never in springtime. Not in April. Nor is this a card – the envelope is the sort supplied in stationery sets: plain white with matching paper. Very sensible, nothing fancy. Why would she write to me? We have never exchanged letters – only cards; just a card at Christmas, the way you do with people. They get on to your list and you carry on sending cards to one another, year after year, knowing full well you'll probably never set eyes on each other again.

I make the envelope wait until I've finished breakfast and rinsed my swimsuit. It sits implacable, sneering almost. I can't put it off indefinitely.

There are two sheets inside, unlined paper, each written on one side only and folded in half. Even as I extract them and smooth them flat, I still cannot imagine her reason for communicating like this. All that we had in common is long gone.

The address in the top right is the one she's lived at for the past decade.

Dear Katy – a blast from the past to start us off. No

5

one calls me Katy now. Kate, that's me. Brief, brisk, brusque even.

Dear Katy,

I would like you to come and see me. Perhaps you could write suggesting a suitable date, as I have difficulty hearing on the telephone. I would be happy to pay any expenses you incur for the journey, including a taxi to and from the railway station.

At this point the long sloping letters run out of space. As I turn the page, I wonder why she thinks I would be travelling by train. Probably never realized I had passed my test. I catch myself dwelling on the mechanics of the journey because this is a far safer area of speculation than considering the reason she wants me to make it.

I feel sure you will understand what I want to discuss with you and why. Please come as soon as you are able, as I must find out what happened to my son.

Yours sincerely,
E. J. Ivanisovic

The letters go fuzzy in my hand, so I put them down on the table where they dance around like a formation team, arriving back at the phrase *what happened to my son*, whenever I glance back at them. Pyrotechnics fizz and flash in my mind.

It's like the rule of three in a fairy story. In stories everything happens in threes. Three little pigs, three bears, two ugly sisters plus Cinderella makes three. Two idle prompts from Marjorie, then this letter. Marjorie thinks murder is ingenious. She thinks actions in the name of love are always for good.

What does Mrs Ivanisovic think? What does she know? Why does she ask now – after so very, very long?

Too late now to return the letter unopened, marked not known at this address. Why, why had I maintained the contact? I could have dropped it years ago. Seasons Greetings. Merry Bloody Christmas. Was it because, at the back of my mind, I was always afraid she guessed too much? Yet how could she?

'Your son is dead,' I said, addressing thin air above the letter. At least you have a grave to mourn at. Not like Trudie's parents. Trudie who saw it all. Trudie whose coincidental disappearance you scarcely remarked upon. Was she so easily forgotten? Or does some octogenarian widow still vainly await her return? Another grieving mother who has no address to write to: someone without the means to reach into the past, demanding answers.

Every night and day I pray, in hope that I may find you.

But Trudie is not to be found. I saw the earth fall on to her, clod by clod, under the yellow light of the torch. Murder is not ingenious. Murder is cruel, dirty, fetid. Murder is sliding on piled earth in the dark. Sights you never want to see, a dead white face in a flickering beam, not flinching when the soil hits it.

TWO

Trudie's arrival cast a shadow over our little group from the very beginning. Literally. She appeared one afternoon while we were sitting on the beach and stood between us and the sun.

The first thing I ever noticed about her was her feet. Bare brown feet – sunburnt rather than dirty – which protruded from beneath the broderie anglais trim around the hem of her maxi. Each of her toenails had been varnished in a different colour: scarlet, black, fuchsia pink. One nail had pale blue glitter polish – glam rock making its mark on the beaches of mid-Wales.

'I thought for a minute it was Cat Stevens,' she said. She rolled her r's in a soft blur of an accent which I couldn't quite place. It reminded me of summer-scented roses and cream teas.

Danny stopped strumming and we all looked up. When I remember it now, it's as though Trudie towered over us, a huge dark figure against the cloudless blue. I can see the sun's rays shooting out from around her head – thunder flashes again. Of course that wasn't really the way of it at all. I couldn't see her properly because I'd forgotten my sunglasses. It was no doubt this foolish omission which rendered everything impossibly bright that day. For everyone else it was just a glorious day beside the sea.

Naturally Danny loved the Cat Stevens thing. He

really did look a little bit like him – and although he always denied it, he'd played up to the likeness by growing a little goatee. He had the same dark hair and thoughtful eyes as the singer. A lot of people remarked on it. He and Trudie immediately struck up a conversation, but I was disadvantaged by the glare: forced to avoid looking directly at the newcomer, while conscious of a vague uneasy jealousy as she invaded our group. It was not just that until then I had been the only female. Confident people always put me on the back foot. I could no more have walked up to a trio of strangers than sprouted wings and flown across the dunes: but Trudie – Trudie was something else. Within a matter of minutes she had flopped down beside us on the sand and was dueting with Danny. A love song, as if you couldn't have guessed. Some Anne Murray number about a child conceived in love.

I wanted to drop her a signal – some casual sign of possession, just to let her know that Danny was spoken for – but there's not a lot you can do when the object of your affections is cross-legged on a beach, cradling an acoustic guitar. The wretched instrument sticks out in both directions, precluding all but the most overt gestures of affection. Anyway, I didn't want to appear completely freaked out and uncool about her presence, so I bided my time, acting the appreciative audience while I sized her up.

She was taller than me and her hair was much darker, though worn like mine in the regulation style of the moment – a long uncut mane, parted down the centre and falling halfway down her back, where it finished in a cascade of split ends. She was wearing an embroidered cheesecloth smock over her full-length cotton skirt, and carrying two bags which she had dumped beside her when she sat down: one a tasselled Greek bag in blues and browns; the other a small tapestry holdall – which seemed a funny thing to have on a beach.

I realized Simon was studying her too. In the normal scheme of things, I thought, Simon ought to pair up with Trudie for the rest of the day. That would transform us into a neat two boy, two girl foursome. It would be better if Simon had a girlfriend. There was no obvious reason why he never quite clicked with girls, because he was not at all bad-looking. He had the sort of straight blond hair which was very much admired at the time, blue eyes and a ready smile. He was thoughtful and polite in a way which had all but gone out of fashion, and he gave out an impression of gentleness, because he was softly spoken and had an unusual delivery – with every word enunciated carefully, as if specially chosen from a vast lexicon in his head. He was also rather quiet until you got to know him, which inevitably meant that Danny was the one people noticed.

All the same it was Simon who asked Trudie, 'Do you live round here?', following up her negative with 'Where are you from?' and getting that strange offhand reply: 'Here and there. Nowhere in particular.'

This didn't faze us at all. It was very 1972 to affect the persona of a mysterious hippy love child, who drifted from place to place, when you were in fact a schoolgirl from Bristol, with a Saturday job in Woolworth's and a respectable career in banking ahead of you, once your O-level results were out.

Naturally, when Trudie asked similar questions of us, she got equally nebulous responses. We said we had driven across from Herefordshire, where we were currently living together in a great big house in the middle of nowhere. We may even have given the impression it was some kind of squat or commune. I don't think the conditions of our tenure were specified, and

I'm sure the fact that we were holidaying students, temporarily escaping the mundanities of Geography Field Trips and Teacher Training, was never mentioned at all.

The upshot of all this was that we had known Trudie scarcely half an hour before she casually suggested 'hitching a ride' with us. An alarm bell began to ring in my head, faint but insistent. I blotted it out. There could be no harm in giving this girl a lift (although an affectionate display between Danny and me was a necessary precursor to avoiding any misunderstandings). Yet still the doubt persisted – we did not know her at all, and she did not know us. My cautious mother had drilled me never to accept, still less solicit, lifts with strangers. All the more reason to do it, said a voice in my head. You're not a kid now, are you?

Simon offered to buy us all ice creams. He ran the words together – eyescream. It's a Brummie thing. Trudie loved it. Not that Simon had the accent: he was well spoken enough to be sneered at as 'posh', but we always said 'eyescream' – it was one of our catch-phrases.

Danny said he wanted mint chocolate chip as usual and I asked for tutti-frutti. In those pre-Magnum days, when ice cream had barely begun to reach out beyond strawberry and vanilla, tutti-frutti was still a bit exotic.

'Ooh – I love the way you said that,' Trudie exclaimed. 'Tutti-frutti – go on, say it again.'

The joke was clearly on me, and I wasn't amused by the way she aped my Midland accent. 'He knows what I want,' I said, attempting to make light of it with a smile.

'Go on, Katy,' Danny joined in. 'Say tutti-frutti for us.'

'Tutti-bloody-frutti,' I said, affecting my Lady Muck voice. 'Come on, Si, I'll help you carry them.'

11

Simon and I set off to stumble our way through the soft sand at the top of the beach. Trudie's barefoot approach was undoubtedly the most practical, and after a few steps I removed my flip-flops and made much better progress.

We joined the short queue at the ice-cream kiosk.

'Do you really think we ought to give Trudie a lift?' I asked. 'We don't know anything about her. We don't even know how old she is.'

Simon could generally be counted on to take a more sensible line than Danny. Danny had a tendency to seize the moment with the confident enthusiasm of one upon whom Dame Fortune invariably smiles. Simon considered briefly before saying: 'I don't think she's as old as she looks – but I'm guessing she's about eighteen.'

It was halfway towards being a question, so I pretended to consider this while squinting into the distance, to see what she and Danny were up to. 'Perhaps we should ask her,' I suggested.

'Mmm.' We were on the point of being served and Simon had become distracted by the operation of extracting coins from the pocket of his jeans – no easy task when they were such a tight fit.

'We might get into trouble if she's only a school kid.' I affected all the concern of someone not quite out of her own teens. 'We don't want to be accused of kidnapping her or something.'

'But she's coming of her own free will,' said Simon. 'It was her idea. A mint choc chip, a rum 'n' raisin and two tutti-fruttis, please,' adding for my benefit, 'I'll ask her, if it's bugging you.'

There was no further opportunity to discuss the matter because as soon as he was handed the first two cones, Simon set off across the beach, leaving me to trudge behind him with the other two ice creams dribbling on to my fingers.

'Yeuch,' I said, licking my hands. 'Sticky.'

'Hey, Trudie,' said Simon, handing her ice cream across. 'How old are you, by the way?'

Ah, that wonderful tact and guile for which the young adult male is so famous.

Trudie's lips curved into a smile. 'Old enough,' she said, dropping a wink which made the others smile.

Thus the matter was settled. We would give Trudie a lift to Herefordshire. Her final destination sealed over a tutti-frutti ice cream.

THREE

I have become quite adept at appearing to give my full attention when I am only half listening. Thus while Marjorie twitters indignantly about someone called George, I ponder the problem of the small white envelope which has been sitting for two days behind my clock, out of sight but never out of mind. George is undoubtedly one of those people I am supposed to know about – a person Marjorie has probably mentioned many times previously, whose role in her life I am assumed to have committed to memory.

'I said to Mary Goldinghey, his minutes bear no relation to what was actually said at the committee meeting – and it's not the first time either.'

I make appropriate sounds of disapproval, while trying to recall what committee this can be – not the WI obviously, unless they've started taking men. Of course girls can join the Scouts now, so who knows?

As far as I can recall, Marjorie sits on several committees. In fact half the world seems to spend its life sitting on committees, presumably in order to organize the other half. I am definitely in the other half – not that I need organizing, but because I mistrust committees. Committees rely on discussions in which the most forthright get to air their views, before arriving at a majority decision which binds everyone. Being an outvoted minority has blighted my life.

I take my shampoo (*guaranteed to revitalize coloured hair*) into the shower, and this provides a temporary escape from her bleating. The water gushes out, obliterating everything else – Marjorie's voice, the smell of the chlorine, the piped muzak. Hits from the musicals this morning – session singers belting out 'The Phantom of the Opera', for goodness sake. When I put my head right under and close my eyes against the jets, even the harsh strip lighting is blotted out, and with it the reality of my tracery of veins and cellulite. I didn't have cellulite in 1972. I don't think anyone else did either. Isn't it one of those things that's been invented since? We weren't so big on things to do with cells back then: cellulite, cell phones, stem cell research were all in the future.

Marjorie resumes her indignation meeting while I am getting dry. 'Basically it's dishonest. If you minute something and it isn't exactly what was said, well, it's a downright lie, isn't it?'

I banish another sentence beginning *Dear Mrs Ivanisovic* to the back of my mind before saying out loud, 'I suppose if it's a complicated discussion, it's sometimes possible to make a mistake.' Always looking to give the benefit of the doubt, that's me. Always the diplomat. Too busy trying not to offend. That's how you end up squashed into the back seat of a Ford Anglia with some girl you've only known a couple of hours. That's how it all begins – being too polite to demur. Another person might have said there wasn't enough room – but good old Katy will just budge up; crush herself into the corner of the oven-like interior, whose back windows don't open more than half an inch. Air conditioning? Are you kidding me? In 1972?

Marjorie isn't having this notion of an accidental misunderstanding. The minutes have been falsified. Her very being is affronted by the episode. I idly wonder what is at stake – a vote of thanks? Someone claiming half a dozen more second-class stamps than was their due? 'I have never done anything dishonest in my life,' she says primly. 'I will not be associated with any sort of dishonesty – nor with people who tell lies.'

A mad urge comes over me to take her hand and bid her a solemn farewell. If she doesn't fancy being tainted by association with George and his dodgy minute-taking, then boy would she flip her lid if she knew a bit more about one of the companions with whom she takes her daily dip. I don't do it, of course. I just toss her my usual 'See you tomorrow'.

On the way home I am free to give my uninterrupted attention to the problem of Mrs Ivanisovic. She has known my address since forever – so why not write before? Has something happened to prompt her? The existence of this unknown factor worries me more than anything. Has an old memory resurfaced – a piece of the jigsaw that doesn't quite fit? And if so, would she be likely to mention it to anyone else? Or could it be something to do with the place itself? Does she know something I don't? Has someone found something? I don't always get a paper – I might easily have missed a small news item. They can do such a lot with so little nowadays. It isn't just cells that have come on in leaps and bounds – there have been huge advances in forensics, stuff we never dreamed of like DNA: which *is* cells, now I come to think about it.

Maybe I should drive out and take a look. I suppose the public footpath still runs right alongside the boundary. If there was any activity I'd be able to spot it. There's Bettis Wood as well. I don't want to go back, but maybe I ought to. The thought flares dangerously. I put it aside while I continue to ponder Mrs Ivanisovic's letter. It's not a good idea to leave it unanswered for too long. A blank refusal might be disastrous when I don't know what cards she holds.

16

If it was an ordinary problem I could mull it over with friends. Over the years I've accumulated some good ones – people who have all sorts of knowledge and life experience, and who between them can advise on anything from income tax to growing geraniums – but this part of my life is a closed book to them and I wouldn't dream of confiding in my brother, still less my sister.

My sister is one of those people you start off making allowances for because they're only six years old and one day wake up to the fact that you're still doing it when they're cracking on towards fifty. That's the way it has always been with me and my sister. She grew up accustomed to evading family responsibilities, so she came to expect automatic exemption from them. Anyway, there is always some pressing thing going on in her life: trouble with a man, or trouble without a man – there was the whole starting-a-new-life-in-Spain thing that failed to materialize, the trauma of her first divorce, the drama of her second . . .

By a strange trick of the light, my sister's complete unreliability in any sort of family crisis has never been a source of irritation to anyone but me. My sister's role was to be the youngest. I was the one upon whom expectations invariably fell, in spite of the fact that, so far as my parents were concerned, I was the scatty, emotionally suspect child, who could not entirely be relied upon – the inherent contradiction seemingly lost on everyone but me.

But then again maybe there is something useful my family can offer in the present situation after all, because from nowhere in particular I suddenly recall my father and the Garden Shed Protocol. My mother loathed our ramshackle garden shed, so after much procrastination my father promised to replace it – but somehow the plans he made to this end were always mysteriously thwarted. Materials were ordered, his best intentions regularly restated, but somehow the new shed failed to appear. On the weekend eventually named for the commencement of this long-awaited project, he was unaccountably called in to work at the last minute and the job was postponed yet again. I often wondered how he managed to arrange that telephone summons – or maybe the gods really were on his side. The new shed was never built.

And so it will be with the visit to Mrs Ivanisovic. After breakfast I frame my reply.

Dear Mrs Ivanisovic,

It was a nice surprise to hear from you and I trust you are keeping well. I would very much like to come up and visit you, but unfortunately I cannot manage this for a few weeks due to various commitments. I note that you have difficulty hearing on the telephone, so I will drop you a line when my diary is not so full. I look forward to seeing you sometime in the near future.

Very best wishes,

Katy Mayfield

Katy? Well, why not?

In fact there is very little in my diary which cannot be moved if needs be. I took early retirement eighteen months ago, when my mother died. I am a completely free agent, which means that I can drive out towards Hereford this afternoon, park my car and take a stroll along the footpath which runs from the house down into the woods – assuming I really want to.

I've been kidding myself for years that I can do as I please, but in reality the puppet strings have only been cut in the past eighteen months – until then it had always fallen to me to be on call for my parents. I never developed any real empathy with them – too great a barrier of assumptions and secrets divided us: but I was pliable and trapped by geographical proximity and complex loyalties. Maybe I never outgrew a vague sense of owing my parents a payback for being such a disappointment to them – or maybe I vainly hoped to redeem myself. Not that it mattered either way – 'their' Katy was too indelibly drawn to be changed. For my siblings, too, I suspect I am a presence rather than a person – their sister Kate, who is there to pick up family duties, provide a cash loan or lend a sympathetic ear (my sister); or who is an occasional duty to be undertaken, a bit like walking the dog, only far less frequently (my brother).

One of these periodic family excursions took place last summer, when I visited a motor museum with my brother and his wife, children and grandchildren. I am not particularly fond of these jaunts and I do not imagine my presence enhances the experience for them; but these occasional get-togethers cannot be avoided – like visits to the dentist, one must be stoical and get through it with partially frozen face and brave attempts at a smile whenever someone makes a joke. One thing I did bring away from the visit was an appreciation of how very small the cars of my youth appear to have been.

There wasn't a Ford Anglia in the display, but they had other makes and models of a similar vintage, and I marvelled at the rear passenger space – accessed by tipping forward a front seat, then clambering through a gap small enough to challenge a contortionist. People boasted of screwing in the back seats of cars, but God alone knows how such an undertaking would have been accomplished.

Cars were slower then and had fewer dual carriageways to travel on, which meant that any but a local destination turned into an endless trek. When I was a child a long car journey was planned like a military campaign, the boot loaded with supplies for the road – sandwiches wrapped in greaseproof paper, flasks of tea, blankets in case of hypothermia, spare Sherpas. With the rashness of youth, Simon, Danny and I had made no such preparations before setting off to the coast, equipped with nothing save what we stood up in and Danny's guitar. There were no emergency rations and nor had we written out the route in bold capitals, packed a torch to read it by after dark, or given much thought to how long the journey might take. Detailed planning was for parents, not free spirits like us.

In this careless frame of mind we lingered on the beach into the early evening, with no one bothering to consider where Trudie might be expecting us to take her. When we finally climbed into the car, Simon did wonder aloud how long it would take us to drive back; but as he and Danny couldn't agree on how long it had taken to get there in the first place, they eventually settled on a mutual notion that the return journey would be quicker than the outward one. I didn't contribute to the discussion at all. I was tired and sunburnt and every breath I took tasted of overheated vinyl.

Thanks to a misunderstanding between the driver and the navigator, we got hopelessly lost along a network of minor roads, whose signposts all led to places beginning with double L, none of which we could pronounce and none of which existed according to our rudimentary road atlas. Trudie thought this was hilarious, as did Danny and Simon. I sat silently in my corner, steaming in every sense.

When we eventually got back on the right road, Danny suggested we pull in at a pub. He spotted that something was wrong as soon as I climbed out of the car.

'Are you okay?' he asked, momentarily placing a cool hand on my forehead. 'You're very warm.'

'I've got an awful headache,' I said.

'Probably had too much sun. You've hardly eaten anything all day either. We'll soon revive you with some beer and sandwiches.'

The pub only had crisps, but the alcohol went straight to my head so I was soon in a much improved frame of mind, joining in with the laughter which was provoking glares of disapproval from the locals. We were accustomed to the hostility our long hair and beads generated in most males over the age of sixty (had they fought a war, just so that we could hang about in pubs looking like that?) and we only laughed all the louder. We were young and free and the world belonged to us.

We had travelled quite a number of miles beyond the pub when I became vaguely aware, from Trudie's remarks, that she not only hadn't the slightest idea of where we were, but was equally uncertain about where we were going. Only when she asked with no more than idle curiosity, 'What's at Hereford?' did it dawn on me that we might have a real problem. I had just decided that a direct question about where she wanted to be dropped off was overdue, when the car started to bounce more alarmingly than usual, forcing Simon to pull into the side of the road.

Trudie and I sat on the dusty grass verge while the lads set about changing the flat tyre. Dusk was descending and the few cars which passed us had their headlights on. Trudie started to hum. Another Cat Stevens number – she was evidently a fan.

I took my opportunity. 'Where are you going exactly?'

The humming stopped. She had been watching the operations with the car jack, but now she turned to face me. It was already too dark to see her expression. 'I'm not sure,' she said. 'I suppose I'm going wherever you guys take me. I saw you sitting on the beach and I just knew my fate was bound up with yours. I'm mediumistic, you see. Sometimes I just know things. It's a gift. I get it from my grandmother.'

I wasn't too sure if there was such a word as mediumistic, but even so I got her drift. I'd met them before, these fashionably fey types, with their mysterious gifts and intuitions.

'I can read palms,' she continued. 'Here – let me do yours.' She held out her hand and I complied, resting my upturned hand on her long slim fingers, while my sceptical mind thought it was too dark to see anything, even if there had been anything to see.

Trudie did not attempt to peer at my lifeline, however. Instead she ran the fingertips of her free hand gently across my palm, looking not at me but at the pale sliver of moon which had just appeared in the sky. A tingle of excitement coursed around the roots of my hair, and the thin steel bangles on my wrist trembled against one another, encircling our hands in a series of barely audible vibrations, like a thousand tiny bells, ringing out a warning from worlds away. When she spoke again it was in a soft rich voice, too low to be audible to the wheel changers.

'You've got an older brother and a younger sister,' she said. 'So you're the middle child, which isn't an easy thing to be. You like children – in fact you want to work with them. You'd like to be a teacher, but I can't tell if you will be or not. There's something in the way – an obstacle of some kind – it's up to you whether you overcome it or not.'

So much for that, I thought. We had been chatting for hours by then and I'd probably let slip clues about myself and my family and the fact that I was at teacher training college.

'I expect you want to know about your love life.' I fancied I detected a trace of mischief in her voice. 'People always do.'

My hand was warm beneath her touch; the pressure of her finger had become a caress. 'Danny is the first great love of your life – but it isn't going to last.'

'That's enough,' I said rather sharply, pulling my hand away.

Trudie didn't seem offended. She continued to affect a dreamy tone. 'There was something else there. Something dark which I couldn't understand.'

My sunburnt flesh was reacting to the cooler air. Goosebumps had broken out on my bare arms. 'Are you guys going to be much longer?' I called out.

'Doing the best we can,' Simon replied, rather tersely.

A single white star had appeared above the horizon.

'I think the moon's fascinating, don't you?' asked Trudie. 'Have you noticed the way, when we're travelling in the car, it seems to follow us?'

I was just deciding how to answer this, when she started singing softly to herself.

'I'm being followed by a moonshadow, moonshadow, moonshadow . . .'

FOUR

I've been back several times before, but it doesn't get any easier. I recognize the sickly sensation of panic which arrives just west of Mortimer's Cross, and know that in another mile or two I'll be removing my hands from the steering wheel, one at a time, to wipe them on the legs of my jeans. I am travelling in silence, because radio stations cannot be trusted not to play the wrong song at the wrong moment. I also blot out any urge to sing or hum, lest my subconscious similarly betrays me. Instead I concentrate on the visuals. It's too early for the trees to be in leaf and many wayside fields have yet to turn green. Signposts point the way to villages with half-remembered names: full of ancient churches and half-timbered cottages, oozing olde worlde charm.

I've driven past before, but until today I've never stopped. This afternoon I approach from the south and turn into the new car park at the edge of Bettis Wood, about a quarter of a mile short of the house itself. I am reassured to find that it looks like any other woodland car park. There's an illustrated noticeboard explaining what sort of things a visitor might hope to encounter – presumably designed by some wildly optimistic council employee, given that it includes deer, foxes and some rare orchids. A separate notice exhorts us to take our litter home, warning of the fine for non-compliance – and yes, there are waymarked trails, colour-coded to make things easier for the littlies. Not a word about murder or the local ghost stories. Both airbrushed out on grounds of poor taste and general unsavouriness, no doubt.

I find it isn't so bad as I anticipated. I challenge myself to walk as far as a nearby clearing where there are three empty picnic tables. Greatly daring, I sit down at one of them, half expecting something to happen – but of course nothing does.

The woods smell different. Spring dampness with a hint of wild garlic – not the dusty warmth of late summer which we knew; the leaden afternoons which presaged thunder in the evening. The very ground beneath our feet was different – the impatient shuffle of last year's dried-up leaves, the twigs snapping underfoot, brittle as our nerves in the moments leading up to that never to be forgotten scream. Somewhere behind me a bird flaps away, the sudden sound making me jump and stifle a cry. Time to move on.

Another car pulls into the car park and two women get out. I judge them to be about ten years younger than me, sensibly dressed in jeans and body-warmers, come to walk their dogs. They glance my way, wondering no doubt what this strange woman is doing, sitting all alone at a picnic table in April. I wonder whether they walk in tandem for security. Woods are dangerous places in which to be alone. The dogs tumble out and are allowed to run free, a lead dangling casually from each woman's hand. They set off along a path which takes them away from the picnic area, their owners following, one of them glancing back at me a couple of times before they go out of sight.

I decide to leave my car where it is and walk up the road to the house. From what I can remember there is nowhere to park, except directly outside the house itself and I don't want to do that. Once I reach the house I can turn off the road and follow the public footpath, which will bring me back through the woods to the car park. When an inner scream rises at the very thought, I suppress it with the reassurance that I am not fully committed to this plan. I can just as easily retrace my steps down the road if I want to. There will be no loss of face. There is no one to goad me – *Go on, Katy – you're not scared, are you?*

The road has grown steeper with the passage of time. There is more traffic, too, and I eat its dust as I walk purposefully up the hill, the surrounding landscape blotted out by high hedgerows. As I ascend the final rise the rooftop comes into sight – just the ridge and chimney pots at first, more of it emerging as I get nearer: then the house itself – closer to the road than I remember – much more visible than when I knew it, now that the overgrown shrubs and rose bushes which screened it from the road have been cut back or cleared away. It's actually quite hard to believe that it is the same house. The brownish-grey roughcast walls have been rendered gleaming white, while the old-fashioned metal window frames, whose dirty panes we never cleaned, have been replaced by modern double glazing. It is still an ugly house, but at least it's no longer forlorn and neglected.

There doesn't appear to be anyone about, so I slow my pace to a dawdle, so as to have a good look. The front garden is full of daffodils and I notice a child's ball, lying forgotten in some long grass near the front gate. A family home then.

The public footpath still runs along the south-eastern edge of the garden, its position indicated by a smart wooden fingerpost. The path looks well trodden but not too muddy. The shrubbery of yore has been replaced by a neat thorn hedge, well established and grown almost to head height. In a year or two this will afford complete privacy, but for the moment I can easily pick out the bedroom window which used to be mine.

The south-eastern side of the house isn't visible from the road, so this is the first time I've looked up at that window in thirty-five years. I am half conscious that I have stopped walking. I stand staring up at the window, as if expecting to see someone there. I remind myself that an unseen occupant of the house may even now be watching me – wondering what I am doing and why I am staring at their house. Maybe they are reaching for the phone – ready to alert the Neighbourhood Watch to the presence of a batty middle-aged woman, lurking on the public footpath with a queer look in her eye.

For all this, I cannot move. They are not real for me, these new occupants. I cannot imagine them. The person I see beyond that window is not a youth of the twenty-first century, equipped with laptop and PlayStation. He is tall and slender, with dark hair falling on to the shoulders of his leather jacket which has creases at the elbows. He moves about the room with confident ease, humming a familiar tune, and when he turns, his face lights up in a smile of recognition, his dark eyes full of mischief and love.

I find that I am crying. Not the delicate romantic crying which makes young men place a protective arm around one's shoulders. These are large untidy tears, which form undignified drips from my not quite double chin – as embarrassing and inappropriate to my years as dancing on the table, or snogging in public.

Almost without thinking I start to hurry along the path. I can see enough of the house and garden to gather that there is nothing untoward. No one has disturbed the most significant element in our landscaping. The garden's secret is safe.

I don't check my pace until I have got well beyond

the point where the garden ends. I am more than halfway across the field and only a matter of yards separates me from the edge of the wood. Now I hesitate. The dog walkers are probably right about safety in numbers. There doesn't appear to be anyone else about, either to adopt the role of local rapist, or merely to wonder at my abrupt about-face. *You're not scared, are you, Katy?*

I try not to stare at the house as I return along the path, lest the occupants really have noticed my interest; but in the end I can't help myself. I wonder who built it in the first place. It probably dates from the 1920s or '30s – a big house, intended for someone with enough money to pay for help with cleaning and gardening, and yet so ugly and utilitarian.

I still remember the unspoken disappointment of our first arrival. We travelled by Ford Anglia of course. Simon driving, Danny (navigating after a fashion) and me in the back, surrounded by all the luggage which didn't fit into the boot. We'd come past all those gorgeous black and white cottages and I had built myself up to expect something equally picturesque, but on a much larger scale. After all, the owner had been described to me as Simon's rich uncle and Simon's remit was to assume the role of caretaker–gardener for the summer, which implied grandeur by the bucketload to me.

The reality was a let-down. An angular house in dirty brown pebbledash, whose front door opened on to a dark, fusty interior. Simon's bachelor uncle had already been away for several weeks and the house had assumed a neglected attitude. Our footsteps echoed on the stone floor of the hall. Dead bluebottles lay on the window sills.

I felt better when we explored the garden, which had a wild beauty in spite of the abundance of weeds. Roses

28

upturned their faces in welcome, clematis trailed artistically from branches and trellis alike, geraniums flopped happily across the path. The lawn was almost knee high.

Simon's uncle had left him with a plan of work to be accomplished in the garden. He wanted a pool and rock garden built in his absence, and the rest of the garden tidied up and generally maintained. That was the payback for living in his house rent-free for the whole summer. Simon was in charge of the Garden Master Plan and Danny was to help with the labouring. I was along to take care of the cooking and cleaning. Not that I had any great experience in either sphere, but the qualification of being Danny's girlfriend outweighed any other questions as to my suitability. In truth Simon didn't know a whole lot about gardening and Danny knew still less – but Simon was his uncle's nephew, and Danny was Simon's best friend, and these factors overrode all other considerations.

Now, as I walk alongside the garden again, I find it so neat and manicured as to be all but alien to its former self. As I turn on to the road and head for the car park, I fancy I can hear someone singing – but it's only the birds, trilling away as they always did. Too easy to imagine things here. Too easy to hear a woman's cry in the screech of a jackdaw.

I quicken my pace so that by the time I reach the car I'm as breathless as I was going up the hill. The two women are just returning with their dogs. Irrationally frantic lest they wonder what I am still doing here alone, I fumble the operation of opening the car and drop the keys. I grab them up and fling open the door. Suppose they approach, to see if I'm all right. I dive into the driver's seat and start the engine. Stop – slow down. Just drive slowly and calmly away. Give them a smile. That will allay any suspicions. Suspicions of what, for goodness sake? Anyone can take a walk.

It's being on my own. People – I need to be with people. I decide to text Hilly and see what she's doing this evening. Not here. I'll drive into Kington and get a coffee first. Hilly is the perfect antidote. She understands everything but knows nothing. The ideal friend for me in fact.

When Hilary Bennington and I first struck up a rapport, the college staff were inclined to discourage it. We were subtly propelled into the company of other students, encouraged to mix with girls who had fewer 'problems': but ultimately nothing could prevent us being drawn together. You may wonder at the staff's interest in my personal friendships, which is hardly the norm in an average academic institution – but of course both Hilly and I were watched intensively for any sign that we were cracking up.

This discomfiting level of attention would manifest itself in random, supposedly casual approaches from lecturers – 'Are you okay, Katy?' – just like that – stopped in the corridor with the enquiry; not infrequently posed in the Special Voice, the sugary, slightly anxious tone reserved for someone who may *not* be okay – someone who must be kept an eye on, because they may not be coping. Hilly and I were both in that category – fragile and damaged, girls who had buckled under personal tragedy, then resumed their studies after a year off. This in itself united us. We looked the same as our classmates – but we were different. Hilly had watched her father fall victim to a heart attack, knelt helplessly at his side while they waited for the ambulance – and I too had crumbled in the face of bereavement.

By the time we returned to college the familiar faces from our own year had qualified and moved on. Our new classmates were far too kind. The forced friendliness – half a dozen people making room for you in the coffee lounge, the concerned faces, the careful avoidance of certain topics which invariably led to awkward silences – all of it like the constant application of pressure to a bruise.

Hilly and I shored each other up. We sat up together when sleep wouldn't come. We never probed, never questioned, never asked if the other was 'okay'. We were just together and it was enough – a relationship in which each could give and receive what was needful. We saw each other through the final year at college and the probationary year of teaching. We shared a flat for a while – until Hilly got married, in fact. Her husband died three years ago and this has brought us closer together again. We've started going on holiday together. Like Marjorie and her friend Pam – except that Marjorie and Pam are both widows – which Hilly and I are not.

In Kington I manage to find a cake shop, where I order tea and a scone – with (what the hell!) jam and cream. I text Hilly and get a message straight back, confirming her availability. Good.

Somehow I feel much better – as if I've slammed the door on the untidy muddle of the past. Locked it all away in a dark cupboard to which no one else has a key.

FIVE

Dear Katy,
I am sorry to inconvenience you, but I am afraid
I must ask you to come and see me as soon as
possible. I am sure neither of us would wish you to
leave it too late.
                              Yours sincerely,
                              E.J. Ivanisovic

It's a first-class stamp this time. Same notepaper,
same slightly unsteady hand. Tone noticeably different.
The first missive was no more than a polite request.
This is a command – with a threat thrown in. It is
blackmail, pure and simple, this phrase *neither of us*
would wish you to leave it too late.

How long is too late? How fast is as soon as possible?
Nor can I put out feelers on the phone, because the
damn woman's deaf, apparently.

I sit staring at the letter. Only one sheet this time.
Not wasting words. Logic says she can't really know
anything at all. Then again, when was life ever logical?
And there is always Factor X. The one thing you
haven't allowed for, which creeps up from nowhere
and catches you unawares. I don't even bother
considering an extension of the Garden Shed Protocol.
The letter reads *don't mess with me* in every syllable.
Loud and clear – *Get yourself here, or you are going to*
regret it. Message received and understood.

Unfortunately 'here' is an address in Sedgefield, which happens to be a couple of hundred miles away. When Mr Ivanisovic retired, they moved north to be near her family. That's where she's from, Mrs Ivanisovic – not some distant Eastern European shore. She's a farmer's daughter from County Durham. It must have been a shock to the system when she became Mrs Ivanisovic. Long before the great Goran made his mark at Wimbledon, she must have had to spell it out for people a thousand times.

They were an oddly matched couple, the Ivanisovics. She was quiet, reserved, raised no doubt in expectation of marrying into good local stock. Danny's father was the opposite – dark where she was fair, excitable and slightly exotic – a wild Balkan transplanted into English soil, who arrived here in the thirties on an engineering scholarship, joined forces with us to fight the Germans, found peacetime employment in the Midlands and never went home, having fallen for a Durham lass somewhere along the way. Oddly it was he, not she, whose accent occasionally betrayed their northern connections. Mrs Ivanisovic had perfect BBC diction.

Danny took after his father in looks. He also flirted with his father's Roman Catholicism, preferring the sensual feast of the Catholic Mass to the earnest Protestant persuasion of his mother – for here too the Ivanisovics stood poles apart: he the bells and smells of Father McMahon's Roman enclave, she the jam and Jerusalem of the red-brick edifice on the opposite side of the road. Devoted to one another despite their differences, they also doted on their only child. His loss haemorrhaged the happiness from their lives faster than blood from a severed artery.

From a note in one of her Christmas cards I learned that Mr Ivanisovic had died not very long after the move to Sedgefield. I could imagine her, dignified in widowhood, not giving way to a public display of emotion. I am surprised to find that I cannot picture her clearly any more. She was younger than him, I think – possibly by some margin. I was a bit in awe of her, although she was always very nice to me. This second letter seems wrong somehow: out of character. But if anyone was going to remember Trudie and start asking about her, it would be Danny's mother. She knew Trudie was staying in the house and must have belatedly begun to wonder what had happened to her – which is still a long way from guessing the truth.

Then in a flash I *do* remember Mrs Ivanisovic's face. I can see her sitting in Simon's uncle's drawing room, perched on the edge of a sofa, balancing a cup and saucer. I recall her expression, somewhere between bemusement and exasperation, as Trudie announced, 'They picked me up on the beach – like a sea shell – and brought me home.'

This was typical of Trudie – a charming falsehood, delivered in such a way as to have you half smiling, half believing it. If truth be told it had been Trudie who latched on to us, and we certainly never intended to bring her home; but by the time the puncture was fixed it had become obvious we wouldn't get back to the house until nearly midnight. Rural England and Wales closed down at half past ten, and as we drove through darkened villages it became clear there was nothing for it but to offer Trudie a bed for the night.

We were all shattered by the time we got back to the house. I began to shiver as soon as we climbed out of the warm car interior, crossing my arms and rubbing them. Danny noticed and cuddled me close while we waited for Simon to unlock the front door. The house felt particularly empty and unwelcoming. My flip-flops slapped against the stone floor of the hall and our voices echoed, unnaturally loud. I watched Trudie's face as she looked around, trying to gauge what she made of it. Simon said she could have the room with the brass bedstead, so I showed her the big cupboard where the sheets were kept, then left her to it.

The three of us had already been in residence for a couple of weeks by then, but the programme of work in the garden had been slow to get under way. Free from the constraints of home and studies, we could squander whole days in bed or cruise around the countryside in Simon's car. We talked and laughed for hours on end, familiarity not yet having exhausted our interest in one another's opinions. Life was suddenly full of exciting new opportunities, like swimming naked in the reservoir, or getting drunk on too many vodka and limes. Although nothing like so sheltered as I had been, Simon and Danny were equally infused with this sense of freedom. Like kids let out to play, we were full of ideas – without our parents to hold us back there was nothing we might not do. There was much talk of visiting local beauty spots, ancient abbeys and ruined castles: plans which mostly failed to materialize, falling victim to late nights and a general reluctance to rise before noon. Danny had already begun to think up bigger and better plans. 'Next year we could go to Italy,' he said. 'See Rome and Florence – maybe Venice.'

'Yesterday you wanted to see Spain,' I protested.

'We could go there too. How about driving down through Europe? We could take a tent, spend the summer on the road?'

His enthusiasm was infectious. Practicalities didn't come into it. Next summer's Grand Tour of Europe became a frequent topic of conversation in those early days. It went without saying that Simon was included in these plans – apart from anything else, he was the only one of us who could drive.

In the meantime, although the lawn had been tamed and some desultory weeding undertaken, the landscaping was still no more than a series of sketches and a heap of good intentions. Nor had I become successfully established in my domestic role. I occasionally undertook a little dusting, which I didn't mind because it entailed handling and examining the large collection of objects which littered the downstairs rooms – many of which I guessed were antiques and perhaps quite valuable. But my efforts never extended much beyond the first distraction to present itself, whether that be one of the musty books I discovered, or some fresh diversion dreamed up by Simon and Danny. My suntan improved with every day that passed, but this progress was not matched in the kitchen, where my lamentable culinary skills condemned us to a diet limited to anything which came with instructions on the packet: a repertoire of Vesta curries and fish fingers, about which in these early days there were only occasional complaints.

The large kitchen where these meals were prepared and consumed occupied one corner of the ground floor. It was grimly old-fashioned, painted in hospital green and cream with a quarry-tiled floor which was cold underfoot whatever the temperature elsewhere. Since our arrival it had become habitually untidy in spite of my sporadic efforts to keep abreast of the washing-up. There were always dirty cups and plates lying about, and a precariously balanced pyramid of kitchenware on the drainer – much of which never saw the inside of a cupboard at all, being recalled into use before anyone got round to putting it away.

On the morning after our trip to the coast, Danny and I followed our usual practice of lying in bed until the middle of the morning. When I finally got out of bed and wandered down to the kitchen, I was surprised

– and I have to admit somewhat piqued – to find Trudie standing at the sink. She had looped her hair out of the way and was busily rinsing suds from a mixing bowl, which she placed on the draining board while I watched. The crockery mountain had vanished, replaced by a couple of recently used utensils and the bowl. There was a lidded saucepan simmering on the stove, and a distinct smell of baking emanated from the oven.

She must have heard my approach, because she turned to smile at me. 'I hope it's all right. I'm making lunch for everyone. Home-made soup and fruit cake. I found what I needed in the pantry. It's to say thank you for letting me stay the night.'

I was about to mumble something ungracious, but the moment was transformed by Simon's arrival; he entered the room, sniffing like a dog who's been denied food too long, drawn no doubt by the unaccustomed smell of proper cooking.

We didn't normally dignify our midday snacking with the name of lunch, but that day we sat at the big kitchen table, eating like civilized human beings. Towards the end of the meal, Simon announced that he was driving into town for some shopping.

'Great,' said Danny. 'If you cash in all the empties, it'll probably pay for next week's food.'

Simon grinned. The amount of drink we were getting through had become a standing joke. 'I've got to go to the off-licence anyway – can't have the beer running low.'

At this point Trudie said she would have to gather her things ready for a lift into town, and Simon surprised us all by suddenly asking Trudie if she wouldn't like to stick around for a few days.

Trudie jumped at the chance. 'You guys are great,' she said. 'And this house – the garden is fab. I feel like I could stay here for ever.'

'You could help Katy with the cooking and stuff,' Simon said.

I was half cross and half relieved to have my role as sole cook and bottle washer unexpectedly usurped. I didn't really expect Simon to solicit my views on the subject before inviting Trudie to chip in. I wasn't used to consultation: at home my parents called the shots – here it was Simon or Danny.

So when Trudie accompanied Simon on the trip into Kington that afternoon, she left her tapestry holdall behind. At the time it didn't particularly trouble me that, although Trudie chattered a lot, we still knew almost nothing about her. I was far more concerned about whether she had lost interest in Danny and latched on to Simon. I was certainly happy to interpret Simon's invitation as a sign that something might be developing between them.

Left to ourselves, Danny and I went out to lie on the grass. It was too hot to do anything else. Apart from a solitary aeroplane trail, the sky was a sheet of uninterrupted blue. I had just started to wonder what it was that Trudie saw in the house and garden, when Danny interrupted my train of thought.

'I wonder how much longer this weather's going to last,' he mused.

'You'd better hope it doesn't break before you get started,' I said. 'It'll be horrible if you have to dig in the rain.'

'There's still masses of time.'

'I know. Almost another three months before Simon's uncle is due back.'

'I bet it isn't this hot in the Limousine,' said Danny.

'I hope Cecile remembers to post those cards,' I said.

Cecile was the buddy from college with whom I had supposedly travelled to France, to spend the summer picking fruit at her grandpa's farm. I had given her a pack of lettercards to post back to my parents at suitable intervals, pre-written with innocuous messages to the effect that I was having fun, the work was quite tiring, the weather good, Cecile's family kind to me and similar bland nonsense: all of which would help convince them that I was safely occupied overseas, under the chaperonage of my friend's family, rather than fucking my boyfriend in rural Herefordshire. It wasn't done, you see, respectable single girls shacking up with their boyfriends for the summer – not in my family anyway.

When Simon and Trudie returned that afternoon, she had a carrier bag full of fruit and veg. That night we feasted on sausages, jacket potatoes and fresh greens. As I helped myself to more gravy, I found I was warming to Trudie by the minute. It was the first decent meal we'd eaten in a fortnight.

Simon seemed to think that Trudie completed our team – with her to help me, he said, he and Danny could concentrate on the garden (not that I had noticed the cooking and housework distracting them over-much). He proposed they commence the pond excavation the following day, even making some corny remark like 'full steam ahead', to which Danny raised a half-drunk bottle of Newcastle Brown in salute.

It was nice, I thought, for Simon to have someone – because that surely must be the way the wind was blowing. And not just anyone either; because there could be no denying that Trudie was beautiful. I suppose I hadn't taken proper notice of her the day before, but I could see it now. She had well-proportioned features, dark brown eyes, and lips which could have been used in cosmetic ads. Moreover the loose-fitting smock and maxi skirt she'd been wearing on the beach had concealed her figure, which today's cut-down denim shorts and white cotton shirt, rolled up under her bust, made very obvious. Trudie was positively stunning. No wonder Simon wanted her to stay.

All this made Trudie dangerously memorable. Mrs Ivanisovic only met her once – but it must have been enough.

I don't want to face up to the letter, but what choice do I have?

Dear Mrs Ivanisovic,
I will visit you at 2 p.m. on Wednesday 25th, unless I hear from you that this date is inconvenient.
Yours sincerely,
K. Mayfield

SIX

Work began on the pond the day after Trudie joined our ménage. By the end of the morning the true magnitude of the task had become clear. Simon had delineated the proposed outline with a long piece of string, held down by a series of stones. Two hours of digging had produced a small uneven hole in the centre of this area, the greater portion of which was still unbroken ground.

After a break for cheese sandwiches and beer, the boys continued their efforts while Trudie set to work in the kitchen, peeling potatoes for our evening meal. Not wishing to be perceived a slacker, I took a duster from the cupboard in the pantry and headed for the room at the front of the house which we had christened the library. I started with the objects on the desk, then the desk itself, gathering a ridge of pale fluff on my duster, which I flicked on to the carpet, being unsure what else to do with it. After this I turned my attention to a small bookshelf which stood under the window. The books had faded spines, rusty browns and blue blacks, with titles printed in gold. I picked one out at random and opened it – tiny black print on stiff paper which had faded to a delicate shade resembling milky coffee; splotched here and there with spots of darker brown, as if some of the coffee granules had not quite dissolved. Someone had written on the flyleaf in black ink: *For my god-daughter Emily from Aunt Grace.* I replaced it next to *Travels in Persia and Kurdistan*, working my way down, vaguely flicking my duster across the contents of the upper two shelves, then kneeling on the red and black carpet to better reach the bottom one.

On the bottom shelf there was a pile of magazines, marginally less ancient than their hardback companions, the top one of which had been left folded open, as if someone had been reading it and not quite managed to finish the item of interest before it got tidied away. The uppermost article was headed *An Intriguing Local Mystery*, and when I pulled it out for a better look I saw that the accompanying picture was captioned *Local beauty spot Bettis Wood*.

I settled down to read, the duster in my hand forgotten.

Ludlow Castle has its White Lady and Hergest Hall is said to be haunted by the shade of Black Vaughn, but how many people know that Bettis Wood has a ghost of its own? Ever since Agnes Payne was murdered in the woods on a hot summer's night in 1912, strange sights and sounds have been regularly reported there and local folk avoid the woods after dark.

Agnes Payne lived in a cottage about a mile from the woods with her husband Tom and their three small children. Tom was the local carpenter and had a reputation as something of a ladies' man. All that summer he had been doing work for a wealthy widow called Martha Stokesby and, if local gossip was to be believed, he and Mrs Stokesby had become more than mere friends.

On the evening of 13th August, Tom finished work at Mrs Stokesby's house rather later than usual and called at the inn for a glass of beer on his

way home. Later that evening, a neighbour ob-
served Agnes setting out from her cottage alone. It
was not the first time she had been seen setting out
alone for a late-evening stroll, but it would be the
last.

According to Tom Payne, when he arrived home
he found his children safely asleep, but his wife was
unaccountably absent. He walked a little way along
the road, but returned to the cottage when unable to
find her. At first light he roused his nearest
neighbours and a search was undertaken. Agnes
was discovered in Bettis Wood, where she had been
strangled with a silk scarf. Payne said the scarf did
not belong to his wife and its origin was never
identified.

Tom Payne was the chief suspect and had no alibi
– but then a new witness came forward, a pedlar
called Joel Rimey, who had been camping on the
edge of the wood on the night of the murder. Rimey
said he had seen a woman very like Agnes, in
company with a man whom he could also describe.
They had been walking along a footpath heading
into the woods, at a spot not very far from where
Agnes' body was found. His description of the
woman exactly fitted Agnes, right down to her
paisley-patterned shawl; but the man he described –
a bearded man with a dark coat and hat – was
nothing like Tom Payne, who was clean shaven.

No arrest was ever made and the mystery remains
unsolved to this day, but sometimes, late at night –

'What have you got there?' asked Trudie.

I gave a little squeak of alarm. 'God, you startled
me. I'm just reading this magazine I found. It's about
the wood down below. There's a ghost story.'

'Wow,' said Trudie. 'Let me see.'

I scanned the final sentence before handing it over; then waited in silence while she read it in her turn. When she had finished, she looked up at me with wide eyes. 'So that's it,' she said.

'What?'

'Ever since I got here, I've had these funny feelings about the wood. I've been looking at it out of my bedroom window and something has been kind of drawing me to it. It must be her – Agnes.'

'Oh, come off it,' I said. 'You never said anything about it until now.'

Trudie shrugged, as if to indicate she didn't much care whether I believed her or not. 'I told you, I've got a gift.' She swept out of the room before I could say anything else.

Abandoned to my dusting, I made a few more random swipes around the picture frames, before it struck me that perhaps I should have cautioned Trudie about mentioning the murder of Agnes Payne in front of Danny. I returned to the kitchen but the peeled potatoes were already in their pan of water and Trudie had decamped.

By the time I caught up with her in the garden, I realized I was too late. After leaving me she had evidently gone straight back to the kitchen to make a pot of tea for the workers, which she had already taken outside. Simon's uncle's house was so old-fashioned that there weren't any mugs, just cups and saucers: some plain everyday green and white ones and a bone china service decorated in a pattern of pink roses. The latter looked scarily fragile to me, but of course this was the set which Trudie had selected to carry into the garden for an afternoon tea break.

As I approached, I could hear her saying, '. . . and now her ghost haunts the woods. I suppose she'll never rest until she gets justice.'

'That doesn't seem very likely now,' said Simon. 'When did you say it was – 1912? That's sixty years ago. The guy'll be dead by now.'

'If it was a guy,' said Trudie. 'There's the Other Woman, too.'

'I thought you said she was seen going into the wood with a man.'

'Well, yes – but it could have been a woman, disguised as a man.'

'It could have been her husband, wearing a false beard,' I said, flopping on to the grass next to Danny, who leant across to greet me with a peck on the cheek.

'I doubt it,' said Trudie. 'I mean, surely she would have recognized her own husband.'

'All the more reason for her to go into the woods with him.'

'But why the false beard?'

'Hang on,' said Simon. 'I've got it. What about the poacher bloke? Maybe he did it, then said he'd seen her with someone else, to throw everyone off the scent.'

'Pedlar,' I said. 'He was a pedlar.'

Secretly I was just relieved at the half-jokey level of interest the story had provoked – because, until then, I had been doing the avoidance-of-certain-topics thing. I hadn't quite been down the track of the Special Voice, but I had been careful not to mention either sudden death or the Timmins Prize. I was probably being over-sensitive, but the circumstances of Danny's winning the prize had been marred by tragedy and I sensed that he felt awkward about it. The prize was awarded by the faculty every year, to the geography student who gained the highest mark in the exams which marked the mid-point of the degree course. In the run-up to the exams it had been generally accepted that only two students were in serious contention that year – Danny Ivanisovic and a girl called Rachel Hewitt.

Rachel Hewitt was a real golden girl: that rare combination of academic and socialite – popular, lively, clever. When she failed to show up for lectures one Monday morning, everyone was surprised but not overly concerned. Rachel had mentioned that she was thinking about going home for the weekend, so when friends knocked on her door in Halls and got no reply, they assumed she had decided to go at the last minute, then missed her train back on Sunday evening. When she still failed to appear on Monday afternoon this theory started to falter, and by Tuesday evening someone got anxious enough to phone her family – who said they hadn't seen her at all. At this point Security were alerted. When they opened Rachel's door with the pass key, they found her lying on the bed wearing the same clothes in which she had last been seen the previous Friday. She had been strangled.

The window of her room was open and only one floor up. It was in a part of the building immediately above a flat-roof extension – an easy enough entry and escape route for her killer; although he could equally have let himself out into the corridor to make his getaway. The doors had Yale locks which sprang shut if you didn't wedge them.

There had previously been reports of a prowler on the campus. One girl claimed to have seen a shadowy face at the window when she was taking a shower; someone else had startled a guy mooching around the parked cars late at night. For the rest of the year, male students set up night-time patrols of the grounds, but nothing further was seen. The police interviewed dozens of possible suspects and witnesses, but the investigation appeared to get nowhere. The whole faculty was agog with it; and of course Danny became the recipient of the wretched Timmins Prize – which, as Simon pointed out, he would probably have won anyway – but Rachel Hewitt's death had turned the whole thing sour, making any kind of celebration inappropriate. For my own parents, the whole episode was confirmation of their wisdom in insisting on my staying at home in Birmingham to study. To the danger of lax morals in halls of residence could now be added the dangers of lax security. They had always been worried that, if not kept a strict eye on, Katy would get into some sort of trouble.

The boys soon lost interest in the story of Agnes Payne and neither of them mentioned Rachel Hewitt – there was really no reason why they should. Once their tea was finished they went back to digging, neither willing to be the first to admit that they'd had enough for the day, or that the work was much harder than originally envisaged. However, when I went out later that afternoon to tell them our food was almost ready, Simon was holding out his blistered hands for Danny's inspection, turning them over and forlornly displaying broken nails.

'Jeez,' said Danny. 'Don't be such a girl.'

They were both laughing, but I could see that underneath it Simon really hated the way his hands were getting messed up.

'Come on,' I said. 'Stop messing about. The meal's nearly ready.' The word 'meal' was a cop-out, because I knew that Simon called it dinner whereas I was used to calling it tea.

'We're coming right now,' Danny said. 'You look good enough to eat yourself.' He picked me up bodily and gave me a hug while he pretended to gnaw at my neck, tickling me while I shrieked and made futile attempts to get away.

That evening we sat in the garden until it was too dark to see. Danny played his guitar and we sang: sometimes all together, sometimes just him.

'You've got a smashing voice,' Trudie told him. 'And you're nice-looking as well. You could make it as a pop star, I bet. Simon, don't you think Danny would look great on *Top of the Pops*?'

Simon didn't answer because he was discouraging a spider who had taken an interest in his can of beer.

'Go on,' urged Trudie. 'Sing something else.'

'Shall we give them "Bridge over Troubled Water", Si?' Danny suggested.

Whether doing Simon and Garfunkel or Morecambe and Wise, they were a polished double act. They went back a long way – an enduring friendship with its own private jokes, which inevitably meant that they often referred to people and events I had never heard of. I desperately tried not to mind that Simon knew so much more about Danny than I did, recalling that without Simon there would be no rich uncle's house, and without the house no chance of spending the whole summer with Danny. But whenever Simon was around I couldn't entirely escape the feeling that I was the newcomer in our trio. No wonder it irritated me like hell that by the end of our first full day as a quartet Trudie was behaving as if she had known the others for years.

SEVEN

After Trudie's arrival our days fell into more of a pattern: while the lads worked on the big garden project, Trudie and I would engage in our housekeeping duties for a while, then lie in the sun, reading the books and magazines we found in the house. When the boys tired of digging – which was not infrequently – we played hand tennis or rounders, using a bat improvised from a piece of old chair leg discovered in the shed. Then Simon found an ancient croquet set and we played with that too – using rules of our own devising. In the evenings we talked and sang and played cards – mostly daft games like Cheat and Crazy Eights – forced to manufacture our own entertainment because the house had no television set.

'Weird,' said Trudie. 'Fancy having no phone and no telly.'

'He doesn't live here most of the time,' said Simon. 'It used to be my grandmother's house until she died, and she always preferred the wireless.'

'Weird,' repeated Trudie.

There was an old radiogram in one of the downstairs rooms, but we could not coax anything from it, beyond a few snatches of foreign babbling and a lot of static. We relied instead on a battery-operated transistor radio, permanently tuned to Radio 1. We caught occasional news bulletins, but everything seemed to be happening a world or two away.

Trudie had only been with us for a couple of days when the teapot with the pink roses on it disappeared. It was Trudie herself who drew our attention to the loss, which indeed the rest of us might never have spotted at all, because she was the only one who ever used the best tea service. Soon afterwards we missed an ugly vase which had previously languished on the kitchen window sill – a hideous yellow object, from which a cluster of purple pansies stood out in relief; then the washing-up liquid vanished, followed by a pair of nail scissors which Simon had left on the kitchen table. The two latter items reappeared within a matter of hours, both in exactly the same place from whence they had vanished, but the vase and teapot were not returned. During the next couple of weeks a whole variety of objects went walkabout – most of them being found again, hours or sometimes days after they were missed.

My first theory was that Trudie was organizing these little disturbances to draw attention to herself and her 'gifts', which had not been taken particularly seriously by anyone to date. Then I began to wonder whether it was all an elaborate scheme to cover up the fact that she had broken the teapot and was too afraid to own up to it. When I noticed the disappearance of a glass paperweight from the library, I developed a new idea. Trudie never seemed to be short of cash and I speculated that some of the household ornaments and china might be finding their way to the antique shops in Leominster. Whenever Simon drove into town, Trudie invariably went along, usually with her Greek bag slung over her shoulder.

I put this theory to Danny as we lay in bed one night, but he didn't rate it very highly. Danny had taken to Trudie and he was always loyal to people he liked; besides which, he lacked my feminine curiosity. The fact that Trudie managed to sidestep all my casual enquiries about who she was and where she came from had apparently passed him by completely. Whenever I drew this to his attention he only speculated that perhaps she was being deliberately mysterious – 'She may not want to admit she's younger than us and hasn't been around much yet.'

'All the same, those things haven't grown legs and walked away by themselves. Don't you think we ought to say something to Simon?'

'Trudie says it's the ghost of Murdered Agnes, trying to attract our attention,' said Danny, mischievously.

I snorted. 'Murdered Agnes, my foot. It only started after Trudie arrived. I think we should ask Simon if she went off on her own at all, when they went to Leominster together the other day. There's going to be hell to pay if his uncle gets back and finds loads of stuff missing.'

Danny was in an infuriating mood and pretended to snore. I was not going to be deflected. 'I'm going to tell Simon tomorrow,' I said.

'Tell him what?'

'What I think.'

'Anyone would think you don't like Trudie,' he said.

'Of course I like her,' I said. 'That's not the point.' Or maybe it was the point. I pondered this as I lay in the darkened bedroom, watching the place where the curtains made a paler patch against the wall. Ever since her arrival, Trudie had joked and flirted with Danny and I had had to pretend not to mind. While I had no objection to the presence of someone who would get Simon out of our hair, maybe I wasn't so keen on the idea of an unattached Trudie floating around. I told myself it was nonsense of course – in spite of her various idiosyncrasies, I couldn't help liking Trudie. She was warm and friendly and very easygoing. She did more than her share of the cooking and washing-up and was happy to fall in with whatever anyone suggested by way of recreation. She just happened to be one of those people who habitually throws an arm around someone's shoulders, or ruffles their hair – there was really nothing in it – and anyway Danny never took the slightest notice. I wasn't jealous of her, if that was what he meant.

Although the pond excavation had ascended our list of priorities, we still enjoyed a lie-in every morning. It was almost eleven when I got up the next day and no one else was stirring. The first thing I saw on entering the kitchen was the paperweight from the library. Like a number of other items, it had reappeared in the centre of the kitchen table, rather than the spot from which it had originally vanished. I knew Trudie must have put it there, but it spooked me all the same. I comforted myself with the thought that it was safe and sound. Hopefully everything would be returned in due course – then no one would get into any trouble over missing valuables. The fact that I had threatened to voice my suspicions to Simon the night before made me feel hot with embarrassment.

Although I think we were all secretly convinced that Trudie was behind the missing objects, we more than half pretended to go along with her talk of restless spirits and poltergeists. It was a bit of a laugh and there was no point getting into a direct confrontation over it. The items were mostly trivial and invariably reappeared; and besides, there was no hard evidence of Trudie's involvement. If challenged she could have argued that any one of us might equally be responsible. Pushing the point was tantamount to accusing her of telling lies, so we kept schtum – which in turn developed into a sort of vague acceptance of the presence of Agnes Payne.

All of us were pretty light-hearted about this – even Trudie, who affected to believe herself more closely in tune with these matters than the rest of us. It was a sort of running joke – when anything at all was mislaid (a not infrequent occurrence in a household as disorganized as ours) someone would incline their head and say knowingly, 'Agnes again . . .' But although Agnes managed to defuse the difficulties which stemmed from our general untidiness, there was no conveniently insubstantial scapegoat for the various other problems which cropped up with depressing regularity: when one or other of us rose with a head throbbing from the previous night's over-indulgence to discover something disgusting blocking the sink, or when our bare feet encountered dried mud which had been trodden in the day before.

The day the paperweight made its reappearance was particularly hot and sticky, so all of us were grateful for the onset of evening when the temperature reduced to a more tolerable Regulo 3. It was still stuffy indoors, so we had carried our food outside and were all sitting on the parched grass, nursing plates of fish fingers and beans (I had taken a turn to provide our meal), when there was an almighty crash behind us. I shrieked, Danny swore, Simon and Trudie both jumped up.

'Jesus-Moses, what the hell was that?' exclaimed Danny.

Simon was standing up, looking towards the house. 'There's something on the terrace,' he said.

The terrace was a paved area which ran along one side of the building. There was grass growing between some of the slabs, but apart from that it was uniformly grey. We could all see the garish splash of yellow and purple which had appeared on the stones, where Simon was pointing.

We abandoned our plates on the lawn before approaching the spot uncertainly, with no one apparently in any hurry to get there first. It was an anticlimax. A jagged chunk of pottery was lying a few inches from the wall of the house. It was a fragment of the ugly vase which had previously stood on the kitchen window sill. The thing had evidently smashed with considerable force, because the other pieces had flown several feet across the paved area and beyond.

'There's no one around,' said Simon. 'Where the heck has it come from?'

We all looked up. Trudie's open bedroom window was immediately above the point where the vase had fallen.

'It's been open all day,' she said, in answer to an unasked question.

'Do you think someone's got into the house?' I asked.

After a brief debate, the boys decided to undertake a thorough search of the premises, having first stationed Trudie and me at the front and back doors respectively. I stood in the kitchen, hopping from one foot to the other and straining to catch any sound from elsewhere in the house. As usual I had fallen in without demur: biddable Katy who always goes along with everything, then ends up standing with her heart in her mouth, waiting for the Mad Axe Man to appear.

But it was Simon who eventually entered via the door from the hall, to report that there was no sign of any intruder.

'I don't believe there was anyone else here,' Trudie announced, when we had reassembled on the back lawn. 'I think it was a sign that Agnes is getting more restless. Maybe she wants us to do something for her – hold a seance or something.'

Danny was poking at his congealed beans with his knife. 'I'm a Catholic,' he said. 'We don't go in for that sort of shit.'

'I don't think we ought to start messing around with stuff like that,' I said. I couldn't help thinking that the way the vase had made its dramatic entrance – right under Trudie's open window – was highly suggestive. She couldn't have thrown it out herself, because she had been sitting with the rest of us in plain view: but maybe she had found some way of rigging it, so that the vase would inevitably topple out of the window at some point during the evening.

'If we go on ignoring her, things may get worse,' Trudie persisted.

'Well, *I* don't want to do it,' I said, confidently expecting Danny to second this opinion; but he was preoccupied with organizing the plate in his lap, and didn't appear to hear me.

'I don't mind giving it a go,' said Simon. 'I don't see what harm it could do.'

'Well, if everyone else wants to do it, I don't mind joining in,' said Danny. Ignatius Loyola he certainly wasn't.

'You're not scared, are you, Katy?' Simon asked. 'I thought you said you didn't believe in ghosts and all that sort of stuff, when we were talking about it the other night.'

I sensed the mockery in his voice. I hated being teased. 'No, I'm not, and no, I don't.'

'Looks like three to one anyway,' said Simon. 'Democratic decision of the majority.'

'You don't have to be there if you don't want to,' said Danny, in a vaguely conciliatory tone. I tried to catch his eye, but he was still poking at his plate and didn't notice. He had to be joking. There was no way I was going to sit somewhere on my own in that big empty house, while the other three had a shot at calling up the spirits. I was about to say something else when he burst out: 'Bloody hell. There's a bug in my food.'

55

Trudie leant across, so that her hair draped over his shoulder. 'It's not,' she said. 'It's just a bit of burnt breadcrumb.'

'It's obvious Trudie fixed the vase to fall out of the window,' I said crossly.

She rounded on me at once. 'What do you mean?'

'What I said. It's just another of your little stunts – to draw attention to yourself.'

'Don't be ridiculous,' Simon said. 'How could Trudie possibly have made the vase fall out of the window when she was sitting here with us?'

'There are ways of doing it.'

'All right then, name one.' Simon threw out the challenge with a triumphant sideways glance in Trudie's direction.

'I don't know. I'm not a member of the Magic Circle.'

'Well, neither is she.'

'How would you know? We don't know anything about her.'

Danny put his plate on the grass before reaching over to squeeze my knee. 'Come on, Katy,' he said. 'Let's not make a big deal out of it.'

'Well, I'm fed up with all this silly Agnes business. Things disappearing and everyone pretending to believe in it all. Simon doesn't really believe in it. He's only pretending he does now to be provocative—'

'How would you know what I believe?' Simon interrupted.

'You're only backing Trudie up because you always disagree with me about everything on principle.'

'Maybe that's because you're always wrong.'

'Come on, guys,' Danny pleaded. 'You're ruining the whole evening.'

'You know what I think?' asked Simon. 'I think you're just plain scared – you're accusing Trudie because the idea of calling up the spirits scares the hell out of you.'

'That's not true!'

'Of course it isn't,' said Danny smoothly. 'You're not really bothered, are you, Katy? You'll join us for a bit of the old voodoo and magic if it makes everyone happy?'

He had edged across, so that he could put his arm around me. He obviously hadn't a clue how much the whole idea put the wind up me – I knew he would never have pushed it if he had – but unless I was prepared to invite Simon's ridicule by making any more fuss, I could see I was cornered. 'I don't mind,' I said, as casually as I could. 'I'm in, if everyone else wants to do it.'

EIGHT

Marjorie's friend Pam has started swimming again. The knee op went well apparently, so the surgeon has given her the all clear. While this does afford me a bit of breathing space from Marjorie, it also introduces another torment, because all the time I'm swimming, I'm constantly aware of their voices echoing off the roof of the pool, like two birds shrieking in an aviary (either that or a jungle), an impression enhanced by the unexpected appearance of plastic ivy and imitation banana trees which sprouted overnight around the pool on Thursday last. (The Leisure Services committee evidently has a year-end surplus.) The miniature tree ferns (which Pam thinks are pineapples) don't survive the week, on account of their resemblance to oversized hand grenades, which the local youths are briefly able to lob at one another until an edict from Health and Safety intervenes. However, the plastic creepers have been allowed to stay, so with Pam and Marjorie supplying the sound effects, we only need a monkey or two swinging from the rafters to complete the tropical illusion.

It's just three days until I am due to keep my appointment with Mrs Ivanisovic. I'm going to book the Travelodge when I get home after swimming – something I've put off until now, vaguely hoping that if I don't make any firm arrangements the trip to Sedgefield won't happen. I have waited in vain for some word from Mrs I to say that the 25th is inconvenient, but there's been nothing. Silence. Just an ominous silence.

By poor timing, I find myself in the changing room with Marjorie and Pam.

'He didn't!' Marjorie is saying.

They both affect mock horror at whatever it is 'he' did, but this is followed by a lot of inappropriately girlish laughter and shrieking, indicative of delight rather than disapproval. I eventually work out that 'he' is a man who has been making advances to Pam. 'Honestly,' she says. 'I said to him – at *our* age . . .'

It is obvious that for all her protestations Pam is thrilled by this attention – like a fourteen-year-old the morning after her first date, recounting her experiences behind the bike sheds. Don't some women ever grow out of this terrible susceptibility to male attention? Just before I activate the shower, I overhear Pam proclaiming shrilly, 'I was all of a flutter.'

All of a flutter. How well that describes it. I can still remember the moment when Danny first asked for my phone number. False modesty aside, I suppose I must have been quite pretty by the time I got to college. By then I'd got the braces off my teeth and lost most of the spots; but shyness and lack of confidence still bedevilled me. My parents kept me on a tight rein, and after an all girls' school I went to a training college where female students outnumbered the males by six to one, so I hadn't exactly been overrun with offers of dates.

Cecile was my best friend in that first year at college. Neither of us was a huge success socially: I was shy and tended to shrink into corners, while poor old Cecile was downright plain. Tell people your friend is half French and they expect Brigitte Bardot; but Cecile took after the other side of her ancestry and looked like

59

what she was – an earnest Jewish girl, with dark hair and glasses. She did well at college, then threw up her career to marry a rabbi and raise a family in Hendon, severing her Gallic Catholic connections almost entirely. We don't exchange Christmas cards, because she doesn't do Christmas.

In those days Cecile was far more lively than I was. I dreamed of excitement and romance, but was uncertain how to get any. Cecile was convinced that the route lay via hanging out in places almost exclusively patronized by members of the opposite sex and, with this in mind, she dragged me to watch Kung Fu films and listen to dodgy local bands, in virtual certainty that these were the natural habitats of the male. Alas, Cecile had failed to allow for the darkness which is the norm in cinemas and blacked-out upper rooms in city centre pubs – and when we were not completely overlooked in the gloom, we invariably got lumbered with the dull, acne-covered types, who made a half of bitter last all evening and had fingers greasy from the chips they bought on the way home.

I can't recall which of us initiated a trip to the fair; but my going was an act of defiance, because according to my parents funfairs were full of rough lads and common girls, and consequently not the sort of places they wanted me to hang about in – this naturally imbued visiting fairs with an allure which drew me like a magnet. The fair was being held on Billesley Common. As we approached, the smell of frying onions and greasy doughnuts reached us, mingled with the damp earthy scent of the flattened winter grass, slimy underfoot thanks to the passage of the approaching multitude. My heart quickened to the sound of half a dozen tunes playing at once, punctuated by laughter and screams: a micro-world of pulsating lights enclosed within a circle of trailers and caravans.

Once inside the barrier we drifted among the crowds, assessing the cost of the rides. The bigger ones were expensive and, without boyfriends to pay for us, we couldn't afford to have many goes. I found myself noticing that my mother had been right about the number of common-looking girls inhabiting the place. They all appeared to be having much more fun than we were, whether screaming as the man spun them on the waltzers, or pigging on candyfloss while their boyfriends threw hoops or darts, or fished for plastic ducks in the hope of winning them a prize. Up close everything looked tatty and I began to wonder why we had been so eager to come. 'Shall we go on the bumper cars?' I asked, half-heartedly. I thought I was talking to Cecile, but when I turned it was to find that two men had managed to sidle between us. The one nearest to me had an anaemic-looking moustache and piggy eyes. 'All right then, darlin',' he said. 'You hop in with me.' His mate burst out laughing. They both smelled beery. It was barely eight o'clock – quite early for drunks. I decided to ignore them, but when I tried to sidestep past the one who had spoken I accidentally stood on his foot. He glared at me and grabbed my arm, probably thinking it had been deliberate. I am not sure what he had in mind, but the situation was arrested by the intervention of a voice from my left.

'Let go of her arm and beat it.'

There was something about the voice which made Piggy Eyes automatically loose his hold and take a step back. His companion had already decided discretion was the better part and was moving off into the crowd, beckoning his mate to follow. I turned to get a look at my rescuer and saw two guys of our own age, taller than the drunks, one fair, one dark, both good-looking.

'He didn't hurt you, did he?' It was the dark-haired one who spoke. I exchanged a swift look of disbelief

61

with Cecile. He was the sort of rescuer dreamed up by the serial writers at *Jackie* – far too gorgeous to be true.

I assured him that I was fine.

'Maybe you ought to stick with us for a while, just in case those two troglodytes are hanging around anywhere. I'm Danny, by the way – and this is Simon.'

'I'm Katy,' I said. 'And this is Cecile.'

The tawdry funfair was instantly transformed into a place of magic. Danny took my hand and began to steer me through the crowd, leaving Simon to pair up with Cecile and follow us. Two minutes later we were crushed together in a dodgem, Danny handling the car with one hand, while he kept the other arm protectively around my shoulders.

We had been on several other rides and were on our way to the twister, when I spotted the giant stuffed toys at the back of the rifle range. There was a rabbit dressed in top hat and tails and I let out a little squeal of delight at the sight of it.

Danny halted in his tracks. 'Would you like one?' he asked.

'You have to hit a bull's-eye,' I protested. 'No one ever does.'

Danny grinned at me. 'I will,' he said. 'I always get what I want.' I loved the certainty in his voice, and the way his eyes met mine as he said it, with their unmistakable implication that his desires ran to more than mere stuffed rabbits.

The three of us watched while Danny handed over his money and took aim. We were all laughing, urging him on, and we groaned collectively when his first three shots missed by a mile. Danny gestured to the man behind the counter that he wanted another go.

'It doesn't matter,' I said quickly. I had scarcely known him half an hour, and he probably didn't have money to throw away on toy rabbits.

'Come on,' said Simon a bit impatiently. 'Let's go on the twister.'

But Danny was already pushing a pound note at the stallholder and picking up the rifle again. His whole body exuded focus and concentration. His next three shots also went wide of the mark.

'They rig the guns, you know,' said Simon, keeping his voice low, and a wary eye on the stallholder who was only a few feet away from us, taking money from another hopeful punter. 'Twist the sights or something. You won't get one,' he added in a louder voice for Danny's benefit.

'I really don't mind . . .' I began.

The stallholder had ambled back towards us. He gave Simon a hostile glare. 'You sayin' this is a crooked game, son?'

At that moment Danny fired again and scored a bull's-eye. He tossed the rifle down and threw his arms above his head like a cup-winning goal scorer, extending the gesture of victory my way, until he had enveloped me in a hug.

'Well done, mate.' The guy behind the stall pulled down a giant rabbit, which at Danny's gesture he handed across to me, taking the opportunity to eyeball Simon at the same time. Simon stepped back smartly, but Danny was oblivious of any tension – totally immersed in his moment of triumph. His determination to satisfy my whim, coupled with the fact that he was far and away the best-looking boy who had ever shown the slightest interest in me, ensured that I was beyond being 'all of a flutter' – I was soaring on fully fledged wings.

Although Cecile had paired off with Simon, their association went no further than one foursome to the cinema with Danny and me. Cecile and Simon just didn't hit it off. 'He was hopeless,' she said afterwards, 'like trying to kiss a flatfish.'

After that, Danny and I went out a couple of times on our own. There was no opportunity for more than this before he and Simon went back to university, the very word inducing terror in my heart, with its guaranteed complement of scheming females who probably couldn't wait to get their claws into him. I was secretly terrified that I would never hear from him again, but he rang me almost every day and about once a month he came down to Birmingham on the train – each brief visit like a colourful explosion against an otherwise grey canvas.

When Danny *was* around he made things happen. While I only talked about going down to London for the day, he went to buy the tickets. He introduced me to rock concerts, folk clubs and Chinese food. The boundaries of my life expanded from home and college to seemingly encompass the whole world. I was finally taking part in life, instead of being a mere spectator. I think it was when the flowers arrived on my birthday – not just any old flowers, but a bunch of red roses – a gesture both impossibly expensive and incredibly romantic – that the relationship leapt up several notches from merely 'seeing' one another, to a grand passion. From then on I was sold.

In those days a boyfriend proved you weren't a failure or a freak. Having one all but defined your worth as a person. Friends from college who had seen the two of us together sidled up to say, 'He's gorgeous. Where did you get him?' Danny charmed everyone who met him and I basked in the envy he generated. Of course I could rely on my parents to strike a discordant note. Although they made Danny superficially welcome, in private they grumbled that I was 'infatuated' and becoming 'besotted' with someone I 'hardly knew'.

'You're not in love with him, you know,' my mother chided. 'You're in love with the idea of falling in love.'

I was familiar with her Rodgers and Hart LP and ignored the reference. 'You're too young to know your own mind yet, Katy,' she persisted. 'You've always had your head in the clouds. It's very easy to imagine you're in love with the first boy who comes along, you know.' It was absolutely typical of her to pour cold water on what was shaping up to be the best time of my life. She never understood that when you're dancing on top of the mountain, the last thing you want to do is look down.

It was about three months after our first meeting that Danny raised the idea of spending the summer at Simon's uncle's. 'Say you'll come,' he begged. 'We'll have a great time.'

'Will it be all right with Simon?' I asked. I had only met Simon a handful of times by then, but Danny had no hesitation in assuring me that it wouldn't be a problem at all. 'The more the merrier,' he said, from which I construed that there would be a whole crowd of us, living as a sort of commune in a big old house, having loads of fun all through the summer.

The prospect of a whole summer living with Danny was the stuff of wildest dreams. In those days, only the most avant-garde of couples lived together openly before marriage. Respectable couples from provincial lower middle class backgrounds 'went out' before getting publicly 'engaged'. At this stage the more liberal of parents might have agreed to the occasional overnight stay, or winked at the obvious connotation of joint holidays, or flats officially shared with same sex friends; but for most of us the expected fiction was a white wedding dress and 'tonight's the night' jokes at the reception.

I knew better than to broach the Uncle's-House-in-Hereford plan at home – my parents would never have agreed to it, and I knew that if I fabricated any of the arrangements Hereford was close enough for them to come out and check up on me. So with Cecile's connivance I came up with an alternative which would keep them well at bay. Although I was nineteen years old, there was no question of making my own decision about how to spend the summer – there was a long debate about the France proposal, with my brother Edward offering an opinion and even my little sister chipping in with her fourpennyworth, before my parents conceded that the fruit-picking plan might be suitable, subject to various conditions being satisfied. In fact, by the start of the summer holidays, my parents were feeling rather smug about their decision to allow me to go to France with Cecile. They made no secret of the fact that an incidental benefit of the scheme would be to keep me apart from Danny, about whom they regularly cautioned me not to get 'too serious' because it might affect my studies. Too serious. God!

By the time I have finished in the shower, Pam has moved across to the hairdryers, where she is using the mirror to guide her application of face paint. The process requires a degree of concentration which precludes her from conversing with Marjorie, who instead turns her attention to me.

'I saw you in Menlove Avenue, last night.' She tosses the words in my direction with barely an upward glance, continuing to fold her damp costume into her towel and pack various other items into her swimming bag, prior to departure.

There is no trace of accusation in her tone, but she has caught me unawares. Startled, I don't dare to meet her eye – stay focused on the utilitarian white tiling and carry on towelling my thighs. Playing for time, I say, 'Menlove Avenue?' as if I've never heard of it. 'Where is that, exactly?'

'It's in Kings Heath off Harding Lane.' Unfortunately my affecting ignorance has merely served to intrigue her. 'You were there last night,' she prompts encouragingly. 'Waiting to pick someone up, it looked like.' There is no subtlety about Marjorie's nosiness. Another person might sense evasion and back off, but she doesn't retreat an inch.

'No,' I said. 'Can't have been me – I didn't go out at all last night.' I don't look at her. Dry between each toe as if my life depends on it.

'Well, I *thought* it was you. Of course, it was dark.' She pauses for a millisecond – long enough for me to inhale thankfully, then almost choke as she adds, 'I said to my friend Gwenda, it's Kate from swimming – I know that car.'

'It can't have been mine.' God, why won't the bloody woman just shut up and go home? 'Not unless someone's borrowing it without me knowing.' Try to make a joke – that might do it.

Marjorie has her jacket on and her bag zipped, but she continues to linger. 'Isn't it strange? When Gwenda came to let me in, she said, "Do you know, Marjorie, I'm sure that must be an unmarked police car. There's been someone sitting in it for almost half an hour. They must be watching one of the houses."'

'Well, maybe that was it,' I suggest. 'Perhaps it was the police.'

'Oh, I don't think so – not in Menlove Avenue. It's such a *nice* road.'

Rescuers come in unlikely guises. It is Pam's turn to give Marjorie a lift, and by now she's completed her toilette in readiness for the bridge club, or wherever it is they propose to occupy themselves this morning, and is standing rather obviously by the changing-room door. Good manners prevent Marjorie from keeping her waiting any longer. Only when they have gone do

I notice that the background muzak is still playing – hits from the musicals again. Elaine Page is belting out 'Don't Cry For Me, Argentina'. I wish she'd shut up too.

NINE

The night of the vase smashing marked the appearance of the first obvious rift in our little group. Until then we had all managed to sidestep any real arguments. Like children charged to be on our best behaviour at a birthday party, none of us wanted to 'spoil things' by making a fuss; and until then we had been careful to defuse any disagreements by backing down or making a joke. Unfortunately party manners tend to have a finite lifespan.

I was already upset about the decision to hold a seance, and the sight of Trudie fawning around Danny when she collected the plates at the end of our meal was another match to the touchpaper. I followed her into the kitchen in silence. We didn't usually bother with pudding, but earlier that day I'd included a block of ice cream in the shopping and now I went to extract it from the fridge, while Trudie rinsed out the dishes. As I opened the fridge door, I saw that the ice cream had been put on a shelf, rather than in the ice compartment. Globs of vanilla had already escaped from the packet and dripped on to everything underneath.

'Trudie, you idiot, you were supposed to have put this in the ice box.'

'It wasn't me who put it away.'

'Well, it wasn't me.'

'Keep your hair on. It'll probably be okay.'

'No it won't. It's gone all runny.'

Simon had followed us inside. 'What's up?'

'Trudie put the ice cream on the ordinary shelves in the fridge,' I said accusingly.

'It wasn't me,' Trudie repeated.

'And now it's completely ruined.'

Simon reached for a bottle of beer and opened it with a flourish. 'Well, it's not the end of the world.'

'It's such a waste of money,' I protested.

'It isn't your money, is it?' Simon spoke with unaccustomed sharpness. 'And I don't suppose it was Trudie who left it to melt, either.'

I was so taken aback that for a moment I didn't know what to say. Trudie was occupied with the dirty crocks and Simon was opening a second bottle of beer. They both had their backs to me.

'It was Trudie who put the shopping away.' I immediately wished I hadn't spoken. I heard myself with their ears – a petulant child trying to excuse herself, when everyone knows she is the guilty party.

'That would be par for the course,' said Simon. 'Since Trudie does all the rest of the work round here.'

'That's not fair,' I protested. 'I cooked the dinner tonight.'

'Oh yes,' said Simon. 'I'd forgotten our gourmet feast – burnt fish fingers and baked beans – the exception that proves the rule.'

He walked out of the kitchen and Trudie swept after him without a backward glance, leaving me oddly shaken. I took as long as possible cleaning up the melted ice cream. Eventually Danny came in to see where I'd got to.

'What have the others been saying about me?' I asked.

'Nothing. What do you mean?'

'The ice cream had melted. I said it was Trudie's fault and Simon had a go at me.'

Danny's anxious expression was replaced with a grin. 'Is that all? Come on, don't go crying over spilt ice cream. Simon was probably sticking up for Trudie because she's sweet on him. Take no notice.'

'But—'

'No buts. Come on, you're at least three drinks behind everyone else. Simon and Trudie are fine. You shouldn't take silly little things to heart.' He hugged me and we went outside. As we walked hand in hand across the grass, I decided he was right about Trudie. Of course she had been pursuing Simon all along – the feints in Danny's direction being no more than a ruse to make Simon jealous. As we approached them, Simon made a grab for her and Trudie jumped up and ran towards the house, shrieking with laughter. Simon scrambled to his feet and pursued her. He could take much bigger strides and soon had her cornered at the edge of the rose bed, where Trudie was reluctant to make an incursion in her bare feet.

'Come on, Danny,' he called. 'Let's throw her into our hole.'

Danny shouted an excuse about being too tired, so Simon pretended to frogmarch her across the lawn, while Trudie continued to struggle and squeal, although she was clearly loving every minute. They flopped on to the grass opposite us and began to trade jibes about gardeners' boys and kitchen maids. I tried to smile and play along, but inside I experienced a growing sense of uncertainty. I had been one of the original three musketeers, but my perception of our respective positions in the group had just been jolted again.

There was one consolation: if Danny was right then Trudie was going all out after Simon. I watched Simon and Trudie together the following day but, in spite of Danny's reassuring assessment, I still couldn't determine exactly how things stood. On the one hand they went off together for a couple of long talks *à deux* in the garden; but there was no obvious chemistry between them. I noticed Trudie touch his arm a couple of times, but it was no more than a friendly gesture. I reassured myself that since Simon and Trudie were both attractive people, who apparently got on well together, it could only be a matter of time before their relationship progressed to another level. Meantime it was just one more thing for Milady Mystery to keep up her sleeve; because although Trudie had by now discovered a good deal about us, so far as we were concerned she remained an enigma – always responding to our enquiries in the vaguest terms. 'I'm just travelling around,' she said once. 'I'm from everywhere and nowhere. Like the song.'

When I finally did receive an intimation of Trudie's background, it came completely out of the blue. This startling revelation took place on the pavement outside W. H. Smith in Hereford. We had all four gone into town for the afternoon, ostensibly to obtain a replacement for a broken string on Danny's guitar. While Danny and Simon were pursuing this errand in the music shop, Trudie had taken the opportunity to pop into Smith's for a magazine. It was crowded in the shop so I hung around by the door, idly picking up a newspaper from the stand and glancing through it.

The jolt came somewhere about page five. *Concern is mounting over the safety of missing schoolgirl Trudie Finch.* It was the photograph which had first caught my eye. A standard school head-and-shoulders shot of a girl in a V-neck sweater, school blouse and striped tie. Her long dark hair was tied in two bunches, one above each ear. It was unmistakably Trudie.

She chose that moment to breeze out of the shop. I couldn't say anything. I just pointed to the picture.

Trudie was absolutely calm. She took the paper from me, refolded it and placed it back in the stand. Then she took me gently by the arm and propelled me a few yards down the street.

'Pretend you haven't seen it,' she said.

'But I *have* seen it.'

'Just pretend you haven't. If you haven't seen it, then nothing has changed and you don't need to worry about it, or mention it to the others.'

'Aren't you afraid someone is going to recognize you, if you keep coming into town?'

Trudie shrugged. 'From a school mug shot? Come off it. And you won't betray me, will you? You're my friend.'

'Of course I am,' I said, 'but—'

She grabbed my arm and held her finger to her lips. 'Shh.' She had spotted the lads emerging from the music store, only a few feet away. There wasn't time for anything more. Without giving any word or sign of agreement, I had somehow become complicit in her conspiracy.

I suppose there were any number of things I could have said or done at this point – any one of which might have led to the safe return home of missing schoolgirl Trudie Finch. I know I ought to have considered the anguish of her parents but, without knowing any of the facts, my sympathies drifted unerringly in the direction of the runaway. It was not just the usual conspiracy of youth against the older generation: in my case it went deeper than that. Was I not a kind of fugitive myself, enjoying a clandestine respite from the overbearing attentions of my parents? If Trudie's family was anything like mine, I thought, no wonder she had done a bunk, and good luck to her. She looked at least sixteen, even in the school photograph.

'Can we go into the cathedral now?' Trudie was asking. 'I love it in there.'

Trudie was right. I didn't need to know about it. I would pretend I had never spent those idle moments looking through the paper. Nothing had changed. And if anyone did chance to discover that Trudie had been staying with us (which was extremely unlikely, as we had so little contact with the outside world), as Simon had said on the beach that first afternoon, it wasn't as if we had kidnapped her or anything.

As soon as we got back from Hereford (another day without any work done on the pond) I set about preparing our meal for the second night running – just to show Simon how wrong he was. In the meantime Trudie prowled from room to room, deciding which one had the most promising atmosphere in which to contact the spirit world. I viewed this surveying operation with considerable scepticism, suspecting that Trudie was trying to engender an atmosphere which was as creepy as possible in order to put the wind up us. The room eventually designated most propitious for holding a seance was a large unoccupied bedroom at the front of the house. It not only had a double bed and an old-fashioned suite of wardrobe and dresser, but also boasted a chaise longue, which was positioned on a circular rug between the dressing table and the foot of the bed.

Working to Trudie's instructions, Simon and Danny moved the chaise longue to one side and rolled up the rug. This left a large empty space on the green and grey lino, in the centre of which Trudie placed an empty jam jar with a couple of joss sticks in it. These she lit – to purify the room, she said, although I was certain it was merely to help contrive a sense of weirdness. She had also acquired some candles from the pantry – the stumpy white ones which every well-regulated household kept to hand in case of power cuts – and these she stood on saucers: first dribbling a puddle of wax to cement each one in place. When each of the lighted candles had been carefully positioned and the one used for dribbling extinguished, Trudie declared the preparations complete but for one last thing – a crucifix.

We all looked at Danny. He habitually wore a small gold crucifix on a chain round his neck. The chain was fine enough to be unobtrusive, and long enough that the crucifix itself was out of sight unless he removed his shirt, when it could be seen nestling among his chest hair: but of course we had all seen him in this degree of undress on an almost daily basis and therefore knew of its existence.

'There might be something else in the house we could use,' ventured Simon, clearly sensing Danny's reluctance.

Trudie fell in with this willingly enough, but although we wandered from room to room, scrutinizing the objects which cluttered every surface, peering into cupboards and checking high shelves, no suitable religious artefact could be found.

We ended up back in the seance room. 'It'll have to be Danny's crucifix,' said Trudie.

No one said anything for a moment, then Danny himself broke the silence. 'Will you unfasten it, Katy? I hardly ever take it off.'

He turned his back to facilitate the operation. I had to move his hair aside to reach the catch. He had recently complained that the catch was faulty and occasionally came undone by itself, but tonight it seemed to take forever to disengage, as if reluctant to leave its owner's neck.

Trudie took it from me and placed it almost reverently on the lino, beside the jam jar containing the joss sticks, which were smoking steadily.

'Now what?' asked Simon.

'Now we have to leave everything like this until it gets dark,' said Trudie. 'Long after dark,' she corrected herself. 'Midnight would probably be the best time, so I suggest we come back here at quarter to twelve, ready to begin.'

She ushered us out, closing the door behind us. No one spoke: indeed we all but tiptoed away. I had to try very hard to stop myself imagining that there was already something else in that room – something which had arrived the moment the latch clicked shut.

TEN

I don't do anniversaries as a rule. I don't take flowers to the cemetery or put an ad in the newspaper. One day is the same as another: we remember what we want to remember – and sometimes what we want to forget.

I make an exception for Hilly. I know it is the third anniversary of Trevor's death on the 24th and I make a point of spending it with her, because I know she'll find it hard to cope alone. Her daughters live too far away to be of assistance – Bethany is in Edinburgh, Sophie not even in the same time zone. So Hilly and I go out to dinner. This is much better than staying in the house, which still speaks loudly of Trevor – although he has been gone from it a thousand days and more.

Hilly is grateful. 'You don't want to hear me going on about Trev,' she says: to which I say I don't mind and she does go on a bit, saying what a good husband he was and how much they loved each other never quite realizing just how painful this line of conversation is for me – dear Hilly – never knowing how much this still touches me on the raw.

Hilly was never what you would have called pretty. She's always been a rather square, solid person, to tell the truth, but she has worn well and maturity suits her. She doesn't succumb to my petty vanities, the Keep Fit and the dyed hair. Hers is grey, cropped short in a slightly masculine style, which helps tone down her bohemian taste in clothes – the big earrings and drapey scarves, embroidered tops and baggy trousers. Hilly has always been what Marjorie would call 'a bit arty'. She likes the theatre and plays the piano, and recently she's taken up painting, which she has turned out to be rather good at – although way too modest to admit it.

I know she misses Trevor terribly – thinks they were soulmates. He was too good to be true, really. The sort of guy no one ever had a bad word for. I met him on a course – it was about maths teaching, as far as I can remember. We hit it off straight away and, somehow or other, I ended up introducing him to my flatmate – Hilly. My mistake.

Hilly was still very quiet at that stage. She'd begun to regain her confidence, but she hadn't had a boyfriend in all the time I'd known her, so the speed of the Trevor thing took me by surprise. I went away for one weekend to attend my grandparents' Golden Wedding and I came back to find Trevor had spent the night. Next thing anyone knew, the church was booked and Hilly was sporting an engagement ring. Apart from the two of them, I was the only one who knew for sure that Hilly was pregnant. We were so close then, Hilly and I. We depended on each other.

When Sophie and Bethany got older, they did the maths and actually used to tease their parents about this 'shotgun wedding' – they knew they were on safe ground, because everyone could see what a devoted couple their parents were. Hilly always said the baby made no difference – they would have ended up together eventually – it was meant to be. I never begged to differ. What was the point? I didn't want to lose my best friend.

We are well down our bottle of wine before Hilly says: 'Tell me about this thing with Danny's mother. Did you manage to find out why she wants to see you so badly?'

I have already mentioned receiving a letter from Mrs Ivanisovic, so I am prepared for this. 'Poor old thing hasn't got long to go, I suppose. She probably just wants someone to reminisce with – someone who knew Danny. I think most of her close family are dead now. The ones that are left probably don't remember him.'

'It must be awful to outlive your children,' Hilly says.

'It *would* be fairer if we all died in age order,' I say, half laughing.

Hilly nods. 'Look at my mother. It's a terrible thing to say, I know, but I have sometimes thought she would be better off dead – and yet she looks set to go on for ever.'

'Anyway, I got this second letter asking me to go and see her, so I've promised to drive up there tomorrow.'

Hilly looks surprised and concerned. 'That's very good of you, Kate. Does she realize how far it is for you?'

'I suppose she must do. I couldn't refuse her really, poor old thing.'

'You're so good,' says Hilly. She means it too. Hilly is always convinced of my goodness and will have nothing said to the contrary. In fact, Hilly is invariably prepared to think well of everyone. She's such a gentle soul herself that she finds it difficult to encompass any notion of evil in others. Deliberate misdeeds occasion her not only pain, but genuine bewilderment. She cannot conceive of how anyone could set out to deliberately harm another. Half a century of life experience has done nothing to dent this innocent faith in human nature – it is part of her charm.

No wonder it was dangerous to introduce her to Trevor. They were two of a kind in many ways. He became one of those rare, saintly headmasters, beloved even of the bad kids. Thirty years' worth of pupils turned out for his funeral. They had to relay the service outside on loudspeakers. You couldn't see the coffin for flowers.

Hilly has brought some brochures for us to look through while we drink our coffee. We're planning a holiday to the Greek islands – sunshine and archaeology – with Shirley Valentine type romance entirely off the agenda. The brochures have been conveyed to the restaurant in Hilly's bag, the latest in a long succession of massive handbags with which she is always equipped. It's another family joke, Hilly's bags. Whenever anyone expresses a need for any item, however large or obscure, the girls always announce that 'Mum has probably got one in her bag.'

I know all the family jokes, you see – the ones about the shotgun wedding and the giant handbags – because I am almost one of the family, like a sort of honorary relation, or old family retainer. Hilly and Trevor's girls never guessing how I once hoped to be so much more.

After I drop Hilly off, I don't go straight home. Instead I drive in the opposite direction. The route is so familiar that I could do it blindfold. I slow down to make the turn into Menlove Avenue, then let the car creep the last hundred yards or so down the wide tree-lined road, before I finally park, halfway between two street lamps. I switch off the lights, kill the engine, and sit in the quiet darkness, staring at the lighted windows of a house a few doors away. A lot of the houses are dark already, but the occupants of this one seldom retire much before eleven-thirty.

With the engine stilled I can hear the thin breeze working the tree branches overheard. When another car turns into the road I sit very still, my fingers poised ready to fire the ignition, but the other vehicle passes by without noticing me and goes out of sight round the bend. I keep glancing around, more alive than ever to the risks I run in coming here since the conversation with Marjorie a couple of days ago. I just can't understand why I didn't see her. She must have parked a lot further down the road and gone into one of the houses behind me; from which I deduce that her friend must live at the Harding Lane end of the road. As a precaution I've got the car facing in the opposite direction tonight – to make sure that she can't sneak up on me. I really ought not to have come at all. I can't afford to let her catch me a second time.

I spend a few minutes staring at each of the houses in turn, wondering which of them is inhabited by the pesky Gwenda: hoping I've chosen a spot which is obscured from her net curtain twitching by the row of trees which edges the pavement.

Some of the houses in Menlove Avenue have acquired UPVC window frames or trendy blinds, but the one I come to see hasn't changed much in twenty years. The front garden still runs its annual cycle of daffodils, roses and fallen leaves. There used to be a stone sundial but that went a long time ago – vandalized perhaps, or pinched; it goes on even in the better neighbourhoods these days, in spite of what Marjorie might like to think. They've had those orangey-brown curtains up for about three years. The previous pair were a blue and silver stripe.

From where I'm sitting, I can see when their hall light goes on; then the upstairs bay is illuminated, almost to the second when its ground-floor counterpart goes dark. I can't see inside the bedroom from this angle, but I glimpse the hand that draws the curtains – a woman's hand – or maybe it's a man's – impossible to see from this distance. Sometimes I imagine I can see more than I really do.

The bedroom curtains are pale beige with a pattern of flowers. The curtains must be lined because once drawn they trap the light inside, reducing it to a pale glow against the darker brickwork; and after a few minutes this dims still further. They must have switched off the main light – probably sitting up in bed, reading perhaps, or supping Horlicks by the light of the bedside lamp. I don't know why I imagine bedside lamps rather than wall lights.

Another car takes me by surprise. I failed to notice its approach and shrink back into my seat in the split second that the headlights sweep across me. It continues out of sight, leaving me alone to my vigil.

When the window goes completely dark, I start the engine and drive away.

ELEVEN

Each of us approached the upcoming seance in our own way, keeping whatever doubts we entertained to ourselves. I put a good face on it – not wanting to be labelled a scaredy cat. It wasn't that I was scared of the supernatural – which I didn't entirely believe in: I was much more afraid of becoming so taut with nerves that I jumped or squealed at anything, thereby attracting ridicule when it turned out to be a great big tease. Simon seemed much as usual. He told us a long involved story which culminated in a fellow student accidentally ending up locked out of his room, standing stark naked on a ledge outside his window. Simon's deliberate drawl invariably added to our hilarity, but somehow I sensed that tonight no one was giving him their full attention. Trudie seemed charged with nervous excitement, as if possessed of a secret she was dying to share with the rest of us, but could not. She was planning a virtuoso performance, no doubt about it, I thought. Yet, of the four of us, I fancy it was Danny who was most affected. I don't think the others noticed, but I detected an artificial heartiness in his voice and saw his fingers stray several times towards his neck, seeking the missing talisman.

As the sun was dipping behind the shrubbery, Trudie observed that she felt chilly and went inside to put on something warmer. I got up and followed her into the house to use the bathroom. When I emerged on to the landing, Trudie was just coming out of her bedroom. On catching sight of me she beckoned excitedly, saying, 'Come and see.'

I accompanied her into the room, picking my way across the tangle of discarded clothing strewn across the floor. Trudie's bedroom window faced west and was high enough to afford a view over the shrubbery, straight down the hill to Bettis Wood. The sun's topmost edge was disappearing behind the tree tops, which were strangely aglow with its dying light.

'Look,' she whispered. 'Red, like blood. I've never seen it do that before. It's a sign.'

'It's just the sunset. A trick of the light.'

Trudie shook her head. 'It's a sign,' she said emphatically. Something in her voice unnerved me. I was uncomfortably aware that Trudie was no longer the ringmaster, putting on a show for us. Trudie believed in this stuff and was scared by it. She was no longer in control.

The red glow faded from the tree tops – the change took a matter of seconds, then the sun was gone and the wood stood greenish black in the dusk, just as usual. The moment was over. The sound of Danny's guitar drifted up to us from the lawn. He was playing 'Moonshadow'.

'What do you think the lyrics mean?' asked Trudie – and I noted with relief that she seemed back to normal.

'I dunno – they're a bit weird, aren't they?'

'I think the moonshadow is your fate,' she said. 'Everyone is pursued by their moonshadow and it always catches up with you, in the end. You just have to accept whatever comes.'

I didn't bother to reply. I had wasted too many school lunch breaks dissecting lyrics to divine their inner meanings.

When we got back to the garden, Danny and Simon were talking about the time when they had seen Ralph

McTell at Birmingham Town Hall, Danny punctuating their remarks with occasional chords on his guitar. Everything seemed calm and ordinary again, except for Danny every so often glancing at his watch. By eleven-thirty we began to run out of conversation. The air had become oppressive, but I decided a storm couldn't be imminent because the stars were still visible. Danny had been checking his watch at increasingly frequent intervals, until I begged him to desist as it was getting on my nerves.

'Why don't we go up now and get it over with?' he suggested, feigning a disinterested tone. 'Then we can all go to bed. I don't know about anyone else, but I'm cream-crackered.'

'Might as well,' agreed Simon. 'I don't suppose your ghosts can tell the time anyway – do you reckon they're on British Summer Time or not?'

Trudie didn't rise to the bait. 'Fine,' she said. 'If everyone's ready, let's go up.'

As we rose to our feet, a breeze like a breath of hot air shimmered across the garden. Suddenly I didn't want to go into the house at all. It loomed over us, a dark hulk of a place, full of whispers and secrets – when we got inside and Simon switched on the kitchen lights, the glare seemed intense. We stood for a moment, blinking and uncertain, like burglars caught in the act.

Trudie led the way upstairs. She had apparently regained her confidence, automatically assuming leadership of the project. Simon's foot caught against the corner of a wooden chest which stood on the landing at the top of the stairs: the resultant bang echoed around the stairwell.

'Bloody hell, man,' said Danny. 'Talk about waking the dead. There's no need to give them advance notice.'

He spoke in obvious jest, but there was no trace of irony in Trudie's reply. 'It's all right. She already knows we're coming. She's pleased. It's what she wants.'

We had become accustomed to referring to Murdered Agnes in this casual fashion, but Trudie's statement chilled me; it conjured up a mental image of Murdered Agnes calmly awaiting us in the chosen room. When Trudie opened the door, I was almost surprised to find everything just as we had left it. The air was heady with incense and the candles were still burning. It came to me that they ought not to have been. They should have burnt out long ago. I reminded myself that Trudie had slipped away several times during the evening, presumably to replenish them.

In accordance with the instructions Trudie had issued earlier, we sat cross-legged in a circle on the floor, holding hands. In best dinner-party fashion, we arranged ourselves boy, girl, boy, girl, maintaining the silence which Trudie had emphasized was essential. 'Once the circle is made, it mustn't be broken,' she'd warned us, so I had my plan of action clear – keep quiet and hold hands – which suited me just fine.

Once we were settled into position, a stillness fell upon the room. The candle flames had been disturbed by our movements, but now they burned steady and clear. From where I was sitting I could see a line of light from the landing, where the door and the floorboards didn't quite meet. I had tinkered with ouija and seances at school, as teenage girls did and probably still do; but these sessions had invariably dissolved into giggles, or else a member of the party had succumbed to the temptation to make strange noises and had to be ticked off by the rest for not taking the enterprise seriously. I had half expected Danny or Simon to adopt this line, but neither of them did. The silence became intense – eventually broken by Trudie's voice, low, melodious, inviting: 'You can come to us. We are ready.'

There was another pause. I noticed Danny's crucifix, twinkling mischievously in the candlelight.

'I can see her.' Trudie exhaled the words softly.

I raised my eyes to see where Trudie was looking – for a split second anticipating a vision of Murdered Agnes in the room with us: but Trudie's eyes were closed. Whatever she was seeing was safely confined in her head.

Danny squeezed my hand, whether in reassurance or to share the joke, I never knew. I didn't look at him.

Trudie began to speak in a low, dreamy voice. In spite of our proximity, I could barely hear her. 'She's going into the wood. She isn't afraid – in fact she's laughing and happy . . . It's getting dark among the trees, so I can't see her very well – wait, Agnes – don't go so fast . . . There's a man – a man with dark hair and a beard . . .'

So much for that, I thought. It's exactly what was printed in the magazine.

'He's her friend, so Agnes isn't afraid. Wait . . .' I felt the hairs rising on the back of my neck in direct parallel with the increasing tension in Trudie's voice. 'He's not with her – she's on her own – looking around – lost in the dark – dark all around . . .' Trudie's voice rose. I calmed myself with the thought that she was one hell of an actress.

'No!' She almost shouted the word. 'Agnes – he's come up behind her – Agnes – I see her now – clearly. She has long dark hair – she looks like me—' Trudie burst into noisy sobs. 'It is me – she has my face.'

As I broke away, I realized that my nails must have been digging into the backs of Simon's fingers. I scrambled round behind Danny to reach Trudie, putting my arms around her and holding her, cradling her back and forth like a child while the candles, which had been disturbed by these sudden movements, sent our shadows gyrating wildly across the walls and ceiling. 'It's all right,' I said. 'It's all right.'

'You shouldn't have broken the circle,' she whispered through tears.

Simon stood up and switched on the lights. Danny retrieved his crucifix and snuffed out the candles. As Trudie clambered to her feet, the first rumbles of thunder reverberated through the house. Simon took over as comforter. I heard him offering to sleep in Trudie's room with her, to which she mumbled her thanks.

The storm which had been so slow in coming intensified in the space of a moment, the thunder bouncing off the roof, chasing us on to the landing. While Simon escorted Trudie to her room, his arm draped protectively around her shoulders, Danny and I almost ran into our own little sanctuary, shutting the door behind us as if barring the way against foes unseen, then laughing nervously at each other while throwing our clothes off in an unspoken contest to be first into bed. Meantime the storm continued at full tilt – B movie thunder, with lightning illuminating the room at regular intervals.

Our familiar bed was an island of normality, a safe haven from Trudie and all her nonsense. Once naked under the sheets I huddled against Danny, feeling the cool shape of his crucifix imprinting itself in my cheek. He planted a couple of kisses on the top of my head, before asking: 'Do you think she really saw anything?'

'Well, she thinks she did: but she was very worked up beforehand. The whole thing is probably a product of her own imagination.'

'More than likely,' agreed Danny. He sounded relieved. I had never thought of him as superstitious. Maybe it was his Catholic upbringing – the constant presence of all those long-dead saints, hovering about in the ether, awaiting the intercessions of the faithful.

'If she suggests doing anything like this again, I don't think we should agree to it,' I said.

'No,' he agreed at once. 'She'll only get upset.'

I lay in his arms, mentally reliving Trudie's distress. Trudie had become altogether too wrapped up in the story of Murdered Agnes. Was it right to allow a schoolgirl to frighten herself half to death? I had somehow acquiesced to keeping Trudie's secret by default, but now I began to question the rightness of it afresh.

A flash of lightning all but coincided with a thunderclap.

'Wow,' he said. 'The storm must be almost directly overhead.' Another simultaneous flash and bang confirmed the truth of this, half deafening me and causing both of us to jump involuntarily, then laugh at each other.

'There's a way of calculating how far away the storm is,' Danny said. 'You count the number of seconds between seeing the flash and hearing the bang; then multiply it by one number and divide by another and it gives you the distance in miles.'

The moment for a tête-à-tête about runaway schoolgirl Trudie Finch had passed: lost in the tumult of the storm.

I assumed Simon's overnight stay in Trudie's room would prove the catalyst in their relationship, but after that one night Simon went back to sleeping alone. There was no upping of the tempo between them, but there was no obvious awkwardness either. I confess that I was baffled. Trudie seemed to grow daily ever more beautiful. How could Simon possibly be immune to her? As the days passed I caught myself admiring her more and more. I started hauling my T-shirt up and knotting it under the bust, but somehow it never looked so good on me. Maybe Simon found her a bit too immature, with her imaginings and amateur dramatics – although there could be no doubt that her fear on the night of the seance had been real. I decided it would be a kindness to find ways of distracting Trudie from her unfortunate preoccupation with the late Agnes Payne.

Nor was Trudie the only one who needed distractions. My initial euphoria at being perpetually on holiday was gradually beginning to wane. The heat pressed down on us, day after day, its heaviness infecting everything: even time slowed to a crawl, making our days stretch out endlessly, each a little longer than the one before. We were effectively stranded at the house unless Simon was available to drive us – but Simon and Danny were focusing on their work in the garden, keeping their bargain with Simon's uncle. Once or twice I caught myself wondering if it wouldn't have been more fun going to France with Cecile – thoughts which I banished at once, not only because they felt disloyal to Danny, but also because they made mock of my own choices. No one had forced me to go to Herefordshire.

At the outset, of course, I had anticipated a much livelier household altogether. I didn't realize until the last minute that the party would be confined to the three of us, and by then I was so excited that it didn't seem to matter. There had been such a sense of enthusiasm and purpose at the beginning – a week before departure day we met for an evening in a pub, where we drew up shopping lists and Simon showed us sketches of the proposed new garden features, which we discussed with a zest which was never quite recaptured once the actual digging began. By the end of that evening, no one could have faulted our team spirit or total commitment to the endeavour. It never occurred to me to question whether Simon and I could spend the whole summer cooped up in the same house. I blithely assumed that our mutual fondness for Danny would give us enough in common.

The house itself provided its own set of disappointments and frustrations. There was no mains gas, so we relied on an ancient electric cooker whose rings took an age to warm up, then burned everything the instant I turned away. Needless to say the saucepans were not non-stick, so they invariably required a sustained attack with a Brillo pad. I was engaged in one such session when Simon walked into the kitchen, a couple of days after the seance.

'I hate this bloody house,' I said, flinging the dirty pan into the suds with enough force to send a miniature tidal wave across the big white sink.

'Well, go home then,' Simon retorted crossly.

'You know perfectly well that I can't go home,' I began, but he had already gone.

Wounded, I abandoned the washing-up and sought out Danny, who was kneeling in the excavation, attacking some old tree roots with a pair of secateurs. He stopped work and squinted up at me. 'What's up?'

'Simon has just been horrible to me, in the kitchen.'

'Why? What happened?'

'He said if I didn't like it here, I should go home.'

Danny hesitated a second, before saying, 'Well . . . that's not unreasonable . . .'

'He snapped at me.'

'I'm sure it was nothing to get upset about. He won't have meant anything. Si's the nicest guy in the world.'

'Whose side are you on?'

'I'm not on anyone's side,' said Danny, evenly. 'But it's a hot day and Si's probably tired. We all have to make occasional allowances for one another. There's sure to be a few disagreements. You're too sensitive, sweetie, that's the trouble. Just forget about it, okay?'

Danny was right of course. We all had to make an effort not to provoke unnecessary arguments. I didn't encounter Simon again until the end of the afternoon, when neither of us referred to the exchange in the kitchen. By then Danny was in a particularly ebullient mood, determined to keep us all laughing, topping up our glasses before we had emptied them. I knew I ought to try harder for his sake – he so much wanted Simon and me to get along – but his refusal to choose between us kept drifting back into my thoughts. I recalled the balloon debates my school had been fond of holding, where the premise was that someone had to be voted out of the basket in order to keep the balloon in the air. Suppose Danny were faced with a choice between me and Simon – who would he vote to save?

Danny and I were up unusually early next morning. I made some tea and toast and by the time we had eaten it the others still weren't stirring, so we went for a walk outside. The grass was still damp and my sandals flicked dew drops on to my toes where they glistened like tiny jewels. Alongside the rose bed there was an old stone bench where it was dry enough to sit down and we paused there, listening to the birds.

'You look incredibly beautiful this morning,' he said. 'The roses are framing your face, like a halo. No, don't move,' he added, as I turned to look at the flowers. 'Just stay exactly as you are. God, I wish I'd remembered my camera.' Another thought struck him. 'Wait there – stay exactly as you are. I'll be back in a minute.'

He headed off for the house without waiting for me to answer. I sat obediently as instructed, like a sitter for a portrait, until he returned carrying his guitar. Without a word he sat cross-legged at my feet and began to play. I recognized the tune at once and when he began to sing the lyrics a lump rose in my throat and

I knew that whatever happened I would remember the moment for ever – the brightness of the morning, the hazy scent of the roses and Danny on the grass at my feet.

He had just reached the final verse when a thin stream of water hit him. The song ended in an abrupt discord. We both turned to see Trudie in the act of discharging a second stream from the plastic water pistol in her hand, before she raced away round the side of the house. Danny leapt off in pursuit, leaving his guitar on the grass. I picked it up and began walking after them. When I caught up I found them facing one another, both white-faced and angry. The water pistol lay crushed at their feet.

'You've hurt my wrist,' Trudie said accusingly. 'And you have no right to break my things.' She marched off in high dudgeon.

I linked my arm through his. 'She's so childish,' I said. 'Take no notice.'

'But she ruined it.'

'No, really, it was beautiful.'

'No,' he said obstinately. 'She spoiled our moment.'

'We'll have lots of other moments.'

Just then Simon's head appeared from an upstairs window, calling to Danny that he would be down in a minute. Although I was vaguely cross with Trudie, I knew she had only intended it as a joke, so once the guys started work I deliberately sought her out, in the interests of peacekeeping.

After we had undertaken a bit of half-hearted tidying up, Trudie raised the question of going down to the wood. Although the wood was only a couple of fields away and a footpath which ran along one side of the garden took you straight into it, we had never got round to going there. It would be fair to say that none of us had taken the least interest in the wood until

Trudie became fixated on the Agnes Payne story, since when she had regularly suggested we explore it together. Fortunately there had always been some good reason for putting the idea on hold – we needed to drive into town for some milk, or there wasn't enough time before we had to start preparing the evening meal: but when she raised it on the day of the water pistol incident I couldn't think of a single excuse, so I fell back on 'I'd much rather stay here and read,' which sounded lame even as I said it.

'Oh, come on, Katy,' she said. 'You're not scared, are you?'

She had unknowingly hit upon the magic formula with which my elder brother had habitually goaded me into all manner of rash actions throughout my childhood.

'Of course not,' I said. 'I'd just rather stay here, that's all.'

'You *are* scared.' Trudie was obviously amused.

'No I'm not.' I made a great show of marking my place and putting my book to one side. 'I'll come if you really want to go down there.'

I couldn't recall ever seeing anyone use the footpath which ran along the side of the property, and it was decidedly overgrown. As we picked our way along it in single file, I privately reassured myself that my reluctance to visit the woods was actually on Trudie's account. She was so imaginative and highly strung, and would only start rabbiting on about the whole murder business. However, if she insisted we go, then I might as well humour her. Once her curiosity was satisfied, she might even start to lose interest in the wretched business.

From a distance Bettis Wood had appeared dark and dense, but, as we got closer, I could see it was a far less daunting prospect than it first appeared. The trees were well spaced and mostly deciduous, providing lacy green curtains of shade which opened out on to occasional windows of clear blue sky. Within yards of the entrance the path became a tangle of interconnected routes, worn by the random passage of rabbits and other explorers. We walked across threadbare carpets of dried-up leaves, which were the same faded orange as the hard sandy ground underneath them.

We had not gone very far into the wood when we reached a clearing which local children had evidently transformed into something approximating an adventure playground. In addition to a rope swing and a plank resting across a fallen log for a see-saw, there had been an attempt to construct an ambitious scramble net suspended between two trees, using a variety of bits of old rope and a couple of plastic-coated washing lines.

'Great,' said Trudie, making straight for the rope swing, where she fitted the knot between her thighs and pushed off.

We took turns with the rope swing before experimenting with the see-saw, for which we discovered we were far too tall.

'What a gorgeous place for kids to come and play,' said Trudie.

'I wonder who uses it?' I said. 'There's hardly anyone living round here.'

'I suppose one family would be enough – and they probably come from the other direction. Isn't there another way into the woods, further down the road from the house?'

My spirits were lifted by the discovery that Bettis Wood was after all a happy place, where children came to play. In my mind's eye, Hammer Horror had been replaced by gambolling badgers and Mrs Tiggywinkle trotting along the woodland floor. Even Trudie's half-hearted speculation, 'I wonder whereabouts they found Agnes,' failed to put a dent in my sylvan idyll.

When we had exhausted all the playground had to offer, we flopped down on a patch of grass. I lay back and watched the sunshine filtering through the leaves. I found that by closing each eye in turn, I could make one of the branches overhead appear to dodge from one side of the sun to the other. I had given up on asking Trudie where she came from, so instead I tried another tack. 'What are you going to do when summer's over?'

'Go back home, I suppose.'

'But I thought you'd run away.'

'I didn't run away – I walked. Anyway I guess my parents will have learned their lesson by then.'

'Has it ever occurred to you that they're worried out of their minds? They probably think you're dead.'

'That's stupid,' she said – but I fancied there was a faint uncertainty in her voice. 'Why on earth would they think that?'

'Because that's what everyone always thinks.'

'They don't.'

'Of course they do. Parents think you're lying unidentified in some mortuary whenever you miss the last bus.'

'I s'pose.'

'You could always ring them. Or ring someone else. Just to let them know you're safe.'

There was a minute or two of silence, and when Trudie spoke again it was to complain about the endless amount of time Simon had spent in the bathroom that morning. 'I was dying for the loo. Honestly – I've never known anyone take so long. He must be the vainest man in the universe. Have you seen the way he spends ages tying that bandanna round his head before they start digging?'

Bitching about Simon provided us with a pleasant diversion. After a while Trudie had another turn on the rope swing and then we decided to walk back to the house.

TWELVE

I have brought Mrs Ivanisovic's letter with me – ostensibly as an aide-memoire for her address, although this, together with the contents of her letters, is burned indelibly on to my mind. She lives in an establishment called Broadoaks. This has been her address for about ten years, but since our communication is normally restricted to an annual exchange of cards, I have no idea what sort of place Broadoaks is. When I substituted this address in my Monet's Garden Address Book, I mentally classified it as accommodation for the elderly, but since Mrs I is still capable of penning a few lines coherently, I assume it is not for 'the elderly confused' – which is the politely euphemistic definition applied to the institution which Hilly's mother presently inhabits.

As I drive across the Tees Viaduct, I wonder how I will recognize Mrs Ivanisovic. She will be an old woman now, with grey hair – maybe a stick, or a zimmer frame. When I first met Danny's mother I already classified her as old. With the arrogance of youth, I thought her life was all but over. Twenty-five seemed past it to me then, thirty positively ancient. Danny's mother was tall, slender, gracious. She wore tailored clothes bought from expensive shops, had her hair done once a week and varnished her nails. She was probably younger than I am now.

In spite of our assumed status as radical free spirits, beneath our frayed jeans and be-sloganned T-shirts we were deeply conventional. When invited to meet Danny's parents, I was appropriately nervous beforehand and cared what they thought of me. The invitation was to join them for Sunday tea – a ritual then observed to a greater or lesser degree by the majority of households throughout the land. When we arrived at his front gate, I was alarmed to find that his parents lived in a detached house, set back from the road. This signified money and particular standards of behaviour. I slid into the house alongside Danny, uneasily aware of the solid-looking furniture, lined curtains and prints on the walls which hadn't come from Woolworth's. Nothing home-made or out of a Littlewood's catalogue here.

I was terrified of shaming myself by using the wrong cutlery, or being offered something exotic to eat and not knowing how to tackle it – but in fact the tea we were served was virtually identical to the one with which Danny had been entertained at my home a week earlier. Ham sandwiches on white bread. A dish of pickled onions. Milky tea. Three sorts of cake: chocolate swiss roll, Battenburg and Viennese Whirls – Continental names to betray our utter Englishness.

Mr and Mrs Ivanisovic were kind to me, and after tea they encouraged Danny to fetch his guitar and play for us. They were obviously convinced of Danny's brilliance in every sphere of endeavour – which made a point of commonality between us.

Does she still remember that first Sunday tea? Is she wondering how she will recognize me?

I find Broadoaks easily. There is a large sign at the open gates – very tasteful – just the name in dark brown, edged with gold on a cream background; nothing about 'home' or 'elderly'.

The drive curves around a huge circular lawn, which is home to the mature trees that screen the building. It's a sunny day, unusually warm for the time of year: a state of affairs which a couple of residents are taking advantage of. There's a lady in a wheelchair, with a crocheted blanket covering her lower half; a bent-backed woman walking slowly down the drive, supported by two metal sticks. I hope neither of these is Mrs Ivanisovic. It would be too embarrassing to drive straight past with no sign of recognition. Neither of them gives my car more than a passing glance, so they are clearly not expecting anyone.

I park in one of the spaces assigned to visitors and head for the front door, which stands open. The hall is reminiscent of the entrance to an old-fashioned country house hotel. I have been expecting the institutional modernity of the place to which I have occasionally accompanied Hilly, but Broadoaks is much more up-market and presumably comes with a hefty price tag. And why not – Mrs Ivanisovic has no one to leave her money to.

I can't see any obvious means of attracting anyone's attention, but there is hardly time to speculate on what to do before a woman appears to ask if she can help me. I am expecting twin set and pearls, but she is in a fashionable skirt and top, with chunky modern jewellery.

'I'm here to see Mrs Ivanisovic,' I say.

'You must be Katy Mayfield.' The smile broadens further. Trained to reassure, she cannot be expected to guess how much this greeting unsettles me. 'If you'll take a seat, I'll see if Betty is ready for you.' She gestures me to a group of winged armchairs which stand where the hall broadens out under the stairs. Once she has seen me safely to a seat, she vanishes through a door to the right of the main entrance.

My arrival has evidently been broadcast in advance – and I note that I am to be Katy for the day. And

Betty – I remember this now – her Christian name is Elizabeth. He was Stan – probably short for Stanislaus or something like that – and she was Betty: tall, slim, gracious Betty, who was probably not so old then as I am now.

I sit taking in the cream paintwork, the brass door handles and the tell-tale handrails, stair lifts and ramps. How can anyone who needs to live here possibly threaten me?

The greeter with the chunky necklace is back – standing at the door, beckoning. 'We've got the all clear.'

She doesn't enter the room herself, but instead holds the door wide open for me, then closes it when I am inside. It is unexpected. I hadn't realized the door led straight into Mrs Ivanisovic's room. I am unprepared – stand startled for a moment.

Mrs Ivanisovic is propped up on the bed, supported by a small mountain of pillows. Her white hair has been recently combed into place and she is fully dressed – a lilac cardigan which matches the veins in her hands, a grey skirt which ends just below the knee, failing to conceal the bony shins and ankles which look frail as the bone china from which we once upon a time drank tea together. I take all this in, together with the oxygen cylinder beside the bed – an ugly intrusion among the pastel-coloured bed linen and dainty knick-knacks – while she in turn appraises me. Her pale lips mouth a smile, but her eyes do not. She holds out her hand: 'Katy?'

Her skin reminds me of creased tissue paper, so when I take her hand I am surprised to feel its smooth warmth. I am frightened to apply the slightest pressure, lest her metacarpals snap at my touch.

THIRTEEN

When Trudie and I got back from our walk in the woods, we found the boys on the point of setting out to Leominster. We were only just in time to scramble into the back of the car, indignant at being almost left behind. Driving with the windows down generated a welcome draught, but once in town the air tasted of dust and exhaust fumes and I half wished we hadn't come along. While Simon and Danny pursued an errand in the record shop, Trudie and I gravitated towards Dorothy Perkins. In my case visiting the shops was essentially a spectator sport, because I had too little money left to buy anything. My parents had provided me with the fare to France, but that had gone into the pool from which we did our grocery shopping. However, this lack of funds didn't prevent me from riffling through the rails of clothes, and inspecting the cosmetics on the Biba counter alongside Trudie. I was in the process of testing the lipsticks when I realized she was no longer beside me. It was only a small branch – the sort of place in which it was impossible to lose track of anyone, unless you deliberately set out to. I hung about for a few minutes, thinking she must have decided to try something on, but when I eventually checked the changing rooms they were empty. After that I went into the street and stood looking up and down, uncertain what to do. We didn't always stick together in town, but nor did we generally abandon one another without a word. At the edge of my vision I caught sight of someone slipping out of one of the phone boxes at the far end of the street. I only glimpsed the figure as it crossed the narrow pavement and vanished into the adjacent shops, but I knew it was Trudie.

I walked slowly towards the phone booths. There were several shops she might have gone into – all I had to do was wait her out. Sure enough a few minutes later Trudie emerged from an antique shop, busily tucking something into her Greek bag.

'Did you buy something?' I asked.

She hadn't seen me standing there. For a second her eyes registered surprise, then became guarded as she said quickly, 'Oh no. I only went in to look at something.'

'I thought you were putting something into your bag.'

She erased a decidedly shifty look with a smile. 'Oh that – a tissue. I'd just wiped my nose.' I knew it was a lie. Whatever she'd had in her hand, it wasn't a balled tissue. Anyway, she hadn't got hay fever or anything like that. Ever the mind reader, she added, 'The dust in the shop made me sneeze.'

'Why did you sneak off by yourself?'

'I didn't. What's wrong with you? Why the third degree?'

'Hey.' Danny's shout made us swivel towards the far end of the street, but then an echoing 'Hey' set us instinctively turning to look in the opposite direction. For a second I thought it was some strange trick of the acoustics: but a guy was waving – not at us, but beyond us to Danny and Simon. I turned to see Danny raise a hand in acknowledgement and the three of them converged at the point where we were waiting outside the shop.

The newcomer was wearing a Grateful Dead T-shirt and dangling a motorbike helmet from one hand. It quickly became evident that 'Josser', as he appeared to be called, knew Simon and Danny from university. He hailed from somewhere up north – a fact betrayed by his sing-song accent and elongated vowels – and was thus the very last person they had expected to bump into in Leominster. After mutual expressions of surprise, Josser explained that he was down for the summer, camping in a friend's garden and earning his keep by fruit picking.

While these preliminaries were being covered, I took a good look at Josser, taking in his greasy shoulder-length hair and clothes which gave no indication of a recent encounter with a washing machine. He had a noticeable gap between his upper front teeth and there was something about his smile which repulsed me, so that I shrank instinctively nearer to Danny when he looked my way. I hated the way his muddy brown eyes appraised Trudie and me from head to toe, like a greedy diner excited at the arrival of the sweet trolley.

On our side Danny predictably did most of the talking, managing to sound friendly while being deliberately vague about exactly where we were living. Each time Josser raised the question Danny evaded him as neatly as a winger at the top of his game, but I noticed that, whereas Danny managed to appear friendly, Simon's forced smile soon faded and at the first opportunity he interjected something about it being time for us to start back.

At this Josser said he didn't plan on staying in town either. 'I only came in to buy some fags. There's not a lot of action here, is there? Right dead and alive hole.'

'We're parked just round the corner.' Simon waved his hand vaguely in the direction and half turned – an obvious preliminary to saying goodbye.

'I bet it's the same place I've left my bike,' said Josser, cheerfully falling into step with us.

Unfortunately this proved to be correct. Josser's motorbike, a black monster with scarlet and yellow flames painted down the sides and a luggage box attached to the back, was parked a mere three vehicles away from ours. When we got level with it Josser began to wax lyrical on the machine's many virtues, while three-quarters of our party edged pointedly towards the Anglia: only Trudie was taking an interest in the bike and of course we couldn't go without her. It was impossible to decide whether she was genuinely oblivious, or just perversely determined not to pick up the collective vibe.

'Ever been on the pillion of a bike?' Josser addressed me directly, and I had to admit that I had not.

'You've never lived,' he said. 'Hop on. Let me take you for a run. I love giving the ladies a ride.'

'No, thank you,' I said, so primly that I sounded (and felt) a complete fool.

He turned to Trudie. 'How about you?'

'I'd love to,' said Trudie.

At that moment I could cheerfully have broken her neck. Simon and Danny exchanged looks but Trudie was immune to their disapproval. Josser had already opened the shiny box on the back of his bike and produced a spare crash helmet.

'Ooh,' said Trudie. 'It's got a death's head on it.'

'Yeah,' said Josser. 'I'm a Hell's Angel, evenings and weekends.'

Only Trudie laughed.

'We want to go back now,' Simon told her pointedly. 'You're going to get left behind.'

'That's okay,' said Josser. 'I'll follow you. That way no one's held up and she still gets to ride the machine. Don't drive too slowly now. I want to give this lady a thrill.'

Trudie giggled. I felt so cross I could have slapped her. She turned to Josser. 'Do I have to hold on to you?'

'As tight as you like.' Josser winked in my direction, but I pretended not to see.

He fastened the strap of the crash helmet for her, while the three of us stood by. It had been perfectly obvious to me that Simon and Danny wanted to shake him off as soon as possible, but instead here we were about to lead him back to where we lived. He climbed aboard the bike and Trudie got on after him in the exaggerated ostrich-like movement of someone completely unaccustomed to two-wheeled transportation. She settled into position, with her long brown legs following the line of his dirty jeans. I had a sudden vision of her coming off the bike and what would happen as her bare flesh met the tarmac at speed.

'Come on,' said Simon, abruptly.

'We shouldn't have let her,' I said, as we climbed into the car. 'Suppose they have an accident.'

'We can't stop her,' said Danny. 'Don't go too fast, Si, okay?'

'You think I was going to?' asked Simon. 'This'll be our slowest drive back ever.'

I watched over my shoulder as the bike followed us into the line of traffic heading out of town. Once in open country Simon proceeded at a steady thirty-five. Josser drew up close behind us, sitting on our tail while Simon did his best to ignore him. Suddenly Josser's patience gave out and he roared the bike's engine, swooping round us and heading into the distance like a rocket. Trudie was past before I had time to register her expression.

'What the fuck does he think he's doing?' Danny thumped the dashboard in frustration.

'Stupid prat,' said Simon. 'Ought I try to catch him?'

'Don't,' I said. 'If you go faster, so will he. If you don't he'll have to slow down, otherwise he'll lose us.'

'Trudie will be able to tell him the way,' said Simon, grimly. 'What an idiot.'

We did not see them again until we reached the house. When we turned in between the gateposts the bike was standing outside the front door, arrogantly pleased with itself. The riders had already dismounted. Trudie was in the act of removing the helmet and shaking out her long hair. Josser was standing beside her looking smug. Although there had never been any suggestion of a race, there was no doubt that Josser had notched up a victory. It was also evident that Josser wasn't planning to leave immediately – an impression confirmed by hearing Trudie's words as we got out of the Anglia: 'We've got some beer, if you fancy that.'

'A beer would be great.' His grin encompassed all of us. I hated the way his lips split wide apart, as if his teeth wanted to climb out of his mouth.

Simon opened the front door without a word, unable to countermand Trudie's invitation without giving way to an uncharacteristic display of bad manners.

'What a place,' said Josser, as he stepped into the hall.

'In here,' said Simon in a flat, expressionless voice, as he led the way into the drawing room.

'What do you think you're playing at.' I hissed, as I followed Trudie into the kitchen, 'inviting him in like that?'

Trudie looked genuinely surprised. 'I couldn't leave him standing outside – not after he'd given me a ride on his bike. Anyway, he said he was thirsty.'

'Of course he did. That's because he wanted to get inside. Couldn't you see that Simon didn't want him coming back here?'

'I thought he was their friend from university,' protested Trudie. 'If they didn't want to get talking with him, why did Danny shout to him in the first place?'

'He didn't shout at him, you nitwit. He was shouting to us.'

'Oh well – what's the harm? He won't stay long.'

'Well, don't encourage him,' I said. 'One beer. Don't take bottles in – just pour him a tumblerful – then he's got to go. Okay?' I started to hunt around for some clean glasses.

'Okay. Can you see where the tray has gone?'

We couldn't find the tray, so we carried the drinks in between us, me with one in each hand, Trudie balancing the other trio on a dinner plate.

'Waited on by a pair of beautiful girls,' said Josser. 'Isn't this the life?' When no one answered, he continued: 'I'd say you fellas have got it made. Place like this to shack up in, a couple of lasses. What's the secret of your success? Or maybe it's better not to ask – some secrets best kept, eh, fellas?' His tone was superficially friendly, but as he took an exploratory drink his eyes tracked from Simon to Danny and back again, and his expression was calculating.

'Have you seen anyone else from uni since term ended?' asked Simon. His tone reminded me of the one my mother employed when she had decided it was time to move on from an unsavoury topic.

'Nah – I went home for a bit, caught up with a few mates, but I was running short of brass, so I came down on this fruit-picking lark. Andy – you know Andy who's on the engineering course – said I could doss at his place. Nothing like this though. It's a grand spot, this. Room for a few more here, I reckon.'

'So,' said Simon, crisply. 'Do you make much money – fruit picking?'

'No, it's crap. Hardly keeps me in beer and fags. Bloody hard work, too. So what is it you're doing here then?'

'Gardening,' said Danny.

I sat watching everyone, saying nothing at all. Trudie was also uncharacteristically quiet. By now she had realized her mistake in being over-friendly with Josser and was probably worried about the extent to which she had annoyed the rest of us. Simon was doing his best to keep up a flow of superficially polite conversation until Josser had finished his beer, but his discomfiture was palpable. It was Danny, however, who surprised me most. I gradually realized that most of the tension in the room was emanating from him. Beneath his normal calm exterior, he was taut with anger. It radiated out of him like an invisible force field, until gradually each of us in the room became aware of it – all except Josser, who blabbed on and on completely impervious, constantly working the conversation back to the subject of our accommodation until he eventually said: 'Tell you the truth, I'm getting a bit sick of Andy's. Maybe I could move out here for a while. I'm pretty discreet – won't tell tales out of school, as they say.'

'You can't, I'm afraid. We've made an arrangement with the owner. Numbers are strictly limited to the four of us.' Simon didn't look at Josser as he spoke. He made as if to take another drink, but found his glass was empty.

Josser stretched his legs out in front of him. They reached right under the coffee table, the worn soles of his boots protruding out the other side. 'Rules were made to be broken. I don't suppose the "arrangement" includes your little harem either.' (He pronounced it hareem.) 'Come to that, I don't suppose the harem know everything there is to know about you two. They're not from the university, are they? So they won't have heard the rumours.'

He got no further. Danny's dive took him completely by surprise. The dregs of his beer went flying. (The glass – miraculously intact – landed several feet away on the hearth rug.) It was so quick that I didn't actually see the blow land. I seemed to be the only one who didn't move. Trudie sprang to her feet with a little cry and Simon jumped between Danny and Josser before anyone had time to say a word. For a second it was like looking at a still from an action movie. The overturned coffee table, Trudie frozen with horror, still clutching her empty glass, Danny poised to strike again while Josser cowered back in the corner of the sofa, a hand curled defensively in front of his mouth. When Simon broke the silence his voice was shaking. 'Just go,' he said.

Josser hesitated. When he moved his hand, I could see there was blood on his lips. Tears sprang into my eyes, not out of any sympathy for Josser, but in shock at the sudden eruption of violence. The situation was poised on a dangerous fulcrum. Josser was easily as tall as Danny and bulky with it. For all I knew, he hadn't been joking with his intimations of a semi-wild biker lifestyle. Maybe he carried a knife – or had a lot of biker friends.

'Go on,' said Simon. 'Piss off.' Simon's precise diction tended to give swear words an unintentionally comic inflection, but the message was undiluted.

Josser rose slowly, keeping a wary eye on Danny who stood like a statue, with Simon's restraining hand resting softly on his arm. We followed our departing guest at a distance, watching in silence as he fumbled with the front door: all four of us advancing on to the step to see him fasten on his helmet, then kick his bike into life. As he flung a leg across it, he shouted something against the roar of the engine.

Trudie was standing next to me. 'What did he say?' she whispered.

'I don't know,' I said. 'Something insulting – something about poofs.'

The guys had both turned back inside the house. Trudie hastened after them. 'I'm really, really sorry,' she began. 'I wouldn't have gone on the bike with him if I'd known how much trouble it would cause.'

'Don't worry about it.' With Josser's departure, Danny had reverted back to his usual easy-going self. 'He's just a wanker. He won't bother us again.' He gave Trudie a quick hug to demonstrate his equanimity. Simon followed his lead by squeezing her shoulder, but unlike Danny he still looked upset.

Then Danny noticed me. 'Hey, what's this?' He brushed away my solitary tear with his forefinger. 'Don't be upset. He's gone now. It's all over.' He gave me a hug too, following it up with a kiss. 'Come on. Let's forget all about it.'

Danny seemed to have no trouble putting the whole episode behind him, and the rest of us did our best to follow his lead. Simon had picked up a bottle of vodka in town and that night, after we had consumed the better part of it between us, we attempted to dance Cossack style on the lawn. Before very long I had fallen over so often that it didn't seem worth getting up. 'The world looks really weird from down here,' I said. No one took any notice. Simon and Trudie were engaged in a contest to see who could whirl round and round longest before they collapsed. Danny was urging them on. The lights from the kitchen windows cast long shadows across the ground. I reached out to grab a handful of light, but my fingers closed on the cold grass instead. Simon and Trudie stumbled into one another and fell in a heap.

Danny appeared above me – as tall as the Eiffel Tower. 'Come on,' he said. 'Let's go to bed.'

He offered a hand and I pulled myself upright. The

house was still stuffy with summer heat. 'I won't be able to sleep,' I protested.

'Who said anything about sleeping?' he said.

We were woken at around one in the morning by a loud shattering of glass, the echo of which was followed by a motorbike roaring away. A speedy reconnaissance revealed that a pane in the drawing-room window had been smashed. We gathered round in various states of undress, staring at the half brick which lay in the centre of a pool of broken glass.

Simon looked at Danny. 'Josser,' he said.

'Unless Murdered Agnes—' Trudie began.

'Don't start all that crap,' said Danny, a trifle more sharply than usual. 'Not unless you expect us to believe she's taken to riding a motorbike.'

'It has to be Josser,' said Simon.

'But why should he bother coming all the way out here?' I asked.

'I assume we're looking for something more sophisticated than to get back at Danny for thumping him,' said Simon sarcastically. 'But I don't think we're likely to come up with anything. There's nothing clever or sophisticated about Josser. He's just a nasty piece of work – that's all.' He saw the way Trudie was looking at him and continued more calmly: 'There was a guy last term – Josser thought he'd found out some stuff about him and threatened to spread it around. He made this guy's life a complete misery . . .' His voice faltered unexpectedly.

Trudie and I both stared at him. 'It was a good mate of Simon's,' Danny said – far too quickly. I wondered what Josser could possibly have found out about Simon, which he would want kept quiet.

'I'll get the bugger when term starts,' said Danny.

'I doubt if he'll be going back,' said Simon. 'He's probably failed his exams. He hardly ever turned up for lectures.' The thought seemed to cheer him.

'Well, he'll be sorry if I ever see him again,' said Danny grimly

The night air flooded in through the broken pane, making me shiver. 'What are we going to do about the window?'

'Leave it for tonight. It only needs a piece of glass cutting to the right size and some putty,' said Danny. 'I know how to do it. I helped my dad fix that broken window, after we put a cricket ball through it.'

'After you did, you mean,' said Simon.

'It was your fault,' grinned Danny. 'You bowled a googly.'

'You leave my googlies out of this.'

'I'm going back to bed,' Trudie announced and as if on cue the three of them all moved towards the door.

'Are you sure we ought to leave the window like this?' I asked.

'Yeah. We'll sort it out in the morning.'

I hung back doubtfully, but when no one else seemed minded to do anything about the broken glass on the carpet I scuttled after Danny, not wanting to be left alone with the hole. The blackness outside menaced me. I felt as if more than fresh air would come creeping in, given half a chance.

Back in bed, I couldn't get the broken window pane out of my head. In my mind's eye I saw Josser silencing his motorbike a good way down the lane before creeping up to the house and reaching in through the jagged hole, his dirty fingers pawing around for the window catch. The next thing I knew, Danny was comforting me in the darkness. 'Shh, shh, what is it? Come on, Katy. You must have been dreaming. There's nothing to be scared of. Just cuddle up next to me.'

FOURTEEN

I don't ask Mrs Ivanisovic how she is. It would be futile, pointless. I let her make the conversational running – which clearly costs her an effort, every sentence like climbing a mountain, leaving her exhausted and breathless.

'I hardly recognized you,' she says. 'You're still very pretty.'

We both know this isn't true, but I let it pass.

'Are you still teaching?'

'No, I took early retirement, after my mother died.'

She inclines her head a fraction, the acknowledgement with which the very elderly greet tidings of death. 'And your father?'

'He died quite a few years ago.'

Another nod to the inevitable. There is a pause while she gathers herself for another effort, so I fill the gap, telling her about my brother and his family; mentioning by way of an afterthought that my sister has been divorced twice. I cannot honestly be sure that she ever met them – I think they attended Danny's funeral, no more connection than that – but she is clearly grateful for my attempts to carry the burden of conversation.

When I fall silent she says: 'You never married.'

'No.'

'Was there ever anyone else? Did you never find anyone after Danny?'

'There was one person – someone I met later – but it wasn't possible.' I surprise myself with my candour.

I am telling Mrs Ivanisovic something I have never confided to anyone before.

She inclines her head in acceptance. 'You were his one great love,' she says. It is no more than a whisper, her voice no louder than rose petals falling on to damp earth. 'He would have married you. You would have been my daughter.'

I do not reply – cannot look at her. Instead I look out of the window, across the wide expanse of lawn to where a distant figure is moving impossibly slowly along the drive. I realize it is the same bent-backed old lady I saw on my way in. Everything moves slowly at Broadoaks. The faint tick of the bedside clock marks the seconds at a more restrained pace than it would in the outside world.

'Have they given you any tea?' she asks, and on receiving my denial she presses her bedside buzzer, which summons a uniformed nurse. 'We would like some tea, please,' says Mrs Ivanisovic, while I wonder if the nurse is privately thinking she has better things to do than fetch cups of tea for Mrs Ivanisovic and her visitors.

When the nurse leaves us alone again there is another brief silence. I wonder what I can possibly say to break it. Ridiculous questions come into my mind. Are they kind to you? How many people does it take to keep up the grounds? All impossibly stupid and irrelevant. Mrs Ivanisovic has pulled down her oxygen mask and is breathing into it. I feel absurdly embarrassed by this – as though I have caught her in a state of undress – so I look away, taking in the rest of her room which until now has been hidden behind my left shoulder.

There is a second armchair, of the same sturdy build as the model I am occupying, a circular table with a vase of flowers on it, a wardrobe, and a television set which sits on top of the sideboard affair which runs along the wall facing the window. The television is flanked by various framed photographs – the one of Danny prominently placed. I stand up and cross the room for a better look, realizing with a start that I recognize the shirt he is wearing. It's a cheesecloth shirt, in thin pale stripes of yellow, blue and white. I was with him the day he bought it in Oasis. I struggle to focus on this, because it has suddenly become important. The shopping trip in question was undertaken just days before our departure for Hereford – so when was this picture taken? I stare beyond him into the background. It's an outdoor snapshot – head and shoulders – Danny in front of a flowering bush of some description. None of us had a camera with us in Hereford. Did Mrs Ivanisovic bring one, when she came to see us that day?

She answers my question almost as if she has read my mind. 'It's the last photo we ever took of him. It was taken in our garden, just before you went away for the summer.' She pauses, the speech a drain on her resources, waiting to regain her breath. 'Stan had forgotten it was in the camera. It wasn't developed until after Danny was dead.'

A tap on the door precedes the reappearance of the nurse, bearing a tray. Two cups of tea, paper packets of sugar, a plate containing a carefully arranged quartet of Bourbon biscuits.

We both thank her as she sets the tray down. I take my tea, more to observe the formalities than because I want it. When I offer to pass Mrs Ivanisovic's cup, she shakes her head.

There is another silence while I drink my tea. They are becoming awkward, these silences. It isn't what I expected. I have not driven half the length of the country to sit drinking tea and looking out of the

116

window. I eke out the tea as long as possible, while inwardly contemplating the contents of her first letter. Sooner or later one of us has to mention it – start the ball rolling – or should I just drink my tea, then look at my watch and say it's been nice to see her again, but I have to be going?

I finish my tea and return the cup to the tray. I offer Mrs Ivanisovic her tea again and this time she takes it. Her hands are unsteady. When she lifts the cup from the saucer, it wobbles dangerously, a massively weighty, unstable load. She manages a couple of sips without incident, before indicating with a gesture that she wishes to be relieved of it. Only when I have placed the cup and saucer next to mine does she speak again.

'Please go to the top drawer – see – yes, there. Reach out that book and bring it to me.'

The book is the uppermost item in the drawer: one of those expensive fabric-covered jobs, scarlet with gold embroidery. The sort of book some women use as a journal or to copy out bits of favourite poetry. She thanks me as I place it in her hands: then opens it carefully. There appear to be several bits of paper lying loose inside the front cover, but she ignores them, turning a few leaves to reach a point where a single sheet of folded newspaper is pressed between two blank pages. She extracts it and hands it to me. 'Open it,' she says.

It has been folded in half and half again, the creases impressed into the paper by years of storage. It is a report of the inquest into Danny's death. I don't have to read it, because I was there. Instead I look up, to find her eyes looking straight into mine.

'That wasn't the whole truth, was it, Katy?'

Words rise in my throat, but they die away before they can reach her; dissolving when they meet the air, like the remains in an ancient tomb.

'There *is* something else, isn't there? I have always known there was something more.' My silence appears to fuel her conviction. 'Stan persuaded me not to say anything at the inquest. He even made me promise not to raise it with you. He said you had suffered so much, just as we had, and nothing would bring Danny back . . .'

I continue to sit dumbly holding the sheet of newspaper while she leaves the words hanging in the air.

'I have to know the *whole* truth, Katy.' When she speaks again, her voice has taken on a surprising degree of strength and urgency. 'You see, I *know* there is something else – something Danny was trying to tell me before he died.'

The door opens, heralding the return of the nurse. If she knocked to warn us of her entrance, neither of us have heard it. She is a lumpen intrusion, her navy uniform stretched over her huge bottom, her senses dead to everything beyond the immediate purpose of her visit, completely oblivious to the atmosphere within the room.

'Now then, Betty,' she says, her brisk cheeriness slicing straight through the situation, impervious to any signs of tension. 'I'm afraid I'm going to have to ask your visitor to wait outside for a few minutes.' To me she adds: 'It won't take more than five minutes, dear. You can just wait out in the hall, or have a little stroll in the garden.'

Mrs Ivanisovic merely shrinks further back into her pillows, apparently resigned to the interruption. Bristling at Big Bottom's patronizing tone, I find myself standing stupidly in the hall, still holding the old news cutting. In an absurdly furtive gesture I hastily fold it back into quarters and stuff it into my handbag, just before the member of staff I encountered on arrival emerges – apparently from a cupboard under the stairs, where I assume she lies in wait for unwary visitors.

Feeling an explanation is warranted, I say, 'I'm just waiting while the nurse is in there.'

'Ah yes. Poor Betty. She has been so excited about your coming. So nice for her to have a visitor. She sees people so seldom – she's very much on her own in the world, I'm afraid.'

The words sting me like hailstones. She should have had Danny. Danny should have been here – and as for me, I might have been her daughter.

FIFTEEN

The broken window inevitably meant another stop to work on the pond. Simon remembered seeing a hardware store in Leominster, which had a notice advertising glass cut to size, so we drove back in search of it the next day. We soon located the right shop and were on the point of going inside when Trudie said: 'I don't have to come with you for the glass, do I? Only there's something else I want to look at.'

'Okay,' said Simon. 'But don't be too long.'

Trudie immediately walked off in a way which made it perfectly obvious that I was excluded from her errand. I went into the hardware shop with the others: but once they were busy giving the assistant their measurements I excused myself, murmuring something about waiting outside. Back in the street I headed straight for the phone booths, where I had spotted her the day before. Once I'd established they were empty, I peered into the window of the shop from which she had emerged the day before, but there were no signs of life. My original idea that she was stealing from the house had returned with a vengeance, although I was forced to concede that whatever she was pilfering, it had to be something pretty small – something which would slot unobtrusively into her Greek bag.

I was wondering what to do next, when I caught sight of Trudie all but running towards me. Even from a distance I could see she was agitated.

'I've just met Josser,' she gasped.

'Where?'

'Down there, coming out of the off-licence. I almost bumped right into him. I didn't know what to do, so I just said hello, and tried to walk on.'

'Well?'

'He sort of stood in my way and said—' here she affected a queer facsimile of Josser's accent – '"I don't know what's going on in that big house out there, but there's things you girls oughter know . . ."'

'What did you say?'

'I didn't say anything. I was trying to get past.'

'Didn't you ask him if he'd put our window through last night?'

'No, I didn't. Would you have? I tried to get round him and he took hold of my arm.' Trudie glanced down involuntarily, as if expecting the contact to have left a lasting stain. 'Then he started rabbiting on about some other stuff, so I jerked my arm to make him let go; then I turned and nearly ran back this way. He smelt horrible too. Do you think I should say anything to the others?'

I thought for a few seconds. 'No. Danny might want to go after him and it's no good getting into a fight in a public place . . . and we don't want any more midnight visits or smashed windows, either.'

'What do you think he means – about things we ought to know?'

'Nothing,' I said firmly. 'From what Danny says, they hardly know him at all. He's just being mean and trying to scare us. Come on – Simon said not to be long.'

I set a pace which didn't encourage talking and when we rounded the corner I saw the boys were waiting for us by the car. Neither of them was in very good humour: for some reason the glass could not be cut immediately, so someone would have to return for it next day. Simon was trying to calculate whether it would need to be transported in the back of the car, although Danny was still optimistic that it might fit in the boot. 'We ought to have measured the boot before we set out,' Simon was saying. 'Even if it had been ready this afternoon, with all of us, we might not have fitted the glass into the car as well.'

The interior of the Anglia felt airless and the seats frazzled bare flesh at the merest touch. As we drove out of town Simon continued to carp, saying that tomorrow he would get up early and collect the glass first thing, instead of wasting half a day. I thought this was a bit rich, considering Simon liked a lie-in as much as anyone else. I was about to point out that he was as much responsible for any delay as the rest of us, when out of nowhere Trudie piped up, 'Who's Rachel Hewitt?'

The car swerved so violently that I had to grab the back of Danny's seat. 'Sorry about that,' said Simon. 'I thought that kid was going to run out into the road.'

'Rachel Hewitt's dead. Why do you want to know about Rachel Hewitt?' asked Danny.

'Oh heck,' said Trudie. 'Was she a friend of yours?'

'Not particularly,' said Danny. 'She was on the same course as me at uni. Someone broke into her room one night and strangled her.' His tone was completely matter of fact.

Trudie audibly sucked in a breath. 'Wow – did they get anyone for it?'

'Not so far as I know,' said Danny. 'They hadn't arrested anyone by the end of term.'

Simon asked: 'What on earth made you ask about Rachel Hewitt?'

'I met Josser in Leominster. He mentioned her – said she was crazy about Danny.'

'That's crap,' said Simon. 'Anyway, Josser wouldn't have known much about who Rachel Hewitt was or wasn't into – she was well out of his league.'

'Oh, look,' said Danny. 'There's a horse with a foal – see it over on the left . . .'

'Oh, how sweet,' I said. 'Slow down a bit, Si – look at his dear little legs – a perfect Bambi.'

'Bambi was a deer.'

'I know, but he's got the same gangly legs.'

'I think we could still get quite a bit of work done today,' Danny addressed Simon. 'It's not four o'clock yet.'

By the time we got back to the house my head felt fuzzy with the heat. I decided to try running a bowl of cold water and putting my feet in it – it was the nearest thing I could think of to a cool dip. We'd had a kiddies' paddling pool when I was little. Just a simple blow-up one, two pale blue plastic rings and a white plastic bottom covered in pictures of shells and fishes, although any illusion of the seaside was always spoiled by the tiny bits of grass which found their way in on our bare feet. I entertained a wistful longing for it, while I ran the kitchen tap.

My bowl of cold water provoked nothing but mirth from the others. 'You look like an old woman,' Trudie said, passing me on her way out to sunbathe.

The cold water failed to do the trick, so I went to lie down on our bed. The open window caught a hint of breeze and funnelled it in my direction. I thought about Trudie's question in the car. She did have an awful habit of blurting things out, without stopping to think what effect it might have on people. Of course she wasn't to know that there might be any particular sensitivities about Rachel Hewitt. Then I remembered what she claimed Josser had said – 'Rachel Hewitt was crazy about Danny' – and I wondered if she had been mischief-making after all. If there had been any truth in this assertion, then it was surely not the most tactful thing to bring up in front of us both. It was rubbish of course. Just Josser trying to stir things because Danny had punched him in the mouth. I drifted into a hazy half-sleep, during which Josser's words echoed every now and then, reminding me of my anxiety while Danny was out of my sight at university. 'Well, you needn't have worried,' said a small, sensible voice in my head. 'Danny is crazy about you – not about Rachel Hewitt or anyone else – just about you.'

The next thing I knew, Danny was rousing me. He was sitting on the edge of the bed, holding a glass of lemonade. 'Are you all right? I didn't realize you'd come up here.'

'I was too hot,' I said. 'I must have fallen asleep.'

'You look a bit pale.' He handed me the glass, a thoughtful frown drawing his eyebrows together. 'You should have told me you weren't feeling well. I don't like to think of you being up here by yourself – you might have needed something.'

'I'm feeling much better now.' I sat up properly and swung my feet on to the floor. 'What time is it?'

'It's half six. We've packed up for the day and Trudie's got dinner ready. Do you feel up to eating anything?'

'I'm fine now,' I insisted.

We went downstairs together. Trudie had made a cheese and onion flan, with roast potatoes and peas, which she was spooning on to four plates. She looked up as I entered the kitchen. 'Where did you get to? You promised to help with the potatoes, or had you forgotten?'

I had forgotten, but before I could open my mouth Danny cut in to say I hadn't been feeling well. Trudie was instantly all concern, but I saw the way Simon's lip curled.

We took our plates and cutlery into the garden. The outside temperature had become bearable, but I declined the offer of cider in favour of another cold lemonade. It was the first time we had all been together since we got back to the house and Trudie wasted no time in embarking on the topic which had obviously been uppermost in her mind for several hours.

'It must be exciting, being involved in a real life murder. Tell me again what happened to this girl you were at university with.'

'There's nothing to tell really,' said Danny. 'She was on my course and we lived in the same hall of residence – although I didn't know her all that well. Someone – some pervert, I suppose – climbed into her window and strangled her.'

Trudie looked deflated. Danny's slightly bored delivery had completely undermined whatever sensational tittle-tattle she had been anticipating. She forked up a lump of potato and masticated thoughtfully, before saying, 'Josser said this girl was mad about you.'

'So what?' said Simon. 'Danny's a good-looking bloke. Loads of girls are mad about him.'

'Was she ever your girlfriend?' Trudie persisted.

'No. Katy's my girlfriend.' Danny leant across to squeeze my shoulder.

'Danny could have had anyone he wanted,' Simon said, 'but he chose Katy.' The note of sarcastic incredulity was not lost on any of us.

I rose to the bait. 'Meaning?'

'Just a joke, darling.' Simon was smirking. He knew he had riled me.

'At least someone wants *me*.' As soon as the words were out of my mouth, I knew I shouldn't have said them. I saw Simon redden and Danny frown.

'I wonder how difficult it would be to strangle someone,' Trudie mused.

'Depends how annoying they are, I should imagine,' said Simon. He didn't need to look at me – I understood perfectly what he was getting at. 'I fancy a walk – is anyone else up for it? Trudie was saying the girls went down to the wood yesterday. I wouldn't mind seeing what it's like down there myself.'

Danny hesitated. 'Maybe Katy shouldn't go: she wasn't very well this afternoon.' He turned to me, 'I'll stay here with you, shall I?'

I acquiesced readily. The further away from Simon the better, so far as I was concerned. Danny volunteered to clear away and I helped him wash up: which seemed only fair since Trudie had done all the cooking again. We were about halfway into the job when Danny said, 'I wish you would try to be a bit nicer to Simon.'

'Maybe you should ask him to be a bit nicer to me.'

Danny chose to ignore the point. 'It's so great when the three of us get along together – like we did at the beginning. It was perfect – and that's the way I like things. I want everything to be perfect between you and me.'

'But Simon—'

Danny didn't allow me to get any further. He kissed his forefinger and placed it against my lips. 'I always get what I want, remember? And I want everything to be perfect, so it will be.'

With the evening sun slanting in at the kitchen window and Danny silhouetted against it, it was easy to imagine him sweeping aside all obstacles to our happiness. He was by turns my forceful handsome warrior and my parfit gentil knyght. He kissed me properly, taking me up bodily and perching me on the table, the better to do so. 'You're so beautiful,' he whispered into my hair. 'Sometimes I can hardly believe you're mine.' Distracted by Danny's kisses, I did not even think to question the veracity of this alleged honeymoon period, in which Simon and I had been the best of pals.

Next morning Simon was as good as his word: he rose early and was back at the house with the pane of glass before ten o'clock. Replacing the window proved to be a major task, involving all four of us attempting to hold the pane in place, while simultaneously getting in each other's way and issuing contradictory instructions to one another. The end result looked awful. Even after Simon had trimmed the surplus putty with a dinner knife, it bulged around the glass with the appearance of badly managed pastry. The surface was a blur of fingerprints, as if a thousand phantom hands had come pawing at the window: an effect I found so creepy that I voluntarily set to work to clean them all off. The others left me to it. It was a desperately tedious job. Each time I cleaned the outside I managed to miss some marks, which were instantly visible once I got back into the drawing room, and every time I went outside again I spotted a few more marks on the inside of the pane. Eventually I gave up the unequal struggle and went to find Trudie in the garden.

She was lying stretched out on the dry grass in her bikini. Her eyes were closed and there was a bottle of suntan lotion lying beside her, with a single white drip suspended halfway down its label. Cleaning the glass had made my arms ache, so the sight of such indolence irritated me.

'Who were you phoning, the other day?'

The question made her jump. Either that or she hadn't heard me approaching.

'No one. What are you talking about? There isn't a phone here.'

'In Leominster.' I flopped down beside her. 'I saw you come out of a phone box, the day before yesterday.'

'Oh – then. I wasn't phoning anyone.' She relaxed into her former position.

'Yes you were.' She's such a liar, I thought, unexpectedly angry. 'Why else would you be in a phone box?'

'I wanted to see if there was a Yellow Pages, but of course there wasn't. They've always been pinched, haven't they? The phone books and Yellow Pages.'

'Why did you want a Yellow Pages?'

'I wanted to look at the antique dealers. If you must know, I wanted to see if any of them advertised any special interests.'

'Come off it,' I said. I was convinced that she was giving me the runaround. 'You were in a street full of antique dealers. You didn't need to look them up in the Yellow Pages. You were calling someone.'

'Well, what if I was?' she suddenly snapped. 'I don't see that it's any of your business, anyway.'

This silenced me. It was absolutely true of course. If Trudie wanted to make half a dozen phone calls, it was really nothing to do with me at all. Nor was it anything to do with me if she wanted to visit the local antique shops – unless of course she was stealing from Simon's uncle. I thought about the way she had sneaked off on her own, two days running. Had she anticipated that I would ask her what she had been up to? It occurred to me that the alleged encounter with Josser had provided a distraction at a very convenient moment.

'Did you really bump into Josser in Leominster?' I asked, trying to sound natural and friendly.

'Of course I did.' Trudie sounded natural and friendly again too. 'It frightened the life out of me. He's such a creepy sod.'

'You didn't think that when you went for a ride on his motorbike.'

'That was then – before he came round and left his calling card through our window.'

'Do you think he'll come back again?'

A cloud edged in front of the sun, blocking some of the heat. Trudie sat up and half turned towards me. 'I shouldn't think so. He'll be one of those people who just comes into your life story, then goes out of it again. You know, like Colonel Careless.'

'What?'

'Colonel Careless – the bloke who hid with King Charles II in an oak tree. He just appears on the stage of English history for that one day; then he's never heard of again.'

'You're making that up,' I said, laughing. 'Nobody could possibly have been called Colonel Careless.'

'It's true – honestly. We did it in History.'

'Come on, Trudie.' We were both laughing now. Keeping my tone light, I said, 'So are you going to tell me why you gave me the slip in Dorothy Perkins?'

Trudie considered this for a moment, looking arch, with her head on one side. 'Well, all right then,' she said, affecting a reluctant conspiratorial tone. 'Since you're dying to know, and I think you can keep a secret . . .' She paused theatrically. 'My grandmother gave me the most valuable gift I possess . . .'

I wasn't in the mood for any of her fairy stories or wind-ups so I faked a yawn, holding my mouth wide open and patting my fingers repeatedly against my lips. I was getting very tired of hearing about Trudie and her 'gift'.

'You obviously don't really want to know,' she said, getting to her feet and walking back towards the house. I let her go. She got into a huff periodically but it never lasted very long.

SIXTEEN

In spite of being young and fit, Simon and Danny found the pond excavation hard going. They suffered from blistered hands and sunburn in the early days, coupled with the frustration of seemingly getting nowhere. Sometimes they spent an hour or more just extracting tree roots, or a whole morning hacking away a rotten stump. They dug out wheelbarrowloads of stones, which they hauled away to provide foundations for the rockery – often the only man-made sound in the garden was the distinctive chink of a stone tossed into the bucket. Once or twice we thought we heard a motorbike roaring along the lane, but, as Trudie said, plenty of people had motorbikes.

While the boys were engaged with their building project, Trudie and I amused ourselves as best we could. The two of us had fallen into the habit of walking down to the woods together. It was a way of escaping from the house for a while and, with no one to overhear, we could indulge in the sort of conversations which held no interest for the boys, to say nothing of seizing the opportunity to grumble about the way they left their dirty socks lying around and forgot to flush the loo. Lately everyone had a grievance of some sort and none of us were slow to air them. Even our woodland excursions became the subject of a spat between Simon and Trudie, when he complained one afternoon that she had not been on hand to provide him with a cup of tea.

'I'm not your bloody slave, you know,' she said. 'I'm a free agent. I can come and go as I please.'

'This isn't a frigging holiday camp,' Simon snarled. 'You can't expect a free ride.'

'I do more than my fair share, so screw you,' she shouted. 'If you don't want me here, I can soon find somewhere else.'

'Pack it in, Simon,' I said. 'Trudie works really hard. It didn't hurt you to make your own tea just for once.'

'If I'm not wanted—' Trudie began, but I managed to soothe her down with platitudes while Simon stumped off – probably to sulk.

After what seemed like an eternity they finally finished digging out the pond. The eventual result was an irregular oval about ten feet by six at its widest points and deep enough to allow for two or three feet of water. Simon ordered sand for the lining and we all stood round when the lorry arrived to deliver it, toasting the first significant landmark in the project.

The arrival of the sand signalled another fall-off in the work rate. It was a milestone and as such felt like a good excuse for a couple of days off. Danny was all for a return trip to the seaside, but Simon said it was too expensive in petrol, so we settled for a walk on Hergest Ridge instead. The heat was less intense that day and from the top of the ridge it was possible to see banks of cloud, creeping in from Wales.

'If it rains,' said Danny, with more than a shade of hope in his voice, 'we won't be able to work on the pond tomorrow.'

'I wish it would rain,' I said. 'I'm fed up with this hot, sticky weather.'

'I'll make it rain for you,' said Trudie. 'What we need is for that dark cloud over there to come over here and shed on us. Whistle for wind, someone, and I'll do a rain dance.'

Simon obediently began to whistle – a traditional tune which I half knew, but couldn't put a name to. Trudie stepped out of her sandals, did a couple of exploratory steps across the grass, then started to dance – graceful and unselfconscious, her long gauzy skirt swirling around her strong brown feet and ankles. She unwound the silk scarf she'd been wearing round her neck and whirled it above her head, like an offering to the gods, against the darkening sky. Simon switched to a verse of 'Greensleeves' and from that to 'Spanish Ladies' while Trudie danced and danced. It was as if she had forgotten us, forgotten the whole world.

We became so fixated on Trudie that we hardly noticed the progress of the clouds. The first spots of rain took us by surprise. They splotched our clothing with damp circles, the size of a 10p piece.

'Hey, Trudie, you can stop now,' exclaimed Danny.

Simon aborted his whistling mid-bar and Trudie spun to a halt, staring up at the sky.

'I made it rain,' she said, doubtfully – repeating the words with something approaching elation: 'I made it rain.'

The shower didn't amount to much, which was just as well considering how far we were from shelter; but the boys addressed Trudie as Rain Goddess for the rest of the day, allowing her to precede us everywhere and bowing her in and out of the pub at Old Radnor – much to the bemusement of the locals. This success in conjuring up a shower reawakened Trudie's fascination with her so-called mystical side, and on the homeward journey she and Simon started talking about the Agnes Payne mystery again. I wished they would shut up about it. Bettis Wood was a happy, sunlit place for me just then, and I didn't want it invaded by the shadowy deeds of long ago.

When we reached the house, the lads fell to discussing the pond again. Simon was starting to worry about the stages of the operation which were still to come – in particular the concreting. Neither he nor Danny had any experience of using concrete, so Simon had obtained a book on the subject of constructing garden water features, from the library in Kington. The contents were not reassuring. Danny's theory that 'you slap together a bit of sand and cement, then add water till it looks about right,' was apparently somewhat wide of the mark. Simon's book was full of cautionary tales about what would happen to your concrete if you didn't get the mix or application right. It ended up by stating: *Concrete laying is a skill that demands considerable knowledge and practice. If you are at all unsure of your ability to do a satisfactory job, employ a professional to do it for you.*

Which was all very well, but Simon's uncle had only left enough money to cover raw materials and the hire of a concrete mixer. Manpower and expertise would cost extra – and we didn't know how much. In the end, Simon decided he would go into town the next day and make some enquiries. 'Asking costs nothing,' he said.

Trudie elected to go with him, while Danny and I stayed behind at the house. With Simon gone Danny opted for some lighter work, and spent half an hour clearing the last small patch of weeds out of the rose bed by the terrace, before throwing himself down on the lawn and saying he was whacked. I joined him there and we sat discussing what we might do next, while drinking tepid glasses of orange squash (we had run out of ice cubes as usual).

'Let's walk down to the woods,' Danny suggested. 'Get away from this place for a while.'

It was another sunny day with a few picture-book fluffy clouds almost stationary in the sky. As we turned into the road I could already feel the back of my dress sticking to me. Insects hummed and butterflies skimmed the field. We had to go in single file down the path, but once inside the wood we walked hand in hand.

'It's really nice to have you to myself,' he said. 'We don't often get a chance to go somewhere on our own.'

I squeezed his hand in acknowledgement.

'You look like a fairy in that dress,' he said.

'Funny-looking fairy,' I said.

The garment in question was a bit of a joke between us. It was one of those over-priced boutique buys which I had quickly regretted: a cotton dress which fell straight from shoulder to hem, with a dozen tiny buttons leading up to a plain round neck – yellow with a big white daisy on the front. After one wash it had shrunk to a length which was positively indecent, and, far from making me look like a fairy, it probably gave the impression of an urban street walker. I almost never wore it, but I was so far behind with the washing that I hadn't anything else clean to put on. Tomorrow, I thought, I will have to drag out the twin tub and tackle the pile of clothes in the corner of the bedroom floor.

We walked on for a bit, eventually sitting down in one of the grassy dells not far from the playground. After exchanging a few kisses, we began to roll around together on the grass – half playful, half in earnest. I realized my dress had rucked up around my waist and tried to pull it down.

'Don't,' he murmured, between kisses. 'Let's do it here, out in the forest.'

Presumably this was his idea of Free Love and all that back-to-nature stuff, but I could only focus on lower middle class proprieties and creepy-crawlies.

'No,' I squeaked, as his thumb engaged with the waistband of my pants. 'We can't. Not here. Let's go back to the house.'

'No,' he said, with his mouth close to my ear, full of lust and mischief. 'Here.'

'It's more comfortable in bed,' I protested, aiding rather than impeding his assault on my knickers by trying to wriggle away.

'Much more romantic here,' he said, kissing me again.

At that precise moment I couldn't think of anything less romantic than the prickle of bent grass under my bare bottom, but it was clear that Danny would not be deflected. I tried a last protest. 'Someone may see us. Suppose someone's coming.'

'Someone is coming, babe – and it could be you.'

I didn't want to upset Danny by repelling him with the violent refusal my every instinct cried out to make. My only hope was a random bird watcher or someone out walking their dog, but Bettis Wood was deserted as usual. Even so, I covered myself up as quickly as possible afterwards, urging him to do the same. It would be just typical for this to be the one afternoon when some pillar of the Parish Council brought her grandchildren through the wood, to hunt for pine cones or something.

'You're not upset, are you?' Danny asked, as we set off for home.

'No – of course not. Why should I be?' I didn't want to make a big thing out of it. Didn't want to be accused of being a prude.

'It was good for you, right?'

For a second I thought he had picked up on my unease, but then I decided it was no more than a routine enquiry – a question to which I always answered in the affirmative – so I nodded, even while I set about dismissing the uncomfortable conjunction from my mind. The truth was that by then I had come to the conclusion that sex was not all it was cracked up to be. Danny was the first boy I had slept with and the idea had turned out to be far more exciting than the actuality.

When we emerged from the wood, Danny led the way back along the path and I followed a pace or two behind. It wasn't a situation conducive to conversation, so I was left with my own thoughts. I decided that I would switch on the immersion heater as soon as we got in, so that I could have a bath later. Tomorrow I would get up early and do the washing. I hated that stupid dress – I should never have allowed things to get so far behind that I had nothing else to wear. I was conscious that lately some aspects of the housekeeping had been neglected more than usual. When Trudie first joined us, it was generally she who had initiated things like the washing and ironing; whereas I tended to have a mass of good intentions, which never quite came to fruition. Lately Trudie's initial enthusiasm had worn off.

When we reached the top of the footpath and came out on to the road, there was a glint of sunlight on metal, visible through the bushes.

'Si's back,' said Danny. A fraction of a second later we turned in between the lilac and the rhododendron which marked the gateposts and he added, 'Blimey O'Reilly – that's Mum and Dad's car, parked next to Si's.'

We both automatically quickened pace. As we entered the house we met Simon in the hall.

'It's your mother.' He addressed Danny. 'There's nothing the matter. She just drove out here to see how you are.'

At that moment we came into line with the open door of the drawing room and caught sight of Mrs Ivanisovic and she of us, so no chance for me to sidle upstairs and pretend to be out. There was nothing for it but to look pleased and walk right in.

She was being entertained to tea by Trudie, who was singularly inappropriately clad for the task, in a pair of cut-down denims, to which a splash patch saying *Try it, you'll like it*, had been sewn; and a bikini top from which her breasts strained to escape every time she leaned forward, which she was doing now, to pour tea from the best teapot. Amid everything else, I noticed that Murdered Agnes must have anticipated visitors, since she had kindly returned the teapot in the nick of time.

'Hello, darling,' Mrs Ivanisovic greeted Danny, who went across to kiss her on the cheek. 'And Katy. How are you?'

'Very well, thank you.' I hung back in the doorway, conscious of my dishevelled appearance in general and that awful dress in particular. Why hadn't I just stuck with my underwear and a big badge which said *Trollop* on it, for goodness sake? 'We've just been for a walk in the wood,' I said, belatedly reaching up to tidy my hair: an operation which sent a dead leaf fluttering on to the carpet.

Mrs Ivanisovic didn't have to say the words 'Dressed like that?' out loud, because her face said it for her. I sat down on one of the sofas opposite her, thereby enabling my skirt to shame me still further by boldly riding up to expose the remaining inches of my thighs.

'Tea?' asked Trudie, brightly. She appeared to be vastly amused by the whole thing. Why the heck couldn't she have slipped upstairs and put a T-shirt on?

We stumbled through a superficially conventional conversation – Mrs I saying it had been 'quite an adventure' finding us, Danny telling her all about the work in the garden and promising to take her for a look round as soon as we had finished our tea. While we talked, I saw the drawing room through fresh eyes. We didn't use it very much, but the silent pointers to our sporadic periods of occupation were unflattering. There was a pile of Simon's uncle's LPs on the floor in front of the radiogram: someone had extracted them from the cupboard and, having looked through them, left them to slide sideways across the floor. The uppermost and perhaps most recent addition to the collection – a live recording of *The Goon Show* – had become the resting place for a stained teaspoon and a saucerless cup, one of several miscellaneous items of crockery which were lying about. There was dust everywhere and a stale smell of sluttish neglect.

Every so often I felt Mrs Ivanisovic's eyes on me. I imagined the aroma of recent copulation mingling with my sweat and heading in an invisible stream, straight as an arrow up her patrician nose. I wondered what other clues might be shouting out from my person, apart from bringing half the forest floor back in my hair. My face burned hot while I sipped tea and listened to her telling Danny all about what was flowering in their garden at home.

She was obviously curious about Trudie, who Simon had been at pains to explain 'was only staying for a couple of nights': as he said afterwards, the Ivanisovics knew his parents, who in turn might talk to his uncle, who would not be happy to find his property had been used as open house by all and sundry.

When Trudie made her silly remark about being picked up on the beach like a sea shell, I began to sweat hot and cold lest Mrs I's next question be to ask when we had gone to the beach – some idiot would be sure to blurt out that it was several weeks ago; but luckily Mrs I turned to Trudie instead and said, 'I'm afraid I didn't catch your name.'

'Trudie.' There was a pause, both women smiling at each other. It was obvious Mrs I was expecting the addition of a surname. Trudie could easily have ignored the hint, because Mrs I was far too polite to press the point and say 'Trudie what?' – but of course, Trudie couldn't leave it.

'Trudie Eccles,' she said, with too obvious a trace of mirth.

Danny's mother checked slightly. I knew she must have spotted the recording of *The Goon Show*. Oh Lord – say something somebody, quick, before Trudie goes and makes things even worse.

'What's the weather been like in Brum?' asked Simon. I could have kissed him on the spot.

We made an ill-assorted group that afternoon. None of us belonged in our surroundings – we four having the appearance of campers at a pop festival, scantily clad and slightly grubby, while she, cool as a cucumber in spite of having driven sixty miles on a hot day, was far too smart for the room in her navy and white summer frock, white matching shoes and handbag.

I was relieved when the time came to escort her round the garden, in which she took a polite interest; like a visiting dignitary, asking all the right questions. She declined to approach the earthworks too closely, for fear of dirtying her shoes, but she admired our work on the rose beds and advised that some of the shrubs had got so out of hand they needed cutting down altogether.

At the conclusion of the garden tour she said she would have to be getting back. The journey had taken longer than she anticipated and Mr Ivanisovic would be worried if he got in from work and she wasn't there. It had been lovely seeing us, she added, and seeing what we were getting up to: I felt the colour rise in my face, feeling that Mrs Ivanisovic knew exactly what I'd been getting up to, as surely as if she had stood in the wood and watched us. Thank heavens there had never been any direct communication between my parents and

Danny's. It was one of the reasons I had been confident I could get away with the fruit-picking-in-France story – and now I was doubly grateful.

It was at this point that she mentioned she had a few items for us in the boot of her car. Trudie had already diverted into the kitchen to tidy up the tea things, but the rest of us followed Mrs Ivanisovic round to her car – a shiny new Wolseley Six, the boot of which was opened to reveal a treasure trove of goodies.

'Mason's pop,' said Danny. 'Great.'

In addition to half a dozen bottles of pop, I could see a big tin of biscuits, various canned goods, four or five Party Sevens and a couple of punnets of strawberries. Simon and Danny set about unloading this booty, while I stood to one side next to Mrs Ivanisovic. Normally I would have helped carry things inside, but I knew I couldn't bend over the boot without revealing my knickers, so I stayed put.

We watched them carry their first load in silence. I wished I could think of something to say, and when she opened her mouth to speak, I thought it would surely be to ask why I wasn't helping; however I didn't have time to frame a convincing excuse about a back problem before her actual words rendered me speechless.

'Stan and I are so pleased to hear that you and Danny are going to get married.' As my mouth gaped open, she emitted a twinkly little laugh, before continuing, 'Now don't bother to deny it. I know it's supposed to be a secret, but naturally Danny had to tell us, before you came away.'

A secret, I thought. You bet it's a secret. So much of a bloody secret, even *I* don't know anything about it.

'I just wanted you to know that Stan and I are very happy that Danny has chosen you.'

I didn't know how to reply. Fortunately I was saved

the trouble because my intended and his best buddy reappeared at that moment for another load, profuse in their thanks and delighted to discover a cache of crisps and Cheesy Wotsits towards the back of the boot. As they carted this new load in through the front door, Mrs Ivanisovic lowered her voice and said in a conspiratorial tone: 'I hope you don't mind my saying, dear, but that little dress leaves nothing to the imagination – and it really doesn't suit you at all.'

I was beyond speech. It was not merely my embarrassment which threatened to shatter me into a thousand little pieces, right there and then on the drive. I was considerably shocked, not to say needled, by the whole secret engagement business. She had chosen words which, while apparently bestowing a seal of approval on our forthcoming union, had also implied that I ought to be honoured by Danny's choosing me. Apparently that was the way she thought these things worked – Danny took his pick and I had no say whatever in the matter. How dare he tell his parents – as if everything was all decided – before he'd asked me. Even my compliant nature had its limits.

On reflection I also found it extremely unsettling that he chose to confide *any* important personal things to his parents, in preference to confiding in me. I had convinced myself that I knew Danny better than he knew himself. I had been coasting along on the crest of a wave, but Mrs Ivanisovic had abruptly grounded me on the shingle. As I watched them embrace while she made her farewells, I felt completely excluded – a confused outsider who watches tribal rituals not entirely understood – transported in an instant from being the central person in his life to a mere bystander. She finally got into the car and we watched while she started the engine, then made a series of short darts across the gravel until she eventually got the car facing the open gates. The steering wheel looked massive: far too large for her tiny delicate hands. She looked over her shoulder and smiled as she gave us a final wave.

'Bye, Mum,' Danny called as she turned on to the road, one chrome wing mirror scraping past the lilac, the other almost touching the rhododendron. 'Wow,' he said, turning to me with a broad grin. 'That was a surprise.'

'You're not kidding,' I said.

SEVENTEEN

The memory of my appearance that day had the power to shame me for many years. Even as I stand in the hall at Broadoaks, pretending to look at a framed print of a hunting scene, the thought of it is enough to bring a faint warmth to my cheeks. I wonder if Mrs Ivanisovic remembers it as clearly as I do. I imagine she does. Every detail of that encounter must be etched on her memory – every detail of the last time she saw Danny alive.

Then I remember that the day she came to tea was not the last time. A dangerous thought flares like a lightning strike, illuminating a vision of Danny in a hospital bed, with his mother keeping her vigil alongside it. He never regained consciousness. Surely that was what they said at the inquest. I tumble out the news clipping, but it's just a summary of what happened: there's nothing absolutely specific.

As I prowl along the hall, examining the framed prints without registering them, I remind myself that she cannot possibly know anything. If she had, she would have gone to the police – or at the very least, challenged me with it years ago. Then I think about the promise she made to Stan. Their compassion because they knew I had suffered too. They had perceived my loss as being in the same league as their own – as if I were already a member of their family.

I might have been her daughter. That's the theory – the idea she has hung on to for more than thirty years

– that I might have married Danny and borne his children. If that had happened, she and Stan wouldn't have left Birmingham to be nearer her relatives in Durham. They would have stayed, in order to be close to Danny and their grandchildren. She would never have come here to Broadoaks. When the time came, it would have been some other nursing home – somewhere nearer to us, her family. All of our lives would have been completely different. I would not be here now, miles from home, booked into a Travelodge for the evening and missing my badminton night. Maybe there wouldn't have been time for regular badminton nights, amid the business of husband and family.

I stop there and rewind back to reality. There would never have been this husband and family. The whole idea of my marrying Danny and becoming Mrs Ivanisovic Junior was a complete fantasy from start to finish. I had never seriously contemplated marrying Danny. I was just a student in college, for goodness sake. We didn't know each other that well. He was just my boyfriend. Oh, we'd talked of loving each other, but love was a state most of our contemporaries fell in and out of every other week. It wasn't *serious*. It wasn't like committing to spend a whole lifetime together. It had never occurred to me that Danny had marriage in mind. He'd never mentioned it – not even as a joke. I remember all too clearly my astonishment when she dropped that bombshell – but of course, she still believes it. Danny had told her we were going to get married. I hadn't denied it. No one had ever disabused her of the idea.

Big Bottom emerges from Mrs Ivanisovic's room, bearing a tray shrouded by a large sheet of green paper towel, under which various lumps and bumps chink ominously. 'You can go back now,' she says. She has a self-satisfied smirk – someone in whom power is vested, telling visitors like me when to come and go.

Whatever unspeakable procedures Mrs Ivanisovic has been subjected to, she looks no better for them. I notice there is a hint of blue about her lips. Somewhere inside this tired old body are the remains of that graceful young woman, the farmer's daughter who married Danny's father, bore his son. Somewhere in there is that woman in the navy and white dress.

I return to my chair and she gestures towards my bag, having evidently guessed where I have concealed her newspaper cutting. I extract it, placing it on the bedside table without opening it out.

'It all came out at the inquest.' I hope my voice is strong and confident. 'There is really nothing else to say.'

She closes her eyes and shakes her head slowly. 'Stan and I could not believe it. Danny was so full of life – so happy. He would never have taken his own life – not without a reason. Katy – could it possibly have been an accident?'

I swallow hard, but the lump won't go away, so I have to swallow again. 'No. I'm sure it wasn't an accident.'

'How can you be sure?' Her response is swifter than I expect.

I meet her eyes, keep my voice steady. 'The evidence. The evidence was of a huge overdose. It can't have been an accident.'

'Then why?' Her voice has reverted to a whisper, which hovers unanswered in the space between us. I struggle to restrain a rising scream. Why doesn't she stop asking me questions and just tell me what she knows?

After a while she takes another turn with her oxygen, while I avert my gaze out of the window. There is no one in sight now, not even the bent-backed old lady.

'A boy came to see us.' I turn at her words, wondering what is coming next. 'A boy from the university. He said he was a friend of Danny's but I don't believe he was. He said things about Danny and Simon – terrible, stupid things. Stan threw him out. He could not – could not accept anything like that. It was against his faith.'

She pauses. I wonder if I am expected to reply, or if there is more. Her eyes are closed again. The lids flutter. Is she sleeping? Has she suffered some kind of collapse? Ought I to call for a nurse – press the buzzer? I am still hesitating when she opens her eyes – carries on as if there has been no interruption. 'I know that Danny was normal. You and he were going to be married. And Simon – Simon had girlfriends too – there was that girl in the bikini.'

She *has* remembered. She has remembered Trudie. Tracer shells erupt somewhere in the back of my head. Is she going to ask me why Trudie was never mentioned at the inquest? Is that the additional detail she has been puzzling over all these years – why no one mentioned that other girl who had been staying at the house, the girl who was there when she visited us only a few days before?

'I know there is something more. Katy – I beg you to tell me everything that happened. All these years of wondering ... I don't care what it is ... or how terrible. I am ready for the truth.'

I hide my need to differ behind silence. I don't think Mrs Ivanisovic is ready for the truth – I don't think she ever will be. Eventually I manage to say, 'I know it must be terrible – specially with Danny being your only son.'

Her reply knocks me sideways.

'He wasn't my only son. We had another son – Stephen.'

Small wonder I do a double take at this. Danny's being an only child had been an essential part of him –

a cornerstone of his person. The idea of a brother is somehow unthinkable. Then I catch on.

'He died too.' The words slip between my lips on an outgoing breath, entering the room so discreetly that I don't think she hears them at all. A little more loudly, I say: 'He died before Danny was born.' It is a confident statement, but she contradicts it at once.

'He was a younger brother. Nearly three years younger than Danny.'

'He was born after Danny? Then why did Danny always say he was an only child?'

'He forgot about Stephen. We made him forget. It was for the best.'

I wait in silence, still not entirely able to grasp the idea of this other child, yet at the same time thinking how the loss of one child would make the survivor doubly precious.

'Danny was not quite three when Stephen was born. Stephen was quite different from Danny – fair hair, different features.' She rested again before continuing. 'We were in the garden one day, myself and the two children that is. Stan was at work. I was sitting on the rug, playing with baby Stephen while Danny made sand pies. He kept bringing them over and I had to pretend to eat them. Then I heard the telephone ringing. I was going to carry Stephen inside with me, but then I thought I would only be a minute and he couldn't possibly come to any harm.'

She isn't looking at me any more. Her eyes are fixed on the opposite wall. I don't need to follow her gaze, because I can already see the scene, played out before my eyes like a faded reel of cine film. I see her hesitate before hurrying across the grass, leaving the baby sitting on the rug and the little boy with the dark curls, playing with his bucket and spade nearby.

'Stephen was nine months old and he'd never

crawled more than a few inches before rolling over and giving up. Everyone said he would be an early walker, because he'd been such a poor crawler. As I was going into the house, I called to Danny, "Look after the baby" – the way you do to small children. I wasn't away more than a minute or two, but when I got back Stephen was gone. Danny was still playing in the sand pit, but I couldn't see Stephen at all. "Where's baby Stephen?" I said, and Danny just stared at me. I had frightened him, you see. He had never seen me afraid, so when I shouted like that, it scared him.'

In spite of myself, I feel my heart beating faster in sympathy with hers. In spite of her dispassionate tone, I stand alongside the distraught young woman of long ago, staring at the empty rug, the abandoned baby toys.

'I should never have said it. You should never make a child responsible for their brothers and sisters. I should never have left them alone. I found Stephen in the garden pond. It was my fault, but I had made Danny feel responsible. It distressed him terribly. He began to have nightmares – to imagine all kinds of things. Stan and I agreed that no child should grow up under a shadow like that – feeling responsible for something which was not their fault – always wondering whether they were somehow to blame. Everyone else knew it was a terrible accident: but Danny wasn't old enough to understand that. We decided the best thing to do would be to forget Stephen. That way Danny would never have to ask himself if he could have saved his little brother that day. We told relatives never to speak of it – we promised never to mention Stephen again, even between ourselves. We destroyed all his photographs, got rid of the cot and the pram, gave the baby clothes to the Church Mission – and it worked. After a few months, Danny stopped asking about Stephen. After a year or so, he didn't remember him ever being there at all.'

'But you,' I ask. 'What about you?'

'I was not entitled to memories,' she says. 'Besides, we had to think of Danny.'

And what about Stephen? I want to add. It chills me, this notion that the identity of one child was expendable for the sake of another. This short-lived scrap of humanity, whose photographs had been destroyed, whose very existence had been denied: sacrificed to the well-being of his elder brother.

Then I remember her own torture – a second's carelessness which resulted in a lifetime of remorse – silently marking the birthdays of that other child, the lost child who was never spoken of. The guilty knowledge like a piece of ice in your heart. I had thought her an overly fond, indulgent parent – but now I understand she had been more. She built a fortress of secrets to protect her surviving son, then suffered the wretchedness of imprisonment within it, carrying the burden of unspoken truth alone.

I can see that she is on the point of drifting off again. I decide it's now or never. 'You said there was something you knew about – something about Danny's death that you never mentioned at the inquest.'

'When Danny was in hospital – after it happened – I would sit holding his hand, hour on hour. I sometimes wondered why you never came – but they said you were ill too . . . they said you were in shock.' She pauses for some confirmation, but I wait for her to continue, afraid that now I've brought her to this point, finally steeled myself to hear whatever she is going to say, any diversion may prove fatal to her willingness to confide or my resolve to hear her. When she realizes I am not going to reply, she picks up where she left off. 'I would sit holding his hand, and talking

149

to him. They said it might help, so I talked and talked. I begged him to come back to us ... begged him to live.' The length of the pause is unbearable, but I am determined not to break it. 'One afternoon, I realized that he was responding: squeezing my hand in answer to questions. The nurses said it was just a reflex, but I knew it wasn't. I'm not sure if even Stan believed me, but Danny and I were so very close – if anyone could get through to him, it would have been me.'

Her eyelids are drooping again. She tries to keep them open, but it's a losing battle.

'The medication,' she whispers. 'So sorry.'

'That's okay. Don't worry.' I am whispering too. I don't know why.

'Come and see me again,' she hisses urgently. 'Come again – a week today.'

This is crazy – I live a couple of hundred miles away. I tell myself that there is nothing to fear from her. Surely I am not going to take these fantasy communications seriously. It's only a step away from table tapping. Is it the time bomb of the knowledge that she *does* have – the faintest possibility that she will say to one of her non-existent visitors, 'I wonder what happened to Simon's girlfriend, Trudie.' Or perhaps it is something else that makes me say: 'Okay. A week today.'

EIGHTEEN

I intended to tackle Danny about what his mother had said straight away – but Simon got in first. The moment the Wolseley had vanished down the lane he began to tell Danny all about a builder in Kington, who had been unexpectedly let down on a job and was therefore available to come and do the concreting for us the day after tomorrow. The builder had quoted him a price, and they had shaken hands on it. 'If we work flat out,' Simon said, 'we can have the sand base installed before he gets here.' He was unmistakably relieved that everything was working out so well.

'Was he wearing a Stetson?' asked Danny.

Simon grinned. 'I know, I know, he could be a complete cowboy. But whoever he is, he'll surely make a better job of it than we could.'

Danny didn't seem inclined to argue with this. By now we had drifted into the kitchen, where Trudie was washing up the cups – perhaps like me smitten with a sense that things had been allowed to slide. I didn't require an audience for our discussion, so I signalled Danny to come upstairs, but Trudie intervened: 'Don't go away, you two. I've got some corned beef and salad for tea, and I want a hand getting things ready.'

While Trudie sliced cucumber and tomatoes, I set about opening the corned beef tin and Simon laid the table. Danny excused himself on the grounds that he needed the bathroom. This enforced engagement with the workaday realities of our life made my conversation with Mrs Ivanisovic seem fantastical. I was more than half convinced that it was all a stupid misunderstanding, which Danny would iron out in minutes flat. I wound the metal key all round the corned beef tin, then without thinking I attempted to prise the two halves apart using my fingers. The raw edge of the tin bit into the ball of my thumb, producing an instant stream of bright red blood. It splashed steadily on to the floor while I gaped at it in horrified surprise. Luckily Simon saw what had happened and came instantly to my aid, pulling out a kitchen chair and instructing me to sit down, while he produced a tissue from his jeans pocket which he told me to hold against my thumb.

'It won't stop bleeding,' I said. 'Look, it's soaking through the tissue already.'

'Don't worry,' he said. By now he had opened the drawer where the clean tea towels were kept and extracted one of the most faded. 'It won't be a deep cut. It's bleeding so much because there's a pulse in your thumb. Here—' he took my hand and replaced the tissue with the clean tea towel – 'keep your hand wrapped in this for a few minutes and hold it up – like this – to give it a chance to stop bleeding, while I get a plaster.' Something in his voice completely reassured me. Trudie had stopped what she was doing, but seeing that Simon had taken charge she went back to her chopping board. By the time he returned a couple of minutes later with a strip of Elastoplast and a pair of nail scissors, my knees had stopped wobbling and I had dared to investigate the injured thumb, which had already all but stopped bleeding as he had predicted.

'Better?' he asked, as he took a look at the cut before cutting a piece of plaster to size.

'Yes, thanks.'

He squatted on his heels in front of me to apply the plaster. When he'd finished his eyes met mine and I felt oddly ashamed – as if he knew all the nasty thoughts I had ever entertained about him. 'Thank you,' I said meekly.

'No probs. Better just sit here for a few minutes. It can knock you sick when something like that happens.' He took over the corned beef tin and levered it open with the aid of a dinner knife, extracting the meat and slicing it neatly into eight pieces, putting two on each plate – every action performed with the elegant precision which characterized all his movements.

By the time Danny reappeared our meal was on the table. While we ate our corned beef, lettuce, tomato and cucumber – all of which would have been vastly improved by the addition of some salad cream if only we had remembered to buy some – Simon and Trudie chattered about their trip into town and the work that still needed to be done before the builder came. The two of them had called in at the library to return Simon's book about garden ponds and while they were there Trudie had come across a local interest book called *Mayhem, Murder and Mystery* which she had persuaded Simon to take out on his ticket. Needless to say the Agnes Payne case was in there, and of course Trudie could hardly wait to read it.

'I've been thinking a lot about Agnes,' said Trudie.

'What's new,' I muttered under my breath, but no one took any notice.

'I think we might be able to make contact with her in the wood. I bet her ghost walks there.'

'A midnight ghost walk?' Simon grinned. 'Spooky.'

I tried to catch Danny's eye, but he didn't see me. 'You can hang about down there all you like, but I bet she doesn't appear,' he said.

Trudie rose to the challenge. 'How much do you want to bet?'

My attempt to kick him under the table misfired and I banged my toe against the table leg instead.

'How much have you got?'

'A hundred pounds,' said Trudie.

'You haven't,' said Danny. A hundred pounds was a fortune to us. What on earth would Trudie be doing with a hundred pounds?

Trudie was rattled. She didn't like her word being doubted. In a movement she'd scraped back her chair and was thundering up the stairs to her room.

'Don't,' I pleaded. 'Don't get her started. We don't want to have a ghost hunt in the woods. She'll only get upset again.'

'Cool it,' said Danny. 'She doesn't have that sort of money. You watch. She'll be back in a minute, saying Murdered Agnes has pinched it or something.'

Trudie's feet sounded again on the stairs. She entered the kitchen with her hands behind her back, then produced a fistful of notes with a flourish.

'Ruddy hell,' said Simon. 'That little lot would pay the builder and then some.'

'It's all yours,' she said. 'If Agnes doesn't show up.'

'You can't take that bet,' I said to Danny. 'You don't have that sort of money to gamble with.'

'We shouldn't anyway,' said Simon. 'It's all right, Trudie. We don't want to take your money.'

'Maybe we should bet with different stakes,' suggested Danny.

Trudie sniffed. 'Such as what?'

'I dunno. Like us doing the cooking for a week or – hey, this is it – if you lose, you have to swim naked in the new pond. How about that?'

'This is getting stupid,' I said. 'Anyway, we're not going down to the woods in the dark looking for ghosts. It's a crazy idea.'

None of them were listening to me. Trudie and

Danny were exchanging more and more outrageous ideas for bets. Pinching a policeman's helmet. Streaking through the cathedral. Fed up with the lot of them, I went upstairs to run a bath. The bathroom was immediately above the kitchen and I could hear them laughing and shouting across one another, their voices fainter than a steady drip, somewhere near to hand.

The lower half of the bathroom was tiled in institutional white. A single line of green tiles marked the point where the tiling ended and the cream-painted walls and ceiling began. The window was filled with frosted glass in a pattern of tiny dimples. There were probably nicer bathrooms in convents or prisons. The immersion heater hadn't been on long, so the water wasn't really warm enough. I shed my clothes and climbed in anyway, soaping myself aggressively, as if I could wash away the peculiar humiliations of the day. I lay right down in the water, watching my hair spread out with a thread of green moss floating amongst it. There was just enough heat in the water to dull the tiles with a mantle of steam. Every so often a bead formed, growing imperceptibly until it overbalanced and ran down the wall, giving a sense of constant movement within the room, always at the periphery of my vision.

I thought about Mrs Ivanisovic giving me motherly advice about my dress. I didn't like the idea of Mrs Ivanisovic for a mother-in-law. She was a bit too much to live up to. It came to me that loads of girls would simply love to be in my position. Danny was such a catch – good-looking, intelligent and funny. His parents were well off. Maybe I was crazy – maybe I should marry him. Then I saw red again. How dare he discuss something like this with his parents, without talking to me first. Then again, surely the whole thing must be some ghastly misunderstanding. What on earth had he told them? Could he really have said that we were getting married? He certainly had some explaining to do, as soon as I could get him on my own for five minutes.

After my bath, I spent ages combing the tangles out of my wet hair. I didn't want to put on the same dirty clothes I had worn through the day; but this only left me with a skimpy wrap-around dressing gown, even more indecent than the daisy dress. Not that I minded about staying upstairs and missing out on another evening with Trudie and Simon. I couldn't be bothered to listen to Trudie going on about Agnes Payne again, or the funny librarian with her hair in a bun, or Simon's dealings with the builder. And if I stayed where I was, pretty soon Danny would come up to see what I was doing, at which point I could have things out with him in private. In the meantime I occupied myself with sorting our dirty clothes into piles, ready for washing the next day.

After a while I noticed it had gone quiet downstairs – for a heart-stopping moment I wondered if they had taken it into their heads to go down to the woods. I all but choked at the thought of being left in the house on my own, with the birds well embarked on their evening songs and the sun getting low. I stole across the landing, reaching the top of the stairs just in time to be reassured by another burst of hearty laughter from below. They've opened the beer, I thought. They sound half pissed already.

I skulked back to my bedroom, feeling forgotten and excluded, but as I turned to close the bedroom door I caught sight of the door of the seance room, which was moving to and fro, sucked back and forth by an occasional gust of air. I decided to ignore it, but as I turned away it thudded softly against the frame again, annoying and insistent, goading me to do something about it. I crossed the landing and tentatively pushed the door open. The room was on the eastern side of the house, so the warmth of the day was long gone and the furniture draped in evening shadows. Everything had been left exactly as it was on the night the seance broke up. No attempt had been made to tidy up – although someone had been in and opened a window and this was obviously what had been making the door bang. I was just thinking that the easiest solution would be to shut the door and walk away when I noticed that the breeze had lifted one of the curtains over the sill, where it had apparently become caught on something outside. I knew that if I left it, it would get soaked when it next rained, or else the wind might drag at it until it ripped. It wouldn't be my fault of course. I hadn't opened the damn window in the first place. Then I thought about Simon explaining things to his uncle: there had already been one or two minor breakages – although these might be excused in the ordinary run of things. Damage to the curtains would be harder to justify – specially in a room which we were not ostensibly using – but in order to rescue the curtain and close the window, I would have to walk right across the room.

You're not scared, are you, Katy?

Leaving the door wide open, I scuttled across the room. It was cold next to the open window and the shiny fabric of the curtains felt like ice. The material had snagged on the outside brickwork, but it came away easily and there didn't appear to be any actual damage. I lifted the curtain inside then pulled the window shut. The movement created a sudden draught which made the door slam so violently that it shook the whole room. It seemed much darker in there now that I was facing away from the window. I stumbled back across the floor with the bang echoing in my ears. I almost fell over the rolled-up rug and then my bare feet sent the jar which had held the joss sticks skittering across the lino. When I reached the door I rattled at the handle frantically. Why wouldn't the bloody thing open?

'Danny,' I tried to yell, but a strangled sound came out instead: something between a gurgle and a sob.

In the midst of my panic I remembered that the door opened inwards. I yanked it towards me so violently that it scraped over my big toe, then all but ran across the landing and scrambled into bed, shivering like a wet dog. I pulled the blankets over me and huddled under them in my dressing gown, welcoming their warmth and weight. I thought I would lie awake and wait for Danny, but within a few minutes I had fallen asleep.

I must have slept deeply that night, because I didn't hear Danny come to bed. When I woke next morning he was sleeping soundly beside me, lying perfectly still except for the motion of his breath. The novelty of sharing a bed had yet to pall, but whereas the sight of him sleeping usually brought a smile to my lips, this morning it was an irritant. He smelled of stale beer and I slid myself away from him, as if to avoid contamination. He didn't stir as I climbed out of bed, straightened my dressing gown, then headed downstairs with an armful of dirty laundry.

There was no one in the kitchen, but evidence of the previous night's jollifications cluttered the table. I hauled the twin tub across the floor, fitted the rubber hose on to the tap and waited while the machine filled. Simon had said something about an early start, but the kitchen clock was already approaching ten, belying their good intentions. When the machine was full I set the temperature and bundled the washing in. It wouldn't hurt it to soak while the water was warming up.

I had just finished when Danny ambled into the room. He had evidently come straight from bed, pausing only to pull on a pair of jeans. His hair was tousled and he looked half asleep.

'Hey,' he greeted me with a stifled yawn, approaching for a kiss, then registering surprise when I ducked aside, putting the table between us. 'What's wrong?' he asked.

'Your mother, that's what,' I said. Now the moment had arrived, I scarcely knew where to begin.

'My mother? What's she done to freak you out?'

'Do you know what she said to me, yesterday afternoon? She told me that she and your dad are very pleased about us getting married.'

To my utter amazement, Danny's face broke into a grin. 'Well, that's nice to know,' he said.

'What?' I exploded.

'Well, that's good, right? I mean, imagine how awkward it would be if they didn't like you.'

'Danny, this is not some kind of joke. Have you told your parents we're getting married – without even consulting me? You – you can't do things like that.'

'But baby . . .' He advanced, still smiling, ready for an embrace.

I dodged again, moving across towards the pantry. If anything his whole demeanour only served to increase my fury. 'How dare you,' I spluttered. 'How dare you just assume I'll marry you – and talk to them about it, before talking to me.'

He stopped smiling. 'Just because you have a problem with your parents, doesn't mean everyone else does. I'm close to my folks, so I tell them stuff, savvy?'

'Not stuff about you and me.' I was yelling now. 'Not stuff that hasn't been decided. How can you say we're getting married? How can you possibly say that when you haven't asked me?'

159

'I always get what I want.' He tried to reassert the smile, but it didn't quite come off. He was annoyed because I was shouting at him.

'Don't be so fucking arrogant,' I yelled.

'Don't swear at me, you bitch.'

Simon appeared in the doorway, his face anxious. 'What gives?'

I folded my arms defensively around my dressing gown: standing half naked in front of Simon would do nothing for my dignity. Inwardly I was reeling. Danny and I had never really quarrelled before. I had expected understanding and contrition. I hadn't anticipated that he would bite back.

'A lovers' tiff,' said Danny. 'It's nothing. Katy has got herself upset over something. Wrong time of the month, I guess.'

'I'm going upstairs,' I snapped.

Danny turned his back, affecting to be busy with something by the sink.

'Danny, come upstairs, please.'

'Don't order me around, okay?' He tossed the words over his shoulder. 'I'll come up when I'm ready.'

I stood in the doorway a moment longer, but neither of them were looking my way so I returned to our room to wait him out. I thought he would have to come upstairs for some clothes and shoes, but after a while I realized he and Simon must have gone outside to work. The boots they wore in the garden were kept in the back porch, but even so Danny must have put his on without any socks, in order to avoid coming back upstairs. I hope he gives himself blisters, I thought.

After half an hour or so I was driven downstairs again by hunger. I remembered the strawberries Mrs Ivanisovic had brought the day before and wondered if the others would mind me taking my share for a late breakfast; but when I looked in the fridge there was no sign of them. Then I spotted the empty punnets, tossed alongside the plastic pedal bin which was overflowing as usual. Trudie chose this moment to enter via the back door.

'Where have all the strawberries gone?' I asked.

'We ate them last night,' Trudie said. 'After you'd gone to bed.'

She didn't even bother to say sorry.

'You rotten greedy pigs.' The words emerged much louder than I had intended.

Simon had appeared behind Trudie. 'Now what's wrong?' he asked.

'Katy's got a strop on, because we didn't save her any strawberries,' said Trudie.

'For God's sake,' muttered Simon. 'Here, Trudie, you take the bottle opener and I'll carry the beer.'

They left me on my own in the kitchen. After a moment I resumed my search for something to eat, eventually resorting to bread and jam: slamming the jam pot and knife down on the table and deliberately not bothering to clear up after myself. The washing machine had already finished, so once I had swilled the jam from my fingers, I transferred my first lot of washing into the spin-dryer and started the second lot in the wash tub. Only now did a fresh problem occur to me: I couldn't go and hang the washing out in my dressing gown, because reaching up to peg things on the line was absolutely out of the question. Moreover I had burnt my boats – I couldn't slip into some dirty knickers just for the duration of a trip to the washing line, because every stitch of clothing I had with me was now in one or other half of the twin tub.

As I hauled the tangle of clothing out of the spin-dryer, unravelling the socks and bras, shaking the worst creases out of the larger items, I was all but crying with frustration. My bikini bottoms emerged

161

somewhere around the middle of the load. That was it. I would put on my bikini. It didn't really matter that it was damp – it would only be the same as getting out of the sea after a swim.

Once outside, I discovered there was a cool breeze which didn't particularly favour swimwear. The washing line was strung between two metal posts in clear view of the pond, but far enough away to make conversation impractical. Danny was at work inside the hole, but I deliberately avoided looking in his direction, keeping my back to him while I steadily worked my way through the basket of damp clothes.

When everything was pegged out I returned to the house. I reckoned the sun combined with the breeze wouldn't take too long to dry some of the lighter things. In the meantime, I decided to make myself another snack and a cup of tea to have sitting up in bed, where I could abandon the damp bikini in favour of my dressing gown, while I read *Frenchman's Creek*. My discussion with Danny would just have to go on hold until I was in a more favourable position to conduct it on my terms.

I peeled off the bikini as soon as I got upstairs. The dressing-table mirror was flanked by two wooden poles topped with circular finials, and I hung my bikini top and bottoms one from each of them. I was back in my dressing gown and about to hop into bed, when it came to me that with the laundry mountain gone I could greatly enhance the appearance of our bedroom by effecting one or two other minor improvements. I collected up the pages of an old Sunday newspaper which Danny and I had discarded sheet by sheet after reading them in bed, balled the whole lot and tossed it on to the landing, ready to be taken downstairs. Between bites of jam sandwich and sips of tea, I gathered up my hairdryer and various scattered shoes, then tidied the top of the dressing table, which I dusted with a paper tissue. I was just pausing to survey the results when a footfall on the landing made me jump.

'Hey there,' said Danny. He advanced across the room and hugged me, before I could say or do anything. 'Better now?' he asked.

I twitched his arms away. 'What do you mean? Better now?'

'I mean tantrum over. Ready to make love not war.' The impish smile, which normally melted me, only contrived to make me feel a whole lot madder.

'Danny,' I said, 'this is not over. You have done something wrong here and you have to acknowledge it.'

'Come on, Katy.' He advanced a step forward, as I took a step back. 'We know how this is going to end. Come to Danny. You know you want to . . . Coming into the garden like that, flaunting yourself in front of me.'

'I was not!' I burned with indignation. I had never flaunted myself in my life.

'Come off it.' He took hold of the bikini bottoms between finger and thumb. 'They aren't even dry.'

'I didn't have anything else to wear,' I said coldly.

'You were coming on to me. Trying to get me to follow you upstairs.'

'I was not. But since you are here, you can start by apologizing for the various things you've done – like calling me a bitch this morning – and telling your parents I'm going to marry you – which incidentally I am not.'

His composure snapped abruptly. 'What is wrong with you today?' he yelled. 'You're just not making sense, Katy. All you want to do is fight with me. I don't understand what's got into you. I thought you loved me. You're right. This isn't over.' With that he turned and walked out of the room.

I watched him go in silence. As I listened to him descending the stairs I found that I was shaking. In my idealized vision of our rural love nest, I had not troubled to anticipate what might happen if we had a major row: I was unexpectedly adrift without co-ordinates to steer by. I heard the sound of his feet along the hallway and the dull thud of the kitchen door. In the silence which followed I fell on to the unmade bed and wept.

NINETEEN

Danny had scarcely been gone more than a minute before Trudie arrived in the room. She immediately sat next to me on the bed and put her arms around me. She was wearing the cut-down denims and bikini top of the day before, and she smelled of sunshine and crushed rose petals.

'He's made you cry, the bastard,' she whispered. 'Don't cry, darling. He's not worth it. You're too good for him, far, far too good.'

She stroked my hair and kissed the top of my head, which was rather more demonstrative than would have been the norm between Cecile and me, but didn't seem odd coming from Trudie.

'He told his parents we were getting married,' I sobbed. 'I couldn't believe it. He's never even asked me. Then when I told him off about it, he called me a bitch.'

'Don't cry over him; he isn't worth it. You'll never marry him,' said Trudie, using the tone of certainty she employed for all her predictions.

I realized that my dressing gown had come adrift at the front; one of Trudie's hands had wandered inside, comforting and caressing.

'Tru-die,' I murmured. 'My dressing gown . . .' I got no further. She kissed me full on the lips and I don't know what surprised me more – the fact that she had done so, or how much I liked it.

When she drew back, her eyes were full of mischief,

165

like we were engaged in some massive practical joke. Her hands were still inside my dressing gown.

'Look, Trudie,' I said. 'I'm not – I mean – I'm Danny's girlfriend – and – and you're Simon's.'

She actually laughed at this – a warm sound – not mocking, but rather inviting me to join the fun. 'Simon's friend,' she corrected. 'Not his girlfriend. Simon doesn't like girls. Not in that way.'

I gaped at her. My knowledge of homosexuality was restricted to an almost comic-book perception of mincing, effeminate men. There had been rumours, no more, about a bachelor schoolteacher once – but I hadn't believed them, vaguely assuming that homosexual men inhabited some other, utterly separate parallel universe. The idea that such a man might have been living right under my nose was astonishing – and yet, as soon as she said it, I knew instinctively that she was right.

'Wouldn't it be convenient if Danny felt the same way Simon did,' she said. 'Then you and I . . .' Her words trailed off as she bent forward to kiss my neck.

'No,' I said. 'You see, I'm not.'

Trudie looked up. 'Not what? Not a lezzie, do you mean? It's not an exclusive club, you know,' she chided, gently. 'You don't have to get a certificate or anything – to say you can join in.'

I thought of the splash patch on her shorts. *Try it, you'll like it.*

Trudie shrugged out of her top in a single movement. Her bare skin was against mine. I let my hands delve into her thick soft hair. It didn't feel wrong. In some vague sense, it didn't seem to count as cheating on Danny – how could you cheat with a girl? My dressing gown had fallen away completely and next thing I knew, Trudie was sliding out of her shorts. There was something incredibly graceful about the way she

166

removed her clothes – and underneath she was so very beautiful, golden brown all over, except for the pale, delicate areas which never saw the sun. I made no further protests.

Afterwards we lay facing one another with the sheet pulled up to our waists and our legs casually entwined beneath it, talking as easily as if we hopped into bed together every day.

'How did you find out about Simon?' I asked. (I was naïve still – assuming Trudie had spotted some secret signal I had missed.)

'He told me,' Trudie said. 'We talk a lot.'

I was mildly stung by this. I had known him longer than Trudie, but he had never confided in me.

'Did you mind?' I asked. 'That he didn't fancy you?'

Trudie flicked aside a long strand of hair which had fallen across her face. 'Course not. I don't mind going out with lads – but I prefer to do it with girls.'

I tried to keep my face from registering shock. In spite of all that we had just engaged in, I found the idea rather difficult to absorb. 'But you don't mind boys?' I was still trying to make sense of it, searching for some context.

'It depends on the boy. I'd go out with Simon or Danny if they asked me – but not somebody like that awful Josser. Did I tell you I saw him in town again yesterday? He tried to speak, but I just ignored him.'

'I keep hearing a bike in the lane,' I said. 'I hope it isn't him – snooping around.'

'Anyway, I prefer to have girls,' Trudie reiterated. 'That's why they threw me out of school. Me and another girl. They got our parents in and agreed between themselves that we had to be separated. I'm supposed to be starting a new school in September and I'm never to make contact with Bev again. That's why I ran – left.'

'Trudie – how old are you?' I was propped up on one elbow, looking straight at her. She had her back to the bedroom door, which was ajar, and for a second I thought I saw the gap darken, signifying the presence of someone on the landing. 'Who's there?' I said sharply.

Trudie turned immediately, but there was no answer and nothing to be seen. 'It's only Murdered Agnes,' she said cheerfully. It was her stock answer to any creak of the floorboards or fleeting shadow.

'Suppose it was Simon or Danny.' I spoke without conviction: it had been no more than a shadow at the periphery of my vision. I wasn't confident there had been anything there at all.

'It won't have been,' she assured me. 'They're both working flat out to be in time for the builder – anyway, what if it was?'

Trudie's casual attitude to our being discovered in bed together was a wake-up call. I was supposed to be Danny's girlfriend. I might be mad at him and I might not think what I had just done with Trudie constituted quite the same level of infidelity as going with another man; but I couldn't kid myself that he would be exactly delighted to find me in bed with our female housemate. Bottom line here – this was not on the same level of friendship as going shopping with Cecile.

'Look, Trudie,' I said. 'This was great and everything, but I don't think we should say anything about it to Danny – or Simon. Not yet, anyway.' (Not ever, said a voice in my head. This is bent, for goodness sake – this is an episode you don't share with anyone – end of story.)

'Okay.' Trudie wasn't in the least perturbed. 'I can keep a secret.'

'Good. I need to sort things out, you see, between me and Danny.'

'Of course.' Trudie leaned forward to brush her lips against my forehead. 'I won't say a word. Not until everything is sorted out – then maybe you could move into my room?'

'We'd better get up now,' I said quickly. 'They'll wonder where we've been – and what we've been doing.'

'Oh, tell them we've been cleaning up,' said Trudie, airily. 'They'll never notice any difference.'

Trudie dressed almost as swiftly as she had shed her clothes and having done so she went down to retrieve the dry washing for me. Then she hung about while I got into some clothes – a pair of cut-downs and a cheesecloth top, still warm from the line – and gave me another kiss before we walked downstairs together. My heart was pounding as we entered the kitchen, but the boys were still outside. I set up the ironing board and began to work my way through the basket of dry washing, focusing on the job in hand as if my life depended on it, while Trudie glided around the kitchen making our evening meal.

Her proximity unnerved me. She kept singing to herself – little snatches of songs, while the sunshine danced across the ceiling whenever she moved a knife or some other utensil. She fetched me a glass of water without my having to ask, smiling as she put it down beside me. I tried to smile back, but all the time I was wondering about Danny. Our earlier fight had yet to be resolved. And what on earth would he say if he found out about me and Trudie? Then there was Trudie herself: as the glow of our sojourn in bed faded, I was beginning to question what madness had possessed me. Talk of moving into her bedroom was nothing short of crazy. I had come here as Danny's girlfriend – I was *still* Danny's girlfriend. Normal girls didn't move into a double bed together. What the hell had I been thinking, letting her climb into my bed, encouraging her to do those things?

The guys worked outside until approaching eight o'clock, which gave me time to both finish all the ironing and work up a positive fever of nerves. We ate at the kitchen table that night. I am not sure whether anyone else sensed that the atmosphere was edgy. Perhaps it was only me, preoccupied by competing uncertainties, desperate to avoid catching Trudie's eye lest I inadvertently betray myself to the others. I kept glancing in Danny's direction, but he was concentrating on his meal. We weren't exactly not speaking, but we didn't say a lot to one another either – which left most of the talking to Simon and Trudie.

'What's the plan for tonight?' Simon asked as we were finishing our meal.

'Maybe Danny could play for us,' I suggested, by way of an olive branch.

'I don't feel like it,' said Danny. 'How about our little wager, Trudie? It's a fine dry night.'

'There's not much moonlight,' said Trudie.

'You never said there had to be any.' There was a faint sneer in Danny's voice. 'Not backing down, are we?'

'Of course not,' said Trudie. 'I was just thinking about seeing our way in the dark, that was all.'

'There's a torch in my car,' said Simon.

'One torch between four,' I interposed – but Danny was way ahead of me.

'There's a flashlight in the pantry,' he said. 'And a small torch.'

'Oh honestly,' I tried to sound dismissive. 'Who wants to go stumbling round the woods by torchlight?'

'We do, don't we, Si?' said Danny. 'Been looking forward to it all day. You don't have to come if you don't want to.' He stood up to get another beer, passing close behind my chair. 'Chicken,' he said, in a voice too low for the others to catch.

I was caught between the devil and the deep blue sea. It was already growing dark outside. I didn't want to join in with the excursion to Bettis Wood; but neither did I want to stay on my own in the house.

'I'm up for it,' Simon was saying. 'We don't need any special equipment, do we, Trudie? Joss sticks? Candles? Medallions of St Theresa of the Roses, anything like that?'

Trudie took it in good part. 'Nothing at all – only torches.'

'We don't have to wait till midnight, do we?' asked Danny. 'Because I'll be asleep by then. I'm absolutely knackered.'

'Worth it though,' said Simon. 'All we've got to do is layer in the sand tomorrow. Then we'll be ready for the concrete man, the day after.'

'We can go now, if you want,' said Trudie. 'The time is almost right for something to happen. I can sense it. In fact things are happening for some people already.'

I glanced at her nervously. Several times during our meal she had come close to saying too much. Simon was watching me and I experienced the alarming sensation that he knew exactly what Trudie was getting at. I felt the colour rising in my face.

'So,' said Danny. 'It's agreed. Tonight's the night for the ghost hunt.'

'How about you, Katy?' Simon's eyes were still on me. 'Are you coming with us or not?'

'Of course,' I said. 'Count me in.' Safety in numbers. At least the others would be with me in the wood – better than staying alone in the big empty house.

There was quite a delay before we set out. Trudie and I both decided to put some warmer clothes on, but whereas I dithered in the bedroom uncertain what to wear, she must have changed quickly and was already standing in the hall with Simon when I came downstairs. They had evidently been talking, but as I approached he cut off abruptly and went into the kitchen. I caught his last words though – '. . . get hurt if you don't leave her alone . . .'

'What's he talking about?' I hissed, as I joined her in the hall.

'He's just being an old woman,' she said. 'He's got a problem with you and me.'

'What do you mean – you and me? You haven't told him, have you?'

'I didn't have to. He walked past the bedroom this afternoon and saw us.'

'Oh God,' I whispered. 'He'll tell Danny for sure.'

'Well, someone's got to,' said Trudie. She spoke so carelessly – as if it didn't matter at all.

'No,' I said. 'He mustn't ever find out. Don't you understand? You've got to make Simon promise.'

Trudie just looked at me and laughed. She pushed open the kitchen door and went sailing in. I trailed in after her, praying that she would keep her mouth shut, but knowing full well that she might choose to say something at any moment – she was utterly irresponsible.

We found both the boys in the kitchen, faffing about because the batteries in the smallest torch were nearly dead. Some spare batteries were finally located on the top shelf of the pantry and inserted into the torch, after which there was still the whole locking-up-the-house fandango. Only when we were standing outside the locked front door did Simon extract his torch from the car boot, at which point it became evident that it had been in there for some time. When he switched it on it emitted no more than a sickly orange glow, which faltered a couple of times before settling into a jaundiced beam.

172

'It needs new batteries.'

'Have we got any the right size?'

'Oh, do come on,' I exclaimed. 'Let's go if we're going. At this rate we'll be hanging around all night.'

Simon hesitated. No one appeared to be inclined to unlock the door and embark on another search for batteries, so he shrugged and said he thought it would be all right and we finally set off. The footpath which ran down the side of the field looked strange and unfamiliar – as if it took on a completely new aspect after dark, showing a side of its character we didn't normally see. Not frightening, I told myself – just different.

Trudie led the way as eager as a child on a trip to the circus. I had chosen clothing which I thought appropriate to the undertaking – jeans with a long-sleeved cotton shirt buttoned over the top – but Trudie had gone for the Bus Stop look: full-length skirt, smock top, floppy cardigan and a long silk scarf wound round her neck. She had commandeered the small torch and as she set off along the footpath, I saw it cleaving the darkness like a pale spear. Danny walked immediately behind Trudie, carrying the big flashlight; then came Simon, assisted by his much feebler beam, and I was last in line – without any means of illuminating the path at all. Under normal circumstances Danny would have been alongside me every step of the way, but I guessed he was teaching me a lesson.

Simon's torch was focused well ahead of where I was putting my feet, so I found it best to keep my eyes away from the lights and concentrate hard on where I was going. Noises play tricks in the dark. I almost convinced myself that I could hear someone breathing behind me on the path; but when I stopped to listen there was nothing there. I hurried on again, not wanting to be left behind.

Once inside the wood we were surrounded by the sound of the trees. Their movements seemed louder at night. Branches creaked as if taking advantage of the darkness to stretch and flex more freely than they felt able to do in daylight. Now that we were no longer confined to single file, I manoeuvred myself so that I was walking slightly to the right of Simon. Until then he had been between me and the others, and it was only when I drew level with him that I realized Trudie had got some way ahead of us.

'Trudie,' I called. 'Hang on. We don't want to get separated.'

I don't think she heard me. My words had not emerged as loudly as I intended, and the noise of the trees increased at just the wrong moment.

'It's okay,' said Simon. 'She said the playground was the place to go. We know where it is. We'll soon catch her up.'

'*If you go down to the woods today, be sure of a big surprise*,' sang Danny.

Trudie was getting too far ahead. 'Trudie,' I called again.

At that moment the two torches alongside me were both extinguished. Someone – Danny, I was almost sure – emitted one of those maniacal cackles of laughter: the stage villain about to pounce on his prey.

'Come on, guys,' I said. 'Stop pratting about.' My voice sounded hollow and squeaky in the dark, a strange mixture of annoyance and pleading. No one responded. There was a rustle to my left and I braced myself for whatever surprise was about to come out of the dark. I hated them in that moment – hated all three of them. Any minute now they were going to jump out and make me scream. It was the sort of stunt my big brother used to pull all the time. I stood rigid in the darkness, experiencing a familiar sense of rising panic, while fighting down the urge to cry. My tears had always been big brother's victory. *Katy's such a cry-baby.* 'Come on,' I said again. 'You're not being fair. I'm the only one who hasn't got a torch. Switch them back on.'

I was greeted by another mad cackle of laughter, which appeared to come from further away than the first. This was followed by Simon's voice from somewhere on my left. 'Fuck it. The battery must have gone.'

He sounded genuine. I clenched my hands at my sides. There was no need to panic. Danny was close at hand with a big flashlight.

'Danny,' I called out.

The silence mocked me.

'Danny.'

The stupid sod. He was obviously determined to carry his little joke through to the end. A treacherous voice in my head whispered that it was all my own fault. If I had made it up with Danny, I wouldn't be standing in the dark right now. I decided to appeal to Simon instead.

'Simon,' I called.

'Katy – where are you?' His reply came from further away than I had expected and I couldn't determine the exact direction.

'I'm here.' Even as I said it, I knew how useless a response it was.

'My torch has come back on again but it's really faint. Can you see me?'

I cast around desperately. Surely I ought to be able to see his light, however dim. He couldn't be more than half a dozen yards away.

'I can't see you.' I felt around with my hands – encountered nothing – took a couple of steps forward, then recoiled as something brushed against my face. 'I can't see you,' I repeated, a note of hysteria rising in my voice despite my attempts to suppress it. 'I've lost the path.'

'Don't worry. Stay put and I'll get Danny to bring the big torch.'

'No,' I shouted. 'Simon, wait.'

He didn't answer. Guessing that Danny had gone on ahead, Simon presumably intended to carry on along the track until he found him. He was going to leave me completely on my own.

Just then I caught sight of the small torch beam moving between the trees. Trudie – the architect of this whole disastrous undertaking – was somewhere not far ahead. I stumbled towards the light and fell heavily, my knees crashing on to something hard – probably a fallen log. It hurt so much I thought my kneecaps must be shattered, but tentative experiment demonstrated that I could still move them. I felt the knees of my jeans and found they were cold but dry, so I evidently wasn't bleeding to death either. I scrambled to my feet and peered into the darkness again, trying to pick up the light of her torch where I thought I had seen it last. My fear was subjugated by anger. I remembered the mischief in her eyes – how she had flirted with us one after another – but it was me who had succumbed. And now she was going to let Danny know what had happened at the very first opportunity.

I glimpsed the flicker of a torch ahead of me again and began to follow it: a will-o'-the-wisp treacherously leading me deeper into the wood. I soon lost sight of it, but not before I had regained the path. At least that was something – all I had to do was stay on it until I reached the playground. Even without the confusing brightness of the torches there was barely enough light for me to pick my way forward and the shifting shadows of the branches made everything uncertain: creating an illusion of movement, so that the ground

176

itself appeared to be undulating to and fro. The wind had risen and the trees responded with louder moans, but these and every other noise were instantly obliterated by Trudie's scream. She only had time to cry out once, but the sound seemed to echo around the wood for an eternity.

TWENTY

Pam's shrieks of laughter echo all over the pool. They bounce down from the ceiling, reverberate from the plate glass windows, chase unsuspecting patrons into the changing rooms. I despise this squealing over nothing, long for the restoration of tranquillity. Until Pam's return, we 'Early Bird Swimmers', as the poster advertising the session describes us, plodded up and down in relative peace and quiet – but now she is back, ripping up our eardrums until I long to shout, 'Be quiet. Shut up, for goodness sake, and give us all a break.' Marjorie joins in with this dawn chorus of merriment. Squawking along in disharmony, loving every minute. I try not to wish Pam ill, but I cannot help thinking that another bit of knee surgery would be such a reprieve for the rest of us.

Almost a week has gone by since I was last in the changing room with them: quite long enough for Marjorie to have forgotten all about the episode in Menlove Avenue. This morning it is Pam who wants to corner me, with a story about her granddaughter. She doesn't know what the schools are coming to – looks to me for confirmation of the parlous state into which the education system has descended. It appears that the grandchild's teacher has entirely failed to appreciate her brilliance – is positively holding the child back. Pam appeals to me for agreement – I must recall meeting little Jolene, back in the Christmas holidays when she was staying up here and Pam brought her swimming. I must have noticed how bright she is.

I do remember Jolene – a suet pudding of a child, with whom I had a brief conversation about her Babar the Elephant sweat shirt. Jolene had not been aware that Babar was a character in a book. I make non-committal remarks, until rescued by Marjorie's intervention: naturally she too has a story about the general incompetence of the teaching profession. I realize that a theory has evolved between Pam and Marjorie that I chose to retire early because of the falling standards they equate to modern-day schooling. This is untrue. My own standards never wavered. Do your best to get through the day and try to stay sane.

I'm just about to escape the pair of them, when Marjorie changes tack completely – abandons the education system in favour of the very last thing I want to hear about. It transpires that, in my absence, she and Pam have been talking about the mysterious sighting of a vehicle identical to mine, apparently parked where I could not possibly have been. This conundrum has injected some interest into their otherwise dull lives, and they have worked it up between them until it has acquired the status of a Matter for Mutual Concern. Marjorie asks whether I have considered the possibility that someone is impersonating me.

It's so preposterous that I burst out laughing. Marjorie looks a bit huffed by this, and explains that what she really means is that someone has made up false number plates and is using them on a car similar to my own. Not, she says, to specifically impersonate me, but for 'criminal purposes'. Pam chips in with confirmation that she has read about such things in the Sunday newspapers.

This time I am ready for them. Numbers are often allocated to car dealerships in batches, I say. This means that cars of the same make and colour sometimes have registrations which are only one digit apart. Surely that must be the solution here. I bought my car locally, so it is highly likely that there is another one driving round the city with virtually the same registration. Pam seems quite taken with this idea, but I can see that Marjorie isn't convinced. Apart from anything else, my solution relies on Marjorie having made a mistake – albeit a small one. Nor does she want to be robbed of a juicy morsel of excitement by the production of a simple rationale.

On the walk home I start to imagine all sorts of scenarios. Marjorie, who is very active in her Neighbourhood Watch, might work herself up to reporting this mysterious occurrence at her local police station – 'just in case', as she would say. Not that they would take any notice. I can almost hear the stalwart desk sergeant thanking her for coming in, while politely shifting into anti-nutter mode. But somehow I can't quite convince myself and the memory of our conversation stays with me all day.

At badminton that evening I play a blinder and kid myself I'm over the jitters. When the session is over I stick around as usual to help put things away and lock up the hall.

'Fancy a drink?' asks Carolyn, our club secretary.

'No, thanks. I'm going to have an early night.' I give her a cheery wave from across the car park. Liar, says my conscience. You know you're not going home.

I don't usually come here twice in close succession – let alone three times in the space of barely a week. I'm uneasily aware that it is getting out of hand. It was the letter. That was what started it all. Meddlesome old women, Mrs Ivanisovic and Marjorie both. What would I do if Marjorie's car was to come round the bend now? Suppose she parked right in front of me. I imagine her getting out of the car, approaching to see exactly who is sitting here in the dark, and me panicking – gunning the car into life and pulling out – not meaning to hit her of course.

Time to put the brakes on.

I have always tried to avoid making my presence too overt. I generally favour the summer months, usually leaving it late, waiting for dusk. The street lamps don't give too much illumination at that time of the year, because the trees cast dappled patterns across the road, half hiding the car in a jigsaw of shadows. Of course winter evenings are also pretty safe because drawn curtains hide me from them, just as they do them from me.

I don't have to see inside the house to know when they are there. There is always the telltale car parked on the drive or lights in the windows. Occasionally I see one of them coming in or going out, but that hasn't happened for a long time. I tell myself that I don't need to come. That there isn't any point really. I can't achieve anything by it – but I am drawn back here all the same. I know the house hasn't changed hands because I check the phone book periodically. Once you have tracked someone down, it isn't so very difficult to keep tabs on them.

But coming here is a two-edged sword. On the one hand it reassures me a little to know where they are – to be so close. Yet equally it focuses that sense of an ever-present danger – the knowledge that a phone call or a knock on the door is all it would take. Up until a few days ago I didn't think anyone had ever noticed me sitting here. If anyone does walk by I'm just a woman waiting in a car. I don't always park in the same place – or come here all that often. I don't look like a stalker – no ski mask or night vision goggles – just an ordinary woman who has grown old waiting. And so long as no one knows about my visits, what possible harm can it do?

Maybe secrets can make stalkers of us all. They say that knowledge is power but secrets are more powerful still – drawing us, holding us in their grip of steel. You can never quite break free despite the passage of the years, because secrets have a life of their own and a way of working themselves to centre stage. The danger is always there, that one way or another a secret is going to find a way out.

TWENTY-ONE

After the scream there were a lot of other noises. A sound of crashing like someone running or falling over. Then voices shouting – I heard Simon calling our names: 'Trudie' and 'Katy' in that order. I found that I couldn't answer him. I had sunk down to a crouching position. Afraid to move. Afraid to breathe. For a moment there was silence again – then I heard Danny's voice. 'Si, Si, where are you? Katy . . .' He began yelling out my name repeatedly. 'Katy . . . Katy . . .'

'I'm here.' When I stood up I saw there was a blob of light coming towards me, winking in and out of sight between the trees. I shouted again and the torch swung in a wide arc, spotlighting trees, clumps of weeds, finally me.

'I'm coming.' I careered towards the figure behind the light, not caring how much I scratched and bruised myself in the process. As I reached Danny and fell against him, Simon loomed breathless out of the darkness. 'My torch has packed up again. Where's Trudie?'

'I don't know.' Danny's voice was taut. 'Did you scream, Katy? Was it you who screamed?'

'No,' I said. 'It wasn't me.'

'It must have been Trudie,' said Simon. 'Where the hell is she?' He raised his voice and shouted again: 'Trudie – Trudie.'

A gust of wind shivered through the canopy above us.

'Shit,' hissed Danny. 'What's happened to her?'

'She was heading for the playground,' I reminded them.

'That can't be very far from here,' said Simon. 'Why can't she hear us? Trudie – *Trudie.*'

'She may be playing some stupid game,' said Danny – but he didn't sound at all convinced.

'We'd better try the playground,' said Simon.

'Link arms,' suggested Danny. 'Make sure we don't get separated again.'

We did as he suggested; me in the centre, Danny on my left lighting the way with his torch and Simon on my right – just like Dorothy setting off to see the wonderful Wizard of Oz, flanked by the Tin Man and the Scarecrow.

It took barely a minute to reach the place we called the playground. For some reason we all stopped dead as soon as the improvised see-saw appeared in the light of Danny's torch. Danny played the beam away from us across the clearing, picking out the familiar shapes of sawn-off tree stumps and the rope swing.

Then his torch fell across Trudie's skirt. That was the thing we saw first – her skirt billowing on to the ground as if she was poised half-way between standing and sitting. When Danny ran the beam upwards we saw the rest of her. She had her back towards us and her hands hung limply at her sides. From the shoulders downwards her body sagged unnaturally within her clothing. Her head lolled forward, where it was entangled in the cat's cradle of string and wire and old washing lines which had been suspended between the two trees, where the kids had tried to make their scramble net. Each of us made a sound of some kind – not proper words – no language was capable of articulating the moment.

Danny was swiftest off the mark. 'Quickly,' he said.

'Katy – you hold the torch.' He thrust it into my hand and ran across the clearing with Simon at his side. I followed them, with the light wavering in my hand as they began to investigate the tangle from which Trudie was suspended.

'I think she's dead,' Simon said.

'No!' The way Trudie was hanging there left little room for doubt, but it was nevertheless unbelievable.

'She can't be,' said Danny. 'Try to hold her up. Let's get her out of this.' He set about the string and wire, managing to dislodge a couple of strands. Trudie's body slumped towards him, the sudden transfer of weight breaking something else with an audible snap, so that the only thing left suspending her was her scarf, twisted around a single piece of wire. Simon disengaged it and Danny lowered Trudie gently to the ground, stepping back on to something as he did so. He automatically bent to pick the object up and found it was the small torch. It was still switched on, but the casing and bulb were broken.

In the meantime Simon had knelt beside Trudie and placed his ear next to her chest. 'She's not breathing,' he said. He grabbed one of her hands and massaged it frantically, before dropping it again.

'What about artificial respiration?' It was all too obvious that Danny was clutching at straws. 'Try loosening her scarf.'

Simon straightened up. 'She's dead,' he repeated, not entirely as though he believed it.

'She can't be.'

'She is, man.' Simon briefly rested a hand on his shoulder. 'We have to go for someone. I'll have to take the car.'

'Right.' Danny nodded. 'Right,' he repeated. 'A doctor – no – the police – but we can't leave her here – alone.'

I stood dumbly between them, gripping our one remaining torch as if my life depended on it. Not looking at Trudie. *Not* looking at Trudie. Not seeing her crumpled skirt, her pale hands. Not looking at her contorted face.

We stood for about a minute in silence. We had reached an unspoken impasse. Which of us would want to walk back alone through the woods – or stay alone with Trudie? But our party was no longer divisible into two pairs and we had only one light between us.

'Please,' I whispered. 'Please can we cover her face?'

Without a word Danny dragged his sweater over his head and complied with my request.

'The police,' said Simon, as if he had never heard of such an organization and was just trying out the word to see how it sounded. A new thought struck him. 'We shouldn't have moved her. Everything should have been left exactly as we found it.'

'We couldn't just leave her hanging there,' Danny exclaimed angrily.

'But they'll want to try to work out what happened.'

'I should have thought it was bloody obvious,' said Danny. 'She dropped her torch and got tangled in these wires in the dark – maybe she lost it as she tripped and fell into them. It was an accident. A fucking accident waiting to happen.' He smashed his fist into what re-mained of the mess of wire and string. It seemed to take hold of his hand, momentarily refusing to let it go – an impromptu reenactment of Trudie's fate. I imagined her struggling desperately in the dark, like an insect caught in a spider's web, pulling the wrong way and thereby tightening the noose around her own neck. I shuddered. Danny worked his hand free and sucked his knuckles where a hank of wire had broken the skin.

'Shit,' Simon all but shouted. 'Shit, shit, shit.' He turned away from us and took a couple of strides into the darkness before returning to stand in the same spot as before. Somewhere in the distance an owl hooted, mocking our predicament.

'Okay,' Simon spoke slowly and deliberately. 'Suppose the police don't believe it was an accident. What then?'

'Meaning?' asked Danny.

'How are we going to explain what we were doing out here in the first place? How are we going to explain how we all got separated and Trudie ended up on her own? And do you think this looks like an accident? Would Trudie really have walked slap bang into this lot with enough force to hang herself?'

I was starting to feel light-headed, positively giddy. In the half-light cast by the torch everything seemed unreal. I finally found my voice. 'Trudie screamed. We all heard her. Maybe it wasn't an accident. Maybe someone attacked her.'

'You mean there was someone else here?'

'There's never anyone else here,' said Danny.

'Well, maybe there was tonight.' Simon's words instantly conjured up a host of possibilities, peopling the deserted woods with half a dozen homicidal maniacs and a thousand pairs of watching eyes.

'Someone might be watching us now,' I said. 'We mustn't split up again, whatever happens.'

'Don't worry,' said Danny. 'We won't.' He placed a protective arm around my shoulder, but it did little to comfort me. Above our heads the trees whispered among themselves, sibilant and conspiratorial.

Simon swore again under his breath. He crouched down and took Trudie's hand briefly between his own. 'She's still warm,' he said.

Well, of course she is, I wanted to shout. She was alive and walking through the woods with us not half an hour ago.

'Suppose it wasn't an accident,' Simon said again.

'You're right,' said Danny suddenly. 'We can't involve the police.'

'I'm not saying don't involve them,' said Simon. 'I'm just saying let's think this through.'

'We can't report this to the police,' said Danny. 'Because if we do, they'll want to know our names and all about us and they'll make a connection between us and Rachel Hewitt. She was strangled. We both lived on the same campus and our names will be on file. They'll think there's a link.'

And in all the ensuing fuss, I thought, my parents will find out that I haven't been in France at all. I pulled myself back in time to hear Simon agreeing that things could get very awkward if the police became involved.

'Wait,' I protested. 'What are you saying? We have to report it.'

'And have the police thinking one of us did it? Anyway, I'm surprised you're so keen to run off and dial 999,' said Simon. 'Seeing that you would be prime suspect.'

'What do you mean? I wasn't at uni with Rachel Hewitt.'

'No, but you never really liked Trudie being around. You've always been jealous of her.'

'That's rubbish! Trudie was my friend.'

'Oh really? Then how come you were always bitching about her? How come you were always picking fights with her?'

'That's crazy,' Danny protested. 'Katy would never hurt anyone – you know that, Si.'

'I wouldn't be too sure. Maybe Katy just lost it. They were always rowing. What was it about this morning – some strawberries?'

I thought my head was going to burst. Trudie was

lying dead at our feet and Simon was dragging up a spat about who had eaten the last of the strawberries.

'If we're going to start making accusations,' I said, 'how about you? Where did you get to, after you abandoned me in the dark?'

'I went to find Danny.'

'It's all my fault,' Danny said. 'I thought I'd creep up on Trudie and give her a fright, but I missed the fork in the path. I got to that place where the plank bridge crosses the stream and I realized I'd gone too far. I was coming back when I heard her scream. If only we'd all stayed together none of this would have happened.'

'Neither of us knows our way around in here as well as you do,' Simon sniped at me.

'I hadn't got a torch,' I said.

'No – but you've got scratches all over your face,' he snapped back. 'Did she put up a fight?'

'Stop it, Si,' Danny rounded on him angrily. 'This is mad. None of us killed Trudie. It was a freak accident – it must have been.'

'I'm just saying how it looks. Suppose the police accuse Katy of killing Trudie.'

'I'll tell them I didn't.' I was all but hysterical. 'Why are you trying to put the blame on me?'

'It doesn't matter whether you did it or not – what matters is whether the police think you did. We can't give you an alibi.'

'And I can't give you one either.'

'Exactly,' Danny cut in. 'Which floats us right up Shit Creek if they try to make a connection with Rachel Hewitt. So let's all calm down, shall we, and stop bandying ridiculous accusations about.'

'You don't think . . .' I hesitated. 'You don't think she would have hanged herself on purpose?'

'That,' said Simon disparagingly, 'is the most stupid thing you've said so far.'

'We have to call the police,' I said – but my voice carried little conviction.

'Not necessarily,' said Danny.

'We can't just leave the body here for someone else to find,' I said.

'Of course not,' said Simon. 'They'd be up at the house, asking first thing.'

'Who knows Trudie's been living here?' Danny broke in abruptly. 'No one. Her folks don't know and her friends don't – when anyone misses her, they won't come looking here.'

'They're already looking for her,' said Simon. 'She ran away from home a couple of months ago.'

I was startled. I thought I was the only one who knew.

'Well, they haven't come looking for her here, have they?' said Danny.

Simon spoke slowly: 'If we try to cover this up and someone finds out, everyone will think we killed her.'

'Then we have to make sure no one finds out,' said Danny.

'What the hell are you talking about?' I asked. 'You don't seem to understand what you're saying. This is Trudie we're talking about – our friend, Trudie.'

I staggered slightly and had to grab Danny's arm for support. Somewhere in my head, fireworks began to explode, blue and silver. All the time we stood there, my eyes kept straying down to look at the heap of clothing inches from my feet. I knew she was dead, but I couldn't take it in. I kept expecting her to move – sit up, whip Danny's sweater from her face and shout, 'Surprise!'

'We'd have to carry her all the way back.' Simon's tone was thoughtful. He was actually weighing up the pros and cons: working it all out. The blues and silvers became blinding.

'We've got all day tomorrow,' said Danny, 'before the guy comes with the concrete.'

I was reeling. 'You can't,' I whispered. 'You can't.'

'The alternative could be one of us spending a long time in prison for something they didn't do.' Danny took the torch from me and shone it around on the ground, as if he was looking for something. 'It's for the best, Katy.' He was talking to me softly, the way you'd explain things to a distraught child. 'Whatever we do now, it can't bring Trudie back. This is really the best way. We both think so.'

Two against one. Democracy in action. Grenades fizzed and banged in my ears. My knees crumpled and I sank to the ground beside Trudie, sobbing wildly, burying my face in the icy folds of her skirt.

TWENTY-TWO

A body is an awkward, heavy burden. Simon and Danny needed both hands to carry Trudie, so I was pressed into service as torch bearer. I led the way, trying to banish from my mind the vision of what was following me. There was no talking, but every so often one of them swore softly as they missed their footing, or their burden caught on something. It seemed to take us forever to get clear of the trees, then stagger uphill along the path through the fields. Trudie's hair and clothing brushed the grass, setting up a constant rustling in accompaniment to the pall bearers' heavy breathing. I felt as if we were making enough noise to be heard in Kington, and that every kind of night creature had come out to watch our grim procession go by, their eyes boring into us as we passed. When we were about two-thirds of the way back up the field, a pair of headlights swept along the road, but they were on the other side of the hedge, too far away to see us. I could hardly breathe as we approached the most vulnerable part of the route – the few yards along the road between the footpath and the front gate, where we would be in full view of any passing vehicle – but the road was deserted.

I led the way around the side of the house without a word. Neither of them had needed to explain where they intended to conceal Trudie's body. I thought of all those cups of tea she had carried outside, all the hours she had watched the hole deepen, never guessing that she was observing the excavation of her own grave.

They laid her down next to the pond. Simon said he needed to fetch the spades from the tool shed, so I accompanied him, lighting the way with the big torch, while Danny walked beside me. 'Why don't you go inside?' he suggested. His voice was all compassion – our quarrel put aside.

I didn't know which prospect was worse – to enter that dark brooding house alone, or stay and witness the gruesome task ahead.

'I'll stay,' I said.

'Sure?' he asked. 'Good girl. We can work faster if you hold the torch for us.'

As we returned across the lawn, me holding the torch, them carrying a spade each, I experienced that sense of unreality again. I half expected to find that Trudie had tired of her part in the charade, had got up and walked away – but she was lying where we had left her.

'This is wrong,' I blurted out. 'I can't do it. We have to tell.'

'If we take out some of the loose stuff we put back in to get it level—' Simon began talking as if he hadn't heard me.

'We can't just bury her . . .' I wailed.

'We have to,' Danny said.

'We can't turn back now. We've got to go through with it, whether you like it or not,' Simon said.

'No,' I protested. My tears had begun to flow freely now. 'There must be some other way.'

'Why don't you go inside?' Danny suggested again.

I shook my head and clung to the torch. They began to discuss the mechanics of it: deciding to remove as much loose earth as they could, put Trudie in the depression this created, then do their best to achieve a smooth surface again, raising the height by a few inches if necessary. Except for the tension in their voices, they might have been working as normal – planning then executing the task, as if this dreadful act was no more than a bit of standard landscape gardening.

When they began to dig I stood above them, my feet occasionally slipping on the pile of loose earth, doing my best to keep the work area floodlit. No one spoke. The light from the big lamp had gradually faded, dimming by degrees until it was little more than a yellowish glow.

'I think the batteries are running low,' I said eventually, stating the obvious.

'We won't be needing the torch for much longer now,' said Danny. 'This is it, Si – we've hit virgin ground.'

Now that it had come to it, neither of them could quite bring themselves to lift her down into the hole. For a moment I thought they were going to funk it, then Simon said, 'Come on' – and they set about the task. It ought to have been reverent and dignified but it was not. Trudie's body was recalcitrant, almost actively resistant. Her arms, legs and voluminous skirt seemed determined to hamper them. She was bundled ignominiously into the hole. As they shovelled earth on top of her, the light wavered madly while I shook with sobs. She was all but covered when the torch gave a threatening flicker.

'It's going out,' I said, panic writ loud in my voice.

'Come on,' said Danny, tossing down another couple of spadefuls in double quick time. 'Let's get inside. We don't want to be stuck out here in the dark.'

Simon needed no second bidding. They threw down their spades and we all but ran for the house, with Simon feeling in his pocket for the door keys as we went. The torch gave up altogether as we reached the front door: leaving us to stand in the darkness while Simon fumbled for the keyhole.

Inside the hall, the first thing I saw when Simon turned on the light was Trudie's denim jacket, hanging over the banister where she had left it several days before. I burst into tears again.

'It's all right, babe. It's all right. It's all over now. All over.' Danny held me tightly while I clung to him. We both caught sight of Simon's harrowed expression at the same moment and held out our arms to him. Group hugs were not the norm in those days, but the events of the night had broken down the usual barriers and constraints. We stood in the hall, locked in a mutual embrace: all our animosity drained away, everything else forgotten in the knowledge of what we had just shared. It was Simon who finally spoke. 'It'll be light in a few hours,' he said. 'We'll have to start work really early if we're going to get the bottom level again, before we can start with the sand.'

'You set your alarm,' said Danny, 'and come and wake me, as soon as you're up.'

Wake him? I thought. How are we ever going to sleep again? Every time I closed my eyes, I saw Trudie's face. I feared sleep, lest it reconfigure the very images I was trying to banish. My eyes fell on the denim jacket. Simon caught me looking at it.

'We'll have to decide what to do with her stuff,' he said.

'In the morning,' said Danny, firmly. 'Now we have to go to bed.' He drew me towards the stairs. Simon followed us, a step or two behind. Danny turned to him. 'Take it easy, man. Okay?'

Simon nodded. 'Goodnight,' he said.

In spite of our angry exchanges earlier I felt sorry for him as we parted on the landing. At least Danny and I had each other. Simon had to spend what was left of the night alone. I thought of the way he had comforted Trudie after the seance – made sure she wasn't left on her own. As I closed the bedroom door behind me I gave an involuntary shiver.

'Cold?' asked Danny. 'Never mind. We'll soon have you safe under the blankets.' He was pulling off his shirt as he spoke. It took me a second or two to realize what was missing.

'Danny – where's your crucifix?'

He looked down. The cross and chain were not there.

'Shit,' he said. 'It must have come off when we were in the wood. I thought I felt something, when we first lifted Trudie up. Bloody hell. I'll have to go back and look for it in the morning.'

A couple of minutes later, when we were lying side by side and Danny had switched off the light, I asked: 'Why does Simon hate me?'

'He doesn't.'

'He must do. He never has a good word to say for me. Tonight he even accused me of killing Trudie. You would have to really hate someone to say a thing like that.' A new thought struck me: 'You don't think he really believes it, do you?'

'Of course not. He wasn't saying that stuff because he believes it. He was just trying to show you how things might look to an outsider – to someone who doesn't know us and doesn't believe it was an accident.'

'Do you believe it was an accident?'

There was a pause before Danny said: 'Yes, I do . . .'

'But that scream—'

'I think she must have stumbled and fallen into the wires. That's when she screamed. She would have struggled to get free, but once she completely lost her footing, her weight would have tightened the ropes and the scarf around her neck.' He paused because I was crying again, my breath coming in a series of ragged sobs. Danny stroked my bare arms and shoulders. 'It was must have been very quick,' he said. 'She probably didn't suffer.'

After that we didn't talk very much. I eventually stopped crying, but my head pounded like the worst hangover in history. Danny slept fitfully, myself not at all. I had never realized before that the birds start to sing before it gets light, a choir of tormentors, their volume swelling as the curtains grew paler. At last I heard some movement on the landing – Simon's bare feet entering the bathroom. Danny heard it too and slid carefully out of bed, moving around the room with exaggerated care.

'I'm not asleep,' I said, at which he relaxed perceptibly and began to move normally. I sat up in bed, watching him as he rummaged around for clean pants, then climbed into the rest of his clothes.

'You don't need to get up yet,' he said. 'You should try to sleep.'

'I can't. I may as well get up too.'

I waited until he and Simon had both finished in the bathroom – six bedrooms, but only one bathroom – then I went in there to use it myself. There was no hot water and I needed to wash my hair. It came as something of a surprise. It was as if normal things could never happen again – and yet here I was, thinking that I would have to put the immersion heater on so that I could wash my hair. In the meantime I did my best with cold water. My eyes were red-rimmed and bloodshot; dark shadows of smudged mascara blended with sleeplessness. I looked like something off an Alice Cooper album sleeve.

When I got downstairs, I found the unification of the night before had dissolved. Simon and Danny weren't getting annoyed with one another, merely adopting polarized points of view.

'This takes priority,' Simon was saying. 'I've been out there and you can still see . . .' he didn't finish the sentence.

'I have to find it,' said Danny. He saw me entering the kitchen and turned as if to appeal for my confirmation. 'I'm just telling Si about my crucifix. I'll have to go and look for it.'

'Later,' Simon began.

'I can't lose it,' said Danny. 'It was a present from my father – when I made my first communion. I've worn it ever since.'

'I'm not saying—' Simon tried again, but Danny wasn't listening.

'If I'm not wearing it, Dad will notice straight away. Anyway, I'd never forgive myself if I lost it.'

'Fine,' said Simon, impatiently. 'We get it. But there are things to do here first.'

'No,' said Danny. 'I'm going straight down there to look for it. If I don't and it's just lying about someone else might take it.'

'Who the fuck is going to be mooching around the woods at this time of day?'

'You don't know,' said Danny, obstinately. 'Besides – one of us ought to go back and have a look around where it happened. Make sure there's nothing of Trudie's left lying about.'

'What could there possibly be?' asked Simon, but his eyes registered defeat. It was clear that Danny was not going to be deflected from his chosen course.

Simon sank down on to one of the kitchen chairs. The unwashed plates from our last meal together were still on the table, together with our dirty glasses. Four of everything. An empty Party Seven tin stood on the worktop, and there was a big pan on the stove with a thin layer of Trudie's casserole congealed in the bottom.

Danny had been standing beside the sink, drinking a glass of water. When he had completely drained it, he plonked the empty glass among the assortment of other washing-up which was awaiting attention. 'I'll go now,' he said. 'I'll be back as soon as I can.'

Simon watched his departing figure, saying nothing. Something about Simon had changed. He looked so vulnerable and dejected that for a moment I wanted to put my arms around him; but I thought Danny wouldn't like that, if he happened to look in as he passed the kitchen window. On the other hand – if Simon didn't like girls, which Danny presumably knew, perhaps it didn't matter. I didn't do it anyway.

'I'll help you,' I said. 'Outside, I mean.'

Simon looked up at me: relief mingled with surprise. I had surprised myself. The words were out before I had time to think about them. 'I have to have a cup of coffee first,' I added.

The milk had been left out overnight and there was no more in the fridge, so I had my coffee black. It tasted bitter, in spite of a generous addition of sugar. Simon found some orange cordial which he diluted in a pint glass, drinking about half before setting it aside. There was no talking.

When we were done with our drinks, he led the way out into the garden. I had braced myself for something terrible, but there was very little to see. The freshly dug earth was hummocky in comparison with the smooth surface which had been achieved the day before, but apart from that there was no clue to the pond's new secret at first glance. Then I noticed a gaudy scrap of red and yellow, which I recognized as part of Trudie's skirt. It looked like a small piece of fabric lying in the bottom of the hole, where it might have been blown by the wind: but I knew it was a part of something much larger, which led down to Trudie herself. Simon took up a spadeful of earth and positioned it carefully on top of the telltale remnant.

'When I first came out this morning,' he said, not looking at me, almost apologetic, 'one of her feet was still showing.'

'Just tell me what to do,' I said.

Simon frowned. 'We were going to level the earth, then put an even layer of sand over that,' he said. 'But I think it would save time if we just started putting the sand in and got that level. I don't suppose it matters if the sand is thicker in some places than others.'

I said nothing. I didn't know anything about making ponds – or burying people.

'One of us needs to stand in here and spread the sand, while the other one barrows the sand across from the pile.'

'I'll do that,' I said quickly. 'I'll fetch the sand.'

'It's very heavy work,' said Simon, doubtfully.

'I want to do it. I don't mind.' Anything rather than stand in that hole with Trudie. Anything.

Simon was right about it being hard work. Pushing the loaded barrow wasn't the worst part – it was the filling, hefting shovels of sand from the pile into the wheelbarrow. My shoulders were aching in no time, and little runnels of sweat found their way into my eyes and down my back, despite the fact that it was still early enough in the day to be chilly.

Each time I brought a fresh load to upend into the hole, Simon had managed to hide another small patch of dark earth under a layer of warm orange. My back and shoulders ached with the unaccustomed labour and my arms felt stretched, as if I'd had a preliminary taste of the rack, but I didn't falter. When Simon asked if I wanted to stop for a rest, I shook my head. It seemed right that I should suffer. It was a punishment for the dreadful thing we had done.

Neither of us was wearing a watch, but I estimated we had been working for about an hour when Danny returned. He came round the side of the house, just as I was pushing a wheelbarrow full of sand in the opposite direction. We met at the edge of the pond and I saw the familiar glimmer of the gold chain at his neck before he spoke.

'I found it,' he said. 'And I also found this.' He held out the torch for us to see. It was the one with the dud battery, out of Simon's car.

Simon went white. 'I must have put it down when we first found her. I'd forgotten all about it.'

'Just as well I went back,' said Danny. He wasn't smug, but his tone let us know that he had been right.

A thought struck me. 'What happened to the other torch? The one Trudie was using?'

'I brought it back last night,' said Danny. 'Don't you remember? I found it lying on the ground – broken. I picked it up and put it in my pocket.'

'There wasn't anything else, was there?' asked Simon. He was clearly shaken by this example of our carelessness. It brought home how very easily we might be found out.

'Nothing to say anyone had been there at all,' said Danny.

'What about the kids' climbing net? It'll be obvious something's happened to that.'

Danny hesitated. 'It was already a bit of a mess,' he said. 'Anyway, it might easily have been damaged by the wind or a bird flying into it or something. Maybe even deliberately sabotaged by another gang of kids.'

'Where did you find your crucifix?' I asked. 'Did you have to search very long?'

'No – hardly at all. It was just hanging in amongst that tangle of stuff. I suppose it must have snagged on some wire when I was getting Trudie out of that awful mess. Luckily the chain hasn't broken. The catch must have given way again. It's been dodgy for a while – I'll have to get it fixed.'

In my mind's eye I could see the crucifix hanging there as he described it. The little golden cross marking the place where Trudie had died.

'We've got on really well,' said Simon. He gestured to where almost a third of the bottom was already covered, but his tone was flat, unenthusiastic.

'That's fantastic,' said Danny. There was genuine contrition in his voice as he continued: 'I feel really bad that you guys have had to do so much without me – but I had to go down there.'

'You did the right thing, man,' said Simon. 'My initials are on that torch, in marker pen.' Whatever division had existed between them earlier, the partnership was rock solid again now.

After Danny's return I lingered in the garden for a while, watching them work. Danny transported the sand and Simon spread it, barrowload after barrowload. Gradually it dawned on me that they were finding this attention discomfiting – that they felt I should be elsewhere. My thoughts turned to the house and in particular the state of the kitchen. I would have to go inside sooner or later and tackle the mess. There was no one else to do it now.

TWENTY-THREE

On the eve of my second trip to Sedgefield, the conclusion of my night-school class in Conversational Italian coincides with a cloudburst. My car is at the furthest end of the car park, and naturally I have left my umbrella in the side pocket of the door and consequently get soaked to the skin. To cap off this wonderful evening, no sooner have I got my key in the door than the phone begins to ring.

It's my sister. A rare event. She opens by asking how I am, but this is only a feed for my line, which is 'Fine. How are you?'

Cue leading lady who embarks on a long speech explaining the various problems currently besetting her life. The divorced estate agent she had such high hopes of turns out to have been a dud. Her older daughter Martine is living with someone 'completely unsuitable' in 'some terribly squalid part of Bristol' – meantime her younger daughter, Belinda (Binny to her mother), is suspected of having an eating disorder. Both her ex-husbands are being aggravating – one has just married a much younger woman – a clear act of provocation, apparently. Is it my imagination, or does my sister actually say, 'He has only done it to annoy me'?

She finally gets round to asking: 'So how's your life? Have you seen anything of Eddie lately?' In the dramatic production that is my sister's life, my offstage activities are not liable to amount to much more than being the conduit for occasional news of our mutual sibling – hence the coupling of these two unrelated queries.

'I went out with them for the day, a couple of months ago. They're all fine.'

She takes this as a signal to issue thinly veiled accusations of neglect, implying that neither he nor I ever go out of our way to spend a day with her. This is partly true and in my case not least because of an occasion when I did go out of my way to spend time with her, only to be blown off because some bloke with an Aston Martin asked her out to lunch.

While I'm doodling on the message pad, giving half an ear to all this, a picture of Mrs Ivanisovic grows in my mind: not the frail habituée of Broadoaks, who could be toppled like a pile of leaves in an autumn breeze, but a younger, stronger version, her body taut with focus and determination as she sits at her son's bedside, posing ever more dangerous questions, to which he signals his response with a squeeze of her hand. The vision is abruptly blown apart by my sister announcing that she has the use of a friend's villa in Portugal for a fortnight, and why don't I join her? There's a pool, a lovely restaurant nearby – a market within walking distance if we want to do our own food – and best of all she has enough air miles to bring the plane fares down to next to nothing. 'How about it?' she asks, so heartily that anyone listening in might think a fortnight of each other's company is something we've been simply longing for these past ten years.

'When is it?' I ask. 'I'll have to look in my diary.'

I can tell she is miffed. It's only a couple of weeks away but someone like me ought to be available to accept without demur. I go through the pretence of rustling the pages of my diary while mustering up a tone of regret. 'I'm sorry, Amy, I can't. I've got something on virtually every day. Two lots of theatre tickets, I'm down to play badminton in the club championships—'

'You could scratch,' she interrupts.

'– and I can't let my partners down,' I continue smoothly, as if she hasn't spoken. 'It would mean missing two weeks of night school – and at this stage I'd probably never catch up; and it's the week our book group meets.'

'Surely none of these are exactly matters of life and death?'

'Well – no. But it means letting lots of people down – and I don't like to go back on my word and leave people in the lurch.' (Not even for a jolly in an Aston Martin.)

I don't tell her that I'd actually much rather go to the book group, where wine and conversation will flow and Hilly will come over all earnest, and our Irish friend Brendan will make us laugh, so I try a conciliatory tack. 'Why not go on your own?' I suggest. 'Look on it as an opportunity to pamper yourself, have some quality time. Chill out.'

'It's all very well for you to say that, Kate,' she snaps. 'You're used to being on your own.' Her vision of a lonely spinster travels down the line, as loud and clear as her accompanying words. She really hasn't got a clue.

'Well, I'm sure you'll be able to find someone else. I bet there are lots of people who'd love to go with you.' Actually I'd lay a substantial wager that she has already asked everyone else she knows – otherwise she wouldn't be asking me. 'It's a shame I can't make it. Maybe next time.'

She brings the conversation to an end soon after that. I sign off with a jaunty, 'Enjoy Portugal.'

Once I have put the phone down the silence in the flat seems to intensify. I prowl around fidgeting with things, then retire to bed over-early to endure a restless night, while my inner demons play Join the Dots. By a trick of perspective Mrs Ivanisovic is just a helpless old lady to most people – but her power to menace depends on who you are. I eventually fall into a deep sleep at around five in the morning, which inevitably means I end up oversleeping. I make myself drive all the way to Ferrybridge without a break, as a sort of punishment.

The service station at Ferrybridge is quite crowded. It isn't school holidays, but there are surprising numbers of children about – presumably taken out of school by parents who think a day out at a theme park has an educational value equivalent to whatever the National Curriculum has on offer. I try to find a table well away from these screeching kids and their quarrelsome families. Pam and Marjorie pity me in my childless state – but I don't think I ever saw motherhood as my destiny: I am not naturally the motherly type.

If I am absolutely honest about it, I don't think I originally chose teaching because I especially liked children or wanted to work with them. As my schooling came to an end and my lack of tangible ambition in any particular direction became ever more apparent, the options had narrowed down to Go To University or Go To College. My parents thought university signified too much freedom for an irresponsible scapegrace like me. College had the advantage of being near enough for me to live at home for another couple of years, where I could be kept an eye on. Commercial college was a bit infra dig – my mother hadn't invested in grammar school uniforms and cheese and wine with the PTA only for her daughter to end up a shorthand typist – so teacher training college it was. This seemed okay to me. I didn't look very far ahead in those days and being on the teacher's side of the desk appealed more than being on the pupil's.

There was a blip of course. In the immediate aftermath of Danny's death, I was returned to my parents, too traumatized to continue with my studies: a situation they accepted with a kind of grim resignation. I had always been the awkward middle child, unfavourably compared to my siblings – the one who never quite fitted in and always tended to be a bit of a nuisance. It was so like Katy to have messed up her academic career (such as it was) by getting involved with an unstable boyfriend who had killed himself. Of course they did not actually say this outright – but I knew what they were thinking. My brother and sister would never have given them all this trouble. They dated normal, sensible people who kept their names out of the papers and never gave suicide a second thought. Trust Katy to pick the weirdo.

In the end of course I went back to college and qualified to teach. Teaching is a greedy vocation. It can gobble up your life if you let it, biting off great chunks at a time, demanding your full commitment. Fortunately I needed its total absorption. When I decided to retire early, everyone was surprised. 'You love teaching,' someone said, but I am not really sure if this was true. By focusing so completely on my work, I managed to exclude a great many other things I did not care to think about. Perhaps teaching was also like a mission into which a penitent throws themselves, the way sinners used to undertake work in a leper colony. Every child in every class became a special kind of mission for me – but at night they went home, and at the end of summer term they moved on. I was only a part of their lives, never the whole of it. I suppose this is the difference between me and Mrs Ivanisovic, whose energies were focused on one child alone.

They *were* very close, Danny and his mother. This makes it easier to believe in the alleged deathbed communication between them. She positively adored Danny. Maybe it was the loss of that other child which forged the bond so strongly. No wonder she was devastated when Danny died. And now even Stan has deserted her – Betty Ivanisovic is the lone survivor, hanging on to life by the slenderest of threads. One snip from the cosmic scissors and she will be gone.

I sip my latte (why can't one just buy a straightforward cup of coffee any more?) and ponder the contents of her first letter – her demand for the truth. *I must know*, she says. Why must she? Why do people think it will always be better if they know? Might it occasionally be better *not* to know? Trudie's mother doesn't know. She has been spared the truth and surely it is better that way. She may even yet hold on to the hope that Trudie is still alive. She can retain her memory of a laughing, dark-haired nymph – unsullied by the truth of a mouldering forgotten corpse, lying far from home without the dignity of a proper grave.

TWENTY-FOUR

Since I was clearly surplus to requirements in the garden I returned to the kitchen, where the smell of stale cooking made me want to retch. I flung open the windows to let in some fresh air, and also to establish some semblance of being in touch with the others – I couldn't see or hear them, but I knew they were not far away. I began to clear the contents of the table, scraping plates, tipping out dregs, stacking everything beside the sink, every moment expecting Trudie to come strolling into the room. I knew it was impossible and yet it still seemed highly likely. Far more likely, in fact, than what had actually occurred.

The kitchen sink stood under the window, which meant that anyone working at it necessarily had their back to the room: a position which made me deeply uneasy. I knew the house behind me was empty, but this did nothing to alleviate the sensation of hostile eyes on my back. It was even worse when I left the kitchen. The whole house seemed full of decaying memories. Desiccated cacti gathered dust on the hall table; a forgotten ancestor stared down from an almost blackened painting, watching the door for relatives long since departed. I noticed that Trudie's jacket had vanished from the hall – I guessed that Simon must have put it in her bedroom with her other things, banished immediately the ridiculous thought that Trudie herself had picked it up a moment before, on her way out of the house for a walk. As I mounted the stairs, another thought struck me – how, when things had vanished in the past, the explanation had been provided by Murdered Agnes. Now Trudie . . . I drew back from the thought, took the rest of the stairs at a run.

Breathing hard, I took my towel and shampoo into the bathroom and removed my shirt, ready to wash my hair. The running water seemed unnaturally loud, filling my ears, masking out any other sounds. Was that somebody moving on the landing? I turned off the taps to listen, but there was no one there. When I turned the water back on again a host of doubts came flooding into my head. Wouldn't it have been better to leave Trudie where she was? Had we panicked and done the wrong thing? Surely we were wrong to fear the involvement of the police – they couldn't have pinned anything on any of us without witnesses. And anyway no one knew exactly what had happened. I struggled to focus on the moments leading up to the scream. Danny had been convinced it was an accident – but suppose there really had been someone else in the wood last night. I realized that the basin was all but overflowing. I had to turn off the taps in double quick time and reduce the water level by slopping some down the overflow.

When I bent over the basin to wet my hair, I was instantly beset by the idea that there was someone creeping up behind me. I jerked my head up, sending a cascade of water across the tiles and on to the floor, ran to the bathroom door and shot the bolt, but it didn't help. I had merely locked my fears inside with me and they jostled around the bathroom, trying to gain the upper hand.

It took an age to wash long hair in the hand basin. At home we had a rubber fitment which went over the bath taps – a shower spray, we called it, which made the rinsing easy: but here the operation involved emptying and refilling the sink half a dozen times, trying not to send a shower of water on to the floor every time I lifted my long hair clear of the sink. I had reached the final rinse when a series of loud bangs reverberated through the house. I leapt back from the sink, soaking everything in range, pressing a wet hand against my mouth to stifle a scream. Three loud bangs – three in swift succession. Wasn't three always the number of significance – the harbinger of something dreadful to follow?

For several seconds I stood frozen to the spot. Water trickled unchecked from my hair, damping my bra, a rash of drops standing out across my shoulders like imitation gooseflesh. It had been easy enough to blame any pseudo-supernatural occurrences on a live Trudie. Alien noises in the house could no longer be thus ascribed.

I picked up my towel and dabbed my arms and shoulders with it, before tentatively towelling my hair, eyes fixed on the bathroom door, listening intently for any clue as to the origin of the noise. The sounds had been near at hand – somewhere in the house. I mentally calculated the distance between myself and the guys. It was unlikely that they would have heard anything and there was thus little hope that they would come to investigate. All previous attempts to open the bathroom window had ended in failure. It was assumed to have been painted shut, years before. How loudly would I need to yell . . .?

The three bangs rang out again – and the penny finally dropped. It was the door knocker. There was someone at the front door. My fleeting sense of relief died instantly. This was no time to entertain casual callers, with Simon and Danny out in the garden presiding over the concealment of a dead body. Anyway, we never had casual callers – or indeed any callers at all. The only person who had ever visited us was Mrs Ivanisovic, and she surely wouldn't have returned a mere forty-eight hours later. It must be someone selling something – or maybe Jehovah's Witnesses. If I ignored them they would have to go away.

Then again, suppose it was someone who really did want to speak to one of us – not even specifically one of us, but the occupier, the home owner. Suppose it was someone who had driven all the way out here specially and was not easily put off. Then in a flash it came to me that it must be the builders. I gave a little cry of horror. They had come a day too early and if I didn't get down there in time they would see Simon's car parked out front and guess we were in – maybe assume we couldn't hear the door knocker and go round the back in search of us.

I bundled the towel into a turban round my head and scurried down the stairs, buttoning my shirt as I went, scrambling to reach the front door. Somehow I would have to persuade them to go away.

When I swung the door open, the two men outside did not look at all like builders. They were wearing dark trousers, pale-coloured shirts and plain navy ties. Not quite smart enough to be the Mormons. One of them was standing expectantly at the door, but the other had stepped back and was looking speculatively up at the house, as if assessing for repairs. Perhaps they were exceptionally well-dressed builders.

'Good morning,' said the man nearest the door. He flipped open a little card holder and flashed it in my direction – exactly the way I had seen them do it on the television. 'Sergeant Mathieson, Staffordshire Police. I was hoping for a word with Simon Willis. Is he in?'

I reeled back a step or two into the hall – my face no doubt yelling, *Guilty as charged, get the cuffs on.* Sergeant Mathieson and his colleague were evidently accustomed to generating this reaction and took absolutely no notice.

'Simon,' I stammered. 'Yes, Simon's here. He's in the garden – working in the garden.' Had I already said too much? Did they *know* what he was doing out there? Had they guessed? How the hell had they got here so quickly? I wondered if they had brought their own spades to dig Trudie up, or whether they would want to use ours.

Sergeant Mathieson and his colleague exchanged looks. They obviously thought I was a halfwit.

'Shall we walk around the back and find him?' The other one spoke for the first time, seeming to address both me and his companion.

'No, no,' I said quickly. 'Please come inside.' I stood back, waving an encouraging arm as if in training for traffic duty. 'If you'd like to come in and sit down, I'll go out and get him. That would be quicker,' I added, seeing them hesitate. 'I know exactly where to find him.'

They stepped inside – probably imagining from the way I'd spoken that the house stood in a vast acreage, within which a hunt for Simon might become a time-consuming jaunt through a maze of shrubbery. I showed them into the drawing room, which looked much the same as it had on the day of Mrs Ivanisovic's visit, give or take a bit of dirty crockery. My heart was pounding so hard I thought they must be able to hear it.

'I'm sorry about not answering the door,' I said. 'I was in the middle of washing my hair.' I pointed up at the towel.

Sergeant Mathieson was not interested in my hair-dressing arrangements. 'Do you live here?' he asked.

'No,' I said. 'Well, yes – I'm staying here – for the summer – as a sort of housekeeper.' The thought flitted through my mind as I spoke that officially I was not here at all – I was fruit picking in France. I saw his eyebrows lift as he swept a glance around the room, his eyes meeting those of his colleague at its conclusion. They were evidently unimpressed with the Katy Mayfield school of housekeeping.

'It's not – bad news, is it?' I fished.

'No, love, nothing like that. We need to speak to Mr Willis as part of routine enquiries. So if you could just pop out and fetch him . . .'

'Yes,' I said. 'I'll get him.'

I walked out of the drawing room and across the hall with all the normality I could muster, but once out of their sight I 'popped' through the kitchen with the velocity of a bullet from a gun, racing across the lawn with my hands on my head in order to prevent my towel from coming adrift.

'What the hell's wrong?' asked Danny, clambering out of the hole and advancing a few steps to meet me.

'It's the police,' I gasped out. 'The police are here, asking for Simon.'

Simon stared at me. His face went so white that I thought for a moment he was going to pass out.

Danny appeared marginally calmer. 'Slow down, Katy.' He placed a gentle hand on my arm. 'What makes you think it's the police?'

'I don't think. It *is* the police. They showed me a thingy – a warrant card. Sergeant Mathieson of the Staffordshire Police.' The peculiarity of this suddenly struck me. 'We're not in Staffordshire,' I said.

Danny turned to Simon. 'Do you think it's some-thing to do with the car? Are the tax and insurance up to date?'

'Of course they are,' said Simon. 'Anyway, they

214

wouldn't send someone all the way from Staffordshire just for that.'

'Do you suppose Trudie came from Staffordshire?' I asked.

'She didn't,' said Simon, abruptly. 'Nowhere near.'

'It'll be something to do with uni,' said Danny.

Simon was staring at him. 'Rachel Hewitt,' he said.

'You can't be serious,' said Danny. 'Why would they come all the way down here about that? You've already made a statement.'

'I don't see how it can be anything else,' said Simon. They were talking in low, urgent voices. I was horribly aware that Simon was still standing in the excavation. They had finished covering the bottom in a layer of sand and were working on the sides now. His feet were only a few inches from Trudie. We had put her there to avoid the attention of the Rachel Hewitt murder enquiry, but it looked as if the enquiry had caught up with us, all the same. Somewhere above our heads a young jackdaw emitted a raucous cry like laughter. I was getting to hate those bloody birds.

'Whatever it is they've come about,' said Danny, 'you'd better go and talk to them.'

'Yes,' I urged. 'Otherwise they might come out here, looking for you.'

'There's nothing for them to see,' said Danny. 'But she's right – you'd better go inside. Ought I to come in as well, d'you think?'

'I don't know.' Simon clambered out of the hole and stood beside me. 'Maybe not, if they haven't asked for you. Anyway – we need to keep working if we're going to have this ready for when the bloke comes tomorrow.'

When the bloke comes tomorrow. Until a few minutes before I had half forgotten that their speed was dictated by the imminent arrival of someone whose attention was going to be squarely focused on the place where we had buried Trudie. Feeling sicker than ever, I trailed after Simon as he headed towards the house. While Simon took off his boots and washed his hands at the kitchen sink, I returned to the drawing room to announce: 'Simon's coming now. He's just washing his hands.'

I had expected the two policemen to be prowling round the room, examining everything, looking for clues; but they were sitting on the sofas, perfectly docile. 'Would you like a cup of tea?' I asked.

'That'd be nice, love, yeah,' said Sergeant Mathieson. 'Milk, no sugar.'

'Two sugars for me,' said his companion.

Simon appeared at that moment. He had regained some of his colour, found time to tidy his hair. His clothes looked scruffy – dirty even when compared to the two policemen, but then they had not been labouring outside. He approached Sergeant Mathieson (who happened to be nearest) with his hand extended: 'Simon Willis. How can I help you?'

That was the thing with being as well brought up as Simon, I thought. You could carry things off, whereas I was hopping about like a flea in the background, feeling as though I had to contend with some strange form of Tourette's – only instead of shouting out swear words, it was things like *She's in the garden – she's under the pond.*

I remembered my promise of tea. 'I'll just go and make the tea,' I said. They had dealt with the introductions and Simon was about to sit down in the chair nearest the door. None of them took any notice of me.

I decided to use the best teacups, but as I lifted them out of the kitchen cupboard I remembered who had been the last person to handle them, and this made my hands shake so hard that I almost dropped a pile of saucers. I had to stand still for a moment or two, gripping the edge of the worktop before I could carry on. I had got as far as putting the kettle on and setting out four cups and saucers on a tray, before I remembered that we had no milk. I opened and closed cupboards and explored the contents of the pantry shelves in a frantic search for a tin of Marvel – but there was nothing doing. For a desperate moment I wondered what would be the effect of whitening our tea with salad cream, but then I recalled that we hadn't got any of that either.

Humiliated, I returned to the drawing room and waited for an appropriate pause in which to break my news.

'So you can't think of any reason why it would have been in her room?' Mathieson was asking.

Simon's skin tone was now approaching another extreme. Where he had been deathly pale, his cheeks now burned like guilty sirens. 'No,' he said. At least his voice was emphatically confident, as he added: 'Absolutely none.'

'And you say you'd missed it sometime before? Possibly in the student common room?'

'I can't honestly be sure,' said Simon. 'That's the last time I actually remember that I was going to use it – but – well, I don't know. It's not easy to remember. It wouldn't have seemed very important at the time. I wouldn't have missed it unless I actually looked for it, because – you know – I wanted to use it. I only noticed I hadn't got it when I was packing up to come home.'

'How about your room-mate?'

'I didn't have one,' said Simon. 'I had a room to myself.'

They noticed me lurking empty-handed in the doorway. 'I'm ever so sorry, but I'm afraid we've got no milk. Would you like some orange squash instead?'

Sergeant Mathieson's companion emitted a derisive snort. The sergeant himself – who hadn't seemed all that excited by my offer of tea – now looked distinctly irritated that it wasn't forthcoming. 'Not for me, thanks,' he said. 'What about you, Jim? Do you want some orange squash?' He made the offer sound ridiculous, emphasizing the words 'orange squash' as if he had never heard of anything so ludicrous in his life. His colleague responded with a shake of the head.

'So . . .' Mathieson turned back to Simon. 'You're staying here for the rest of the holidays, are you?'

'Until my uncle gets back at the end of August,' Simon corrected. 'After that I expect I'll go back to my parents' until term starts.'

'And are the other people here all friends from university?'

'No,' I jumped in smartly. 'I'm at teacher training college, in Birmingham.'

'How many of you living here?' asked the other policeman. He said it so casually – as if it wasn't important at all. Did he notice Simon's hesitation?

'Three – just myself, Katy, and our friend Danny, who's working out in the garden.'

Digging a grave, digging a grave, my newly diagnosed Tourette's wanted to shout, but I wouldn't let it.

Just then a new idea gripped me. Suppose they produced a search warrant. Trudie's possessions were still scattered all over her bedroom – with perhaps among them evidence of who she actually was. It wouldn't take the slowest of Mr Plods two minutes to work it out. There was no possible way we could explain it. Something would have to be done about her things. I stood there racking my brains for a plausible reason to go upstairs, so that I could gather all Trudie's stuff together and hide it – but where? And if they found her things all bundled up under a bed or stuffed into the back of a cupboard, wouldn't that look even more suspicious? Couldn't we just say she'd gone out somewhere? But then Simon had already told them there were only three of us – and three into four lots of clothes won't go. One wild idea after another. We ought never to have moved her body – in doing so, we had only made everything appear much, much worse.

'So . . .' Sergeant Mathieson was consulting some notes. 'You don't think you could have lent it to Rachel Hewitt, then?'

I swallowed hard. At least they appeared to have lost interest in the make-up of our household.

'No,' said Simon. 'I'm sure I would have remembered.'

'Why?'

'Because I hardly knew Rachel Hewitt,' Simon said – a bit crossly, I thought. 'So I wouldn't be likely to lend her anything. She wasn't on the same course as me and we didn't live in the same block. I saw her a few times, because our blocks shared a common room – but we used separate kitchens. I don't think we ever spoke to one another.'

Sergeant Mathieson looked as if he might be getting cross too. He had been denied his cup of tea and now he wasn't getting very far with Simon. 'So you've got no idea how your screwdriver came to be in this girl's room? You didn't lend it to her – or anybody else, so far as you can remember – you weren't on her course and you lived in a different block. You haven't got any suggestions at all?'

'I can hazard a guess, if you want me to,' said Simon. 'As I said before, the last time I remember seeing my screwdriver was when I took it down to the common room because someone wanted the plug on the record player fixed – but when I got down there with it, another guy – Keith, I don't know his second name – was already mending it. I didn't go straight back to my room. I stayed and talked for a bit and I suppose I must have put the screwdriver down and forgotten about it. I assume I went back to my room without it and later on someone else picked it up – maybe took it back to their room to use it for something and never returned it. It's like that, I'm afraid. There's a lot of petty thieving goes on. Finders keepers and all that. Maybe Rachel took it herself – who knows?'

'Well, Mr Willis—' Mathieson stood up and his colleague followed suit – 'I think that's all you can help us with – for now. You know where you can find us – if you think of anything else you want to say.'

Simon stood up politely – although neither he nor Mathieson attempted a smile. I scuttled ahead, opening the front door and holding it for them. Simon didn't follow us. They walked straight to their car without looking back, started the engine and drove away. Sergeant Mathieson's colleague made a much better job of turning their car than Mrs Ivanisovic had.

As they disappeared out of the gate, Simon came out of the drawing room.

'It's all right,' I said. 'They've gone.'

We stared at one another – for a moment I thought Simon was going to say something, but then he hesitated as if he had thought better of it.

'What were they talking about?' I asked.

Simon shook his head as if he couldn't quite believe what he was saying. 'They've found a screwdriver – a small one that belonged to me – in Rachel Hewitt's room in Halls. You'd think they'd have found it straight away – they must have searched her room when they first found her – but apparently one of the contractors found it, when they moved her desk to paint behind it – they're redoing her room during the long vac. They moved the desk and the screwdriver had dropped behind it. It might not have been hidden – it may just have fallen down there by accident and be nothing to do with the murder at all.'

'But how did they know it was yours?'

'They didn't – until today. I'd put my initials on it in marker pen – I did it with a lot of my stuff, to try and stop people pinching things.' He gave an ironic laugh. 'They've been working their way through all the students whose initials are SW and MS – they didn't know which way up to read it.'

'You could have said it wasn't yours.'

'What for?' Simon stared at me. 'It is mine, and it would only have made things far worse if I denied it, then someone else told them who it belonged to.'

'I suppose so,' I said. 'But how did they know to find you here?'

'They went to my parents and my parents gave them the address.'

I could tell from his tone that Simon was joining Sergeant Mathieson in the growing band of people who recognized me for a halfwit. I had forgotten that Simon's parents knew where he was. Lucky they hadn't wanted me. My parents would have sent them on a fine old wild-goose chase.

I tried to restore my reputation by exhibiting my practical side. 'We've run out of milk, and all sorts of things,' I said. 'We're going to have to go into Kington.' Simon scarcely appeared to hear me. He was looking beyond me towards the kitchen door, almost as if he could penetrate its solid surface and see far beyond it, into the garden. 'It would be better to get the shopping done now,' I persisted. 'You can carry on working into the evening if you need to, but the shops all close at half five.'

He appeared to consider this. 'You're right,' he said eventually. 'I'll go and tell Danny.'

TWENTY-FIVE

They say it's grim up north, and whoever they are they've undoubtedly got it right this afternoon. Although barely three o'clock, it's so dark that I need to use my headlights. The first spots of rain hit the windscreen just as I am turning into the gates of Broadoaks. Today there is no one in the grounds, which look windswept and unwelcoming under the steely sky.

On my previous visit I came empty-handed, but this time I have brought a box of chocolates – an assortment of milk and plain, because I have no idea which she prefers. I considered flowers, but there were already some in her room last time: probably fresh flowers are all part of the Broadoaks package.

As I make a dash from my parked car, holding my umbrella tilted like a shield to ward off the worst of the weather, I wonder if I ought to let someone know I am here – or just knock and enter her room. I can't see a way of alerting anyone's attention – there doesn't appear to be a bell to ring – but I am rescued by the appearance of the same minion as before. Different necklace this time – some sort of pink rock chippings, strung together any old how – hideous. She takes my dripping umbrella and goes through the same routine as last time. While she's doing this, I suddenly get it. There must be closed-circuit television cameras which enable them to intercept everyone at the door. To make the old ladies feel secure. No expense spared.

She eyes my box of chocolates doubtfully. 'I'm afraid you'll see a big change,' she says. She hesitates with a hand on the knob of Mrs Ivanisovic's door, perhaps trying to prepare me but unable to hit on the right thing to say, before she finally steps aside and holds the door open for me, as she did on my first visit.

Mrs Ivanisovic is in bed – under the covers this time. The bedclothes are up to her chest, the pastel bedspread disappearing under a broad fold of white cotton sheet which is so pristine that I assume Mrs Ivanisovic has scarcely moved since it was made up around her. She looks like a little skeleton clad in borrowed flesh, around which someone has draped clothes belonging to some other third party. Her oxygen mask has become a fixture, held in place by slim bands of pale elastic. It emits the only sound in the room – the shallow wheeze and whisper of her breathing. Her eyes are closed.

I sit in the chair beside the bed, careful not to disturb her. I am still holding the chocolates and I look around for somewhere to put them down, but the top of her bedside cabinet is cluttered with things: a jug, a water glass, a pair of spectacles, a little dispenser of sweeteners (as if she needs to worry about her weight) – all the detritus of her vanishing life.

When my own mother died it was in hospital, in an impersonal bed with metal sides that clanged when moved and an officious-looking chart clipped at its foot. The bed was separated from the rest of the ward by thin cotton curtains, a green and grey fabric which someone employed by the NHS had once mistaken for tasteful – or maybe there had been a job lot of fabric which was going very cheap. It is clear that Mrs Ivanisovic will not be subjected to these indignities. She will be permitted to expire quietly and discreetly at Broadoaks, in a room full of her own things, with a view of the garden (albeit presently obscured by torrential rain).

I sit for about ten minutes while Mrs Ivanisovic remains oblivious to my presence, listening to her breathing, which I gradually realize is mingled with the soft, slow tick of her clock. The two sounds are complementary, if always out of sync.

Eventually I stand up and pad across the room to where I can put the chocolates down on the sideboard, alongside her collection of framed photographs. The majority of the pictures are of Danny and his parents. There is one of Danny's father as a young man and I note the strong resemblance. They have the same eyes. Dark and deep, full of laughter . . .

Mrs Ivanisovic stirs behind me. Only the slightest of movements, but I am aware of it and turn to find her eyes are open. I return to the bedside, but I don't sit down. She is looking up at me, but in such a way that I'm not sure if she sees me.

'It's Katy,' I say, quietly. 'I've come to see you – like I promised.'

She nods – well, hardly that really, just a tiny movement to show she understands, recognizes who I am.

I don't mention the chocolates. Uncertain what to say, I resume my seat and take hold of her hand. I hardly know the woman, but it doesn't seem presumptuous. In fact it feels like the right thing to do. She welcomes this gesture with a gentle squeezing of my fingers. Her flesh feels clammy. She tries to say something, but the oxygen mask defeats her.

'It's okay,' I say. 'Don't try to talk.'

Irritation flickers in her eyes. There is evidently something she wants to convey to me. She gestures with her free hand, which hovers like a butterfly above the bed covers.

'You want me to bring you something? Press your buzzer for the nurse?'

Her head rolls from side to side – so a definite negative on the nurse then.

I turn to see where she seems to be pointing. 'The photographs?' I ask, wondering if she wants me to bring one or two across for her to see – although Lord knows, she must know every detail of them by heart. It is not the photographs however. I track my way steadily round the room, suggesting one thing after another while she shakes her head. Eventually we end up at one of the drawers in the little sideboard. She wants me to open it. I relinquish her hand reluctantly, fearing more newspaper cuttings – but what she's after is a photo album. It is, after all, my interest in the family pictures which has inspired her. She thinks to entertain me by showing me some more.

I carry the album over to her, resting it on the bed propped up in such a way that we can both see it. I can think of worse ways of passing the afternoon. She doesn't seem interested in the earlier pages (Danny's primary school mug shots, interspersed with summer holiday snaps). There is evidently something further on in the album that she particularly wants me to see. When we get to the right page her hand flaps against the bedclothes. It is obvious which picture she thinks I will be interested in. It's a shot of Danny and me holding hands, looking at each other rather than the camera. Was he really so much taller than me? I had all but forgotten. It's a romantic kind of shot – captured spontaneously just before we turned away from one another to smile for the camera.

She starts to gesture urgently. Makes sounds I can't understand.

'It's Danny and me,' I say, trying to sound pleased.

She makes more noises. Jerks her head. I think I understand.

'Do you want me to take the picture?'

She nods, relaxes. Closes her eyes. The whole thing has been too much effort.

I don't want the photograph, so I make no attempt to remove it. In fact I turn the page, finding myself among some completely different subjects: cliffs and wild flowers, still in those washed-out colours which now define our world of thirty years ago.

Her eyes have opened again. She looks down at the new set of pictures, then back at me. I hurriedly turn back to the page of her choice.

'I don't want to spoil your album,' I say. 'And besides—' an inspirational lie occurs to me – 'I already have a copy of this picture.'

She understands now. Sinks back as if relieved. Closes her eyes again. Poor deluded woman, she doesn't want me to lose my chance of acquiring this sentimental relic of a long-ago love. She imagines that I cherish these memories as she does. She has forgotten her question about my finding someone else – forgotten my answer. She thinks I still carry that same old torch – the beacon of love which was going to transform me into the next Mrs Ivanisovic.

I continue my perusal of the family album. There is little else to occupy me. The rain has stopped, but dense grey clouds are still chasing one another beyond the bare branches of the trees.

After a while Mrs Ivanisovic opens her eyes and gestures that she would like to begin our game of Hunt the Thimble again. She makes tiny birdlike gestures while I do the guessing. 'The sideboard?' 'The window sill?' Until we eventually settle on the drawer of the bedside cabinet.

Unlike the rest of the room, the interior of this

drawer has not been kept tidy. It is a tumble of small personal items, including a crumpled tissue, a lipstick, a fat brown envelope with what look like utility bills inside it. I unpack these various items into my lap; none of them is what she seeks. I delve into the prehistoric layer. It is evidently a repository for mementos she wants to keep close. There is an ancient champagne cork and an old theatre programme. In the back corner I find a small jeweller's box – the sort which might contain cuff links, or a pair of smart earrings. The box is covered in a dark brown fabric, worn thin at the corners. She nods at me.

I balance this box on the corner of the bedside cabinet while I carefully replace the lapful of objects I have accumulated during the search, trying to remember their order of extraction as best I can. She closes her eyes again – whether too weary to keep them open or in resignation at my pedantry I cannot tell. As I finally slide the drawer shut her breathing changes. She is taking longer-drawn-out breaths with a shudder at the end of them. She is definitely sleeping.

I pick up the little brown box – holding it in one hand, while opening it with the other. On top of a cushion of dark blue padding sits Danny's crucifix. It catches the light – gives me an impudent wink. From far away I hear familiar laughter – see his face and hear him call my name.

TWENTY-SIX

While Simon went out to fetch Danny I took the opportunity to run up to the bathroom and remove the towel turban from around my head. I normally combed out my hair straight away, so I had not appreciated what half an hour or so of neglect could achieve. My hair had become a tangle of half-dried frizz, kinked in the places where it had been folded under the towel, as effectively as if I'd used curl papers. The only thing for it was to wet it thoroughly again. I was about to fill the wash basin, when I heard Simon bawling my name from downstairs.

'I'm up here,' I shouted, advancing to the top of the stairs. 'I've got to wash my hair again.'

'Don't be stupid,' Simon yelled. 'You wanted to go to Kington – we're going *now.*'

'I can't,' I protested. 'Look at my hair.'

Simon was standing in the hall with Danny just behind him. Both appeared to be on the edge of losing their tempers.

'Can't you wait a minute or two, while I at least wet it? Just look at it.'

'No,' said Simon. 'Come on. If we're going, we go now.'

I considered ignoring him – but something in his face told me not to push it. I stamped down the stairs, then marched through the hall to the front of the house. Simon stood beside the front door, waiting to lock it behind me. I clambered into the back of the car as usual and the others took their places in the front. As Simon started the car I said, 'We should have told the police.'

Neither of them responded. Simon revved the engine fiercely then slammed it into gear so violently that the car emitted a groan of pain. We swerved on to the lane sharply enough to send me sliding halfway across the seat and back.

'Jesus,' Danny objected. 'Let's get there in one piece, shall we?'

'We should have told them,' I said. 'Sergeant Wotsit and the other one. We should have told them about Trudie.'

'Of course we should,' shouted Simon. 'That was the whole idea of hiding her body – so we could tell the Staffordshire Constabulary all about it at the first opportunity.'

'We could have explained it,' I said. 'We could have told them that Trudie had done it herself. We could have said that we got frightened and thought the best thing was to cover it up – but now we realize that wasn't the right thing. We could have said that Trudie threatened to kill herself and went off on her own – and we all went out after her and were too late to save her . . .' I was babbling by now. Clutching one straw after another.

'Quite the little liar, aren't we?' said Simon.

'You know that wouldn't work,' Danny said more gently.

'We have to tell the truth now,' I said. 'Before it's too late.'

'Are you insane?' Simon cut in again. 'Before it's too late? We've buried her – don't you understand that? It was too late from the minute we moved that body out of the wood. There's no going back now.'

I didn't answer. Tears slid down my cheeks and made damp splotches on the front of my shirt. I knew he was right. Our compact had been forged the night before. There was no going back. We drove on in silence, with Simon taking it at a more reasonable speed. I attempted to work a comb through my hair, but even as I tried to concentrate on this, I was aware of a nauseating sensation as we got nearer to the town. It started as mere butterflies in the stomach, gradually progressing into little knots of fear which moved up through my gut. It was not as if anyone in town knew us: but we had made regular visits to the local shops – invariably accompanied by Trudie. Suppose someone asked where she was – just casually – at the till in the mini-market, or in the greengrocer's. 'Where's your friend today?' We had no answer planned, no story agreed. We were the most amateur criminals in history. We weren't going to get away with this for more than half a day.

Simon found a parking space in the square. 'Wait a minute,' I said, as he raised the handbrake and Danny moved to open the door.

'Now what?' asked Simon.

'We've got to get our story straight: in case anyone asks about Trudie.'

'We can do that later,' said Simon, impatiently.

'No – no, we can't. Suppose someone asks about her, in one of the shops.'

'Why would anyone do that?' asked Danny.

'They just might,' I said, stubbornly. 'You know how Trudie was – noticeable – friendly with everyone. Suppose someone does ask – what are we going to say?'

Danny thought for about half a second. 'Just say she's moved on.'

Simon was opening the door. 'Come on,' he said. 'Let's not waste any more time.' He tipped the driver's seat forward and held the door for me to get out. As I straightened up my eyes momentarily met his. There was something in them that made me go cold. Something darker and more desperate than I had ever encountered.

Without another word, the two of them strode off towards the shops, while I scuttled after them. I wondered whether it might be easier to cope if you had experienced a sudden death before. Simon and Danny had already come into contact with a violent death on the campus where they both lived. Did you become anaesthetized? Did it work like a vaccination – a partial cure because of previous exposure to something similar? But their relationship with the death of Rachel Hewitt had been no more than second-hand. They had actually handled Trudie's body – interred it themselves. A vision of Simon's screwdriver shot into my head from nowhere. With it came a miniature bolt of lightning which used my spine as a conductor. Rachel Hewitt had been strangled. I banished the thought angrily. Trudie's death had been an accident – a horrible accident. What we had subsequently agreed to do, while intrinsically wrong, was also understandable – and the arrival of the police that morning was no more than confirmation that our motives had been justified.

In the mini-market I wandered up and down the aisles, haphazardly collecting various items of grocery. Danny put two bottles of whisky into our basket, muttering that it would ensure we got some sleep. It was impossible to concentrate. There weren't many other customers, but I was convinced that such as there were, were all covertly watching us. My haystack hair didn't help matters and when we got to the till, the middle-aged cashier looked pointedly at our two bottles of spirits.

'Let's not go in the greengrocer's,' I said, when we got outside. 'Trudie always used to chat to the man in there.'

'Don't be silly,' said Danny. 'I'll go in on my own, if you like.'

If this was intended to shame me into the errand, it didn't work. I told him what was wanted and left him to deal with the friendly greengrocer alone. Simon stayed with me on the pavement, affecting interest in the contents of the hardware shop window. There was a newsagent next door and by force of habit I extracted one of the papers from the rack which hung beside the door and began to flick through it. I wasn't looking for anything in particular, just killing time, trying to be unnoticeable. Then my eyes caught the words *Trudie Finch* – a small item on an inside page – no photograph this time.

'Simon, look at this.' I held the paper up so that we could both read it.

. . . Trudie Finch phoned a friend to confirm that she is alive and well . . . hopes are mounting that she will return home soon . . .

'Here – are you going to buy that paper or not?' At the first sound of the shout from inside the shop, I hastily refolded the paper and stuffed it back into the stand. I could easily have bought it, but somehow even appearing to be interested in the paper felt like a guilty proclamation in respect of its contents. The proprietor, clad in a brown overall and flat cap, came bustling to the door and pointedly adjusted the paper. 'Bleedin' hippies,' he said.

'She must have phoned a friend,' I hissed, when we had put a few yards between ourselves and the newsagent.

'When – how?'

'That day in Leominster – the day we bumped into

Josser. I saw her coming out of a phone box. Suppose she told them where she was.'

'She can't have,' said Simon. 'If she had, the police would have been round by now. Or her parents would have come looking for her.'

'There have been pictures of her in the paper,' I said. 'Someone might have recognized her.'

'But they haven't, have they? Not everyone reads the paper from cover to cover, you know.'

'It was only a school photograph,' I said. 'She does look a lot older – out of uniform.'

'Well, there you are. And no one has recognized her. Something would have happened by now if they had.' In spite of his confident words Simon's eyes scanned the street nervously, as if he was expecting a challenge at any time.

'He never said a word,' Danny informed us on his return: but he let his hand brush mine – to let me know he understood my anxiety and was on my side.

'Is that everything?' asked Simon. 'Right – let's get back.'

We were mostly silent on the journey home. When Danny tried to initiate a conversation Simon seemed preoccupied and did not respond. I toyed with the idea of telling Danny what we had seen in the paper, but Simon didn't mention it and I was reluctant to embark on a conversation which might force me to say her name. I was afraid I would choke on it. Even without the name I couldn't shake off the tangible pain whenever I allowed myself to think about her. I tried to concentrate on something else, staring straight in front of me, fixing my attention on the back of Danny's head. A small area of his neck was visible, where his hair had fallen to one side. The skin was pale where the sun didn't normally reach it. A thin line of gold chain threaded neatly across the gap. Another series of thoughts crept up on me unawares. Necks led to strangulation and strangulation led back to Rachel Hewitt – and Trudie. Simon's initials on the screwdriver. Simon's initials on the torch.

I had to stop thinking like this . . . Look out of the window – are those horses in that field? . . . Stop it, stop it right now . . . I clenched my hands hard enough to make the nails bite into my palms. I carried on doing it until the pain drove out everything else. Then I threatened myself that I would do it again and again, unless my thoughts kept themselves under control.

Simon and Danny helped me carry the shopping into the house before they went back to work in the garden. After I had put everything away, I returned to the bathroom to stick my head in the wash basin again. I had dreaded the moment, but it wasn't so bad as I expected. No strange noises assailed me; no unseen watchers brooded at my back. I rubbed my hair dry with the towel, then went into the bedroom to use the hairdryer. After a minute or two I caught myself humming. I stopped immediately. I glanced around, half expecting some signal of disapproval; but the familiar inanimate objects around me exuded indifference.

It had been a brief interlude of forgetfulness. No sooner had I stopped humming and banished the song from my mind, than its place was taken by a line of concerns, which formed up to compete for my attention. There was our story – we had to get our story straight – just in case anyone did come asking for Trudie, wanting to know where she had gone. Then there were her things. We would have to dispose of them somehow. We ought to have buried them with her body – but it was too late to think of that now. There was the seance room – that would have to be put to rights. The library book about murder and mystery would have to be returned.

Finally, hopping up and down at the rear of the line, trying desperately to engage my attention, was the thought of what I was to do about Danny. I tried to ignore it but it pestered at me, refusing to stay quiet and wait its turn. I knew just from the way he looked at me, the way his hand brushed mine, that for Danny nothing between us had changed. In his mind we were on course to spend the rest of our lives together – but for me everything had changed. Irrespective of any-thing else, our relationship was doomed now that we had shared in the disposal of Trudie's corpse. I knew that however many years went by I could never look at him again without experiencing the searing pain of those memories. The only possible road to release lay in severing our connections for ever and trying to forget. I was going to have to break the news gently. But not yet – not yet.

In spite of Simon's anxiety about how long it would take, the layer of sand was in place and had received a final watering before I had our dinner on the table. The meal was not a success. The jacket potatoes were hard in the middle, the chicken wings all bones and no meat, and the packet sweet and sour sauce was too watery. We ate in silence, the food turning to cardboard in our mouths, everything needing to be chewed and chewed, until it was rendered into mushy lumps which had to be washed down our throats with the remains of the sour-tasting beer. No one complained. In fact none of us had anything to say at all. Silence filled the kitchen like poison gas, stealthy and invisible. We ate and breathed it, our nerves inflamed by its toxicity.

After dinner Danny helped clear the table without being asked and Simon joined in. We floundered like zombies, drained and exhausted. When Simon and I collided between the table and the sink we apologized to one another as if we were virtual strangers, adopting the exaggerated courtesy which is normally reserved for the very sick or recently bereaved. When I had finished washing up I slumped back into one of the kitchen chairs. Simon had disappeared somewhere and Danny was putting away the last of the cutlery.

'I can't stay here,' I burst out. 'It's driving me crazy. This whole place is driving me crazy. It's full of her – everywhere I look, there's . . . there's stuff reminding me.'

'It feels bad right now,' said Danny. 'But it will get better.'

'It's not just that,' I said. 'It's not safe here. I don't feel safe.'

'It is safe really,' he said. 'No one knows she was here. No one will suspect anything – and tomorrow, when the guy comes with the concrete—'

'No,' I all but screamed at him. 'Don't talk to me about that. Don't make me think about it.'

Simon chose that moment to reappear and I lapsed into silence. He joined me at the table and we just sat there – a weird artificial situation, in which every movement, each foot shuffled, each clearing of a throat was magnified. Our usual evening routine of inconsequential backchat and drinking games was completely inappropriate – singing was out of the question. Normal life had died with Trudie and emptiness stretched before us.

Danny produced one of the bottles of whisky from the pantry and set it in the centre of the table with three tumblers. We watched as if mesmerized while the golden spirit gurgled into the glasses. Danny pushed one each toward Simon and me, then lifted one himself, holding it up as if about to propose a toast. Simon and I looked at him doubtfully.

'It's the best way,' he said. 'Come on.' He lifted his glass and downed it in one.

I had never tasted whisky before. We generally drank beer or cider, though when in funds or attempting sophistication I might have a vodka and lime, or a brandy and Babycham.

'I don't like the taste,' I said after one exploratory sip.

'Haven't we got anything to put in it?' asked Simon.

'Water,' suggested Danny. 'Or ice – you know – scotch on the rocks.'

'We're out of ice,' I said. (We always were.)

Danny carried my glass across to the sink and topped it up with tap water, the way we would the despised orange squash. It was no improvement.

'You can have mine,' I said.

'Try to drink it,' Danny urged. 'It'll help.'

'No – I don't want to.' I pushed the glass away from me, like a kid refusing its greens.

Danny pushed it back. 'It's an acquired taste,' he said. 'You're not giving yourself a chance to acquire it.'

'What are you, my dad or something? I don't have to drink it if I don't want to.' I was suddenly very tired of being told what to do.

Danny backed off at once. 'Don't get upset. I was only trying to help you get some sleep.'

'I'm tired – I'll sleep without the whisky.'

The first part at least was true. I was exhausted: so sapped of energy that I could scarcely think or speak. The second declaration was merely optimistic. By nine o'clock I could not bear to sit there any longer and asked Danny if he was coming to bed. We left Simon alone in the kitchen.

Danny had been right about the soporific effects of the whisky. After a few mumbled declarations of love he fell asleep, while I lay beside him unable to follow where he had led. My mind had been sluggish while we sat in the kitchen, but now it began to race. I kept going back to the moments in the wood. The images had become confused and my memory had begun to play tricks with the soundtrack. It seemed to me that there was something important that I ought to remember, but when I pursued this memory along the path, the trees turned into criss-cross forks of lightning and I had to turn back. Danny seemed to share my restlessness. His body gave a series of twitches and he muttered something inaudible a couple of times. Eventually his whole body gave a start and he woke up. He lay completely still for a moment, then put out an exploratory hand which connected with my thigh.

I took advantage of his wakefulness to ask: 'You remember when we were in the wood – when Trudie screamed?'

'Of course I do.' He spoke cautiously. Or maybe he was half asleep.

'Where were you?' I asked. 'Were you anywhere near Simon? You'd been right by us a couple of minutes before.'

There was a pause. I could hear him breathing steadily in the darkness. 'I couldn't see anyone,' he said. 'I thought I'd play a joke on her. I was going to creep up on her from behind. Then I got a bit disorientated and went too far. For a minute or two, when she screamed, I couldn't find my way back.'

'Did – did you hear anyone, crashing about on the path?'

'Sweetheart, there were all sorts of noises – people yelling and trying to get to one another. Anyway, let's not go over and over it. Try to forget it. It's over now.'

That was Danny, I thought, always ready to turn the page – and sure enough within a couple of minutes he was asleep again. I tried to emulate his approach. It had been a terrible accident and all the agonizing in the world wouldn't bring Trudie back. I tried to settle myself to sleep, but whether my eyes were open or closed I could still see Trudie. Not the dead Trudie – I couldn't allow that image to come screaming into my head – I saw the oh so alive Trudie, dancing for the rain gods on Hergest Ridge, laughing and singing in the garden. I saw her golden body lying next to mine, in the exact same place where Danny lay now. Beautiful, beautiful Trudie. How could she possibly be dead?

I should have wept for her then, but the tears didn't come – just an increasing sense of hopelessness and with it a raging thirst which I tried to ignore; but as I tossed from side to side I became increasingly desperate for a cool drink. I wished Danny would wake up so that I could send him downstairs on my behalf, but he was dead to the world. He had closed the bedroom door, but when I lifted my head I could see the telltale chink of light in the gap at the bottom which meant the landing was still lit up. I stared at this sliver of light for a long time, telling myself that it would only take a few seconds to run down for a glass of water. Eventually I was so desperate that I slipped out of bed and switched on the lamp: partly in order to locate my dressing gown and partly in the vain hope of accidentally waking Danny. He shifted in his sleep, but nothing more, not even flinching when I opened the door and the light from the landing shone directly into his face.

I closed the bedroom door before tiptoeing to the stairs. The house was still swathed in dusty heat. The floorboards grumbled as I passed over them and each stair creaked on a different note, like a badly tuned instrument. My bare feet made a soft, sticky sound on the hall floor.

'Who's there?' Simon's voice stopped me dead. I hadn't realized he was still in the kitchen. It was too late to turn back now.

'It's me – Katy,' I croaked out the words. The fear

and tension in his voice were more unnerving than the shock of encountering him. He was sitting at the kitchen table exactly where we had left him. He stared at me with bloodshot eyes that seemed to expect someone else.

'I'm thirsty,' I said.

'It's the alcohol,' he said.

I didn't bother to remind him that I hadn't partaken. 'It's supposed to make you sleep.'

'Well, it doesn't,' he said, grimly. 'It just gives you a headache and messes with your mind.'

'Danny's asleep,' I said – not exactly to dispute the point, more for something to say.

'Lucky Danny,' said Simon. Then he folded his arms on the table, put his head on to them and began to cry. I wasn't sure what to do. I'd never seen a man cry before. I filled a glass with water, while trying to decide whether it was better to pretend not to notice. I drank the water at one go and refilled the glass. Simon's shoulders continued to heave. His sobs were faint but audible.

'Is there something I can get you, Si?' I asked nervously.

He raised his head and rubbed a bare forearm across his face. It took him a moment before he said: 'Do you really think what we've done is wrong?'

I was taken aback. To start with, I hadn't expected a direct question, and secondly I was confused by the note of accusation in his voice. There was a long pause. When I realized Simon wasn't going to fill it, I said, 'Of course it was wrong – but Trudie was dead when we found her. Nothing could alter that . . .'

'We were supposed to be her friends,' said Simon. 'But we didn't stop it from happening.' His face looked ashen, the way it had when I first told him the police had arrived. He must be very drunk, I thought.

'We couldn't stop it,' I said, in my best reassuring-a-child voice. 'It was an accident. It wasn't our fault.' In my head I heard myself calling out his name and his answer receding into the distance – then footsteps running back along the path. I told myself not to be an idiot. He was probably thinking cause and effect – that if only we had taken more care not to get separated, she might never have dropped her torch and become fatally entangled in the wires; or maybe he was taking it back a stage further and thinking we should never have gone down to the woods at all. I found myself unexpectedly flaring with anger against Trudie. It wasn't our fault, I thought; it was hers. She shouldn't have gone on ahead like that. None of this would have happened if we'd stayed at the house. It was all Trudie's stupid fault for insisting we go into Bettis Wood after dark in the first place. Trudie and all her nonsense about bloody Murdered Agnes. Now the rest of us were stuck with the guilt and uncertainty, and those terrible images which were never going to go away. 'It's not our fault,' I said, robustly. 'We were in a difficult situation and we had to make a choice.' It was true that I might not have agreed with the choice we had made; but we were stuck with it now.

'A choice.' He echoed my words, adopting a strangely ironical note. 'We made our choice.'

'You should go to bed,' I said. 'Try to get some sleep.'

He gave a hollow laugh. 'I don't think I'll ever sleep again. Not now . . . not after today . . .'

'What's this – a midnight conference?' Danny's voice made us both jump.

'I came down to get a drink – and Simon hasn't been to bed at all.'

Danny regarded us irritably. 'Better go to bed, man,' he said to Simon. 'That concrete guy's due here at half eight.' To me he merely said, 'Come on,' and jerked his head towards the stairs. He was right of course. We had to try to get some sleep.

TWENTY-SEVEN

Every picture tells a story. Here I am, just as the fat-bottomed nurse marches in, sitting at Mrs Ivanisovic's bedside examining her valuables while she sleeps. The nurse's face registers an obvious reaction. We gape at one another – her wondering how to handle a visitor who has apparently turned up at the deathbed to indulge in a bit of pilfering, me trying to find the best words to explain.

I open the case and hold it out for her inspection – that way she can see it isn't a diamond bracelet. 'She signalled for me to get it out,' I say. 'I think she wanted to look at it. It belonged to her son.'

'I didn't know she had a son.' She sounds doubtful.

'He's been dead a long time.'

She glances across at the ranks of framed photographs and light dawns. 'Danny,' she murmurs. 'Of course – she *did* have a son, now you mention it. That's him in the photographs, isn't it?'

'That's right.'

She hands back the box and I snap it shut.

'What happened to him, then? Motorbike accident, was it?'

'Suicide.' My voice has dropped to a whisper. It isn't deliberate.

I can see she is intrigued, her original suspicions subsumed by the possibility of some gossip about a patient's family. Suicide has potential connotations of tragedy and drama above and beyond a mere road accident. She leans across me to check the fit of the oxygen mask, a manoeuvre which brings her large bosom into the space which I had thought to claim as mine. I lean back into my chair, enveloped in an aroma of antiseptic handwash and spring-fresh fabric conditioner.

'How long ago was all this then?' Her accent tends toward the sing-song I associate with Newcastle. It reminds me of Josser.

'1972.'

'By – that is a long while. It must have broke her heart, poor soul.' She nods in my direction, trying to imply that state of mutual understanding which encourages shared confidences – in no hurry to get down to the nitty-gritty of patient care while something so interesting is on the conversational menu. 'Why did he kill himself?'

I glance at Mrs Ivanisovic. She appears to be asleep, but how can one really tell? 'No one knows,' I say. 'At the inquest they hinted that it might have been something to do with his being gay.'

'Oh.' She hesitates. 'Did *she* know he was gay?'

'He wasn't,' I said. 'He had a friend who was, which is why some people might have thought that – but he wasn't gay himself.'

'Aah.' She looks smugly knowing. 'Well, maybe he was but he hadn't come out. Lads didn't in them days. Maybe that's why he killed himself – you know – couldn't face telling folk.'

Normally I just keep quiet. Let people think what they want: but something in her tone grates. How dare she think she has it cracked – she who only heard of Danny's death half a minute ago.

'He wasn't gay,' I say.

'Well, you never know—'

244

'*I* know. I was engaged to be married to him when he died.'

As her face reddens in embarrassment, I feel instantly ashamed of myself. She has taken in my ringless wedding finger, my presence at his mother's bedside, and is mortified by the innocent trampling she has done. Moreover I was not even telling the truth. I was not engaged to Danny, whatever he or his parents may have thought – whatever I may have said to score a cheap point over the fat-bottomed nurse, no such arrangement ever existed between us.

'I'm sorry,' she says, sounding it, 'but I'll have to ask you to wait outside for a couple of minutes while I see to Mrs Ivanisovic.'

I leave the room feeling that it is me who should be sorry. The woman with the pink rock chippings round her neck is just crossing the hall.

'Are you popping out for a breather?' she asks. 'I think it's stopped raining.'

'I'll just wait here, thanks. The nurse is in there at the moment.'

Pink Rocks lingers, nodding sympathetically. 'She's a remarkable old lady, isn't she?'

I opt for safe agreement, uncertain precisely what it is about Mrs I that she is referring to.

'Every day this week, Dr Brownlow has come out from seeing her, saying he doesn't expect her to be with us by morning.' While I stand in the hall, wondering if Dr Brownlow is generally noted for such a cheering line in optimism, Pink Rocks twits on about how some people have this remarkable will to live. Maybe she thinks I can derive some comfort from this – or maybe she secretly suspects that I'm a frustrated beneficiary, wondering how much longer Mrs Ivanisovic is going to lie here in Broadoaks, depleting her estate to the tune of a hundred pounds or so with every passing day. I remember the situation we faced with my own mother – the pressure on hospital beds, the wait for suitable nursing-home places. No doubt some other rich old lady is already waiting somewhere – her name down against Mrs Ivanisovic's place – that nice room with its big bay window, so handy for the garden. Her family may have been told that a room will shortly be available. They will be longing for the vacancy to occur – no one actually admitting that this entails the hope of another's swift demise.

Does the nurse think about this as she ministers to her dying patient – wondering who will be the next occupant? Or maybe she is pondering another contradiction – that of the healthy young son who couldn't wait to leave life behind, set against the ancient mother who is holding on to it so tenaciously.

So many people all waiting for one old lady to die. A life flickering to its close. A faltering flame that could be snuffed out in an instant.

When I am allowed to return, I find Mrs Ivanisovic is awake. Her eyes follow my progress from the door to the bedside chair. I notice she is propped a fraction more upright and has a writing pad and pen to hand on the bed. She must have signalled for the nurse to get them out. She appears more alert – I wonder if the nurse has administered something.

'You're looking a little better,' I say.

She raises her eyebrows – a little better, a little worse, what does it matter? She applies pen to pad. The pad has been folded open at a clean page and the pen top has been taken off, so she is free to start writing, but when she begins her efforts are feeble. She takes an age to produce a single word: *Why.* The letters are oversized and uneven. She doesn't bother with a question mark.

'I can't tell you,' I say, shaking my head, affecting to

be at a loss, while employing a version of the double speak with which children were taught to respond in wartime. It is a piece of evasion which has amused me ever since I first read about it – a carefully engineered, typically British loophole. I think about this as Mrs Ivanisovic struggles to manipulate her pen. How during the war, when signposts were taken down to foil the expected invasion, children were instructed to respond to enquiries from strangers seeking directions with the cosy middle class expression 'I cannot say' – thus avoiding the words 'I don't know', which would have been a lie. Thus was the enemy to be thwarted without anyone breaching the commandments.

Mrs Ivanisovic is not going to be put off so easily. She is no mere German paratrooper disguised as a nun; Mrs Ivanisovic is a remarkable woman – hasn't Pink Rocks said so? She is determined not to give up her hold on life until she has winkled out the truth. Now she has completed her next effort and holds up the pad. The letters weave across the page; some look as if they are trying to clamber over others in a general rush for the edge of the paper. *Did you quarrel.*

'Of course we quarrelled sometimes.'

She jabs her pen at the page, her frustration boiling over.

'Please, Mrs Ivanisovic. I have told you everything I can tell you. If you are asking me whether Danny killed himself because we quarrelled, then I can assure you that wasn't the case. If something like that happened, don't you think I would have said so at the inquest?'

She leans back against the pillows. The whisper of her breathing pulses gently across the room, mingled with the soft slow tick of the bedside clock. Another shower patters against the window panes. All these years she has been pondering the question, wondering how it could possibly have come about that her clever, witty, talented son – a handsome young man on the brink of a successful life, last seen in an ebullient mood, happy and in love – could have taken his own life, without a word of explanation or a note of farewell. I reassure myself that she has no answers. Her theories rely on no more than wild guesswork: she imagines that we quarrelled and Danny took his life – in a misguided fit of pique after a lovers' tiff. Or can she do better than this?

I notice that my fingers are hurting. My hands have been resting in my lap and without realizing it I have been clenching my fingers, the nails digging into my palms. I imagine her voice, asking him question after question. 'Was it something to do with Katy? Was it something to do with Trudie?' Some idiosyncrasy in the Broadoaks air conditioning sends a chilly draught across the back of my neck.

She leans forward and works the pen again. It threatens to escape her fingers, wobbles and tracks across the page, as if tempted to express ideas of its own. I watch as she forms the letters, coaxing the pen into the track of an S, then an I. The M is pitiful, shambolic.

'Simon?' I ask.

She nods. I pause, trying to recall her words during my last visit. How some fellow student of Danny's had visited, but been shown the door. The nurse has already brought Josser unbidden into my mind. Was it he who intruded upon the Ivanisovics? It would be just like Josser to imagine there could be capital to be made from feigning close acquaintance with Simon and Danny. When that failed he might have fallen back on innuendo. Before the inquest I hadn't known that Simon's homosexuality was a secret shared by some of his peers at university. I suppose I imagined them all as slow on the uptake as I had been myself.

'It was true what people said about Simon.' I proceed carefully. I don't want to distress her. 'And also – and also that he loved Danny – but he loved him as a friend – not in a sexual way.'

I try to read her expression from what little I can see of her face. She affords me the movement which passes for a nod. She understands and more importantly believes what I am saying. I see that she is drifting again. Her hands slip away from the writing implements, so I remove them. Watch the rain making patterns on the window. After a while the nurse enters to ask if I would like some tea. When I say I would, she nods and vanishes, neither of us alluding to anything which has passed between us previously. She returns with a tray containing not only the necessary accoutrements to provide several cups of tea, but also a plate containing four triangles of egg and cress sandwich and a slice of Madeira cake, all neatly arranged under a sheet of clingfilm.

'How about Mrs Ivanisovic?' I ask.

'I'm sure she won't want anything.'

I survey this unexpected bounty, remembering just in time to say, 'Thank you very much.'

Once she's gone, I reach into my bag in search of a foil of paracetamol tablets. It's rather close in Mrs Ivanisovic's room and I feel a touch headachy. Time was when you could buy a decent-size bottle of painkillers to meet your needs through the whole winter, but now the nanny state will barely allow you a sufficient quantity to see you through a dose of flu. I press the pills upwards until they break through the foil, extracting them slowly and placing them on the bedside table, not taking my eyes off the figure in the bed. Does she know something or doesn't she? How can I be sure? Mrs Ivanisovic makes a small sound – nothing so overt that it could qualify as a snore. Everything about her is fading: the flame which once burned so brightly has grown dim. In my mind's eye I imagine a column of smoke rising from a snuffed-out candle. I realize that I've forgotten what I was doing – continued to absentmindedly liberate the tablets from their packaging until a small group of them has accumulated on the bedside table.

I take two of the paracetamol with my first cup of tea. The second cup accompanies the sandwich and a third helps wash down the cake. Soon after I've finished, a minion I haven't seen before – a pretty girl with auburn hair and a mint green overall – appears to collect the tray. I am only just quick enough to palm the little collection of white tablets, which has been sitting all this time alongside Mrs I's plastic dispenser of sweeteners.

'When you want another cup of tea or anything, you just ring the bell,' the girl says.

It is evidently assumed that I am going to be here for some time.

TWENTY-EIGHT

The 'concrete guy', as Danny called him, showed up promptly at half past eight. I was halfway downstairs when I heard his pick-up arrive, but Simon got to the door ahead of me. I had only expected one workman, but the concrete guy was accompanied by a youth who was perhaps a couple of years younger than myself, and a little terrier dog which ran across to nose about under the lilac. The older man had thinning auburn hair, a check shirt, and trousers whose original colour was now indeterminate, being so spattered with the skimmings of jobs long past. His skin had been reddened by years of exposure to the sun and was dotted with a thousand pale brown freckles. His companion wore workman's jeans and a Rod Stewart T-shirt, so well washed that its lettering had faded to a ghostly grey. They appeared to be perfectly ordinary and could not possibly have imagined the dread with which we shuffled out to greet them, exhibiting all the unwillingness of bad boys sent to the headmaster for the cane. Nobody managed to smile.

It was evident that the concrete guy (who Simon introduced as Vic) mistrusted us on sight, because his opening words included the phrase 'cash up front'. Simon attempted to protest that he understood the arrangement was cash on completion, but once it became apparent that Vic had no intention of unloading his cement mixer until our money was safely in his pocket, Simon backed down and went inside to fetch the cash, leaving the rest of us to stand awkwardly alongside the pick-up. There was no disguising the exchange of satisfied looks which passed between Vic and his sidekick. Local Builders 1, Suspicious-Looking Hippies nil.

Vic pointedly counted the cash before carefully stowing it in the back pocket of his trousers. While this was going on I glanced from Danny to Simon and back again. We would have to be very careful – palpable tension might make the builders suspicious.

'Right then,' said Vic. 'Let's see the job, shall we?'

Simon led the way round the side of the house and across the garden to the pond. While we were still ten yards away Danny gave a shout and began to run. We had all in the same instant seen the little dog shoot ahead and dive into the hole. Sand flew upwards while Danny charged headlong to the rescue and Vic bellowed, 'Gerrout of it, yer bugger.' At the sound of Danny's approach and his master's voice the dog – clearly thinking better of it – emerged and trotted away.

'Thinks 'e's gonna find a bone,' the youth said cheerfully.

I couldn't bring myself to look at Danny, fearing to read in his expression how much the terrier had un-covered. Danny was about to hop down into the hole, but he was checked by Vic, who said, 'Don't worry, we'll soon smooth it out again.' By this time we had all reached the pond and it was too late to do anything anyway. I glanced down at the spot where the wretched dog had been burrowing, but the hole he had made was hidden behind the little pile of sand he had dug out of it. Out of the corner of my eye I saw Simon edging around the pond in order to get a better view. I had a desperate urge to sit down. My ears buzzed and spots danced in front of my eyes. This was it. We were going to be found out – right here, right now.

Simon startled us all by jumping into the sandy hollow and kicking the sand back into place with his boot. 'Bloody dog,' he said. 'We spent ages yesterday, getting it perfectly smooth.'

I saw Vic give him a funny look – probably wondering why Simon was getting so het up over nothing. Danny strolled round to offer Simon a hand back up. I saw him say something quietly and Simon gave a half-nod. Vic didn't appear to notice. He began to survey the job, taking an agonizing length of time to peer into the sand-lined hole from all directions, walking slowly round the outside, humming and hawing and chuntering about the angle of the sides and whether they were too steep to take the mix. Just when I began to be afraid he was going to say it couldn't be done, he jumped into the hole, landing heavily on a spot immediately above Trudie's head. We watched in horror as he began stamping about, leaving his great boot prints all over Simon's smoothed-out sand. I imagined the soil compressing into Trudie's features. It was all too much. I charged headlong across the grass and vomited into the rose bed.

Danny was beside me in a moment, holding my shoulders, uttering words of comfort. 'Come inside,' he said. 'Come on . . .'

I wiped my mouth on the back of my hand, tried to calm myself. I was shaking violently. As if from a long way off I heard Vic ask, 'What's wrong with her then?' and Simon's voice, discreetly lowered – presumably issuing some platitude about a tummy upset.

'I'll go in,' I said. 'You'd better stay out here with Simon.'

Danny only paused to consider this for a moment before nodding. 'You're right,' he said.

I stumbled off in the direction of the kitchen, feeling like a coward and a traitor. Once inside I stood trembling beside the sink, imagining what might happen if the blasted dog jumped into the hole again or Vic took it into his head to start poking about or scraping away some of the sand; but after what seemed like hours I heard the unmistakable monotonous rumble of the concrete mixer. By the time I felt able to return, having washed my face and changed my T-shirt, work was well under way.

'Better?' asked Danny and I nodded, miserably aware of a lingering taste of vomit, which matched the sickness in my heart.

The concrete mixer had been set up close to the pond, where it stood tumbling its contents a few feet from where Vic was at work, kneeling on a big board in the bottom of the pond, using a trowel and flat to apply a smooth layer of concrete like a master chef icing a giant inverted birthday cake.

Not wishing to leave Vic and his mate unsupervised, Simon and Danny had offered to help, affecting a willingness to learn by their involvement. Vic accepted this readily. He evidently liked the idea of having this expanded workforce at his disposal and when I arrived he found a role for me too – I was to act as tea lady, keeping the menfolk continuously supplied.

In truth there was only a limited amount of fetching and carrying for the labourers to do, so Simon, Danny and Gordon (as the youth turned out to be called) were left for long periods with nothing to do but stand about, watching Vic at work. Gordon was a garrulous lad, blissfully oblivious to the level of indifference his observations inspired in us. He tried football, then pop music, and when those lines of conversation failed he diverted to television, but we were not fans of *The Fenn Street Gang* and hadn't seen

Top of the Pops in weeks. His attitude toward us was a mixture of curiosity and condescension. In common with many of those who entered the workforce in their mid-teens, he viewed university students as work-shy parasites, who enjoyed long holidays at the expense of the working classes 'and half of them not doing anything useful after – I mean it's all right if you're studying to be a doctor . . .' Yet at the same time we represented a form of glamorous independence, living out here all summer, not having to keep regular hours and answerable to no one – probably getting up to all kinds of wildness – orgies and drugs, like what was reported in the *Sun.*

We all instinctively understood the need to humour Gordon. He was incurably chatty and sure to tell his mates about the job he had worked on at some funny old place inhabited by a bunch of hippies. Our best hope was to appear uninteresting – because it was soon clear that Gordon assumed all manner of excitement might be available. 'Bet you have some great parties up here,' he said, and '''Ave a lot of friends down, do you, at the weekends?' To these and other enquiries, we responded with a negative. We just worked in the garden and kept the house tidy – dull as ditchwater, that was us.

It was from Vic, however, that the most alarming question of the morning came. He was kneeling on a board in the pond, smoothing concrete across its curving side – the angle of which had not after all proved too steep for the mix to be applied. 'Where's that Trudie, then?' he asked.

There was a horrified silence. Vic was concentrating on what he was doing and didn't see our faces. 'I suppose she's still in bed, is she?'

I stifled my Tourette's. Simon couldn't take his eyes off the place where Vic was kneeling. Danny recovered first. 'She's not here any more,' he said. 'She's moved on.'

255

Nothing more was said on the subject just then, but while Gordon took off on another digression into the world of Slade and T. Rex, I began to speculate frantically about Vic's question. How on earth? Then I remembered that Trudie had accompanied Simon into town, the day he embarked on his quest for a helpful builder. She had evidently introduced herself to Vic – and probably to every other builder they had called on. And they would hardly have forgotten her – it was not every day a Trudie showed up in your yard. It was only a matter of time, that was all. I half wished Sergeant Mathieson would walk around the corner of the house and arrest us there and then, just to get it over with. Simon was standing in front of me and I noticed that, like mine, his T-shirt was soaked in sweat.

'Now then, young lady,' Vic interrupted Gordon's latest monologue – spoke right across him in fact. 'How about another cup of tea?'

I bristled. No one except my father called me young lady – and he only did it because he knew how much I hated it. I swallowed my resentment – on the being patronised front, the score now stood at approximately Local Builders 30, Hippies nil, but we dared not stop humouring them.

'Right ho,' I said.

Gordon went to stand by the concrete mixer, slightly apart from the others. When I approached to get his cup he gave me a knowing wink and said: 'Have to get rid of her, did you?'

'What do you mean?'

'That Trudie – causing trouble, was she – between you and the other lads?'

'No.' I went for indignant, but didn't quite manage it. Instead my voice emerged in a cruel parody of Minnie Mouse. 'We didn't – haven't got rid of her.'

'I thought he said she'd gone.'

256

'She has – but she was only staying with us for a while.'

'Where's she gone then?'

I wasn't prepared for this. It wasn't that he was suspicious – he was just making idle conversation: but we still hadn't worked out exactly what to tell people, which left a real risk that I might pluck something out of the air, only to have Danny or Simon contradict it later – and that *would* make him suspicious. I let the cup I was holding slip out of my fingers. It fell on the grass and didn't break, but it was enough to divert his attention and enable me to make my escape.

When I brought out a fresh brew of tea Gordon hung back until everyone else had taken a cup from the tray, then gestured me to one side, a little way from the others. I didn't like the look of this but I couldn't see any way out, so I followed him a few steps towards the edge of the lawn, as if we had discovered something of mutual interest under a clematis-draped arch.

'You're in trouble, aren't you?' he said, keeping his voice low, eyeing the others to see if they were watching us.

The idea that he must know about Trudie lurched crazily into my head. I couldn't see how – but somehow he must have found out. Maybe he'd been hiding in the woods that night – or detected something amiss with the base of the pool. Irrational as drunks, these thoughts weaved around my mind while he awaited my answer. When none was forthcoming, he said, 'It's all right. I won't say nothing to Vic.' When he lowered his voice the local burr intensified – Trudie would have called him 'a country boy' or 'a local yokel'.

'Nothing about what?' I stuttered.

'About you bein' pregnant. I know the signs, see – sick in the morning and jumpy as a cat. My sister got herself into trouble last year. I can get the address of this clinic off her, if you want.'

257

Only intense indignation prevented me from laughing out loud. 'I am not pregnant,' I said, haughtily. I stalked back to the house in a fine state of high dudgeon. Once in the kitchen I began to laugh. It came out in a gush, like water released by the collapse of a dam. I had to sit down before I buckled under its weight, laughing until it turned into sobs which hurt my throat and wrenched my chest.

The noise of the cement mixer ground on all through the day. My head became so full of it that every turn it took seemed to slice painfully into my brain. The outside temperature had risen to baking point again, weaving a blanket of heat across everything like a deadweight. There had been several thunderstorms already and I guessed we were in for another one. My head started to throb in unison with the mixer, but when I sought refuge in the kitchen the sound intruded even there. We kept the transistor radio on one of the kitchen shelves and in a desperate attempt to blot out the sound of the machine I reached up and turned the lower of the two dials. The radio came to life with a loud crackle of complaint, followed by Johnnie Walker's voice talking about a postcard he had received from some holidaying listeners who hailed from Manchester: a welcome reminder that somewhere in the world people were focusing on normal cheerful things, instead of secrets and death.

'And now,' said Johnnie, 'we have Anne Murray singing 'Danny's Song'.

I waited by the radio intrigued. I hadn't realized there was a song for Danny. An instant later I almost broke the knob in my haste to turn it off. I hadn't known the title of *that* particular number was 'Danny's Song'. It was the song Trudie and Danny had sung as a duet, that first afternoon on the beach. The first song they ever sang together. A terrible vista yawned ahead of me – of a world in which everything led back to just one thing.

Now that I had silenced the radio, the cement mixer seemed if anything louder than before. I remembered that we had a bottle of soluble aspirin somewhere: Trudie had bought it a couple of weeks ago, somewhat annoyed that she had to buy the larger size because the little chemist had run out of bottles of fifty. I hunted about until I found it, unscrewed the cap and prised the lump of cotton wool out of the neck. When I tipped the bottle half a dozen tablets tumbled into my palm before I could stop them and I had to feed all but two back in. These I dissolved in a glass of water, gently agitating it to speed up the process. They were all but gone when Danny popped his head round the door.

'You okay?' he asked. 'I came to tell you that the pond's finished.'

'Why is that bloody machine still going then?'

'He's cleaning it out. They do it with stones.'

No wonder it sounded noisier than ever. Danny went back to join them. After a while the machine stopped. There was a longish period of quiet before I heard the engine of the departing pick-up. It sounded a long way off, although it was really only down the hall and just the other side of the front door. As the sound faded into the distance I experienced a curious sense of desolation. I had not liked Gordon and Vic, but their departure left me feeling stranded. They had their truck to take them away, back to that other world of normal life, where normal people did normal things, but there was no escape for me.

It's the heat, I told myself. It's so oppressive.

I went outside to find the guys. They were standing beside the pond.

'He says we can fill it with water tomorrow,' said Simon, as much to himself as to us.

'It's going to take a lot of filling,' said Danny. 'How long do you reckon it'll take, Si?'

I noticed the way Danny sounded almost cheerful. The sight of the finished pond temporarily lifted my spirits too. After all, the chances of discovery had just been radically reduced in our favour. By contrast Simon's voice was completely flat. 'Ages,' he said. 'Maybe all day.'

'Could be,' Danny agreed. 'How are you feeling?' he asked me.

'A bit better – specially now they've gone.'

'If you don't feel up to making our dinner, I could rustle something up.'

I was on the point of accepting but then I noticed how tired he looked. Dark curls of hair were sticking to his forehead. His clothes were pale with dust from the sacks of sand and cement. 'I'm much better,' I said quickly. 'I'll be all right.'

'Great,' he said. He put his arm around my waist as we walked back towards the house. 'It's all over now, babe,' he whispered into my hair. I wished I could believe him, but I knew he was wrong. It was too hot for displays of physical affection and I disengaged myself as soon as I was decently able.

After we had eaten we sat outside, well away from the newly completed pond. It was obvious that a storm was coming – the sky had faded into shades of mauve and grey and, although we saw no lightning, every so often a prolonged rumble of thunder reached us from far away in the Welsh mountains, sometimes followed by a breeze which rushed through the garden, leaving the trees and bushes whispering nervously among themselves.

Danny had discovered some lemonade at the back of the pantry, which he used to dilute my whisky. I drank quite fast. It was something to do with my hands. Our desperate attempts at conversation were interspersed with lengthy silences. It was as if we had already said everything there was to say to one another – or else that everything left was unsayable. Several times I caught Simon looking at me speculatively, but each time our eyes met he looked away. It was starting to spook me. When Danny went inside to the bathroom, I could stand it no longer. 'Stop staring at me, will you? You're giving me the creeps.'

My shrill protest seemed to annoy him. He fixed me with an unremitting stare. 'You're crazy about Danny, aren't you? I wonder how far you would really go for him. What's your limit, Katy?'

'I don't know what you mean,' I said. There was a wobble in my voice and I edged sideways across the grass, putting an extra couple of feet between us. Rachel Hewitt had been crazy about Danny and look what happened to her. She had been stabbed with Simon's screwdriver – no – wait – that wasn't right – she had been strangled – with Trudie's scarf. I stared into the shrubbery, not wanting to look directly at Simon but conscious that he was still watching me.

Danny flopped down beside us. 'It reckon it must still be over twenty degrees in there,' he said.

I heard him without comprehension. I stole another quick look at Simon, but he was dismantling a daisy he had plucked out of the lawn: picking it apart petal by petal, with ugly ragged nails. From nowhere I remembered how perfectly shaped his nails had been at the beginning of the summer, before they were ruined by the digging. What had Simon been saying a minute or two ago – had he in fact been saying anything at all?

The storm advanced slowly until the thunder was menacing us from close at hand, rolling up the slope from Bettis Wood, challenging us to flinch before it. Although we had been monitoring its approach the first raindrops took us by surprise. We heard them before we felt them, huge drops which had darkened the paving stones of the terrace before we managed to scramble up and dash inside. I weaved unsteadily into the kitchen, banging my arm on the door jamb and grabbing the edge of the table for support. You're drunk, I thought. Madly, disgustingly drunk. The notion was oddly pleasing.

'Phew,' exclaimed Danny. 'The way that rain's pelting down, we won't need to use the hose pipe to fill the pond tomorrow.'

A barrage of thunder drowned Simon's reply. I instinctively put my hands over my ears; as I did so I felt the house vibrate though the soles of my feet.

'I've never known a place like this for storms,' I shouted, my words emerging unnaturally loud in a lull between the thunderclaps. Another prolonged burst of noise – like giants moving their furniture in a flat directly overhead – precluded any reply. For a moment or two the storm was directly above us, then the rain ceased as abruptly as it had begun. The thunder diminished, almost as if it had lost interest in the game. It was as hot as ever – the house was still airless – and outside the evidence of the rain was already evaporating.

I looked across at Simon. His face wore a desperate expression. 'God, this is an awful place,' he burst out.

'We've had worse storms,' I began. 'The night of the seance—'

'Shut up,' Simon shouted. 'Just shut up about that, okay?'

'We've got to clear that up,' I said stubbornly. A combination of Dutch courage and Danny at my side meant that I wasn't about to back down. 'There's still candles lying around – and Trudie's stuff is all over that bedroom. Someone's got to get rid of it.'

Simon grabbed the nearest chair and flung it across the kitchen. 'Shut up about it,' he yelled.

I cowered towards Danny, still not quite giving in. 'I'm only saying it's got to be done.'

Danny gave my arm a squeeze. 'Just leave it for now,' he said. He crossed the kitchen to where the chair lay on its back against the twin tub, calmly lifted it and returned it to its original position by the table, before saying, 'Come on, Si, don't let things get to you. You know Katy only means for the best. We're all on the same side here.'

'Are we?' Simon continued to stare at us, like a creature at bay who thinks an attack may be imminent. I watched him nervously, wondering what he might do next, but Danny evidently entertained no fears. He draped his arm around Simon's shoulders, saying, 'Come on, mate. Let's sit down and have another drink. The way to get through this is not to think about it.'

Simon allowed himself to be steered into a seat at the table. When he spoke again his voice was much steadier. 'Well, I have been thinking. I've been thinking about a certain screwdriver.'

I shivered as if someone had laid its cold metal stem against my bare back. The others didn't notice.

'You managed to explain about the screwdriver. You've got nothing to worry about there – nothing at all.' Danny spoke over his shoulder as he opened the pantry door and reached out the lemonade bottle. He brought it across to the table, saying, 'Come on. Let's have a nightcap.'

Simon didn't reply immediately. When he did speak, Danny was banging about in one of the cupboards looking for something else, so he didn't hear as Simon said to no one in particular, 'Sometimes people can't even see what's under their own noses.'

263

'I don't want another drink,' I said to Danny. 'Let's go to bed.' I wanted to get away from Simon. I didn't like the way his eyes kept flickering from me to Danny and back again.

Danny acquiesced without further discussion and we went upstairs together, leaving Simon alone at the kitchen table. Danny wished him goodnight but Simon had withdrawn into himself, morose and silent. Once we were in bed Danny began to make the inevitable advances, but he desisted as soon as I said I didn't feel like it.

'Sorry. I forgot you haven't been feeling well.' He rolled away from me and lay on his back, with one arm crooked under his head.

'Danny,' I said. 'What was it that Josser found out about Simon?'

'What?'

'Josser – you said he found out something about Simon – what was it?'

'Whatever made you think about Josser? Forget about him. He won't bother us again.'

There was a short silence. He hadn't denied that it was Simon about whom Josser had some kind of intelligence. I wanted to ask whether it was only that Simon was a homosexual, but I was afraid Danny might ask how I knew and I didn't want to go into that just then.

While I was still hesitating Danny spoke again. 'I was thinking,' he said, 'that maybe we should bring our wedding plans forward a bit.'

With the light turned out he was no more than a series of shapes in the darkness. He spoke so casually that without seeing his face I couldn't be sure whether or not this was a joke. I decided it must be.

'What wedding plans?' I gave a half-hearted laugh. 'We don't have any wedding plans.'

'Then let's make some.'

264

'Just like that?'

'Just like that.'

'But we've never even talked about getting married. I mean . . .' I was still uncertain whether he was kidding or not, so I carried on playing it for laughs. 'I haven't picked out a dress or anything.'

'That's just a detail,' he said and in that moment I knew from his voice that it wasn't a joke. 'You can do that once we've set a date. Let's make it soon, Katy. There's nothing to stand in our way.' His voice had taken on an urgency which unnerved me.

'My parents,' I said quickly – for once thinking how useful they were. 'My parents will say I'm too young.' And it's true, I thought frantically, I am too young. I had hardly begun to shake off the shackles they had imposed and now somewhere not very far in the distance I could hear the clang of the matrimonial prison gates.

'Who cares? You're over eighteen. You're mine, Katy. There's nothing to stand in our way – nothing to come between us. Let's seal it – make it official. We'll get married in church, the full works. How about it?'

Somehow I knew it was the church wedding he was soliciting my agreement for – not the marriage itself, which was apparently all decided. This wasn't the moment to decline a proposal, any more than it was the time to make one. It was altogether too bizarre, too unbelievable, lying there in the dark unable to see each other's faces. Besides which I didn't want to instigate any kind of row with Danny just then. Simon's behaviour was becoming dangerously weird: I needed to keep Danny onside as an ally.

'We can't talk about this now.' I tried to keep my voice from betraying all that was going on in my mind. 'We're both far too tired. Let's just sleep on it. Come on, kiss me goodnight.'

TWENTY-NINE

I slept late the next morning and when I awoke it was with a gradual realization that I had sole occupancy of the bed. It was the first decent sleep I'd had for several days and I celebrated with a luxuriant stretch encompassing every limb of my body. This blissful moment was cut short as I turned my head and caught sight of an alien object on the pillow, just inches from my face. I jerked into a sitting position, but my panic subsided as abruptly as it had begun. It was a white rose from the garden. The tribute had been laid on a sheet torn from a shorthand notepad, on which Danny had scrawled *For my one True Love*. There was a trio of kisses underneath the writing.

I sat up in bed with my knees hunched up to my chin: what would once have seemed the ultimate romantic gesture was now a scary demonstration of obsessive intensity. Our conversation the night before had brought back the memory of Mrs Ivanisovic's visit – all but forgotten in what had taken place soon afterwards. This business about us getting married was no mere whim of the moment, hatched as an antidote to the nightmare in which we currently found ourselves. It was a long-term plan, which he had already discussed with his parents. And the longer I let the fantasy engagement go on, the harder it would be to break it off.

Then again I was reliant on Danny as my only ally against Simon. Although I was reluctant to concede it,

266

Simon's increasingly erratic behaviour was starting to really scare me. Maybe I didn't have to disabuse Danny of the marriage thing just yet. It surely wouldn't take him too long to see for himself that our relationship had been blighted for ever by what had happened in the past few days. Given time he would view things in a more rational light. Time and distance would help put everything into its true perspective. None of us could possibly think straight while we were trapped in a pressure cooker.

As I waded through my fog of anxieties a dual imperative emerged: I had to get away from this house with all its terrible associations and I had to escape from the frightening certainty of Danny's love. If the solution was to get away as soon as possible, there remained an obvious problem – where could I go? Not back home, because my parents thought I was with Cecile's family – there were far too many awkward questions to answer there – and the situation would be compounded by the continuing arrival of cheery letters, telling them how much I was enjoying myself in France. One possible option was to actually go to France. I had the address. I spoke the language – well enough to buy a train ticket at least – and Cecile had assured me of a welcome. The flaw in this plan was financial. I had started the summer with very little money and I'd already spent most of it. This wouldn't be a problem once I got to Cecile's grandfather's farm, where I could earn some cash picking fruit. I could get my fare home without any trouble, if only I could get out there in the first place.

Then I remembered Trudie's money. Trudie had at least one hundred pounds stashed somewhere in the house. Easily enough to cover my escape to France. It felt uncomfortably like stealing, but on the other hand the money was no use to Trudie any more. Strictly speaking it belonged to her next of kin, but they weren't ever going to see it, so why shouldn't I put it to good use? I decided that if any one of us was to have the money, Trudie would prefer it to be me. However, as this was not a point I cared to debate with the others, I also decided it would be best not to remind them of its existence.

In the quiet of my bedroom, I began to work out a possible route. I could get Simon to run me to the station in Leominster from where I knew I could get a train to Newport. London-bound trains ran through Newport, and once I got to London it ought to be easy enough to get a connection to the Channel ports. Outside the window a blackbird began to sing loudly – he seemed to be cheering me on.

Before I left I would have to make sure that everything which might incriminate us had been properly taken care of. Danny could be awfully cavalier at times and Simon's reliability was definitely questionable. Rather than trust them to look after things, I would offer to sort out Trudie's bedroom myself – an undertaking which would afford me the opportunity to locate the hundred pounds. I would make a bonfire of her things, wash the bedding and thoroughly clean the room. I knew I could not safely leave until every vestige of her presence was gone.

I found the prospect of positive action comforting. I went into the bathroom and ran the bath tap, holding my hand under the flow to test the temperature. It was icy. No one had thought to switch on the immersion heater. I decided that if they could handle cold baths at public school, then so could I. I ran a few inches of water into the bath and stepped in. Hell's teeth, the upper classes must be tough! I knelt down cautiously – sitting seemed out of the question – and began to soap my goosey flesh, while my nipples stood out in horrified protest. Perhaps cold baths were only used as a punishment. If so then it was appropriate that I should take one, in penance for the wrongs I had already shared in and the additional sins I was about to commit.

Vigorous rubbing with my towel restored the circulation. I dressed swiftly, not forgetting to fill the tooth glass with water and stand Danny's rose in it on the dressing table. No point in provocatively leaving it to die.

When I got downstairs they were both sitting at the kitchen table. One look at Simon was enough to suggest that he had barely slept at all. His jaw was covered in a line of pale stubble and he was wearing the same clothes he had worn the day before. When I walked behind his chair I caught the stale odour of the unwashed.

Danny was opposite him, eating toast and jam. I pecked my lips against the top of his head in passing. 'Hi,' I said. 'Thanks for the flower.'

'Do you happen to know what the date is?' asked Danny.

I didn't. We hadn't got a calendar and hardly ever bought a newspaper. It was difficult enough to keep track of what *day* it was, never mind the date. Puzzled by the question, I racked my brains for any significant date that I had forgotten – a birthday, or anniversary of some kind. 'I don't,' I said. 'Why?'

'It's just this letter came for Simon.' Danny waved an explanatory hand towards the table, where an envelope lay among a clutter of used crocks, garden twine and the shorthand notepad which Danny had used for his love letter. The envelope had been slit across the top, its contents removed, read, then roughly restored. Its arrival was a singular event. Simon's uncle's post had been diverted and none of us ever received any letters. It was the first time the postman had called since our arrival.

'It's from Uncle Arthur,' said Simon. 'He's coming back earlier than planned. On the ninth, according to this letter.'

I took this in for a moment before saying, 'That can't be very far off.'

'It's ages,' said Danny. 'That yoghurt we threw out the other day was dated something in July.'

'Which doesn't mean a whole lot,' said Simon.

'Does that mean we're going to have to leave here?' I asked, a plan fomenting in my mind.

'Don't worry,' said Danny. 'You can stay at mine. Your parents needn't find out.'

'They might,' I said. 'I might bump into them.'

'Unlikely,' he said. 'We live right on the other side of the city.'

I decided not to pursue the point just yet.

'I'm going to turn the water on,' said Simon. 'It's going to take hours to fill the pond.'

I decided it was time to seize my opportunity. 'I know no one likes to think about this,' I said carefully, 'but if Simon's uncle is coming back, it's even more important to get rid of all Trudie's things.' When neither of them replied, I continued: 'I'm willing to collect them all together – make sure we don't miss anything. Then I think we ought to burn it all.'

'That seems like the best thing,' said Danny.

Simon was silent.

'There's the room where we had the seance as well. I could tidy that up too if you like – but I'd need some help, moving the furniture back.'

'No problem,' said Danny. 'We can do that, can't we, Si?'

Simon came out of his trance to make a grudging assent.

Danny regarded me anxiously. 'Are you sure you can handle doing Trudie's things on your own?'

'I can manage,' I said. 'It's better if I do it – girls' stuff and everything.'

Danny gave me a hug – a physical seal of approval on my assumed bravery and selflessness.

'I'll go up now,' I said. 'I may as well get started.'

I all but ran up the stairs, only hesitating when I stood at the bedroom door. I took a deep breath before I opened it. Considering Trudie brought so little luggage with her, she had managed to spread her belongings pretty comprehensively around the room. I stood just inside the door, with my hand on the knob. On the one hand I cavilled at actually shutting myself in the room, but on the other I didn't want to be observed in the act of pocketing Trudie's nest egg – the boys were safely occupied at the moment, but there was no saying how long they would stay outside. I compromised by leaving the door open a crack – not enough for anyone to see what I was doing if they happened to pass by.

The sooner I got it over with, the sooner I could get away. I started by collecting up clothes from the floor. I found the tapestry bag and shovelled them in any old how. The handles were made of fabric as were the loop and toggle fastenings, so I figured it was combustible. The halter neck top which had been Trudie's favourite garden attire was draped from one corner of the open wardrobe door – there was only one garment actually hanging up inside the wardrobe – a white dress which I'd never seen her wear. It went into the bag with the rest.

The book about local mysteries was lying face down on the floor. When I picked it up, I could see that Trudie had been reading about the Agnes Payne case. I closed the book and put it on the window sill; it would have to be returned to the library, next time someone went into Kington. I noticed the sill was very dusty: there were marks on it where things had been put down and subsequently removed – one a perfect set of fingermarks where her hand must have rested, perhaps when she opened or closed the window.

From my vantage point at the window I could see that the boys had already unreeled yards of hose pipe, which Danny was guiding until the open end dangled over the side of the pond. Vic's handiwork had already dried to a much paler shade of orange. Danny's shout of 'Turn it on' reached me faintly through the glass. The awful connotations of the pond's construction did not preclude this from being a big moment. Forgetting my haste I stood like Danny, watching and waiting for the water to arrive. Just when I had become convinced it was never going to, it streamed forth in a confident gush, making a dark wet stain down one side of the concrete as it raced into the lowest level. Here it formed a spreading puddle which had almost covered the bottom by the time Simon joined him. The puddle became an inch of water across the bottom, after which its visible volume increased too slowly to monitor. Simon was right – it was going to take hours to fill.

Suddenly conscious of wasted time, I turned to the assortment of toiletries which stood on the dressing table. Bottles of shampoo and cans of deodorant were unsuitable for burning, so I gathered them together in a stray carrier bag, ready for the dustbin – there was nothing traceable about discarded cans of Us or part-used Biba lip gloss, after all.

I found myself continually drawn back to the window with its view down to the wood and its telltale set of fingerprints in the dust. I tried to concentrate on the task in hand, but it was only a couple of minutes before the marks on the window sill caught my eye again. I swept my hand across to obliterate them. It came away coated in a thin film of dust, which I cleaned off on the counterpane, as assiduously as if it had been someone else's blood.

In one of the dressing-table drawers I found what I was looking for. One hundred pounds in tens and fives, held together in an elastic band and tossed casually among her clean knickers. I stood contemplating the bundle of notes, wondering where to conceal it. I had no pockets and if I openly carried it across to our bedroom, Simon or Danny would be sure to choose that moment to pop upstairs for something and catch me in the act. Another glance outside strengthened this possibility – the water was still running but neither of them was standing beside the pond watching it. The library book offered me a solution. I hid the notes inside the back cover, where the weight of the book flattened the bundle to the extent that no one could possibly have guessed it was there.

Soon the only thing I had left to deal with was Trudie's Greek bag, which was slumped forlornly on a chair under the window. There were only five things inside – her purse, an unopened packet of Handy Andys, a used envelope, a crumpled Kit Kat wrapper and a small volume covered in pale blue imitation leather, which had the word DIARY on the front and the initials T.E.A.F in the bottom right-hand corner, both embossed in fancy gold lettering.

After putting the rubbish with the to-be-burnt items, I sat down on the edge of the bed while I checked the purse, pausing every so often to glance over my shoulder towards the door. In the pouch reserved for cash I found twenty-three pence in coins, which I extracted and piled neatly on the dressing table. In the wallet section there were two one-pound notes, several crumpled till receipts and a torn bus ticket. When I picked up the envelope I noticed it had a foreign stamp. It had been addressed in loopy old-fashioned writing and slit neatly along the top. There was no letter inside, just two adjoining photo booth snaps cut from the strip of four. They were of Trudie and another girl, the pair of them crammed close together in the space designed for solo shots, laughing and acting up. I almost slipped the pictures into the back of the library book with the money. It felt wrong to burn a photo of someone. Common sense reasserted itself. I turned the pictures face downwards so that Trudie's eyes couldn't try to meet mine, then replaced them in the envelope which I pushed well down inside the bag. The purse had a metal clasp and press stud fastening which wouldn't burn so I put it with the other things to be thrown away. Thank goodness Trudie hadn't written her name and address inside it – not like Simon, plastering his initials all over everything, the idiot.

Only the diary remained. I knew I shouldn't, but the urge was strong. It was fastened shut with a dainty little strap and buckle. That buckle wouldn't burn either, but it was so tiny it scarcely mattered. Before opening the diary I skewed myself round so that I was almost facing the bedroom door – that way it would be much harder for anyone to catch me unawares. My fingers were trembling as I undid it. Stupid, I said to myself, it won't bite you.

Someone had written inside the front cover *Happy Christmas 1971 with love from Auntie Edna and Uncle Bob*. Overleaf, on the page reserved for personal details, Trudie had dutifully completed most of the sections. It was all there – her home address and telephone number, who to contact in case of emergency (*Mr and Mrs R.G. Finch above address*), even her blood group. I stared at this information, feeling slightly sick.

Flicking through the first few weeks of the year, it appeared that Trudie had been an enthusiastic diarist. Her small round handwriting detailed successes at school (*Came out top in French again*), visits from relatives (*Granny came for lunch*), and undercurrents of a more serious nature, principally her passion for someone called Bev and her hatred of her parents.

As the year progressed Trudie's resolve to emulate Pepys had evidently faltered. Gaps between entries grew longer until some weeks there was nothing more than an isolated note, *Maths test 64%*, or *Nilsson still number 1*. I fast forwarded too far, finding myself among the virgin pages of early September. The pristine sheets reproached me silently: empty except for the little black dates coupled with symbols marking the state of the moon – a mocking reminder that nothing would ever be recorded on them.

I hastily turned back in time, stopping short as I caught sight of my own name. *Katy doesn't seem to like me much*, Trudie had written, in the early days not long after she had first moved in, w*hich is a shame because I fancy the pants off her.*

Out of the corner of my eye I thought I caught a movement on the landing. I froze, a tangle of conflicting emotions competing with one another and blind panic getting the upper hand. I held my breath, not daring to call out or question who was there. In a moment of déjà vu I heard Trudie's laugh as she said, 'It's only Murdered Agnes.'

I silently closed the diary, my eyes all the time on the gap between the door and its frame. There was nothing to be seen or heard – no suggestion that anyone had been there at all. I stuffed the diary well down among the things to be burnt. I didn't know what else Trudie might have written about me or how recently she had made her last entry.

I gathered up the things which wouldn't burn and carried them down to the dustbin, taking care to bury the purse under much less interesting items. At the back of my mind I entertained the vague idea that such a personal item might be traced back to the missing schoolgirl Trudie Finch.

On my next trip upstairs I stripped off the bedding and collected the towels, carrying them down to the kitchen, where I dragged the twin tub across to the sink and began to fill it with water. Simon entered the room while I was waiting beside it.

'Can you get a bonfire going in the garden?' I said. 'I've got everything ready to burn.'

He took a box of matches from the shelf above the boiler and left without a word.

Once the machine was full I set the controls and fed the sheets and towels into it. Then I took a duster back to the bedroom and made a start on the cleaning, all the time keeping an eye out for some sign that Simon had managed to get the fire started. From the window I could see beyond the garden to Bettis Wood. It wasn't so hot as it had been the day before. Grey clouds hung over the valley, making the trees look gloomy and forbidding. I knew where Simon would build the bonfire. There was a sort of clearing beyond the hydrangeas, where garden fires had obviously been made before. Sure enough after about five minutes a few wisps of smoke began to appear above the bushes. I made sure the diary was bundled up inside one of Trudie's shirts, then carried the bulging bag down to where Simon was feeding a small blaze with some dried-up sticks.

'I got it going with some old newspapers I found in the shed,' he said. 'But it's quite difficult. A lot of the stuff we've cut down is too green to burn.'

'So long as it gets going well enough to get rid of this lot,' I said.

'Is that all there is?'

'Yes. Everything else has gone in the dustbin.' Seeing his look of alarm, I continued hastily, 'It's only deodorant, stuff like that. Nothing personal. Nothing that can be identified.'

I fed the things into the fire a few at a time. In spite of my impatience to get finished in Trudie's room, I was determined to stay and make sure the diary and everything else was safely destroyed. Simon seemed indifferent to whether I was there or not. There was no sound in the little clearing except for an occasional crackle from the blaze. When smoke occasionally billowed in our direction we moved aside as one, but otherwise we might have been inhabiting separate galaxies, steadfastly ignoring each other's existence.

'Where's Danny?' I asked eventually.

'Mooching about somewhere.'

'Any idea what he's doing?'

'No.'

I noticed that his eyes were red-rimmed. It might have been the smoke from the fire or lack of sleep, but I wondered if he had been crying again. It occurred to me that out of us all he had been Trudie's most consistent friend. They had confided in each other. He had known about Trudie running away – and also about the afternoon Trudie and I had spent in bed together. I tried to remember what she had said – that Simon wasn't happy about it. What had he meant that night – when I overheard him in the hallway, saying that someone was going to get hurt? Did he mean emotionally – or had he been threatening her? My thoughts tracked round in wider and wider circles while I shied away from ever reaching the hub – and in the meantime we stood in silence, solemnly observing the effects of fire on different materials. Some burned slowly, blackening, threatening to smother the flames like a fire blanket; others sparked and blazed, while a couple of tops melted, shrinking away like something in a horror film. The process seemed interminable – but I knew I had to make absolutely sure of everything.

Both the bags proved stubborn. Simon had to poke them repeatedly into submission, using a long blackened hoe he had found nearby, which was clearly a veteran of garden fires. Only when everything had been rendered down to ash and blackened lumps did I leave him, still encouraging the bonfire with whatever bits and pieces of garden combustibles he could find, the object of the exercise apparently forgotten, the maintenance of the fire having become an end in itself.

Before returning to the task of cleaning Trudie's room I spun the washing and emptied the machine. I hung the bedding outside to dry, ignoring the proximity of the smoking bonfire. Then I took fresh sheets from the airing cupboard and remade the bed. As I finally dragged the eiderdown into place I startled myself by knocking the library book off the window sill. It landed on the carpet with a muted slap and fell open at the chapter headed *The Murder of Agnes Payne.*

THIRTY

The nurse returns briefly to check on Mrs Ivanisovic from time to time. During one of these visits she switches on the bedside lamp and draws the curtains, making the room at once cosy and conducive to sleep. Images of bedtime stories and mugs of cocoa creep unbidden into my mind.

'She's very peaceful, isn't she?' Fat Bottom nods approvingly as she moves about the room, surprisingly light on her feet for someone carrying so much bulk.

This is the way we all want to go, I suppose – starchy sheets and a clean nightie. Never mind all that raging against the dying of the light – give me a comfortable bed and appropriate analgesia any time.

The lampshade has a pattern of daisies on it – I hadn't noticed this until it was illuminated. *Lead, kindly light, amid th' encircling gloom. The night is dark and I am far from home* – isn't that the right hymn? *To rest forever after earthly strife, In the calm light of everlasting life.* Or, as my generation would more likely have it, *she's climbing the* 'Stairway to Heaven'.

Fat Bottom departs on tiptoe, the door closing behind her with the faintest of clicks. At this point Mrs Ivanisovic opens her eyes and struggles to focus. She says something, but her voice is weak and croaky, and the words are completely obscured by the oxygen mask.

'It's Katy,' I say. 'I'm still here.'

'Katy.' It's very muffled, but there's no mistaking her acknowledgement. Her gaze moves beyond me, searching for something (or is it someone?) behind my right shoulder. I steel myself not to look round. I have learnt that there is never anyone there. Only the consequences of our own actions can haunt us.

Mrs I scans the immediate area until she lights on the bedside table. I follow her look.

'The crucifix? You want the crucifix?'

I take up the faded brown jewellery case and open it, handing her the crucifix and chain so reverently that they could be holy relics. She receives them in the same way: closes her hand around them, then motions me to take them back. When I hold out my hand she places the crucifix and its chain carefully on my palm, then closes my fingers around them. Her intention is clear. She has given them into my keeping. Time stands still as she retains her frail grip on my hand, inside which I can feel the cool weight of the treasure she has bestowed on me. It is like a gesture of forgiveness – a benediction.

I know there will be no more questions. Do I feel a pang of guilt at deceiving her to the very end? I do not – for I am protecting her from a truth far more devastating than anything she has imagined.

When she releases her grip, I withdraw my hand and deposit its contents into my pocket. Her eyes are closed again, her breathing shallow. The clock ticks louder now, taking the leading part in the duet.

My mobile phone tweets softly from the depths of my bag, alerting me to the arrival of a text message. If Mrs Ivanisovic hears it she gives no indication. I fish the phone out and read the message:

How are you? Call me later if you can.

Hilly of course. We always use proper spelling and punctuation in our texts. Two ex-teachers – what do you expect? I reply:

Still with Mrs I. She is very poorly, so I am staying a while longer.

Hilly's reply comes back almost immediately.

Poor you. Thinking of you. Don't ring if too tired.

When I read the message I can hear her voice in my head, saying the words. Darling Hilly – who loves me as a friend, but cannot love me in that other way. 'I'm not like that,' she said, so many years ago – pretty much the exact same words I used with Trudie – the difference being that for Hilly they are true. Sometimes we fall in love with the wrong person – but friends is good – friends for more than thirty years.

THIRTY-ONE

When I bent down to retrieve the library book I noticed something small and shiny under the bed. I dropped on to my knees to see it better and discovered it was a pen – not just any old pen but a fancy stainless steel one, which had been personalized by the engraving of that same quartet of letters TEAF. Was I the only person in the country who didn't have my initials stuck all over everything?

The discovery made my heart lurch. I thought I had managed everything so cleverly and yet here was a dangerous telltale of Trudie's tenancy that I had all but missed. Nor could I decide what to do with the pen. Neither bonfire nor dustbin seemed appropriate.

Several silly distracting thoughts crept into my head before I could stop them. Perhaps Trudie – or was it Agnes – had made the book fall to the floor, just so that I would find the pen. Or maybe finding the pen was entirely incidental and something meant me to read the chapter about Agnes Payne. The rational side of me wasn't having any of this. I had brushed the book off the window sill myself. Naturally it had fallen open at that particular place, because it had been left face down in that position for the best part of three days. If you dropped the book a hundred times it would probably fall open at the Agnes Payne story for no other reason than that.

As I lifted the book my attention was caught by the opening line – *Although the murder of Agnes Payne*

remains officially unsolved ... Although? Why al-
though? In spite of myself I was intrigued. I couldn't
really spare the time but I started to read it anyway.

Although the murder of Agnes Payne remains offi-
cially unsolved, local historian Maisy Gregson is widely
believed to have uncovered the true culprit, more than
half a century after the event. So much for the magazine
article, I thought. The author of that couldn't have
done his homework very thoroughly. I scanned
through the rest of the piece at top speed. It was mostly
repetition of the stuff we already knew – until I reached
the last couple of paragraphs.

Scotland Yard were called in, but the detectives
from London made no more progress than the local
men. The investigation slowly fizzled out and the
case remained unsolved. That is until 1967, when
Maisy Gregson started to write a history of the
parish. One day when she was looking at the old
parish registers, Maisy noticed some entries signed
by a clergyman she had not come across before – an
R.W. Wilkins-Staunton. Maisy subsequently found
an old parish magazine which alluded to the fact
that Reverend Wilkins-Staunton's calling had
taken him across the world – to a teaching post
in Nova Scotia, and from there to a church in
Massachusetts.

Intrigued by the globe-trotting curate, Maisy
made some enquiries with a friendly librarian in
Boston who wrote back with some shocking infor-
mation. Roger Webb Wilkins-Staunton had been
executed in the USA for the murder of one of his
flock in 1931. The murder bore many similarities to
the killing of Agnes Payne, right down to the
victim's membership of Wilkins-Staunton's Bible
Group and the use of an expensive silk scarf. It has

been said for many years that we will never know who killed Agnes Payne – but Maisy Gregson is convinced she knows the answer.

A note at the bottom of the chapter said *See Plate viii*, so I obediently flicked to the glossy central pages expecting to see a picture of Maisy Gregson. The caption below Plate viii, however, identified it as Agnes Payne. It was a rather grainy reproduction of an old photograph, which showed a plain woman in a severe high-necked blouse. Although Agnes was wearing a hat, I could see she had light-coloured hair. She looked nothing like Trudie at all.

I shut the book feeling oddly disappointed. Although I couldn't hear a thing, I felt as if Trudie and Agnes were both screaming at me, trying to tell me what I'd missed.

I left the book and pen lying on the bed while I had a last look round the room. The discovery of the pen made me so nervous that I opened and shut all the drawers again, looked down the back of the dressing table and chest of drawers, even investigated the top of the wardrobe, almost choking myself in an enveloping cloud of dust in the process; but I made no further discoveries.

When I was finally satisfied, I took the pen and book back to my own room. I extracted the money from inside the back cover, putting twenty pounds in my purse and the remainder in the inner pocket of my anorak, which had been hanging unworn in the wardrobe ever since we arrived. Then I set about gathering all my things together, piling them on the bed so that it would only take a matter of minutes to pack them in my rucksack.

I couldn't quite shake off the idea that I should have learned something from Trudie's library book, but the voice of reason reminded me that it only proved how daft and far-fetched Trudie's ideas had been. Murdered Agnes had clearly not been in touch with Trudie. She had no need to be – her mystery had been put to bed by Maisy Wotsername. Moreover she had ultimately received justice in its acutest form. The murderous vicar had been executed for his crimes.

I kept the book to one side ready to take it down-stairs with me, but I hesitated over the pen. It would be very difficult to destroy it but binning it might be too dangerous. Not many people had four initials. Maybe no one but Trudie had that particular combination. I didn't trust the guys to come up with a safe solution; so I decided to keep the discovery to myself and hid the pen in my anorak pocket with the balance of Trudie's money.

The hall was so gloomy that before descending the stairs I switched on the lights, but this only served to increase the sense of depression, highlighting the long wisps of cobweb floating from the ceiling and the film of dust which lay over everything. It was as if the house manufactured dust, I thought; breathing in stale air overnight, then exhaling it as dust the following morning, so that I could never hope to keep pace with it. For some reason this reminded me about the hose pipe, slowly filling the pond. The moment I allowed my guard to slip far enough to allow in one image associated with the pond, it was followed by a host of others that I didn't want to see. I couldn't stand much more of this. I had to get away.

As I entered the kitchen through one door, Simon came in at the other.

'Hi,' I said. 'Have you worked out how long it is until your uncle gets here?' (It occurred to me – too late – that I might have been able to use Trudie's diary to work this out, if only I hadn't been so busy snooping.)

'No, I haven't thought about it.'

That seemed a bit weird. Surely Simon must be wondering how his uncle would take the fact that so much of the projected garden development was still unfinished. He must have sensed what I was thinking, because he added, 'I can't think of anything – I can't think straight at all.'

A brisk barrage of knocking interrupted us. There was someone at the front door – someone who favoured the traditional rat-a-tat-tat approach to making themselves heard. Simon's eyes widened and he gripped the back of the nearest chair, as if he needed its support. I too must have been on the verge of hysteria because for some reason this latest development struck me as extremely funny. 'It'll be the Avon Lady,' I said. 'Shall I go?'

Simon evidently didn't get the joke. After gaping at me for a few seconds, he said, 'You see who it is. I'll wait here.'

I almost skipped along the hall, positively light-headed. We'd already had the builders, the police and the news brought by the postman. What more could Fate throw at us?

The man waiting on the step was tall and thin. He was wearing an old-fashioned tweedy suit and grey sideburns on a scale which outdid Noddy Holder's. In his hands he held a hat which he had presumably just removed. It looked for all the world like a deerstalker. I suppressed a wild urge to laugh. Having run out of other tricks the gods had sent us Sherlock Holmes.

The man regarded me as someone might look at a slug who has invaded their greenhouse. He wasted no time on preliminaries. 'Is Trudie in?'

Aha – the direct approach – trying to catch me off guard. 'No,' I said carefully, not least because I was still

286

fighting to subdue my mirth. 'She doesn't live here any more.'

He regarded me with disbelief. 'Are you sure? She specifically told me this is where I could find her.'

I started to return to my senses. 'Why? I mean – who are you?'

He reached inside his jacket and extracted a card which he held in my direction. I took it from him and discerned that he was an antiques dealer from Leominster. Having read the card I handed it back, uncertain what my next move ought to be. He continued to stand on the front step, evidently expecting an invitation to enter. When none was forthcoming he began to speak, his tone somewhat impatient, his face screwed up as if assailed by a bad smell. 'Trudie came into my shop last week and showed me something rather valuable. It was outside my speciality but I told her I would make enquiries with a friend and it turns out that he is interested. I have come to tell her so.'

'What was it Trudie showed you?'

'I rather think that is between myself and Trudie.'

'It might not have been hers, you see. It might have belonged to someone else. Someone who – lives here.'

'I see. I did explain to the young lady that the question of how she had come by such an item would inevitably arise, before it could be put up for sale. Do you know something about the item in question?'

Oh God. Now he was starting to wonder if we were a ring of antique thieves or something. 'I don't know,' I hedged. 'It depends what the item is. It's not a teapot with roses on it by any chance?'

He drew himself up as if insulted. 'It is a stamp. For your information an Hawaiian Missionary stamp. Now is the girl who called herself Trudie here or isn't she?'

I stared at him. Was it all a joke? What would missionaries be doing with stamps? The sensation that

287

I had stumbled into a Monty Python sketch began to reassert itself. Then I gasped. 'It was on an envelope, wasn't it? It was the thing her grandmother gave her.'

'So she said, yes. Although my friend would require some sort of proof. But you say she doesn't live here any more. In which case are you able to get a message to her, or tell me where she has gone?' His voice was increasingly tetchy. No doubt he had detected my earlier amusement and suspected me of giving him the run around. His irritation made me nervous, but I couldn't pull myself together. I thought about that envelope – that tatty old envelope to which I hadn't given so much as a second glance. In my mind's eye I saw it blackening as the flames crept toward it, then suddenly being engulfed: its precious cargo snatched into instant oblivion.

'You say she's not here?' he repeated. A little white spot had appeared at the end of his nose. I could see he was on the edge of losing his temper.

'No, she's gone.'

'And you don't know where to?'

'No. She didn't say. She hadn't decided.'

'Then I've wasted my time,' he said, abruptly turning towards his car, saying something under his breath that I didn't hear.

The blood pounded in my head. Who else might Trudie have confided her whereabouts to? She had barely been dead a couple of days and already the search for her was narrowing in our direction. Suppose this man had spotted Trudie's name in the papers? She was supposed to be a runaway in hiding, but here she was giving out her address to all and sundry. She had even told him her own name. Her first name anyway. Trudie – that was who he had asked for. Maybe she hadn't said Finch – maybe she'd only said Trudie or maybe Trudie Eccles, or something equally daft. Suppose she had been introducing herself in other antique shops, talking to other dealers.

For a wild fanciful moment I wondered if I ought to find a way to prevent him from leaving. Entice him into the house, poison him with my cooking, then have the boys bury him alongside Trudie. Perhaps that's how mass murderers got started – one thing leading inexorably to another: because once you have begun there's no turning back . . . But I had let my quarry escape. I closed the front door, resigning myself to the fact that I was not successful mass murderer material.

Simon had been listening from the other end of the hall. He retreated into the kitchen at my approach. 'Who was it?' he asked, as I entered the room. 'What did he want?'

I stared at him. I knew he must have heard every word. I didn't have a chance to respond, because just then Danny came in from the garden, saying that he'd turned off the hose pipe and thought the whole thing would look better once there were some plants round the edges. 'Perhaps we ought to go to the plant nursery tomorrow and buy some.'

This gave me my cue. 'Is the nursery towards Leominster? Because I was thinking, you know, with Si's uncle coming back and everything, that the best thing would be for me to go to Cecile's family after all – and I can get a train from Leominster.'

'What are you talking about?' Danny made no attempt to disguise his annoyance. I realized I had sprung it on him too quickly.

'I know you said I could stay with you – but I think this would be safer.'

'No,' said Danny abruptly. 'It wouldn't be. We've got to stick together.'

At that moment I felt more certain than I had ever been that 'together' was not an option. I had to get completely clear of that house and of Danny. I had to find a way of shutting this whole horrible mess into a cupboard and never opening the door on it again.

'Someone's just been here,' said Simon. 'He was looking for Trudie. Katy sent him away.'

Danny turned to me. 'Who was it?'

'Just some old guy – an antiques dealer. Trudie had been into his shop, asking about a stamp.'

'What stamp?'

'Oh, I don't know. Some stamp her grandmother had given her. What does it matter – we've burnt it now anyway. I told him she'd gone away.'

Danny whistled between his teeth. 'Shit. I wonder how many more people are going to turn up here, looking for her.'

'That's just the thing,' I said. 'If we weren't here, we couldn't be asked anything.'

'We need to be here, to give the right answers if anyone does ask.'

'No,' I said. 'I think you're wrong. And can't you see that all the time we're here, together, we're never going to be able to stop thinking about what's happened? Simon's uncle coming back is the best possible thing that could happen. This way none of us has to stay here the whole summer – we can all get away.'

'You have to stay with me,' Danny persisted. 'I don't want you to go to France.'

'It would be for the best,' I said.

Simon had been looking from one to the other of us, saying nothing. I addressed him directly. 'Will you take me into Leominster, Si?'

Danny gave him no opportunity to reply. 'You're not going,' he said. 'You can't go. We're meant to be together. What about us – our future?'

'There is no us – we have no future. Can't you see that? Whenever I'm with you, I'll always be thinking about what happened here. The only way any of us can hope to forget is to stay well away from one another – and even then ...' I trailed off, allowing Danny another opportunity.

'That's crazy. Tell her she's crazy, Si. The only way is to stick together.'

I turned to Simon, deliberately blanking Danny. 'Please will you drive me into Leominster – if not this afternoon then first thing tomorrow?'

'Don't take her,' Danny butted in. 'She doesn't know what she's saying. By tomorrow she'll have changed her mind.'

We both faced Simon, forcing him to choose.

'The nursery isn't on the way to Leominster,' he said. He didn't say it as if he was making a decision; it was just an observation, spoken in a flat tone of voice, as if in response to a different question posed by some other voice we couldn't hear.

I decided to assume he had declined. 'Fine,' I said. 'I'll make my own way.'

Danny tried to put a conciliatory arm around my shoulders. 'Why not sleep on it?' he suggested, in a much kinder tone.

I shrugged him off. 'I'm going to pack,' I said.

THIRTY-TWO

I stamped out of the kitchen, not exactly slamming the door but undoubtedly applying greater force than was necessary. I would show them. Even biddable old Katy had her limits.

The few minutes it took me to shovel everything into my rucksack afforded sufficient time to contemplate the realities of the situation. The afternoon was already well advanced and I was at least four or five miles from the nearest town. I didn't know what time the buses ran, or where they ran to, and even if I could get to Leominster it was probably too late to complete my complicated train journey that night. A bed and breakfast would eat deep into my precious travel fund, even assuming that I could find somewhere to stay. I wasn't equipped for camping. I could try hitch-hiking, but it wasn't recommended for women on their own and sure as eggs were eggs I would fall in with a murderous psychopath and finish up dead in a ditch.

As I fastened the straps of my rucksack I heard the first patter of raindrops on the window. Great – that was all I needed. How long would it take me to walk five miles? When I lifted the rucksack off the bed, I was also forced to consider how far I could actually carry it.

I decided to appeal directly to Simon again. Maybe if Danny wasn't around, I could persuade him to run me into Leominster straight away. I wasn't mad about the idea of being on my own in the car with Simon, but I was spurred on by the thought that an immediate departure might still see me in London that night, if not at the coast itself.

I descended the stairs cautiously because I didn't want to encounter Danny if I could avoid it. I had more than half expected him to follow me upstairs and attempt to convince me of the error of my ways – but he was probably giving me time to cool off. He would not have banked on my being packed and ready to leave in ten minutes flat.

The kitchen door was closed so I got right up to it before I heard voices coming from the other side. Damn it – I had counted on Simon being alone but they were both still in there. I was about to creep away again when I heard my name. I didn't catch what Simon was saying about me, but Danny's reply came through loud and clear. 'Not on your life. Katy stays here with us.'

'I say let her go if she wants to. I could take her to the station this afternoon.'

I laid a hand on the door, elated to discover that Simon had apparently come down on my side.

'She doesn't really want to go,' Danny began, but Simon interrupted him.

'Yes, she does – and we'd be better off without her.'

'Don't say that about Katy.' The sudden anger in Danny's voice took me by surprise. My hand jerked away from the door as if the panels were red hot. 'You just want her out of the way.'

'I'm just thinking about what's best for all of us. And she doesn't know, does she?'

'What do you mean?'

There was a pause. When Simon spoke again his delivery seemed slower and more precise than it had ever been. 'I covered for you. When the police came and asked me about the screwdriver.'

The words stopped me dead. The cold from the stone floor travelled upwards, stiffening me like washing frozen on a clothes line. It seemed to take forever before Danny spoke again.

'I don't know what you're going on about that for.' I found it impossible to gauge his mood. He sounded half amused, half irritated. 'The screwdriver was easy enough to explain. There's no problem about that.'

'Only that it wasn't true,' said Simon.

'What? Are you saying you *don't believe* they found the screwdriver in that girl's room?'

'No. I'm saying I lied about it to the police.'

'Well, that's what friends are for, Si.'

'That's not why I did it. By then we were all up to our necks and I had no choice.'

'Come off it, Si. You did it because you *lurve* me.'

'Piss off,' said Simon, angrily; but the words ended in a sort of sob.

'We're best mates, you and I – always will be, yeah? But don't imagine you can blackmail me with fairy stories about screwdrivers.' Danny's tone hardened as he continued. 'Nothing you or anyone else can do is going to stop me being with Katy. I'm in love with Katy and you just can't take that, can you?'

'You don't know what it's like to really care about someone,' Simon burst out. 'You don't have feelings like other people. You're not – not normal.'

'*I'm* not normal. That's a good one, coming from you! I've started to think I'm the only one who is normal round here. Everyone knows you're as bent as a five bob note.'

'At least I'm honest about it – with myself and other people.' Simon's voice rose to a shout. 'At least I'm not a nutter – why did you do it, you bastard? Why? Why?'

There was no sound from the kitchen for several minutes, then Danny spoke again. He sounded perfectly calm and friendly. 'Look, Si, you're the greatest, right? We're a good team. Butch and the Kid. Laurel and Hardy. Morecambe and Wise.'

A chair scraped across the floor. I couldn't tell which one of them it belonged to. After a moment Danny spoke again. 'The three of us were great together. There wasn't any friction until Trudie came along – how about the Grand Tour of Europe? We're still on for that, right? Nothing's really changed.'

When Simon eventually spoke his voice echoed all the disbelief I was experiencing myself – but there was something more – a sense of utter despair. 'I lied for you. I thought it was the right thing to do – but now I see I was wrong. I've done a terrible thing and ruined my whole life. I can't take back what I told them, even if I wanted to. I'm implicated now whatever happens. So's Katy. I wondered if she was in it too – but she wasn't, was she? It was all you.'

'Si, Si, what are you saying?' Danny was soothing as syrup. 'You're talking rubbish, man. They've got absolutely nothing on any of us. You explained to them what happened about the screwdriver and they went off satisfied.'

'I lied to them about the screwdriver,' said Simon. 'You know I lied, because I lent it to you. You told me you needed to borrow it, to help some girl fix the plug on her hairdryer. You told me you'd lost it.'

There was an explosion inside my head. Blinding white light obliterated everything, laying waste to thought processes. I staggered backwards away from the kitchen; putting out a hand to steady myself against the hall table, feeling my way along the bottom of the banisters like a blind man. I shook physically as the aftershocks continued to pulse through my brain, jangling like a hundred broken mirrors. When I reached the stairs I sank down on to the bottom step, holding my head in my hands, trying to stem the awful pain you only experience when something splinters your soul.

They were shouting at one another now, my fellow conspirators; but the short distance I had put between us, coupled with the thickness of the door, prevented me from hearing what they were saying. I couldn't even distinguish between their voices.

The same idea went round and round in my head like a merry-go-round – Simon thinks he killed her – Simon thinks he killed her – over and over, flashing silver sparks, overheating, until the fairground music became a constant scream.

Danny had killed Rachel Hewitt. Danny had borrowed Simon's screwdriver, and used it as a ruse to gain entry to her room on the pretext of mending her hairdryer. Why? Why? Surely not just to win some stupid academic prize. Only a madman would behave thus. But if Simon was telling the truth, then it was no wonder Danny had been so anxious to conceal Trudie's accident from the authorities. I didn't want to believe it was true but I could see why it might be. Simon hadn't known about the screwdriver being found in Rachel Hewitt's room until after we had buried Trudie – and by then it was too late. He was certainly right about that. By then we had implicated ourselves too deeply for anyone to believe in an accident.

'Hey, what are you doing here?' Danny startled me, opening the kitchen door without warning and emerging into the hall. He came straight to where I was sitting. 'Have you been crying?' His voice was full of genuine concern. His eyes tried to engage with mine. A part of me still wanted to believe in him, even as I wanted to escape.

'I overheard you and Simon. I heard Simon saying things – I know you killed her.'

Danny's face didn't register surprise. He scarcely hesitated. 'It was for you,' he said. 'I did it for you.'

I looked up at him not comprehending. I'd never met the girl.

'She was coming between us,' he said. 'I had to stop her.' His expression sought my understanding – my approval. He was saying that he had killed someone for the love of me.

Then I did understand.

I leapt to my feet and flung myself up the stairs. This must have taken him by surprise, because he didn't move immediately – just stayed where he was at the foot of the staircase, saying, 'Katy . . . Katy – wait.'

By the time I reached the bedroom I could hear him coming after me, so I slammed the door shut and cast around for the nearest movable heavy object, which was an old-fashioned armchair with an upholstered back and seat. I dragged it behind the door and sat on it, just in time to stop him opening the door.

When he realized he couldn't get in he shoved the door a couple of times, jolting me and my chair, but not managing to dislodge us.

'Katy . . .' His gentlest voice, appealing and persuasive, slightly muffled by the solid panels. 'Don't be daft. Let me in.'

'No. Go away.'

'Katy – come on. I need to talk to you – face to face. I need to explain.'

'Go away,' I shrieked.

I could see myself reflected in the long narrow mirror which was set in the wardrobe door. I looked bizarre, enthroned on the high-backed armchair, my face scarlet with the effort of thwarting the intruder, my expression demented.

Danny began to push steadily against the door. My feet started to slip – he was stronger and heavier than me. A dark gap appeared between the door frame and the door, faithfully recorded in the wardrobe mirror; but by the time the gap had opened three or four inches the chair had slid me within reach of the bed. I braced my hands and feet against it, feeling as if my knee joints were liable to snap. Either this additional barrier defeated him or else Danny decided to concede, because the pressure ceased abruptly and I capitalized on his temporary surrender by shunting myself and the armchair back against the door in a single movement.

'Katy, come on – let me come in and talk to you.'

I didn't respond.

'Okay.' Danny attempted a tone of cheerful resignation. 'I'll talk to you from out here.'

I stayed silent.

'We're *supposed* to be together, Katy. We love one another. It's meant to be. You and me – together.' He paused, got nothing in return, continued: 'Trudie was trying to take you away. She was leading you astray, in fact. Can you hear me, Katy? You know what I'm talking about, don't you?'

I said nothing.

After another brief pause he went on. 'I know you can hear me. Listen, babe, I'm not blaming you. She was leading you on – I know that. It's not normal – all that girl with girl stuff. She was . . . defiling you. As soon as Simon told me he'd seen the two of you together, I knew I had to stop her . . . Aren't you going to say anything, Katy?'

I couldn't say anything. I sat in my chair rocking to and fro, my lips and brain frozen.

'Katy, I did it for us. Look – I'm going to come back later when you're feeling calmer and we'll talk it through. You'll see it was the right thing in the end.'

I heard the stairs moan out their discordant concerto as his feet descended. It was weird the way the stairs were sometimes so noisy and sometimes quiet – not like a normal house where you got to know the location of all the loose boards. Here everything was as variable as shifting sands.

I was rooted to the chair, not daring to relinquish my guard on the door in case he came straight back. He wasn't even bothering to deny it. Was I dreaming this? Had I somehow misunderstood?

I forced my mind back to the night in the woods – the first moments when I found myself alone in the dark. I had called out to Danny but his light had disappeared. The only light I had seen was a much smaller one in the distance – Trudie's light, which I had attempted to follow before I lost sight of it among the trees – but Danny had been somewhere between us. He must have switched off his lamp and followed Trudie, crept along in the dark until he caught up with her in the playground.

My eye fell on Trudie's library book, still sitting on the bedside table waiting to be taken downstairs. I recalled Trudie's words on the night of the seance – how she had described the laughing, happy victim entering the woods and the man with the dark hair and beard, of whom she had been unafraid because he was her friend: 'She's on her own – dark all around – he's coming up behind her. She has my face.'

THIRTY-THREE

Once Danny had gone downstairs there was nothing to be heard except the steady patter of rain. The bedroom window had been left open and one or two spots fell inside, where they sat isolated from one another on the window sill, as if each was waiting for one of the others to make a friendly move.

A whole medley of thoughts passed through my mind and I followed them like a child stumbling through a maze, never quite catching up with the rest of the group, unable to see the way out. The most obvious idea was to put on my anorak, grab my rucksack and attempt to put as much distance as possible between myself and the other occupants of the house before my absence was spotted. I only had to get down the stairs, across the hall and out of the front door. It sounded simple but my legs refused to move. Moreover I had to gamble on the key being left in the front door and my ability to negotiate the stairs without setting up a racket. Danny's recently acquired habit of appearing as if from nowhere was an added difficulty. Then it occurred to me that Simon ought to be on my side. Perhaps we could run away together – that way we'd have the advantage of the car.

Another internal voice questioned where I thought I could run to. Wherever I went, there was no escaping from what I knew. The stuff in your head comes with you wherever you go. You can't leave it behind.

I waited a long time for inspiration, but it didn't bother to show up. After a while I heard footsteps on the landing – but it was only someone using the bathroom. I wondered if it was Simon and considered calling out to him, but I dithered about it so long that the footsteps went away again. After that there was another long silence.

Eventually I moved my chair away from the door and opened it a crack. I decided it would be better to do a recce before I risked being caught in the hall, laden with my rucksack. I stepped out of my sandals and crept across to the banisters, where I paused to listen. There was no sound from anywhere else in the house, but as soon as I ventured down a couple of stairs they immediately sprang into full orchestral mode, providing a loud overture to herald my appearance. I stopped dead, clinging to the banister and holding my breath. At that moment I heard the kitchen door opening, but I managed to conquer the urge to race back into the bedroom, because I knew that anyone coming out of the kitchen would have to walk right along the hall before they could see me standing on the topmost stairs.

'Suit yourself, man.' It was Danny's voice. He didn't sound angry; just ordinary – his everyday self.

Simon's reply was no more than a brief mumble: his words failed to reach me.

'Well, you know where I am,' said Danny. He sounded ridiculously breezy.

I was poised for a speedy retreat but he didn't approach the stairs. He must have gone into the drawing room. Damn. If he left the drawing-room door open there was no way I could get past it and into the kitchen without him seeing me. Then I had another idea. If I could slip downstairs and out of the front door, I could go round the other side of the house and back in at the kitchen door, without having to pass the drawing room at all. Simon and I could use the kitchen door to get away via the same route, without Danny realizing that anything was afoot until he heard the sound of Simon's car – and by then it would be too late for him to do anything about it.

It took me an age to bring myself to make a move, after which I took the stairs one at a time, leaving long intervals between any which uttered so much as a squeak. When I finally reached the bottom I padded across to try the front door, but the big mortice lock was secured and there was no sign of the key. Where had Simon last put the keys? Why had we never bothered to establish a hard and fast rule for this sort of thing?

A noise from the drawing room sent me diving through the nearest door – into the room we called the library. I listened for a moment, but there was no sound to indicate that anyone was approaching along the hall. A new idea struck me. The library occupied the front right-hand corner of the house and had windows to two sides, each with top lights and side openers. There was gravel under the front window and a flower bed under the one at the side, neither of which presented an ideal landing for someone with bare feet – but at least they weren't too high off the ground. I tried them all and every one was painted shut. What kind of decorators did Simon's uncle employ? It was probably the same story as the garden – get in some half-baked family member who was short of cash and let them make a mess of the job.

Just then the quiet was shattered by two or three guitar chords. I turned around in double quick time but then I realized that Danny was still safely in the drawing room, where he had begun to strum a familiar tune. At least this covered any slight noises I might make. I had completely exhausted my small store of ideas and I felt dangerously exposed downstairs so I edged cautiously out of the library door and crept back to my room, slightly reassured by the fact that while ex-altar boy Danny was playing 'He's Got The Whole World In His Hands' he was unlikely to come out of the drawing room and see me. Then again, so long as he was in the drawing room, there was no way I could reach Simon in the kitchen.

Perhaps he had forgotten his promise to come up for another chat. I kept my door open a crack, monitoring his position by the music. Every so often there would be a pause in the programme – but then he would begin again, working his way through that extensive familiar repertoire, every song of which would be forever tainted with its own particular horror from now on.

I was hungry by then and dreadfully thirsty. I addressed the latter problem by rinsing out the tooth glass I had used for Danny's rose, and drinking water from the bathroom. I threw the white rose out of the window.

The playing had become more sporadic – he must be getting tired. That was it, of course. Danny always slept like a baby. He could be absolutely relied upon to fall asleep sooner or later. I only had to wait him out. Then I could go down and solicit help from Simon. It would have been useful if Simon himself had come up to bed – but, now I stopped to consider it, I didn't think he'd spent a night in his room since Trudie died – or the first night maybe – but not since.

Down in the drawing room Danny was attempting 'Moonshadow' – attempting it but missing loads of notes. He was either very drunk or very sleepy – possibly both. The guitar eventually fell silent. When the silence had lasted for several minutes I sensed my chance and stole down the stairs. No one had bothered to extinguish the hall lights since I switched them on that afternoon. I got as far as I safely could, then very slowly inched my head sideways until I could see into the drawing room. Danny had his back to the door. Good – and also drat – because if he'd been sitting like that all along, I could probably have got past him ages ago.

I slid along to the furthest end of the hall, turning the knob on the kitchen door as quietly as I could, while holding a finger to my lips ready to shush Simon until I was safely inside. I needn't have bothered. Simon was slumped forward at the kitchen table where he had fallen asleep, with his head resting on one arm. He was facing away from me and beyond his head I could see the neck of the whisky bottle. I was shocked to note that the hands of the clock were recording half past eleven. I had been skulking upstairs for hours and hours.

I made a wide detour round the table, not wanting to startle Simon into shouting out. I saw the fallen glass first, then the aspirin bottle open on the table. His long fair hair had fallen across his face.

'Simon, Simon.' I grabbed at him urgently, entirely forgetting the need for stealth. The arm lying closest to me slid off the table, thudding against my thigh before it fell useless at his side. I drew back his hair, the ends of which were sticky with the vomit which had choked him. His eyes were closed.

'Simon – Simon.'

I took up the fallen arm and tried to find a pulse. I didn't know much about first aid, but maybe if I could clear his airway . . . Even as I thought of this I knew it was pointless. The flesh of his arm felt unnaturally cool.

I stood beside him taking in foolish details: the puddle of whisky which had escaped from the glass when it fell, knocked over accidentally by Simon no doubt. The whisky bottle next to it was the same one Danny had opened two nights before: I recognized it by a small tear in the side of the label. There was still about an inch in the bottom, so Simon couldn't have drunk very much. He hadn't bothered to replace the cap on the aspirin bottle. I automatically rectified this, noting that the bottle was still three parts full.

It came to me that until a few days ago I had never seen a dead body. Now I had seen two. Simon's neither frightened nor repelled me. The pyrotechnics failed to make their usual explosive entrance. Instead I experienced a strange sensation of calm. It arrived in waves, rolling steadily across my consciousness, and with it came a submerged current of anger: a surging rip tide which infused me with a powerful sense of strength and purpose. It seemed to me as if the very creatures of the night were aware of my presence and trembled before it.

I walked calmly from the kitchen to the drawing room, taking a route which brought me in front of the sofa where Danny was slouched with his guitar in front of him, held upright between his knees. He appeared to have been dozing, but as he registered my arrival he gave a lazy smile.

'Katy.' His voice was slurred. The other bottle of whisky was standing at his feet and told its own story. He patted the sofa beside him, enjoining me to take a seat.

'Are you okay, Danny?' I asked. He began to fumble the guitar out of the way and I bent to help him, propping it against an arm of the sofa.

'Thirsty.' He grinned at me stupidly, still patting the vacant cushion at his side.

'Wait there,' I said. 'I'll get you something to drink.'

'Had something to drink.' He winked and nodded in the direction of the bottle on the floor.

I picked it up. 'You're going to have an awful hangover in the morning; but I can cure that. Hang on – I'll be back in a minute.'

I returned to the kitchen where I placed the whisky bottle with its fellow on the table, before reaching a clean half-pint glass from the cupboard. I filled it with water, unscrewed the cap on the aspirin bottle and upended it over the glass, only righting it after perhaps a dozen or more pills had splashed their way to the bottom, where they began to effervesce like an experiment in a chemistry class. There were so many of them that they needed some help, so I got a spoon out of the drawer and stirred the mixture vigorously, but a lot of undissolved residue still kept falling to the bottom. The cloudy liquid looked extremely unappetizing, so I hunted out a bottle of Ribena from the pantry, some of which I trickled in. Then I went back to the drawing room, with the glass in one hand and four aspirin tablets in the other.

Danny's face lit up when he saw me. I don't suppose the Reverend Roger Webb Wilkins-Staunton gave his executioner such an enthusiastic welcome. This time I accepted the invitation to sit down and submitted to a lengthy kiss. He tasted vile. I suppose it was the result of an excess of alcohol in a stale mouth, but in my mind it represented a breath of evil escaping from somewhere deep inside him. I steeled myself not to recoil: told myself that I could endure much more than this, for Simon and for Trudie – and for that Rachel girl too, although I had never known her.

'Come on now,' I said, affecting a motherly bossiness. 'Take these aspirin and have your anti-hangover medicine.'

He was surprisingly biddable. He took the first couple of aspirin – Big Man, you see, taking them two at a time – placed them in his mouth and washed them down with a slug of my concoction. This made him grimace and emit a noise of distaste but I ignored this, impassively handing him the second pair of pills, which went down the same way. Only after this second gulp did he hold up the glass, eyeing the opaque purplish-pink liquid.

'This stuff's disgusting,' he said. 'What the hell is it?'

'Hangover cure,' I said. 'Secret recipe. It's got Ribena in it for vitamin C. Come on, drink up.'

He didn't comply; instead he cradled the glass in both hands, smiling at me foolishly. 'You're not angry with me any more?'

'No,' I said, maintaining my fixed smile. It was the truth. I was beyond anger. I had moved further than that, into uncharted extremes of emotion, for which there were no familiar labels. 'Look out, Danny. You're going to spill it.'

This reminded him to take another drink – two or three sips which didn't reduce the level in the glass by very much.

'It's horrible,' he protested. 'I don't like it.'

'You'll be sorry in the morning,' I said playfully. 'Go on – be a man, drink it all down.'

The challenge to his masculinity won the day. He drained the glass, coughing and spluttering but getting it down. I relieved him of it before he had the opportunity to get interested in the gritty residue which hung on the sides of the glass and coated the bottom.

'It's foul,' he complained.

'Well done,' I said. 'I'll get you something to take the taste away.'

'Kiss me first.' He made a half-hearted lunge in my direction but I was too quick.

'No thanks,' I laughed the moment off. 'I don't want the taste of that stuff in my mouth.' I was no Juliet, to kiss his lips in the hope of sharing her Romeo's fate.

I went back into the kitchen and put together another aspirin and Ribena cocktail. I counted the pills this time – ten of them: the mix wasn't so dense as before. This only left a handful of tablets in the bottle. There must have been more pills in the first dose than I thought.

When I got back to Danny he was half asleep. He struggled to open his eyes and say something. I wasn't sure if this was just the normal effects of alcohol-induced slumber, or whether his hangover cure had already kicked in. I didn't want to leave it to chance.

'Danny – wake up – come on. You need to take some more medicine.'

He mumbled a protest and flopped his hand ineffectually in my direction, but I lifted his head into a more upright position and put the glass to his lips. He was too dopey to cooperate, so a lot of the liquid dribbled out of the corners of his mouth and on to his T-shirt. Lucky it was a purple shirt, I noted irrationally. That way the Ribena wouldn't stain it. I coaxed and persevered until the glass was empty. When I let go of his head it slipped to one side. His eyes were shut. I wondered how long it would take.

I took the glass back to the kitchen planning to wash it out, but the sight of Simon diverted me. Ought I to do something for him? It seemed wrong somehow to just leave him there. On the other hand what could I possibly do? I couldn't lift him on my own. I couldn't summon help, because there wasn't a phone.

Then it hit me – with Simon and Danny dead, how was I going to get away? I couldn't summon a taxi. I had no idea how to work the car. The rain had stopped, but the idea of walking out into the night terrified me. Everything beyond the kitchen window was inky black. The night transformed the window into a mirror, through which I could see a picture of Simon's body slumped at the table, surrounded by a composition entitled *Still Life Arranged by a Suicide*. I averted my eyes, because the scene reflected in the glass was somehow even more horrible than the reality inside. The strange calm which had driven me until now began to dissipate as swiftly as it had arrived. I was stranded in the middle of nowhere, with two corpses on my hands.

This reminded me that I ought to check on Danny. I had expected to find him sleeping peacefully or better still already dead, but he wasn't. He had shifted his position on the sofa and, as I watched, his fingers clenched and unclenched and his body twitched. Beads of sweat had appeared on his forehead. Instead of sounding slow and sleepy his breathing was faster than normal, as if he was running in a race.

I began to panic. Surely an overdose of aspirin sent you quickly off to sleep. Had I messed it up – maybe by mixing in the Ribena? I watched in horror. Why wasn't he just sleeping? Why wasn't he dead? I must have given him enough to stun a rhino.

To my alarm he began to exhibit more signs of movement, make low moaning noises – as if in pain. Then he opened his eyes. He was looking straight at me – and he knew.

Perhaps I should have made a brief speech; told him how he deserved to suffer for what he had inflicted on others: but I couldn't say a word. I couldn't move, not with those bloodshot eyes on me, paralysing every muscle.

He suddenly lunged forward, whether seized by another spasm or in an attempt to reach me I wasn't sure. He fell forwards off the sofa, crashing to the floor with enough force to set the nearby bric-a-brac dancing. His foot caught the guitar which hit the deck in a discordant clang. He reached out a hand but I sidestepped, leaving him to flounder, gasping and jerking like a fish out of water. I was sickened by the sight of him – but not remorseful.

I thought of Trudie dancing for rain on Hergest Ridge, of Simon singing at the wheel of the car. 'Murdering bastard,' I whispered.

It was that word that did it. The M word. I'm a murderess, I thought. I have killed Danny. Except that I hadn't. He made a crablike movement across the carpet, bringing himself close to my feet. Before I could step back his hand closed around my ankle. I screamed and bent down to wrestle him away. For a millisecond those angry red eyes met mine, then I deliberately looked away, concentrating all my attention on prising his fingers from my ankle. He attempted to swing his free hand into the contest but I saw it coming and jerked backwards so hard that he was dragged across the carpet, still clinging on with one hand while the other sought to steady himself. I straightened up and kicked wildly, managing to lunge back another step so that he was at full stretch, his grip loosened sufficiently that another kick saw me free. I ran for my life, across the hall and up the stairs back to my bedroom where I barricaded the door with my faithful armchair. I fell on to it, my heart beating so loudly that I was afraid I wouldn't hear Danny when he came for me.

THIRTY-FOUR

I had gone to pieces again now the deed was done –
and yet I was not sorry. I could not give him the death
he had given Trudie, or put him through the agony of
mind which had persuaded Simon to take his own life,
but I had settled his account. An eye for an eye – isn't
that what God advocated, somewhere along the line?
But although I had forced Danny to pay in full, I think
I knew even then, that in doing so I had committed
myself to a gruelling long-term instalment plan.

Wherever I am, I'm always walking with you.

I lay back in the chair, limp with exhaustion. Twice
I caught myself nodding. Sleep beckoned – tempting
me to relinquish the chair in favour of the bed; but at
the forefront of my mind was the idea that Danny
might be on his way. I compromised by sliding on to
the floor and laying my head on the seat of the chair,
using my arms as pillows. That way, if anyone did try
to gain entry, my weight ought to impede their progress
long enough for me to resume station on the chair.

I slept fitfully, retreating from moments of wakefulness as a prisoner kept long in darkness shrinks before
the light. Eventually I woke to find the sun shining into
the room. I sensed however that it was not the state of
the day which had roused me. Something had changed.
Some alien sound had intruded to alert me. I lifted my
head and listened intently.

A voice called from somewhere inside the house.
'Hello – is anybody home?' It was a man's voice. A

strange voice – one I had never heard before. 'Hello –
Hello-o-o.'

I dragged my chair out of the way and dodged across
the landing. Dust motes floated in the sunlight, as if the
whole of the stairwell was inhabited by a million tiny
spectral beings. From the head of the stairs, I could see
the top of the man's head. It showed pink through
thinning pale gold hair. He was a bulky man, tall and
rather overweight, wearing a creased linen jacket over
a collar and tie and corduroy trousers. Older than my
parents. He had let himself in through the front door,
which was now standing wide open.

He must have spotted my arrival out of the corner
of his eye, because he paused in the act of walking
down the hall to look up and say: 'Oh, there you are'
– a pleasantry cut short by an exclamation as he caught
sight of what awaited him at the far end of the hall. 'Oh
my God.' He hastened out of my sight towards the
kitchen.

I began to descend warily, one reluctant step at a
time. I could hear him repeating the words over and
over: 'Oh my God. Oh my God.'

When I reached the bottom of the stairs and turned
to face the kitchen, I saw what he had seen. Danny was
lying face down on the floor just inside the kitchen
door. In my mind I saw him crawling there, inch by
inch, his eyes blazing.

The newcomer was out of sight. He had evidently
gone further into the kitchen: no doubt he was looking
at Simon, taking in the whisky and the aspirin. 'Oh
God,' I heard him say again.

He reappeared in the doorway. His face was bright
pink and he was sweating. 'Katy – Katy, is it? What on
earth has happened here?'

I stared at him. Eventually I stammered out that I
didn't know – I'd been asleep.

312

Danny was lying on the floor at his feet. I couldn't stop visualizing him dragging himself across the floor, maybe over a period of many hours. I ran outside and retched violently. Nothing much happened. I hadn't eaten for almost twenty-four hours.

'Katy!' The stranger's voice came from inside, alive with urgency. 'Come quickly.'

Something in the tone of his summons made me obey. From the front step I could see that he was down on one knee, bending over Danny.

'Over here,' he said. 'He's still alive. You stay with him, while I drive to the phone box and call an ambulance.'

'No!' I almost screamed it.

I retreated to the doorstep. He must have thought me too afraid to go anywhere near the other body. He only paused for a millisecond before giving way. 'Of course not,' he said. 'You mustn't stay on your own. You'd better come in the car, with me.'

He guided me round the side of his car, holding open the passenger door. 'As quick as you can, Katy,' he said. He'd had a shock himself, but he assumed mine was the greater. He got into the driving seat and started the engine. 'It's too late for Simon,' he said grimly, 'but we may be in time to save Danny. That *is* who it is, I suppose?'

'Yes,' I breathed.

Next minute I was holding on to the edge of the leather seat with both hands as we tore along the lanes. It only took us about two minutes to reach the phone box – one of those isolated boxes which stand at a junction in the middle of nowhere, little used except by the occasional motorist who has broken down. While my companion was making his call, I assessed the situation. There hadn't been much time for explanations so far, but I was going to need one and sooner rather than later. The easiest lie to maintain is always the simplest one. I would say I had been tired the night before and gone to bed early – leaving Simon and Danny downstairs in the kitchen. I'd been so tired in fact that I had fallen asleep on the top of the bed, still in my clothes – no other way to account for my dishevelled appearance – and I had only woken up when this man arrived.

At this point it dawned on me that the man must be Simon's uncle. How else would he have keys to the door and know all our names? It also came to me that it must be the ninth – the day Simon's uncle had warned us he was coming home. I forced myself to concentrate on more important issues. Danny was still alive. Danny was going to tell them everything – well, everything at least about how he came to be sprawled half dead on the kitchen floor. I could try denying it, but my fingerprints were all over everything. Nor would it do any good, me belatedly telling them what I knew about Trudie Finch and Rachel Hewitt. In fact Danny would probably find some clever way out of it, some story that landed me and Simon with sole responsibility for everything.

'Help is on its way,' Simon's uncle announced, as he climbed back into the driver's seat.

I sat dumbly alongside him, not uttering a word on the return journey (which we accomplished only marginally more slowly than the outward one). He seemed to understand from my silence that I didn't want to go back into the house.

'Would you like to stay here?' he asked, when the car stopped outside the front door.

When I nodded he went in alone. I sat contemplating the dashboard. It was faced in polished wood, with a series of little black switches encircled with chrome. I committed it to memory, like a diagram required for a maths test. This seemed more important than wondering what my parents were going to say about me being arrested for murder.

It felt like an age before the ambulance came roaring up, scraping between the lilac and the rhododendron as it turned in at the gate. The ambulance crew glanced briefly in my direction, but Simon's uncle was beckoning from the front step so they left me alone. After a while they brought out the first stretcher. I deliberately didn't look. I heard the ambulance doors being closed and the vehicle racing off into the distance.

Simon's uncle came over to stand beside the car. 'They're sending a separate ambulance for Simon,' he said. 'And also one for you. I've told them you're in shock.'

After a short silence I asked meekly, 'Is Danny still alive?'

'Yes. Don't worry. They'll do everything they can for him.'

The police car came next – travelling at a higher speed than the ambulance, arriving in a cloud of dust. They spoke to Simon's uncle first, then to me. I gave them my name and address and said I didn't know what had happened. I was aware of some sort of consultation nearby but I didn't turn my head. The dashboard occupied most of my attention. The little symbols perplexed me – I was never going to get full marks when it came to the test. I caught the words 'suicide', 'asleep' and 'shock'. After that I lost track a bit. I think the next arrival was another police car, but maybe it was another ambulance. I knew it was just the calm before the storm. They might think it was suicide now, but once they took a few fingerprints . . . once Danny woke up . . .

'They were very close – friends since school . . .' The words floated at me from out of a dream. 'Yes, yes –

here with my full permission – they have been constructing a garden pond . . .'

The attention turned to me. 'I don't want to go to hospital,' I protested. 'I've got to catch a train to France.'

I found myself in hospital all the same. I slept for a long time. Then I woke up and wished I hadn't. My mother and father had appeared at the bedside. My father said, 'You've got a lot of explaining to do, young lady.'

I was about to say that I was saving it all for the judge when my mother cut in to ask how I was feeling. I decided it would be better to close my eyes and feign sleep until visiting hours were over.

Next day the doctor said I could be discharged. The ward sister rang my parents to give them the glad tidings and it was arranged that they would drive down from Birmingham to collect me that afternoon. A kind of peace descended on the ward after that, with the doctors' rounds completed and the visitors still to come. I plucked up courage and buttonholed one of the nurses – a kindly one with a dark blue uniform, whose voice had a distinctive Welsh lilt.

'The boy who was brought in the same day as me – Danny Ivanisovic – is he still alive?'

She looked at me sadly. 'He's in a coma, Katy.'

'Would he be able to recognize me?'

'No, dear. He can't recognize anyone. Would you like me to take you to see him?'

'Yes, please,' I said. It wasn't sentiment which motivated me, so much as the need to embark on a fact-finding mission.

The kindly nurse insisted that I travel by wheelchair. She pushed me along the corridor, through some swing doors then into a side room. Danny was lying in a hospital bed with his eyes closed. A monitor beside the bed registered his hold on life with a steady series of audible beeps. He looked surprisingly clean and tidy. Someone had washed him and combed his dark curls into place.

'His mother and father have been sitting with him,' the Welsh nurse said. 'But they must have popped out for a breath of air.'

I was deeply thankful for that. I didn't want to run into Danny's parents.

'I don't understand,' I said slowly. 'How was it that Simon died but Danny is still alive?'

'This is much more usual,' she said. 'Overdoses are a very unreliable way of trying to kill yourself.'

'I thought you just fell asleep and – and sort of died.'

'That's the trouble,' she said. 'Quite a lot of them do only *sort of* die. They finish up in a coma like this.'

'Do they recover?'

'Some do,' she said.

'Is Danny going to?'

'That's not for me to say, my pet. Come on now, we'd better get you back to the ward.'

My parents arrived an hour later. The doctor had prescribed some tranquillizers and I was grateful to retreat into the sanctuary they provided; able to ignore the questions, the resentful glances. They withheld direct censure because officially I was 'ill'. But I was in no doubt about their true feelings. I was 'their' Katy after all – the one who had always been a bit of a nuisance.

Danny lay in a coma for another twelve days. He died without regaining consciousness. Even so I lived in fear of a knock at the door, a uniformed figure in the hall. The deaths had been sudden and suspicious, so surely the police would investigate.

Not so – the coroner's inquest brought in verdicts of suicide. Simon and Danny had been found close

317

together in a room containing clear evidence of drug and alcohol consumption and no signs of violence. They had enjoyed what was described in court as 'an abnormally close friendship' and Simon was a known homosexual. It was even hinted that Danny had tried to combat his own inclinations by indulging in 'normal' relationships with the opposite sex. A suicide pact was suggested. It's hard to believe how gullible people can be. Give them half a look at a simple solution and they'll lurch towards it like a drunk to a bar.

I was on the Happy Pills for weeks and weeks. My mother complained to her friends that whenever I appeared to be recovering, something invariably happened to set me back. 'We are treading on eggshells all the time,' she grumbled. It was true. However carefully they tried to shield me, something always seemed to crop up. One day in October I decided to go for a walk and because it was chilly I started to put on my anorak. I hadn't worn it since it had been returned from Simon's uncle's along with all my other things. My mother surmised that this factor alone had been enough to upset me: the mere sight of the garment bringing back dreadful memories. She had no idea that it was not the anorak, but the cool slim object my fingers encountered in its inside pocket which sent me tumbling over the abyss.

'So I decided the best thing would be to give it to the Scouts' jumble,' my mother explained later. 'But when Katy found out what I'd done with it, blow me if that didn't send her off into a fit of hysterics as well. She kept on asking me if I'd checked the pockets, but when I asked her what was in them all she would say was 'nothing'. You can't do right for doing wrong with her, you really can't.'

My mother bought me a new coat to replace the one sold at the jumble sale. If the new owner of the anorak ever tried to trace the donor, no word reached us. I daresay the buyer was happy to keep mum about the cash windfall and the shiny pen.

It was not until Christmas that the sky really fell in. Mistaking my moment, I chose Christmas Eve to reveal to my parents that I was pregnant. To say that mutual hysteria followed would be an understatement. The liberality of the sixties had left our family unscathed and the prospect of a grandchild born out of wedlock sent my mother into a frenzy of operatic proportions. By Boxing Day the furore had been replaced by an icy resolve. Tears and recriminations still surfaced from time to time, but my mother's mouth had set into the hard thin line which became its trademark as she grew older and a solution had been arrived at – I would be sent away in the style of an earlier age. Officially convalescing with relatives after my 'breakdown', I would bear my child in the secret shame of a home for unmarried mothers. The whole thing was hushed up to the extent that even now I am uncertain which of our closest relatives got wind of it. When I eventually returned home neither pregnancy nor baby was ever spoken of again – probably less to protect my feelings than to safeguard my siblings, particularly my younger sister, from moral contamination. It was the elephant in our living room, avoidance of which became habitual.

My parents paid for me to be incarcerated for six months in a big old house in Shropshire, where it was a kind of relief to see out my pregnancy in anonymous surroundings. I shared a room with chain-smoking Sharon and Fat Deirdre, the pair of them like a cliché from a television drama.

Nowadays the traditional adoption story consists of a weeping teenage mother, her baby wrested from her arms by a stern-faced nun – but there were no nuns in my story. No nuns or priests, no prayers, no angels. Only demons who came by night to whisper in my ear; poisonous insinuations about the child I was carrying.

He was a very quiet baby. He lay in my arms attempting to focus on my face, almost as if he understood that he needed to imprint it while he had the chance. I knew that ours was a relationship which could never be – what terrible influence might it have upon someone, to discover he was the son of a pair of murderers?

Hilly was among the few people I ever told about the baby. She took a typically Hilly line: 'You gave him life,' she said. 'And his adoptive parents will be giving him love and he'll bring them happiness which they might not otherwise have had – it's a double gift, really.'

I wished I could share her confidence. I used to wonder about him, wonder how he felt. I wished he could know that sometimes rejection is a kindness, not a cruelty. I wished he could understand that it was for his own good.

Then one day I saw him in the playground. It was not the first time I had experienced the disturbing sense that I might be looking at my own child without knowing it – but this time there was something more. This little boy, eight years old and newly moved into the area, had the Mayfield nose and chin. He looked just like my brother Edward at the same age – and thankfully not a bit like Danny. He hadn't been allocated to my class, but the register was readily available and there was his date of birth: 1 May 1973. His school record removed any lingering doubt – there was a note in there from his parents which confirmed that he had been adopted at birth.

Of all the schools in all the world he had walked into mine.

It was when he moved on to senior school that I began to watch the house. It began as a single curiosity visit which developed into a habit. The knowledge of his whereabouts calmed my anxieties about the kind of family he might have been growing up in; but this unexpected proximity also enhanced my fears for him. He appeared to be a happy, healthy child. He was bright, popular, well adjusted. But the legislation which had once guaranteed my anonymity was amended while he was still a child. I knew that once he hit eighteen he had a right to see his files – and get his birth certificate. Mayfield isn't even a common name. He was sure to remember that a Miss Mayfield had taught at his primary school. I became ex-directory as a precaution, but I knew it could never take him long to track me down if he cared to do it.

It is not that I fear what this discovery might do to me. To acknowledge that one once bore a child out of wedlock is no longer a scandal – if anything it has become faintly heroic. In the fashion of our times the unmarried mother of yesteryear has joined the ranks of the Victim. My greatest fear was that once he began to delve, knowing the name of his mother would never be enough. The space for the father's name on his birth certificate was blank: but if he were to seek me out I could scarcely pretend not to know his father's name – and even if I refused to tell he might turn to others. My brother, my sister, any well-meaning halfwit with a memory spanning three decades might point him in the direction of Mrs Ivanisovic – and out would come the story of Danny's death – and he would ask more and more questions, the thought of which made my head spin like a ride on the waltzers when the fairground hand makes the car go faster and faster, until you are choked by your own screams.

So many questions I could never answer. What does a child want to know? Was I ever in love with his father? So easy now to say that I was not – to deny the best times in the knowledge of the worst. Perhaps some questions can't be answered. Perhaps it depends when you ask them. Everything changes. Even Cat Stevens isn't Cat Stevens any more. This is what goes through my mind as I sit outside his parents' house in Menlove Avenue. How easily even now someone could light a touch-paper towards the truth. If I can do one thing for him, it is to keep that burden as mine alone. Let him believe in the teenage mother bullied by nuns or the parents killed in a car crash – any nice little story will do. Let him be content and without curiosity while I carry the secrets for both of us.

I feel safer with the passing years. If he had wanted to know he would have found me by now. Yet I am still drawn to sit outside the house, in spite of knowing that he doesn't live there any more. His parents are still there and maybe in some deep-down unacknowledged part of me there's a hope that I might catch a glimpse of him. The faint possibility that one of my visits will coincide with one of his. There was a strange car parked on the drive one evening last year. I waited over an hour but when the owner finally emerged it was a stranger – too old to be their son – their son and mine.

THIRTY-FIVE

A strange sense of peace hangs over Mrs Ivanisovic's room. I no longer watch the clock or think about what I might be doing elsewhere. When her eyelids flicker I take her hand and hold it; she relaxes, sleeps again.

It doesn't feel wrong for me to be sitting here – although perhaps it should. Am I not the person who destroyed her beloved son? And yet in doing so I have preserved her illusions and dreams – perhaps that counts for something.

It gradually dawns on me that the sounds which have kept me company throughout the evening have ceased. The clock has stopped ticking and Mrs Ivanisovic is no more. Death has entered on tiptoe and borne her quietly away.

I find the bedside buzzer and press it once. It is answered by a different nurse. Fat Bottom must have gone off duty. One look is enough. She nods and says, 'She's gone.' Then she notices that I am still holding Mrs Ivanisovic's hand. 'Would you like a minute?' she asks.

'No. I'm fine.' I lay the hand gently on the cover. 'Is there anything I have to do – anything to sign?'

'Don't worry about that,' the nurse says. 'It was an expected death, so we can deal with all the formalities.'

'That's fine.' I gather myself, prepare to leave.

'Would you like a cup of tea?' she asks. 'Don't feel you have to rush straight off.'

323

'No, really, I'm fine.'

It feels very cool emerging into the night air after several hours in Broadoaks, where the little old ladies live like hothouse blooms in temperatures that would wilt a hardy perennial like me. I get into the car with an odd sense of completion. As if in coming here, I have accomplished something – although I don't know what it is.

As I pull out of the gates an edge of the moon appears from behind the clouds. What was it Trudie once said? The moonshadow is your fate and it follows you everywhere.

I'm being followed by a moonshadow . . . moonshadow . . . moonshadow.

I drive as far as the Tees Viaduct, stop my car and put on the hazard lights. It is too late for there to be much traffic, and there are no policemen around to query why I am illegally parked, obstructing the inside lane up here on the bridge. I get out of the car and walk round to stand next to the rail, where a chilly wind whips at the edges of my jacket and ruffles my hair.

Moonshadow . . . moonshadow . . .

I take the crucifix and chain from my pocket and drop them over the side. They disappear immediately into the blackness. Don't even make a splash. I get back into the car and drive on.

Moonshadow . . . moonshadow . . . I won't have to cry no more.

324

ACKNOWLEDGEMENTS

'Moonshadow' words and music by Yusuf Islam (Cat Stevens) © 1970, reproduced by permission of EMI Music Publishing Ltd, London W8 5SW. 'How Can I Tell You' words and music by Yusuf Islam (Cat Stevens) © 1971, reproduced by permission of EMI Music Publishing Ltd, London W8 5SW. The hymn 'Lead Kindly Light' was written in 1833 by the Venerable John Henry Newman (1801–1890).

I would like to record my gratitude to all the people who have offered help or encouragement in seeing this book into print, but in particular Emma Dickens, Nick Greenall, Jane Conway-Gordon, Krystyna Green and of course my husband Bill.

DISCUSSION POINTS FOR READING GROUPS

(1) Did you find Kate an easy person to identify with? Would you have liked her as a friend? Did you feel she is an honest narrator?

(2) *We've both been going there for quite some time, so Marjorie assumes we know all about each other.* At the very beginning of the story, this question of how well we can ever know one another arises. Did you feel this was a theme which ran through all the relationships described in the novel?

(3) Kate asks: *Why do people think it will always be better if they know? Might it occasionally be better not to know?* Is the whole truth always the best or kindest thing? Was Kate morally obliged to answer Mrs Ivanisovic's questions honestly?

(4) Did you feel that by the end of the novel everyone got their just deserts? Who were the obvious exceptions and why? Is it ever appropriate to take justice into your own hands?

(5) Kate says: *I don't think I ever saw motherhood as my destiny: I am not naturally the motherly type.* Is she being too hard on herself – or is this a realistic self-assessment? Are there any indicators to the contrary?

(6) Was Mrs Ivanisovic a 'good mother'? How much of Danny's behaviour, if any, is attributable to his upbringing? To what extent can parents be held to account for the way their children turn out?

(7) Kate's parents never appear directly, but how much does her relationship with them influence the events of the summer of 1972? What do you feel about her relationship with them and other members of her family? How much of this relationship is driven by the family as a whole and how much by Kate's own attitude?

(8) *Anything for love.* That may be what the lyric tells us, but how far is it appropriate to go for the object of our affections?

(9) *Sometimes we fall in love with the wrong person . . .* Are some people irresistibly attracted to the 'wrong' types? What do you think initially attracted Kate to Danny and vice versa?

(10) Did you feel that the differences between the young Katy and the older Kate were well drawn?

(11) Who was the most attractive or sympathetic character in the novel, and why? If you had to spend a summer with one of the quartet of house sitters, which would you choose?